DUTY BOUND ON THE UNION PACIFIC

One Man's Story of Building Lincoln's Transcontinental Railroad

Lawson McDowell

Publisher's Notice: Portions of this novel are adapted from *Omaha Gold*, a novel published by Rawr Publishing Company and Lawson McDowell in 2010. This expanded retelling includes an updated storyline with additional historical perspective and photographs.

ISBN-13: 978-1493677580

ISBN-10: 1493677586

RAWR Publishing Company
Omaha, Nebraska

Cover Photo - Public domain lithograph by Currier and Ives. Prairie Fires of the Great West

Cover Design – Kathy Dinkel, Visual Statements, Omaha, Nebraska

"Thirst, hunger, the ferocity of Indians are all no more feared, so lightly do we skim these horrible lands. Yet we should not be forgetful of these hardships of the past."

"When I think how the railroad has been pushed through this unwatered wilderness and haunt of savage tribes; how at each stage of the construction, roaring, impromptu cities, full of gold and lust and death, sprang up and then died away again, and are now but wayside stations in the desert; how in these uncouth places pig-tailed Chinese pirates worked side by side with border ruffians and broken men from Europe, talking together in a mixed dialect, mostly oaths, gambling, drinking, quarrelling and murdering like wolves; and then when I go on to remember that all this epical turmoil was conducted by gentlemen in frock coats, and with a view to nothing more extraordinary than a fortune and a subsequent visit to Paris, it seems to me, as if this railway were the one typical achievement of the age in which we live, as if it brought together into one plot all the ends of the world and all the degrees of social rank, and offered to some great writer the busiest, the most extended, and the most varied subject for an enduring literary work. If it be romance, if it be contrast, if it be heroism that we require, what was Troy town to this?"

Robert Louis Stephenson
Across the Plains
Chattus and Windus, London
1892

Acknowledgements

Special thanks to the following individuals and organizations who made this novel possible.

Union Pacific Railroad, Omaha, Nebraska, a 150 year old company that still strives to fulfill the missions assigned by Abraham Lincoln himself.

Union Pacific Railroad Museum, Council Bluffs, Iowa

University of Iowa Library, Iowa City, Iowa - for access to Doctor Thomas Durant's personal papers.

Gary Rosenberg - Douglas County Historical Society, Omaha

Stephen McDowell – Photo selection

Ann Gentle – My editor who proved invaluable, lending to the manuscript sharp eyes and a keen insight.

Most of all, I am grateful to my wife, Virginia, and my family whose tolerance, though tested often, bore the strain.

Principal Characters In The Novel

<u>1800's Historical Characters</u>
Abraham Lincoln, President of the United States
General Ulysses S. Grant, candidate for U. S. President
General Grenville M. Dodge, UPRR Chief Engineer, Congressman
Benjamin Kennedy, Mayor of Omaha.
Oakes Ames, United States Senator from Massachusetts
Dr. Thomas C. Durant, Union Pacific Railroad Vice-President
Peter M. Dey – first Chief Engineer of Union Pacific Railroad
Silas Seymour, Consulting Engineer
George Train, land developer, UPRR promoter, noted orator
General William Tecumseh Sherman
<u>1800's Fictional Characters</u>
Colton Rusk, former officer in the Union Army
Libby Rusk, wife of Colton Rusk
William Rusk, son of Colton and Libby Rusk
Darcy Lonigan, an Irish-American fugitive from New York
Anthony Butler, a Missouri and Western Telegraph Co. employee
Sean Cook, an Omaha orphan
Buck Clayton, a prominent land owner in Bellevue, Nebraska

Contents

DUTY BOUND ON THE UNION PACIFIC

One Man's Story of Building
Lincoln's Transcontinental Railroad

Prologue

The Angel of Death hovered over armies blue and gray, anticipating their wrath. Neither cold winds nor predawn darkness slowed the march to imminent battle. Death's wait would be short.

With the first rays of sunlight, the fury of 26,000 souls erupted in violent settlement of differences.

The horrific sounds of war reached to the heavens—cannon salvos, rifle volleys, the agonized screams of wounded soldiers and horses. Death descended into the carnage for the grim harvest.

Along the front lines, hand-to-hand combat raged. Scores of men fell that morning. And with each desperate charge and ensuing hail of fire, hundreds more joined the ranks of those ahead, crowding the gates of eternity.

By noon, the generals recognized the battle showed signs of waning, though few who fought for their lives noticed change. On the right flank, Confederate resolve crumbled one bloody step at a time. The left side showed similar weaknesses. Union forces were gaining the advantage.

* * * *

ON THE UNION LINES, Major Colton Rusk gathered his lieutenants for a short briefing near the battle's hot center.

"I saw Colonel Dodge and his horse go down fifty yards to the south," Rusk said.

"There's heavy fighting there, sir. That's the third horse the Colonel has lost today."

Rusk had already made his decision.

"Colonel Dodge never stood up. I'm going to get him out. He's not far away, so I'm going on foot with my sergeant. If we don't return, Lieutenant Brady is to take command. Send a message to Major Straub if that happens."

Rusk dismissed the lieutenants and watched them return to the fighting. Then, he and his sergeant left.

Minutes later, Rusk and the sergeant neared Dodge's last known position. They moved up quickly from the rear, crouching low in the bullets and smoke.

The Union battle line had advanced twenty yards, leaving behind a grisly field of killing. Ahead, they saw the enemy counterattacking to retake lost ground. Rusk focused on the battle debris until he spotted the unmistakable uniform of an officer.

"There he is! He's to the right of those dead horses," said Rusk.

"I see him!" the sergeant acknowledged. "That's his coat, alright."

They moved closer stepping across bodies and around an overturned ammunition wagon.

They reached their goal and looked on the unmoving body of Colonel Grenville Dodge.

Rusk spoke decisively. There was urgency in his voice.

"He's breathing. There's no blood around him. Maybe he's not hurt badly. Let's get him to a safer area. Help me pull him to his feet. We'll carry him between us. Let's go, Sergeant."

As they lifted Dodge, three enemy soldiers broke through the Union line. When the rebs saw Union blue coats, they charged with bayonets extended.

The frightening rebel yell would have unnerved many men. Rusk calmly raised his pistol in his free hand and felled them with three dead-on shots.

Five more rebels broke through as Rusk and the sergeant dragged Dodge toward safety.

"Hurry!" Colton yelled. "The rebs are overrunning this area!"

* * * *

DODGE RETURNED to semi-consciousness when jerked to his feet. His first awareness was that the air was gray with smoke against a background of blue sky. He was momentarily confused, unsure of his whereabouts.

Then he heard the stark truth of battle: the reports from Colton's pistol, the explosions, the moans of dying men. The reality of his circumstances fell into place, one piece at a time.

He remembered the artillery concussion that had thrown him off his mount. He raised his head from his chest and looked at the men carrying him.

"Colton. You came for me?"

"Yes, sir. We had to. The enemy is pushing hard on this side. We're losing ground for now. Major Straub is on the way with reinforcements."

"And the overall battle?" Dodge asked weakly.

"The Fourth Iowa is doing well, sir. We've taken the brunt of the attack. You prepared us well for it. We've held against everything they could throw at us. I believe the Iowa boys will have their way before the day is done."

Dodge tried moving his legs, but could not keep pace, taking one step for every three they dragged him.

"I'll get you settled, and then get back to our men," Rusk said.

* * * *

COLONEL DODGE REMAINED on the battlefield two weeks recovering from his wounds. His men had made a critical difference in achieving a Union victory against a superior Confederate force. The victory established Union control of Missouri and Northern Arkansas for the war's duration.

Dodge would soon be promoted to Brigadier General.

Major Colton Rusk's destiny sent him a different, less fortunate direction that afternoon.

Chapter 1

Mr. Lincoln will see you now. Please come with me, sir."

Brigadier General Grenville Dodge stood from the horsehair sofa in the White House reception room. He straightened his uniform coat, double checked his appearance in a nearby mirror, and followed the president's secretary into an inner hallway.

"The president just finished his regular cabinet meeting. Have you met him before today?"

"Yes, ma'am. We met in Iowa before the war."

"Good. Then you know what to expect."

She started up a stairway.

"I'm afraid you're right, ma'am. I do know what to expect."

Grenville Dodge was worried. A summons to travel to Washington to see the president was alarming for a newly appointed brigadier general. The order had come a week earlier at Corinth, Mississippi as he was rebuilding railroads destroyed by retreating Confederates. More disturbing, General Ulysses Grant had personally delivered the order without explanation.

The trip to Washington had given him time to think, probably too much time. Grenville Dodge was prepared to receive a strong reprimand, maybe worse. Now on a White House stairway, he fretted over his concerns.

Dodge knew that newspapers north and south were printing negative stories about his freed slave soldiers. Dodge's all-black regiments were universally unpopular, except within the Union army itself. There, they were appreciated.

Dodge assumed the president knew of the stories. He worried he had caused political problems and that it was time to pay the price.

At the top of a stairway, they entered a hallway. The general almost stumbled as a new likelihood hit him.

The president probably wants to discuss cotton speculation. This meeting could be worse than I imagined.

Dodge considered how his spy network was funded with the proceeds of smuggled cotton shipments. By paying northern sympathizers and freed slaves for information, he had kept a reconnaissance stream flowing to Union commanders. More than once, his spies made critical differences in battle.

He knew the real problem lay in the minds of newspapermen who wanted a scandalous story. They suspected Dodge was pocketing a share of the proceeds. They saw his old boss, Doctor Thomas Durant, getting rich from cotton sales. Dodge's refusal to reveal the names of spies had cast a cloud of doubt over the entire operation.

That's it. The president wants a private discussion about my spy network and the cotton smuggling proceeds.

Entering Abraham Lincoln's office, General Dodge found the president seated at a long walnut table amidst unrolled maps and piles of documents.

As the secretary left, the president closed a military history book he was browsing. He looked at his visitor, smiled warmly, and stood. He towered over the general.

"Grenville, I'm glad to see you. How are your wounds?" The president's voice was deep and warm.

"I'm doing well, Mr. President. The battle at Pea Ridge was a year ago, and I've recovered quickly. Thank you for asking, sir."

The president removed his gold spectacles and laid them on the table. Dodge saw Lincoln looked exhausted. The president's reputation for working tirelessly was well-deserved.

"I am very grateful destiny spared you," Lincoln said sincerely. "How is your family? Where are they weathering the war?"

"They are doing well in Council Bluffs, sir. I miss them, as all soldiers miss their families."

"So they do, Grenville."

The president stepped to the office windows and looked out at the city. The view was of a city bearing the terrible strain of war. The Potomac River in the distance was barely discernable through the blue smoke from thousands of campfires and chimneys. Closer, the Washington Monument stood in the haze. It was less than a third complete, construction stopped for months now. It looked more like a ruin than a grand tribute.

"Too much time has passed since we talked, Grenville. I am sorry for that. I never had a chance to thank you for supporting my nomination and election."

"It wasn't just me, sir. The Iowa delegates felt you were the strongest candidate. They liked your position on the railroads. You are dearly loved in Iowa."

The president smiled. "We'll see how long it lasts. The public is sensitive to bad news. Our progress with the war is less than the country expects."

"We are making headway, sir."

"And your opinion of Grant?"

Lincoln's unexpected question caught Dodge off guard. "If you are asking me about how he is doing, I will tell you General Grant is a great leader, sir. The press is always looking to paint him in a bad light, but I tell you the men under his command will do anything for him. Even before Shiloh he was making a difference."

Lincoln seemed pleased. "I give your opinion great weight, Grenville. I am flooded with advice to the contrary, mostly from Democrats." The president brushed dust off the curtain.

"I do, by the way, agree with you about Grant. Come, let's walk."

The two left the office and walked slowly across the White House grounds. Dodge found himself relaxing in the company of the somber leader. Shortly into the walk, the president changed subjects.

"General Grant tells me you are doing a splendid job rebuilding railroads. You have become indispensable. He is amazed at the speed and durability of your work. Your bridges have earned you a solid reputation. I am not surprised by this, Grenville."

"Thank you, Mr. President. I try to be a good soldier, but railroads are my true passion, sir."

"Business leaders and engineers tell me that you know more about railroad construction than any two experts. Do you recall our last walk and the topics we discussed?"

"Yes, sir, I do. During your visit to Council Bluffs we climbed to the hilltop near downtown and took in the view of Omaha."

"We talked about the nation's need for a railroad to the Pacific Ocean," Lincoln reminded him.

"I remember," Dodge said.

"Last year's Pacific Railroad Act requires me to name the starting point for the transcontinental railroad. I am feeling pressure to make a decision. Do you still think the Platte River Valley is the best route?"

Dodge answered without hesitation. "The Platte route is by far the best. No other route can match its advantages. The buffalo used the route for a million years, then the Indians, and then the fur trappers. For the last thirty years, wagon trains have found it the best route. It has a natural, easy grade with few curves for hundreds of miles."

Lincoln pressed on. "And the best starting point for the railroad?"

"The best beginning point for the road is Council Bluffs, sir. The river there has a good rock bottom, and the channel is stable. The probability that the river will shift is extremely remote," Dodge said.

"I must make a decision soon," Lincoln sighed. "The naysayers tell me a transcontinental railroad is impossible to build. They have given me concern about the engineering obstacles."

"With all due respect, sir, engineers and builders can overcome the hurdles. The concerns will be labor and financing," Dodge said.

"Ah, the financing," said Lincoln. "I believe we may need to amend the railroad legislation with more incentives. Maybe next year Congress can work on the issue. One thing is for sure, Grenville, the country needs this railroad. Without it, it will take decades to settle the West. I am confident that from the ashes of this war the railroad will rise as a great unifying national triumph. The Pacific railroad is a national necessity."

The two men returned to the president's office and continued their discussions over lunch.

The meeting ended in mid-afternoon with cordial handshakes and best wishes. As Dodge left the White House, President Lincoln returned to the office window. The sky had darkened and snowflakes fell on Washington. He watched the general walk toward the street and hoped to see him again.

Lincoln spoke to the snowy scene, "Godspeed to you, Grenville."

He had considered asking Dodge to join the Pacific Railroad construction team, but remained silent. He knew providence and war would determine Dodge's future.

Lincoln watched Dodge's carriage leave. He lingered a moment rubbing his eyebrows before returning to his desk.

Within days, Dodge was wearing his typical baggy pants and supervising reconstruction of a railroad bridge burned by Confederate soldiers. Dark ash and the smell of burnt wood covered him. He picked up a pry bar and joined his men moving a bridge beam.

"Let's go, boys," he shouted enthusiastically. "We can finish this span before dark. Heave to!"

Lincoln and Gen'l Dodge
at Council Bluffs, Aug.1859

Memories Of The Council Bluffs Meeting
Painting by C. Everett Johnson
*From the Bostwick–Frohrdt Collection, Owned by KM3TV and on permanent
loan to The Durham Museum, Omaha, Nebraska*

Chapter 2

California and Oregon-bound emigrants traveling the rough wagon road across Iowa faced one final hardship before reaching Council Bluffs and the Missouri River.

Each of the thousands of wagons on the well-worn road had to climb the long ridge of high bluffs and weave around the narrow valleys before descending into the town and river basin. In those days, trees covered the bluffs and limited the line of sight for most of the climb.

Travelers felt surprise when a magnificent view of the Missouri River Valley unfolded before them. The pasts they were fleeing seemed less troublesome as they gazed upon the land that held their hopes for a new start.

* * * *

IN LATE AFTERNOON a covered wagon completed the arduous climb up the east side of the bluffs. At the summit, four large horses breathed heavily as the driver pulled the reins and talked them to a stop. The dirt trail here was rough. The grease pail hanging under the wagon continued swinging long after the wheels stopped rolling. The spot afforded the three passengers a spectacular view.

The driver sat in the center of the wagon's plank seat. He held the reins loosely as he scanned the horizon. He was thirty-five years old, of average height and weight, and dressed in durable clothing. He wore a felt hat with a wide brim. At his right was a young woman, perhaps in her late twenties. Her features were striking. She wore a full-length blue plaid dress and a bonnet. On the driver's opposite side, an eleven year old boy leaned affectionately against him.

They enjoyed the view while the horses rested. From this distant overlook the family studied the landscape of their future.

Below, they could see the bustling town of Council Bluffs. And while they could not hear the sounds of progress, they could see evidence of it in new construction, freshly cleared lots, and streets crowded with wagons and horse traffic.

Beyond Council Bluffs they could see across the sparsely developed river bottoms to where the wide Missouri River flowed. Across the river, the Nebraska Territory was clearly visible. The buildings in Omaha appeared no bigger than ants. After traveling a thousand miles of wilderness, the family felt inspired by these sights.

The man lifted his arm and pointed to Council Bluffs.

"Libby, I think that big building in the center of town must be the hotel. A real bed tonight will be a welcome change. And look to the right. I think that barn must be a livery stable. See the row of wagons stored in back?"

She replied, fully roused from the boredom of wagon travel.

"I see it! The town looks so perfect, so peaceful. After all we've been through, I can see us settling in a place like this." Her eyes met her husband's.

The man placed an arm around the boy's shoulder, pointed and said, "Look, William. I see the top of a steamboat above the treetops. See it moving? It's headed south to St. Joseph and Kansas City. That's the Missouri River for sure."

The boy spotted smoke billowing from the tall stacks. William gave an animated nod and bounced excitedly on the seat.

"And look there, son. See that tall building? The one I showed your Ma? That's got to be the Pacific Hotel. We'll stay there tonight, maybe in the same room President Lincoln slept in once."

"I can hardly wait, Pa," the young boy said. "There's so many people. Maybe there's kids too."

As Colton Rusk urged the horses forward for the descent into Council Bluffs, the family's hearts brimmed with hope.

The Rusk family reached the outskirts of Council Bluffs before dark. They passed only three homes before reaching the large barn they had seen from the summit. The sign above the double doors announced in four foot tall letters ROB BLACK'S LIVERY & BLACKSMITH.

Colton guided the wagon to the side of the road by the front doors. "We'll stop long enough to see if we can board the horses and wagon. Then we will find a hotel room."

Colton Rusk pulled off his hat and wiped his damp forehead with a rag. Before he could dismount, a brawny blacksmith passed through the front doors and approached the wagon.

* * * *

PROPRIETOR ROB BLACK assessed the sight before him. The four-horse team looked exhausted from their long journey. They breathed heavily in the dusty Iowa air. Flies swarmed them from a nearby garbage pile.

"You folks Mormon?" asked the blacksmith examining the three. "Most arrivals are these days."

"No, regular citizens," the driver replied. "We're just arriving from back east. My name is Colton Rusk. We need to board the team and wagon with our belongings until we make decisions. Can you care for them?"

The blacksmith looked closer at Rusk. The man on the wagon sat tall and straight. He had a look born of confidence and pride.

"We can keep them as long as you need," Black said.

"I will pay a week's charges in advance. We'll go into town first to find lodging. I should return in a bit to leave everything with you."

"That will be fine, sir," Black replied, and then wondered what had driven him to address the stranger as "sir."

Colton finished the transaction with new greenbacks. He handed them down from the wagon secretly thankful to remain seated. Black fingered the unwrinkled bills trying to remember the last time he had seen any.

The wagon moved on, clinking and creaking down the dirt road. The houses they passed were spread far apart with vacant lots between. Many were new, some still under construction.

Libby noticed several showed the warm touches of home. She liked the white picket fences around the yards and curtains in the windows.

William saw that children stopped playing to watch the wagon pass. A boy about William's age held up a hand and waved. William responded in kind.

As evening approached, Council Bluffs lost its bustle. Late shoppers and stragglers hurried along the dirt streets and wooden sidewalks to finish their day before dark.

The Rusk wagon came to a gentle stop at the Pacific Hotel. Colton stood from the board seat and braced mentally for the climb down. The agony came with exertion. It was always waiting, ready to spring up and take over his thoughts and actions. Hard as he tried to master the wicked hurting, when it reared its ugly head the debilitating impact to mind and spirit still shocked him.

Despite the pain, he knew it was important to maintain the joy of the moment.

"If they have a room, we'll take real baths tonight. I think we should celebrate our arrival at the town café. I see it just down the street. William, you stay with the team. Libby, you can come with me if you want, or just stretch your legs. I'll be back in a minute."

* * * *

THE FAMILY'S ARRIVAL had not gone unnoticed. Evil, beady eyes studied the wagon and horses through the dirty window of the saloon across the street. They examined the boy and passed on. The man was of more interest and drew careful scrutiny. He was crippled, or at least badly injured. The eyes watched the pronounced limp as the man walked around the wagon to help his wife down. The cripple, the watcher admitted, had a salient look about him, standing tall and erect despite the obvious pain.

Having assessed the man, the dark eyes glistened as they focused on the wife. She was especially beautiful, he thought, the most enticing women he had seen in a long time. While her husband was in the hotel, she stood serenely on the boardwalk talking with the boy.

The watcher in the bar was Darcy Lonigan, an Irishman. He was a loner, dependent on no one, a man grown tough and mean in the poorer boroughs of New York City.

To say that Lonigan was unattractive was a gross understatement. His facial features were dagger sharp. His skin was raw and pockmarked, giving him unnatural facial shadows. His eyes were small and deep set in the head. The whites of his eyes were yellowish and menacing. His dull brown hair hung long and reminded people of trampled wheat.

If anything about Lonigan was more frightening than his appearance, it was his behavior. He was ill-tempered, foul-mouthed, and mean as a snake.

Lonigan had been orphaned at six years old, his parents killed in a fire at the shoe factory where they had labored for pennies. He lived with a drunken uncle who resented the obligation and expense of a small boy. The uncle provided the bare essentials with no concern for moral guidance.

The boy was unloved, unwanted, and left almost starving to raise himself. Darcy Lonigan turned to crime. He entered his teen years taking what he wanted, when he wanted it, without conscience or remorse.

Lonigan lifted a whiskey glass to his thin lips and remembered another time.

A week after his twenty-first birthday, Lonigan killed a New Jersey store owner in a bungled robbery. He fled, first moving south for several years then west. Since the murder, Lonigan had continued his evil ways without pause. Now in Council Bluffs, he found himself wanting. He had no plan, only needs, and a pretty woman was one of them.

Lonigan watched as the woman waved goodbye to her husband and boy. He watched them turn the wagon at the wide intersection and drive to the east. When the street was quiet again, the lanky Irishman downed his whiskey, threw several coins on the bar, and sauntered out the front door.

On the boardwalk, Lonigan leaned against store front. He looked up and down the street coldly and deliberately. He knew the woman had walked toward the mercantile, but was uncertain where she was now. He waited, assuming she was inside one of the stores across the street. He watched the last stragglers leave the street and hurry home for supper.

In due time, Libby emerged from the mercantile, carrying a small bag of candy for the boy. She looked east, but saw neither Colton nor William returning.

Lonigan straightened, spat on the boardwalk, and started across the street toward her.

He was two buildings away when she stepped into the street and walked away from him toward the City Café. As she entered the café, Lonigan positioned himself near the door. He saw her through the front window talking with the proprietor.

Colton and William, meanwhile, had taken the horse team and wagon to the livery stable and started their return to the hotel. For Colton, the walk was painful. He pushed himself for the sake of exercise, stretching, and healing. They talked about Council Bluffs, the homes they passed and the farm they left behind. They spoke of living in this new city. Soon, the Pacific Hotel was in sight.

Colton was approaching the hotel when he saw Libby. She was on the boardwalk outside the café. He could tell from her mannerisms she was frantic with fear. A man was standing close to her, too close, talking and trying to gather her full attention. Each time she moved to get away from him, the man moved to block her. As Colton crossed the street, he saw the man shift several more times to prevent Libby from leaving.

"Step away, mister," Colton commanded as he came within the final feet.

"Who might ye be?" the man asked with a deep Irish accent.

"This is my wife. Step away now! Last chance for peaceful terms."

Lonigan became loud. "Ha! You? A cripple is telling me what to do? I think this lady probably needs a real man. You're no good for her. Leave us. Take the boy while ye still can." Lonigan doubled his fists.

Lonigan was fast, but Colton was faster. Lonigan went down hard with one powerful blow to the jaw. He was stunned to find himself sprawled on the dirty boardwalk.

Regaining control, Lonigan sprang to his feet pulling a skinning knife from his boot.

"Well, now. See what ye've done? Ye've woke up the wrong passenger this time. That clatter on me jaw will cost ye dearly, pikey," Lonigan snarled.

He lunged at Colton with the razor-sharp knife. In one fluid motion, Colton knocked the knife aside with one hand. With the other he delivered a crushing blow to Lonigan's face. Lonigan went down again, this time unconscious. The knife flew into the street.

Libby ran to her husband and clung to him crying.

"I was so scared Colton. I was scared something terrible was going to happen. He is the devil! I saw it in his eyes."

"Everything will be fine now Libby. He won't get back up."

Below them Lonigan slowly regained his wits. He glared up at Colton, hatred in his eyes. Lonigan feared the powerful man above him, this man who so easily overpowered him despite disability.

Colton held Libby and comforted her. From the corner of his eye he saw Lonigan begin to stir. He turned his head just enough to meet Lonigan's eyes with a dangerous look.

Lonigan abandoned all thought of further action and began nursing his pains. He also nursed a gnawing desire for revenge.

Colton clutched his wife and son close as the three crossed the dirt street and entered the Pacific Hotel.

Behind them Darcy Lonigan slowly got to his feet and eyed the saloon two doors away. Walking away, he spotted Libby's candy bag on the boardwalk. Still rubbing his jaw, the Irishman altered his route and ground the bag under his heel until nothing remained but mangled trash.

Chapter 3

Colton rushed Libby and William through the Pacific Hotel's lobby and up to the second floor.

The desk clerk saw the pretty woman crying as the family entered the front doors and hurried past. He wondered what was happening but did not intrude.

Colton led his family to a small room that was plain even by frontier standards. There was a bed, a dresser, a single wooden chair, and little more. A yellow wash basin with a pitcher and a chamber pot with painted flowers gave the room its only bright colors.

Two open windows looked onto the street. Faded curtains were tied back to catch any breeze in the August heat. William knew the extra blanket and pillow on the bed would make his pallet.

Colton sat with Libby on the bed. She clung to him, still crying. He looked into her swollen, flooded eyes and saw the pain. He let her weep knowing the tears were part of a healing process, not just for the confrontation with Lonigan but for deeper injuries. He held her and stroked her hair telling her how much he loved her. William joined them on the bed. Colton held them in his strong arms, Libby in one, crying, William silent, in the other.

When her crying was spent, she looked up at him. "Thank you Colton. I'll be all right now."

He kissed her cheek tenderly.

"I'll be back," he said motioning William to step outside with him.

He took William into the hallway where he placed several coins in the boy's hand. "Son, go down to the hotel desk clerk and ask if he can have food delivered to our room. He will help you. If you have any problems, come back and get me."

"Yes, Pa," William answered, and he scurried away to the stairwell.

Alone in the hallway, Colton leaned against the wall and ground his forehead into it, lamenting his absence when she needed him most. It had taken her weeks to recover from the hell they left in Maryland. She was stronger now, and for that he was grateful, but he felt helpless to protect her completely.

He rejoined Libby in the room.

"Everything is going to be all right now, Libby. This was an unfortunate incident we can put behind us."

"He was deranged, Colton. He never talked any sense at all. I was so scared without you."

"We can forget him, sweetheart. The fight ended it. We have a great life in store for us here. Let's move ahead. Nothing can stop us from being happy here."

"I'll try. I'll really try. I believe in you, Colton."

They slept in a comfortable feather bed for the first time in weeks.

Libby lay close against her husband and said a prayer of thankfulness. William wrapped himself in the blanket under the windows and soon fell asleep dreaming of campfires, horses, and the night sounds of nature he had grown accustomed to.

Colton slept for two hours before a dream woke him. He had experienced the same dream before. In it, Libby cried pitifully in a darkened room, William watching her. Colton saw a man and woman consoling Libby. Now fully awake, Colton was at a loss for an explanation. He decided the dream was a visualization of the awful events that occurred while he was away at war.

* * * *

DAWN CAME TO Council Bluffs.

Colton slept until daylight. He was the first to rise. He quietly dressed, stretched his aching leg, and slipped downstairs to the lobby. He purchased a newspaper from the desk clerk, a week-old Chicago Tribune, but gladly paid for it. He ambled out of the hotel front doors and across the street.

The moment he entered Webb's Café, the aroma of fresh baked bread and sweet cigar smoke flooded his senses. He felt at home with the sounds of lively discussion. The café was about half full of men sitting two and three to a table. He could tell by looking that the customers ranged from laborers to businessmen and bankers. Colton took an instant liking to the surroundings and sat at a table close to the kitchen.

"What can I get for you, mister?" the owner asked, wiping his hands on a towel.

"Coffee and biscuits sound good."

"Want bacon with that?"

"Sure, that sounds good. And maybe you can help me."

"What do you need, stranger?"

"I'm looking for a railroad office."

"We don't have any railroads yet. I dunno if we'll ever get a railroad at all."

"I was under the impression the Pacific Railroad had officers in the area. I'm looking for a fellow named Durant."

"Durant, eh? Sure everyone in Council Bluffs has heard of Doc Durant, at least by reputation. We hear he intends to establish the railroad in Omaha and skip Council Bluffs entirely. I guess that's okay as long as President Lincoln approves, but that ain't happened so far."

"I am hoping to talk to Mr. Durant. Do you suppose I stand a better chance to find him in Omaha?"

"You won't find him here. If he's in the area, he'll be at the Herndon House Hotel in Omaha. You can catch the Omaha ferry at the end of the street."

"Thanks," said Colton.

The café owner eyed Colton closely. "Say, wasn't that you who had a fight outside the café last night?"

"Yes. I had a problem with a fellow."

"We get strangers passing through all the time. He's almost as new here as you. He's a real troublemaker, that one is. They call him Lonigan. He's been here maybe a couple of weeks. Got a strange look in his eyes, he does. Caused a problem at the saloon last week too. Sheriff put him in jail for three days."

"We settled our differences. It was nothing I couldn't handle," Colton said.

"Say, did he hurt your leg? I seen you limping."

"No, I'm trying to shake a war wound." Colton responded.

"How'd it happen?"

"I was at the Battle of Pea Ridge in Arkansas a year ago."

"At least you're walking. Some of my friends are never coming back. I'll go get your food, friend."

After eating, Colton returned to the Pacific Hotel to find Libby and William just waking. He took them for breakfast and watched closely to ensure they had recovered from the previous night's excitement. When he saw Libby was bubbling with enthusiasm, he announced his plan for a day trip to look for Dr. Durant in Omaha.

To his surprise, Libby and William wanted to stay in Council Bluffs, the town that would probably be their home.

"I've put last night behind me," Libby said. "William and I will be okay as long as we stay around people. I want to explore Council Bluffs. If you're late, we'll be in our room well before dusk."

Colton felt comfortable about his family's safety, but just to be sure, he called on the sheriff to report the incident with Lonigan.

"I'll check on your family later this morning," the sheriff said. "And if I can locate that scoundrel Lonigan, I'll let him cool off in jail until you decide whether to press charges."

By ten o'clock he hired a carriage to take him to the ferry landing.

* * * *

WITH COLTON GONE TO Omaha, Libby and William lulled away the morning. Libby read Colton's newspaper and took time for Bible study. They lunched at the Webb's Café then returned to the hotel.

While William played with stick figures, Libby reflected on their long, difficult journey from Maryland.

She knew Colton's return from the war had saved their lives. His appalling wounds, terrible as they were, had a brighter side. They were the Godsend that returned her husband to her.

Colton's wounds were part of the reason they could never return to farming, but there were other reasons as well. They had no choice but to leave. The journey returned her from the brink of insanity.

She remembered telling Colton about the fears that overwhelmed her when Confederate troops moved onto the farm and established a camp. She could see the rebel soldiers - several thousand - all skinny, many in rags and shoeless. For her, the farm would never be the same.

Rebels cut off contact with the outside world, drove off the hired hands, and butchered the cattle. They refused to allow her and William to leave. Though treated with respect, she was essentially a prisoner in her own home. She never knew if she was a hostage or merely an attraction kept to remind the rebels of their families back home.

After a month of quiet confinement, battle arrived on the front lawn. Union forces attacked one morning attempting to drive the invaders out. The Confederates held fast putting up a fierce defense that lasted three days and raged across their fields. It was a battle that flattened the fences, slaughtered the horses, and reduced the barn to a mound of smoldering ashes.

When the fighting started, Libby and William fled to the cellar. After three days, silence came, and when it lasted a full day, she knew the battle was over. She and William emerged cautiously to daylight. The house was still standing and mostly intact, though bullet holes riddled the south side. A cannon shot had blown a gaping hole in the east wall of the bedroom affording a clear view of the fields. The trees, once beautiful, now stood stripped bare of leaves by artillery concussions. Five men lay dead between her front door and the barn's smoking rubble. Three more bodies were behind the house.

Then, the overwhelming gruesomeness struck home. Beyond her immediate surroundings, she saw hundreds of bodies scattered to the horizons in all directions. Many lay naked in ghastly, inhuman positions, their clothing blasted away by cannon explosions. More were mutilated and covered with dried blood. They lay strewn among the overturned wagons, abandoned cannons, and countless dead horses. It was impossible to hide the sight from William. The horrors of war were inescapable.

Horses gone, she and William walked five miles to the closest farm and found it burned to the ground and abandoned. They returned home to shelter. At least at home they had dozens of jars of preserved food from last fall.

The closest town, Sharpsburg, if it still existed, was twenty-five miles away through hostile territory. The horrors encountered on the walk to nearby farms told her it would be impossible to make the trip. And so, they stayed at their farm completely isolated.

Libby was deeply shocked by the ordeal. She was physically and emotionally incapable of helping herself or William. As happens in such cases, the two reverted to primitive survival behavior.

"Ma?" William had whispered as they watched the last of the lantern oil burned out. "Are we going to die here?"

"No," she replied. "Things will be all right soon." But her voice said otherwise.

Over seven hundred men died on the Rusk farm. Months later, Colton told Libby that the bloody clash had been part of a bigger battle named for a nearby creek. The day Antietam Creek flowed red, over 23,000 men died in the bloodiest day of the Civil War.

After a week, soldiers came to remove the Union Amy's dead. Confederate bodies were left behind, bloating and bursting in the sun for two more weeks, food for clouds of flies and scavengers. The smell of death came in strong waves that staggered the senses. It became unbearable over time. She and William were alone and helpless. She lacked the strength to bury one man.

Even after three weeks, when Union soldiers returned to bury the dead rebels, the graves were shallow. They dug a burial pit less than a hundred yards from the house into which they threw four hundred rotting corpses. Hundreds of shallow graves scattered across the farm made easy pickings for wolves. It was a farm no longer, and to Libby it could never again be home.

When the burial detail finished their morbid work, they told her help would arrive in two days. It never came. Abandoned, Libby and William became two more victims of the battle.

It was three more weeks before Colton arrived in the back of a two-wheel ambulance wagon. Libby and William were nowhere in sight. He frantically searched the farmhouse and found his thin family huddled on the dark cellar floor, unwashed, malnourished, and confused.

The ambulance wagon took them to the church at Sharpsburg, where their recovery began. Colton vowed to take them far away from the war and begin a new life. The trip across America, 1,100 miles to Omaha, was slow by design. The journey worked miracles in Libby and William, restoring hope and health.

Now in Council Bluffs, she was stronger. She could, at times, ignore memories of the life-altering experience. Now she struggled, trying to forget Darcy Lonigan. She worried that the incident was a bad omen. How she hoped she was wrong. She collected her strength and ventured into the town with William to investigate their new surroundings.

* * * *

THE MISSOURI RIVER was low in the late summer season, exposing much of the river bottom and leaving the ferry far from the normal shoreline. A road of sorts extended across the dry, cracked mud flats to the landing. Colton paid the carriage driver and followed the wagon wheel ruts the last hundred yards. This was the least scenic place he had seen on the long journey.

On the ferry, Colton rode with a handful of travelers, a wagon, and a crew of three. He studied the scene and noticed at once the large building dominating the view of Omaha. He asked a fellow passenger about it.

"I can't help but notice that big building on the hilltop. What is it?"

"Why that's the Territorial Capitol, stranger," the other answered.

"What's the other tall building off to the left?" Colton asked. "The one closer to the river."

"That's the Herndon House Hotel at the foot of Farnam Street. It's a good place to stay if you can afford it," the traveler replied.

Colton perked up remembering the Herndon was the best place to find Durant.

Within minutes, the ferry landed in Nebraska Territory. Colton disembarked and crossed the bare flats and natural levee into town. He found Omaha intriguing. Everywhere he looked, he saw robust economic activity. Construction was in full swing in every direction.

He saw no evidence of railroad construction or materials.

As Colton approached the Herndon House he saw it was larger than it appeared from the ferry. It was a solid structure, all brick, standing four stories tall. The upper three floors had balconies. Two carriages waited outside for guests.

Colton entered the main door and saw surprising luxuriousness. He had seen finer hotels in Chicago, but it was clear Herndon House was a high quality establishment. He found the registration desk at the rear of the lobby.

The clerk greeted Colton with a smile, "How can I help you, sir?"

"I'm looking for a railroad man named Durant, Doctor Thomas Durant. Do you know where I can find him?"

"We know Mr. Durant well. He is a guest here, but I haven't seen him for several days. Sometimes he leaves for weeks. Check across the street at the telegraph office. They may know his whereabouts."

After inquiring about room rates Colton walked to the telegraph office. The sign above the door read "Missouri and Western Telegraph Company."

The Herndon House Hotel –Omaha, Nebraska
Courtesy of the Douglas County Historical Society

The telegrapher was busy receiving a message, so Colton waited until he finished before speaking up.

"I'm trying to locate Doctor Thomas Durant. Do you know him?"

"Yes, of course. I do. He left for St. Joseph three days ago."

Colton's face showed disappointment.

"I expect him back on tomorrow evening's boat," the telegrapher added.

"I'll check back tomorrow," Colton said. "I may leave a message for him."

Colton left the telegraph office and spent the next three hours exploring Omaha. He ate lunch at a local café where he met two businessmen who confirmed the city was committed to bring in the railroad.

By late afternoon, Colton realized Omaha was more to his liking than he'd previously thought. Before returning to the ferry, he reserved a room at the Herndon House for the next day and resolved to bring his family to Nebraska. A room at the Herndon, he thought, would be a good use for a part of the funds salvaged from a life and home abandoned. It was money that had ridden 1,100 miles hidden under the wagon.

Colton returned to Council Bluffs that evening tired and hungry. His leg throbbed. That night, the family ate dinner at Webb's Café and shared their day's experiences.

"The sheriff came by this morning to make sure William and I were all right," Libby said.

"I hoped he would," Colton replied. "I talked with him before I left for Omaha."

"The sheriff is sure he can get a conviction if we file charges."

"There will be no charges, Libby. The problem is solved. We're moving on in the morning. Omaha is a nice town. You and William are going to like Nebraska."

Libby and William listened intently.

"Omaha was impressive. The town is about the same size as Council Bluffs, but seems it's growing faster. Our future is in Omaha."

"What about the railroad?" she asked.

"Doctor Durant has an office in Omaha. People say the railroad will have a huge presence there. Dr. Durant promised them the railroad will make its headquarters in Omaha."

Libby warmed quickly to the idea of moving to Omaha.

"Will we take the wagon?"

"Yes. I believe it will be a permanent move. We can rent a house. Maybe within a week we can sell the wagon and horses."

"I can get used to city life. If you think Omaha is the best place for us, we're ready to go, right William?"

William nodded, not fully understanding the implications of the conversation. He could tell his parents were optimistic, and that was enough for him.

"If I can't get a job with the railroad, we should have enough money to make it at least a couple of months. Meanwhile, we need to stay in hotels to be closer to the top people. After camping so long, I think we're ready for a change."

Colton's cheery talk failed to hide his concern. The long trip west was an all or nothing gamble.

* * * *

THE FERRY TRIP to Omaha was routine for the seasoned travelers. Libby and William held on tight as Colton drove the horses over the natural levee and onto the Omaha streets.

He drove to the M. Hunt Livery stable at Sixteenth and Farnam, a carefully chosen destination. Without question it met their boarding and storage needs. Just as important, the Herndon Hotel was within walking distance.

The eight block stroll to the hotel led through the heart of downtown. Colton wanted Libby and William to see firsthand Omaha's charms and possibilities. They ambled from storefront to storefront discovering the town. The bakery, with its perfect breads and cakes, was especially appealing to Libby who often fretted over baking.

Approaching the Herndon Hotel, Colton pointed to the line of waiting carriages. "They're available to take us anywhere we want. Let's hire one this afternoon. We can tour the town. We need to make sure we really like it here."

William and Libby approved the idea and looked forward to the tour. After registering, Colton escorted his family to the Herndon House dining room for lunch. They found one of the most extensive menus they had ever seen. Many items were in French. The family had a fun time selecting their orders.

"I am flabbergasted they offer lobster," Libby said. "It must come by steamboat. Who would ever have imagined such a fine restaurant in the Nebraska Territory?"

They hired a carriage to show them the town. For two hours they explored. Libby declared the day "perfect."

* * * *

AS DUSK APPROACHED, Colton left to conduct business. At the Telegraph Office, he found the telegrapher sweeping the floor. Today, the noisy telegraph clicker was silent.

"Good afternoon," Colton announced to the telegrapher.

"How can I help you?" the telegrapher responded.

"I came to see if you have any updates on Dr. Durant's arrival."

"He's still due tonight. I received a wire from him this morning."

"Good. I need to leave a message for him," Colton said.

"I'll get paper and an envelope for you. He should pick it up late tonight or first thing in the morning. No charge of course."

Colton wrote a one page letter and tucked it into the envelope.

The telegrapher took the envelope. "At the risk of being nosy, are you selling land to Mr. Durant? He's been buying quite a bit lately."

"No. I want to talk to him about a job."

"I doubt if Durant is hiring anyone, so far as I know."

"You are probably right, but I will talk with him nonetheless. If destiny intends for me to have a job here, it shall happen."

"What's your name, friend?" the telegrapher asked.

"I'm Colton Rusk." He extended his hand.

"Pleased to meet you. I'm Anthony Butler. I've been running this office for Mr. Ed Creighton ever since his telegraph lines arrived."

Anthony Butler watched Colton limp to the hotel. He puzzled about what a crippled man could offer a rich New York financier like Doctor Durant. He had the carriage of a soldier, yet this Colton Rusk seemed completely out of place.

Chapter 4

Three hundred miles west of Omaha, a clear stream meandered along the natural boundary dividing the flat plains from rolling sand hills. Narrow and no more than three feet deep, the stream flowed almost year round, stopping only in winter's coldest months.

A thick carpet of prairie grass covered the surrounding plains and dunes, providing a habitat for thousands of well-adapted creatures. It was a beautiful land teeming with life - infinitely more complex than the descriptions of Eastern newspaper men who called it a "vast wasteland of sky and grass."

The small stream, at a point twenty miles south of its junction with the Platte River, ran past a broad, green meadow bordered by groves of ash and cottonwood trees. The high plains to the west and higher dunes to the east provided protection against the full brunt of harsh weather.

At the upper end of the meadow, high enough to be safe from flood waters, a Cheyenne village of fifty or more teepees lay nestled against the tree line. A worn path wove down the sloping land to the stream.

The village afforded easy access to the plains where buffalo grazed and grew fat for Cheyenne hunters. Many generations of the tribe knew this spot as their summer home. A sacred burial ground lay a quarter mile away where parents and grandparents and those from long ago rested forever.

In the cool morning, smoke drifted across the waking village. Villagers coaxed campfires to life and prepared to face another day.

Near the community's south end, a warrior opened a buckskin door flap and stepped from his teepee. He looked at the sun's position and searched for clouds. He was tall and muscled, about thirty years old, and dressed in tan buckskin. A single rare, red feather was tied in his hair with a beaded strip of buckskin. His abrupt appearance caused a bird to abandon its search for food in a nearby garbage heap and fly away.

The Village Awakens
Courtesy of United States Archives

Another warrior emerged from the teepee, a younger reproduction of the man preceding him. He too wore buckskin with a feather in his hair. He was several inches shorter and significantly less muscled. The older Indian, White Eagle, stopped at the ashes of last night's fire and stirred the embers with a stick. He added kindling and surveyed the ashes. When satisfied the fire would start, he spoke to the younger man, Running Elk.

"The old one is awake. We will see him now. Come."

"My dream will disturb him," Running Elk answered his father.

"Your dream is important. You must tell Chogan all you told me. The old one will know what this means."

White Eagle started toward the opposite end of the village. Running Elk followed. They passed through the maze of teepees until almost at the village's' northern edge.

White Eagle stopped at a teepee indistinguishable from any other. He listened, and when he heard sounds from inside, he scratched softly on the deerskin flap and called.

"Chogan. It is White Eagle. I must see you."

From inside came the response, "You may enter."

White Eagle held up his hand signaling his son to wait, then lifted the flap and entered. Inside, he found the grizzled old man sitting quietly chewing a strip of buffalo meat. His woman sat next to him. Their weathered faces looked like tanned leather.

"What is it, White Eagle? Why do you come so early?"

"It is my son Running Elk. You know him. He has had a strange dream, one that is beyond explanation. Will you hear him?"

"Bring the boy to me."

Chogan was the oldest and wisest man in the village. He knew the legends and history of the people. He communed with the Great Spirit and understood his signs. He counseled the Chief, cured the people, and prayed for them.

White Eagle called for his son to enter then sat on the buffalo hide beside Chogan. Running Elk entered the teepee as Chogan's wife stepped outside.

When Running Elk's eyes adjusted to the dimness, he saw his father and Chogan. He stood until invited to sit.

The old man looked at the boy. He was pleased with what he saw.

"Tell me your dream, Running Elk," the old man asked.

Running Elk was nervous in the presence of the ancient medicine man and wondered how to begin his story. He started tentatively

"Last night I dreamed of many days ride to the rising sun. Our chief sent me to learn the ways of our enemy, the white man. I saw many white men in their wagons."

Running Elk paused to measure his audience.

The old man grunted acknowledgement. "Go on," said Chogan.

"I came to a bluff overlooking the white man's village and their strange lodges. In my dream the village lay near many Cheyenne teepees. As I watched, a huge wolf came to the village from the east. He walked on two legs. His jaws were hideous with teeth like flint axes. His eyes hungered for the village and the lands. I was afraid and hid in the grass to watch."

The old man shifted slowly sitting up, as if preparing for bad news.

"Then as the white men came from their lodges, the wolf raged. He killed and ate many. No white men fought him, but welcomed him in their presence. The great wolf destroyed far more than he could eat. His huge teeth cut through their bones and flesh like wind through the tall grasses. Those who begged for life and bowed to him, he spared.

"Then came ten giant horses. The great horses blew smoke and spat fire onto the Cheyenne village. They had huge teeth like the Great Wolf. Our people ran from their teepees. The giant horses burned and crushed our people with their huge hooves. They destroyed the village and all things in it. Our people lived no more. Then the tall wolf helped the devil horses slaughter the buffalo, not as a hunt, but killing all, even the young ones. In the spring, grass came where the village once stood, but I saw no people or buffalo. The tracks of the devil horses remained as if burned into the earth. This is my dream, old one."

Running Elk waited for a response, hoping his father felt no shame for his dream. The old man's chin trembled as he spoke.

"The Great Spirit has given me the same dream. It is a warning. The tall wolf is a new creature I have never seen. The white man will bring him upon us. We must watch for him whose greed brings the end of our people."

Running Elk listened helplessly. He felt the gravity of the moment and looked to the older men for guidance. None came.

"Go now. I must pray about these things." His voice filled with fear. "I will ask the Great Spirit to help us stop the evil that comes."

He reached behind him and picked up prayer feathers. He motioned only once for the two to leave, then began a methodic chant.

White Eagle and Running Elk slipped silently from the teepee and disappeared into the village.

Chapter 5

After months on the trail, the Herndon House dining room was a welcome change for the Rusk family. When William mentioned he'd sure like more of that Herndon pie, the family naturally showed up for dinner without discussion. They could splurge for now.

While they ate, a steamboat arrived from St. Joseph and docked at the foot of Jones Street, seven blocks away. They heard the shrill whistle but remained oblivious to the reaction it caused. Outside there was an excited rush to the riverfront. People walked and ran and rode horses and carriages to meet the arriving steamboat.

The evening riverboats always brought the mail and residents returning from the east. It was a time when young men and women flirted, the adults gossiped, and businessmen checked for inbound shipments. Occasionally the captain, if he had a good musician aboard, allowed an impromptu concert or dance on the deck.

* * * *

DR. THOMAS DURANT waited impatiently while the gangplank lowered. He was aloof and spoke to no one. With minimal jostling, he was the first passenger to disembark and enter the waiting crowd.

"Doc" Durant, as he preferred to be called, was tall and thin. His expensive suit was out of place in a frontier town. The clothing alone gained him special treatment when people subconsciously stepped back from his path. A lifetime of poor posture made him appear sway-backed. He wore an over-length Van Dyke beard that was inconsistent with his stylish clothing. The scraggly beard might have been his most noticeable feature except for the piercing blue eyes. Few could hold his penetrating gaze.

For all the time Durant spent becoming a medical doctor and professor, he didn't find it challenging. This doctor preferred the high stakes business world. Making money was his passion, and he was good at it.

By any standard, Dr. Durant was rich from trading stocks, selling cotton, and building railroads. At home, Durant was sufficiently moneyed to be well-known in New York's elite society.

Dr. Thomas Clark Durant
Public Domain Image from
The United States National Park Service Archives
Photographer Unknown

Long strides took him quickly from the crowded steamboat and past a cargo storage area. Seeing no carriages on the riverfront, he walked to the Missouri and Western Telegraph office. At age forty-three, he was fit enough to make the walk at a brisk pace.

Telegrapher Anthony Butler was still at his post when Durant burst through the doors and bluntly asked, "Where are my messages?"

The startled telegrapher stood. "Here, sir. I have several for you."

Anthony Butler handed Durant a string-bound packet of sealed envelopes. He knew the envelope with Colton Rusk's letter was placed strategically on top. It drew the desired attention.

"What is this?" Durant growled.

Butler responded in a manner calculated to provoke comment. "A crippled fellow came looking for you the past couple of days. He wants to see you about a job. That must be his letter on top."

"I'm hiring no one right now, especially a crippled man."

"He wants to talk to you."

"That won't happen." Durant commented without emotion.

Durant placed the envelopes aside momentarily and wrote four outbound telegrams. He addressed two to New York City, one to Washington, and the fourth to Philadelphia.

Butler read the handwritten telegrams and commented, "I can read them all right, Dr. Durant, but I sure don't understand your codes."

If Durant's demeanor had been icy to that point, it abruptly turned to disdain. He glared incredulously at the telegraph operator. Butler knew from the look that he had crossed an unspoken boundary.

Durant concluded a ten second stare with insult. "Are you stupid, man? You have no business knowing what my messages mean. They're in code to keep the likes of you from understanding them. Why would I want you to understand my thoughts? Don't answer! Just send the telegrams!"

Durant left for his hotel room at the Herndon House.

* * * *

THE REGISTER AT the Herndon House Hotel showed the two largest rooms on the preferred second floor in the name of Dr. Thomas C. Durant. The larger of the two rooms, now converted into an office, afforded a fine view of the riverfront. The furnishings met the doctor's bare-bones specifications with a desk, table, and a small safe.

The second room was a well-appointed sleeping room that remained unused for long periods while the doctor traveled.

The morning after his return to Omaha, Doctor Durant sat alone reading a brief from his Washington lobbyist. As he read, his face turned red with anger. He continued reading, his face becoming more flushed with each word.

Durant spoke resolutely to himself. "These lobbyists are utterly incompetent. They have no idea how to get results. Now I'll have to do things myself."

Outside the office, a man sat leaning back in a wooden chair. He was a secretary of sorts, provided by the hotel to perform clerical work Durant might require. His name was Ray Johnson. He felt the same sense of dread a mariner feels on a dark morning, knowing a storm is surely coming, but unsure exactly when. Johnson's storm came sooner rather than later.

Durant screamed at the closed door. "Johnson!"

The clerk jumped to his feet and entered the office. Durant stood with his back to the clerk staring out a window. Durant spoke, never looking directly at him.

"Prepare a telegram for immediate transmission."

Johnson dropped into an empty chair and fumbled to open his notebook.

"This telegram goes to Daniel Sullivan, Esquire, 5638 Pennsylvania Avenue, Washington, D. C. I hereby appoint you as my lead lobbyist for Congressional affairs. Your salary is increased ten percent effective immediately. Your first duty is to notify lobbyist Douglas Belcher that he is dismissed from my service for lack of performance. I plan to be in Washington soon and will settle with him at that time. Further instructions to follow. Acknowledge by return telegram. T. C. Durant."

He gave the clerk a dismissive wave and returned to watching the street below. As the clerk stood to leave, Durant said, "Wait!"

Johnson stopped. "Yes, Doctor Durant?"

"Why are so many people on the streets? They're all dressed in black. What's going on here?"

"Omaha has its first legal execution this afternoon a half mile west of the capitol. We're going to hang a murderer."

"One of your friends, Johnson? Maybe a family member?"

The clerk seethed, but said nothing.

The Herndon House Hotel – Omaha, Nebraska
From the collections of the Omaha Public Library

Durant's face twisted into a slight smile. "Actually, I'm glad the territory is making progress. Go on now. Deliver my telegram."

Johnson crossed hurriedly to the telegraph office.

Anthony Butler looked up as Johnson came in.

"Durant sent me with a telegram," Johnson called from the door.

"Don't tell me," said Butler smirking. "I'll bet it's urgent and requires immediate transmission, right?"

"Of course it's urgent. No secret code with this one. You'll find it interesting."

Butler examined the message. "You're right," he said. "It's in plain English. I'll send it right away."

"I got to go. If I don't get back soon, there'll be hell to pay."

* * * *

ANY PLEASURE Durant felt hearing about the execution faded quickly when he returned to his desk. He picked up Colton Rusk's letter and read it for the fourth time since last night. He studied every word for hidden meaning and clues to potential problems.

Who was this man Rusk who had a referral from Grenville Dodge? The note was short and direct:

Omaha, Nebraska, August 26, 1863

> **Dr. Thomas Durant**
> **General Grenville Dodge has recommended I contact you regarding Union Pacific's need for hardworking men with energy and vision. I recently arrived in Omaha in anticipation of assisting you in a meaningful way with this historic project. I will appreciate the opportunity to meet with you to discuss the railroad and where I should fit in. Contact me at the Herndon House Hotel.**
>
> **Colton Rusk**

Durant's mind tumbled in paranoid thought. He wondered what dangerous game was in play. Was Rusk a spy? Or, maybe the cripple had something worthwhile to offer.

Durant calmed himself and thought. At the end of his self-debate, he decided he would, indeed, talk with this brazen outsider. He would invest a few guarded minutes to see what developed.

He said the stranger's name aloud. "Colton Rusk."

Decision made, Dr. Durant summoned Johnson who had just returned from the telegraph office.

"A man named Colton Rusk is registered in the hotel. Find him and deliver a message immediately. Instruct him to report to my office at eleven o'clock tomorrow for the meeting he requested. Go!"

Johnson hurried out and soon located Colton with his family in the hotel lobby, returning from an outing. Colton was purchasing a newspaper as Johnson approached.

"Sir, are you Colton Rusk?" Johnson asked.

"I am sir."

"Doctor Thomas Durant will meet with you at eleven o' clock tomorrow morning. His office is on the second floor of this hotel."

"Please tell him I will be there."

Johnson left for the grand stairway to return to his hallway post.

Colton turned to his wife.

"Well, Libby, tomorrow we shall see if we have a future with Lincoln's railroad."

Chapter 6

AUGUST 28, 1863 - THE DURANT INTERVIEW

I feel"—Libby paused, picking the right word—"disappointment. No, actually it's more like fear."

Colton opened the hotel door for her, and followed her into the lobby.

"What are you fearful about?" he asked.

"We spent most of the morning looking for a house and found nothing, not so much as a one-room cabin. It looks like Omaha has nothing to rent or buy."

"Don't get discouraged, Libby. We'll find something," he assured, trying to sound convincing.

"Even the houses under construction on the outskirts of town are already purchased," she persisted. "And Twenty-Fourth Street is so far out. What are we going to do, Colton?"

"We haven't seen everything yet. We'll continue looking tomorrow, and if nothing comes up, we'll look the next day. If worse comes to worse, we'll live in a boarding house for a while. It's too early to worry," Colton said. "For now, I need to get ready for my meeting with Dr. Durant."

* * * *

COLTON STEPPED INTO THE second floor hallway just before eleven o'clock. He saw Johnson in a chair at the end of the hall and approached.

"Good to see you again. I'm here at the time you directed," Colton said.

"Dr. Durant is out for a few minutes. I will show you to his office. You can wait until he returns."

Colton sat alone in the plain office for what seemed like ages before the door opened and Doc Durant entered. He was wearing a long, formal coat, a style with tails Colton had seen only on the East

Coast. It was strange attire for a frontier town sweltering in the August heat.

Durant removed his coat and hung it on a coat stand, revealing more expensive clothing and a gold watch chain.

Colton's impression was that Durant, while not physically large, was an imposing, authoritative figure. Durant's mannerisms showed the subtle arrogance of great wealth: an extended little finger, head high in the air and slightly back. His movements were slow and deliberate, almost to the point of showiness. He exuded confidence.

Colton watched Durant open a leather satchel, remove several papers, and lay them on a side table. Neither spoke. The silence would have unnerved many men, but Colton remained quiet, knowing Durant was taking his measure.

Durant reached his desk and sat without introduction. He neither offered a hand shake nor attempted small talk to break the ice. Instead he began with business-like precision.

"You are Rusk?"

"I am, sir."

"I grant you time to speak with me because you used Grenville Dodge's name."

"Thank you, sir."

"I grant you no more than five minutes. You'll get less if I detect you are wasting my time."

Colton remained silent waiting for the obvious question.

"How do you know General Dodge?" Durant asked.

"He was my colonel when I served in the Iowa Fourth Infantry."

"In what capacity did you serve?"

"I was his Major."

"What were your principal duties?"

"I was in charge of Washington relations, procurement and other sensitive matters."

"What kind of sensitive matters?" Derision dripped from Durant's tone.

"I was responsible for the intelligence team and its funding."

"Ah. Then you are saying you ran Dodge's controversial spy network?"

"That was one of my duties."

"What was your role in funding?" Durant asked.

"I am the person who developed a way to use enemy assets to help the nation's cause. Colonel Dodge liked the concept and authorized it."

"What sort of enemy assets are you talking about?"

"Cotton."

The answer was magical and drew Durant's full focus. His fortune from smuggled Confederate cotton had required General Dodge's help. Durant paused for a closer look at the stranger. He suspiciously examined Colton's commanding appearance, the look of a disciplined military man.

"And you used money from cotton sales for what purpose?" Durant asked.

"We paid informants and Confederate insiders for information."

Durant was still wary. He knew Colton could have gleaned everything up to this point from newspapers. His next question would provide proof absolute.

"What was the name of the steamboat that carried the first cotton shipment north?"

Colton knew it was a trick question and answered without hesitation.

"The first three shipments were not by steamboat. They went by railroad to Ohio with military protection. The fourth shipment went by the steamship *Intrepid* to St. Louis."

Durant relaxed. This man Rusk seemed legitimate. No imposter would have known such details. Durant's manner became less sharp, though without any hint of pleasantness. He decided to fully evaluate Colton Rusk and fired non-stop questions testing him.

"What's wrong with your leg? I heard you're crippled."

"I took shrapnel in action last year in Arkansas."

"When were you assigned to General Dodge?"

"General Meade assigned me to assist Colonel Dodge when the Army absorbed the Iowa Guard. He was still a colonel at that time."

"Where were you before your time with Dodge?"

"Washington. I was in the War Department for two years."

"Doing what?" Durant asked with increasing curiosity.

"I had many duties. My main function was to give private briefings to the newer and less influential senators and representatives. The Generals briefed ranking congressional members."

"What did your briefings cover?"

"My presentations covered the changing military situation. I also sought support for military projects."

"You were a military lobbyist! I hate lobbyists."

Nonetheless, Durant couldn't resist the temptation to further test Rusk.

"Who is Oakes Ames?"

"He is a senator from Massachusetts."

"Have you met with Lincoln?"

"I have."

Durant continued to pepper Colton with questions about the inside workings in Washington. After fifteen minutes, Durant made one of his few positive comments of the day.

"I'm satisfied with your experiences. Frankly, I expected you to be a snake oil salesman."

Next they covered military contacts. Colton proved satisfactorily that he had worked with Ulysses Grant and William Sherman. When Durant paused for a moment, Colton removed a letter from his pocket.

"I have a letter of introduction from General Dodge for you."

Durant snatched the letter and examined it. He knew Dodge's unique handwriting from years of correspondence. He read:

May 23, 1863

Dr. Thomas Durant,

This will introduce to you Major Colton Rusk, retired. Major Rusk served with distinction in the Battle of Pea Ridge, Arkansas while assigned to the Fourth Iowa Infantry.

Beyond his bravery in battle, Major Rusk consistently proved himself invaluable in dealings with the War Department where he was previously assigned. He can write well, keep books, and effectively organize a rabble.

Major Rusk suffered wounds in battle and returns to civilian life a hero. I am personally indebted to him for his service and can recommend him for any position that requires a trusted, intelligent and motivated man. He was also the Iowa 4th's best shot with a pistol.

Gen. Grenville Dodge- Army of the Republic

Durant laid the letter on the desk. "That's Dodge's scribble all right. I'd recognize that horrid scrawl anywhere. Lord knows I've struggled with his letters often enough. In this case, it's mostly legible. That means he gave the letter serious thought. What does Dodge mean when he says he is personally indebted to you?"

"General Dodge believes I saved his life by pulling him clear of a hot situation at Pea Ridge."

"Ah! The Battle of Pea Ridge. The fight that made Dodge famous. The newspapers tell us Dodge saved the entire Union Army in that battle. They rave about his wounds and the bullet holes in his clothing. He had three horses shot out from under him. Out with it, Rusk! Did you save him?"

"I prefer to characterize my actions as performance of duty."

Examining the letter again Durant seemed satisfied.

"You have an acceptable reference. But why are you in Omaha? Why didn't you just go back to wherever you came from?"

"My family and I left Maryland three months ago for a new life. The war took our farm."

Durant walked to the window and stood watching the river.

"Men are like any other tool. If they break or are lost, I replace them. I lost two personal assistants in the last year. A Sioux war party scalped and cut up one in the Wyoming Territory. The other I fired and left in Utah."

Durant returned to his desk.

"My concern is your obvious lack of business talent. If you had any, you wouldn't be here." Durant paused to let his slanderous remark sink in.

"Even so, I may be able to use you. I have need of a trustworthy man who will obey orders immediately and without question. You have been in battle, followed orders, maintained loyalty."

"I meet those requirements," Colton said.

"Before we go further, I want to check your wound. I want to make sure you have no infection; otherwise I'm sure to make a losing investment in you."

"I beg your pardon."

"Drop your pants, Rusk. I want to examine your leg. I'm a qualified medical doctor. I might be able to give you good advice."

Colton Rusk looked to ensure the door was closed and reluctantly unbuckled his belt and lowered his pants.

Durant examined the wound with the cold, uncaring indifference of a farmer inspecting cattle at auction. Upon seeing the mangled thigh, the Doctor made a clucking noise.

"You're lucky the field hospital didn't remove the entire leg. Army doctors are quick to amputate. I probably would have amputated it myself. I see no infection here."

"It still gives me ample trouble," Colton acknowledged.

"Of course it does. You have considerable healing ahead of you. You will never walk normally. My advice is to ignore the pain and stretch the leg regularly. It needs the work. For me, you are an acceptable business risk if you can handle the pain of riding a horse."

"I'll manage," Colton said buckling his pants.

The room fell silent as Durant contemplated his next step.

"I want you to work for me as an assistant handling security and intelligence. You will represent me in dealing with cities, contractors, and others who may have reason to defraud or oppose me. You will work for me directly and report to no other person. You will follow my every command with no conscience, anything short of murder or robbery. You will be duty-bound to act in my personal interest only. Are you interested in building a railroad with these terms?"

"I am," Colton answered

"You've been away from work for a while, so I'll tell you what you're worth. The going rate for a healthy bodied man doing hard labor is three dollars per day. I offer you triple that rate in return for unquestioned loyalty and a good work ethic. That's nine dollars per day and other benefits. Don't try to haggle about the rate. I save negotiating for important matters. Is this offer satisfactory?"

"Yes. I accept." Outwardly Colton was calm, but inside his heart leapt with joy.

"Just to ensure we have the same understanding, if you violate our agreement, I will fire you on the spot. Understood?"

"Understood." Colton responded, trying to reconcile the thrill of a new job against a threat of dismissal, all within in fifteen seconds.

"And I'll test your loyalty in ways you will never suspect. You are my representative. You will speak my views. You will endorse my opinions publicly and privately. Is that understood?"

"Yes, sir."

Durant suddenly changed directions. "Why do you want to be a part of the railroad?"

"Grenville Dodge convinced me that trains are better than horses. They carry people and freight faster and farther than wagons. They carry bigger loads and do it cheaper. I saw it myself in the war."

Durant looked at Colton in astonishment. "Have I just hired an idiot? Your awakening is about twenty-five years late. Railroads are the rage on Wall Street. Railroads will transform our naked continent into a powerful nation."

Durant held up his hand for Colton to remain silent. "Listen to me closely. You need understanding beyond the elementary lessons of troop and cotton trains. Lincoln tells me that over the last twenty years about five million immigrants entered the United States. More are trickling in now. After the war we will see millions more. They are waiting for clearance to board ships all over Europe."

Colton nodded understanding but wisely remained quiet.

"They're going to move west and fill the desert with cities and farms and businesses. How will they get there? Wagons? No. We must have a railroad to the Pacific Ocean. It is essential to the nation. Now is the time to build a railroad to California."

Colton stirred with excitement about the future.

"Before you think I'm a patriot, you need to understand I just gave you a sample of the rousing language used to promote the construction. I personally don't care if a railroad is ever built. What I do care about is profit from building it. Take this lesson to heart: I will help give America its railroad, but my sole goal is to make money."

Durant gave Colton a moment to reflect before continuing.

"You have the limited view of a farm boy soldier. It's time for your thinking to mature. Your horizons need to expand. Go now. Think about this job and be here tomorrow at ten o'clock."

* * * *

THAT EVENING, THE family walked along Farnam Street in a breeze that drove back the summer heat. Libby listened to every detail of Colton's interview.

"Are you sure this is what you want?" she asked. "This seems like a dream come true." She held up the flowers he had given her and breathed in the sweet aroma.

"I'm sure, Libby. This job is exactly what we need. This is where we begin again with a new town, a new job, and a blank slate. Dr. Durant seems to have the drive and brains it takes to succeed. I'd suspect he has iron will."

William looked up at his mother and saw her smiling. He saw the pride in his father's face. He knew enough to understand they were in a good place.

"Maybe Omaha has a school, Pa, with other kids?" William asked.

"I'm sure it has, son. We'll find it soon."

Chapter 7

Colton rose early the morning he was to report for his new job as Dr. Durant's assistant. He walked to the crowded café on Farnam Street for breakfast.

He sat at a table near three men discussing the execution two days earlier. Colton was unfamiliar with the case, so worked his way into the conversation by asking about the man's crime. The men welcomed the chance to rehash the event. Soon Colton was a part of the group.

He introduced himself and asked for advice on finding a home.

"You'll find a realtor's office just around the corner," one said. "But I have to warn you, Omaha is growing so fast I doubt if you find anything soon."

Colton left the café troubled for the first time about where his family would live.

Just before ten o'clock, he stepped into the second floor hallway outside Durant's office, anxious to get started on his new job. Johnson was leaned back in a chair at his usual place.

"I guess I should formally introduce myself. You already know, I am Colton Rusk." He shook hands with the clerk.

"I'm Roy Johnson," the clerk responded.

"I suppose we'll be seeing each other, perhaps working together. Doctor Durant asked me to report for work this morning."

"You a new assistant?"

"Yes."

"He's difficult to work for. You'll find out. He's in the office with George Train right now. I'll see if he's ready for you."

As the clerk stood from his chair, Colton asked, "Are you referring to George Train the orator? The same man who introduced street cars to London?"

"That's right. The famous George Train is in there. He's a lunatic if you ask me."

"I've read about him. He's quite popular you know," said Colton.

"Don't really care. Stay here a minute."

Johnson disappeared into Durant's office. He returned expressionless and gestured Colton inside.

Durant was at his desk; George Train sat opposite him looking exactly like newspaper drawings he'd seen.

Train turned in his chair to face Colton, but it was Durant who spoke first.

"George, this is Colton Rusk, my new assistant. His headquarters will be here in Omaha."

"Really? That makes two of us, Doc."

"With more to come I suspect," added Durant.

Colton looked at Train. He wore extravagant silk pants and a white vest. His fingernails shined with polish white as snow, presumably to match the vest. Instead of shoes, Train wore Italian sandals. Colton caught himself staring and struggled to maintain eye contact. He was almost sure Train had caught him gawking.

Colton reached to shake hands with Train. To his surprise, Train grabbed his own right hand with his left and vigorously shook hands with himself.

"I'm pleased to meet you, Rusk." Then noticing Colton standing dumbfounded added, "Oh don't worry, I never shake hands with other people. Something I learned overseas in another cultured land."

"I'm likewise pleased to meet you," said Colton. And to Durant, Colton said, "Good morning, sir."

Durant was rude and unfriendly. "Rusk, let's get something understood during your first minute here. I don't engage in small talk with employees. You don't need to wish me good morning, or good night, or good luck. I have included the little pleasantries, if you need them, in your generous salary. When you come into my presence, state your business, or if you have nothing to say, have a seat and keep quiet. I'm a busy man. Now sit."

Colton sat. He might have felt like an obedient dog, but he had seen similar behavior in government and military leaders. He had learned to respect candor and unambiguous leadership styles. Colton's military background taught an appreciation for a clear sense of direction in good leaders.

George Train seemed an independent spirit who was willing to push the limits with Durant. He seemed to enjoy making bold inquiries about matters outside his responsibilities. "So, Doc, why did you dismiss your lobbyist? Belcher seemed competent."

The question, perhaps by design, irritated Durant.

"I fired him because he left Washington at the exact instant he was supposed to be cultivating a senator. He wasn't doing his job."

"That's strange," Train pursued. "Why did he leave Washington?"

"He went to be nursemaid for a sick child. He threw his career away for a case of measles. Men take care of business, fight wars, and provide the livelihood. Wives and doctors exist to take care of sick children. I'm a doctor. I know these things."

Train ignored the offensive remark and aimed a grin at Durant.

"We've wasted enough time," Durant scolded. "Let's proceed with our business."

Durant focused on Train.

"We need to acquire more property west of Omaha. I want you to go to Fremont and Columbus in the next few days. Buy property, anything that's for sale. Once we announce our decision to build through those cities, prices will skyrocket. Next month I'll want you to go further west for the same purpose. Leave us for now. I need to talk to Rusk."

Train stood and made an exaggerated bow to his leader.

"Master, I leave you. If you need me, I will be having breakfast and praying the Herndon House may some day prepare a decent egg."

Durant pointed to the door with an exasperated look. "GO! Damn you."

Train departed. Durant closed his eyes and rubbed his forehead trying to calm his nerves. Then he addressed Colton.

"We need to finish your orientation so you can start producing. Where do you plan to live?"

"We're looking for a rent home nearby."

"In other words you have absolutely no idea where you will live." Durant paused a moment then softened. "Admittedly you're new to the area. You have no comprehension that homes in Omaha sell far in advance of construction. The reality is that you won't be able to get a home for six or seven months."

Colton started to speak, but Durant was too quick.

"Because you represent me, however, I will take you under my wing. I own several homes in Omaha. We'll have George Train work up the documents and get you into one as part of your compensation."

Durant screamed at the door. "Johnson! Get in here!"

The clerk opened the door no more than two inches and peered in.

"Go find Train. He's downstairs eating breakfast. Grab him by the collar and drag him back up here."

Johnson snapped the door shut and scurried off.

Within minutes Train knocked on the door, opened it, and stepped inside. "You rang, Master?" he said with a deep bow.

"Stop bowing to me. If you must be subservient, pick the lint off my coat before I go into public. Meanwhile we need to provide Rusk and his family a place to live. I have two homes over on Capital Avenue. Move him into one as part of his salary. Set up a forgivable loan so he can hope to own it someday."

Train nodded once. "A standard arrangement. I'll take care of it, master."

"Well then, do it. Fix him up so we don't have to waste time while he hunts for a house. I can't afford for him to travel back and forth from some God-forsaken ranch on the edge of Indian Country."

Train slipped backward to the door and disappeared.

"Now back to your orientation," Durant said. "I have several assistants. George Train is one of them. He may be a little strange, but he is very influential. He will be a promoter for the railroad. You will serve a different role."

Colton leaned forward.

"You will be my personal representative with authority to fulfill specific instructions. I will rarely allow you to use your own discretion."

Colton nodded and was about to ask for more details about the house when Durant rushed on.

"Questions? No? Let's move ahead. I am leaving for New York tomorrow morning. You and I will stay in touch by coded telegram. You are to check the telegraph office twice daily for my messages."

"Yes, sir," Colton said acknowledging Durant's first clear instruction.

"That brings us to the cipher book," Durant said.

Durant produced a small book and gave it to Colton.

"This is the code book we will use. Most correspondence between us will be in code. My codes drive the telegraphers crazy, but also keep them out of my business. In the back you will find a list of code names for nouns, locations, names, verbs and dollar amounts."

Colton opened the book. It appeared to be a normal calendar notebook with a twenty page reference section at the back. He saw nothing remarkable about it. He looked closer at the list of words and numbers in the back.

"How does your code work?" Colton asked.

Durant explained his system. For a man of Colton's experience, it was easy to understand. The calendar book contained all the codes Colton would ever need.

"It's more than adequate to confuse a layman," Colton commented.

"Let's see how you do. Decode this sentence: Adams inspected 47 horses for Indians in Atlanta. Skin them."

Colton, quickly decoded the sentences. "The sentence actually says: Jones delivering $5,000 for land purchase in St. Joseph. Purchase tract per previous instructions."

"Correct!" Durant exclaimed, almost smiling. "You catch on quickly. Start sending me coded messages tomorrow. Charge expenses to my account."

"Yes, sir," Colton responded.

"As part of your duties you will occasionally deliver documents."

Durant opened a desk drawer and removed a brass box.

"This is a document carrier," he said handing it to Colton. "Any time you are handling one, it will remain locked at all times. You may, for some missions, have a key."

Colton examined the shining document box.

"It's one of a dozen brass boxes that fit in my safe in New York. You will find it also fits quite nicely in the bottom of a standard carpet bag. I'll leave this box for you. You will need it soon."

"Very well," Colton replied.

"Do you own a pistol?"

"Yes."

"Keep it ready. Carry it whenever you transport papers."

"I will," Colton answered.

"The next two months will be demanding for me. I'll be in Chicago for organization meetings to create Union Pacific Railroad. I may need you to react or travel on a moment's notice."

"I'll be awaiting your instructions," Colton said.

"Meanwhile, I want you to get acquainted with mayors and city leaders from St. Joseph to Sioux City. I will give you a letter of introduction and authority. Assure each mayor that I am considering their city as the starting point of Union Pacific. Lincoln will make the final decision based on my input.

"Work each city's underbelly to learn their railroad strategies. No city will be on our railroad route without a significant contribution, mainly to me. Find out their funding potentials and if they are holding back the incentives they can offer. Gain their confidence so that we can have the information we need. I expect good results.

"You're no longer a war spy, so you don't need to steal information. Simply keep your ears open and let them talk. Analyze and track down any rumors that might impact my decisions.

"George Train represents me in specialized areas. If he gives you instructions, no matter how emotional he gets, remind him that you work for me only. You are on my personal staff. Your pay will come from my accounts rather than the railroad.

"George has first choice for using the office while I'm gone, but you are welcome to headquarter here for meetings and paper work."

The orientation continued through lunch and into the afternoon. Durant frequently tested Colton to take a deeper measure of character or gauge his understanding of instructions.

Durant liked Colton's answers. By late afternoon he was convinced Colton was trustworthy, intelligent and appropriately aggressive.

Durant ended the day sending Colton on his first mission. "Go get my dinner and bring it to me. Charge it to my account. After you're through you can go do whatever you do. Be back here in the morning thirty minutes after sunrise."

"What do you want for dinner?" Colton asked.

"The special is fine. I don't really care. All Omaha food tastes the same to me. Just get me something to choke down. Go. GO!"

Colton grinned inwardly and said, "Yes sir." He knew the entire day including the dinner run was nothing more than a test, an exercise to observe submissiveness. Colton knew the game and played it well.

Twenty minutes later Colton was with Libby and William telling them about the day including the surprising news about Durant's providing a house.

"Mr. Durant seems awfully nice to give us a house like that," Libby commented. "I hope it has more than one room," she added in all seriousness.

George Francis Train
Public Domain Photograph
Library of Congress through Wiki Commons

Chapter 8

AUGUST 30, 1863 – DURANT LEAVES FOR NEW YORK

Colton waited in the dark hallway outside Durant's hotel room, ready for his second day's work. He swallowed the last bite of a cold biscuit as Doc emerged from his room at sunrise.

Colton was careful to avoid saying, "Good morning." Instead he quietly reached to carry Durant's carpetbag.

"Let's go. We have work to do, Rusk. First, we stop at the telegraph office. Then we're meeting with the Omaha mayor."

Durant strode through the hotel lobby without glancing at the desk clerk. He led the way to the telegraph office where Anthony Butler was taking over from the night telegrapher. Both telegraphers jumped to attention as Durant burst through the door.

"My telegrams!" he demanded. "And make it quick."

The telegraphers scurried to deliver the morning messages, then stepped back respectfully while Durant opened each envelope and read its contents.

Doc was still looking down at a telegram when he suddenly barked at the telegraphers, "Pay attention! This is Colton Rusk. He is my personal assistant. He has full authority to use any services and charge fees to my account. Is that understood?"

"Yes, sir," both men responded in unison.

"Paper! Get me paper and pen." Within seconds Durant was writing telegrams and referring to his code book.

In the middle of furious writing, Durant suddenly looked up and turned toward Colton with wild, unfocused eyes. His face was turning red. "Blasted stockholders! Soft, wavering daisies. They never make things easy." He returned to writing.

Colton could only wonder at the thoughts that must tumble through Durant's mind.

By the time he'd penned four telegrams, Durant's tirade was spent. He thrust the messages at Butler.

"Transmit these. I am leaving on the noon steamboat to St. Joe. If you get any responses before we cast off, get them to me at once. Otherwise, forward them to me in St. Joe."

The telegraphers watched Durant disappear out the front door bellowing about the treachery of lawyers.

The night telegrapher spoke first. "What an obnoxious bully. He's the worst customer I've ever served. I doubt anyone will rush down to the boat landing with anything for that man."

"Wrong," replied Butler. "If Durant has a bad business meeting because of an undelivered telegram, he will track it back to the responsible individual. Only a few months ago, the office manager in Des Moines failed to deliver an urgent message. Doctor Durant had it tracked back to the manager. The poor man will never work again anywhere as a telegrapher."

* * * *

MAYOR BENJAMIN KENNEDY owned a big general store at Farnam and Thirteenth. Kennedy, a big ruddy-faced man with a full crop of red hair, was popular with Omaha people. He had grown wealthy by providing basic goods to the citizens. Kennedy also furnished provisions for emigrant wagons moving west. He greeted Doc and Colton warmly as they entered the store.

"I thought I had missed seeing you," the mayor said, smiling broadly. "I've been trying to track you down for several days, Doctor."

"I've been out of town and just returned," Durant responded pleasantly. "Fact is, I returned mainly to see you and George Train."

Durant's unexpected cordiality gave Colton transient pause.

Kennedy ushered his guests to a stock room that doubled as an office. He poured coffee for them.

Durant spoke. "Mayor Kennedy, allow me to introduce my personal assistant. This is Colton Rusk. When I am away from Omaha, Rusk will represent me. He is one of my key men and has broad authority to speak on my behalf. He and I will be in daily communication about business matters."

"Nice to meet you, Rusk." The mayor shook Colton's hand.

Colton had excellent skills for reading non-verbal mannerisms. He watched the two leaders exchange small talk. They discussed the murderer hanged two days before and the event's notoriety. On the surface it appeared Kennedy and Durant were friends. Colton also saw subtle, but unmistakable, signs of distrust.

The mayor got down to business. "I am hoping to hear how the railroad is progressing. Our citizens have donated generously to your cause. Just think, you have 500 acres of prime land along the riverfront perfect for locomotive shops and a depot. The other 700-acre gift just outside town will be available for future expansion."

The mayor reached behind several grain bags near the table and produced a brass box. "I have another payment on our cash donation."

He handed the box to Durant who almost licked his lips with greed.

"Our citizens are quite anxious to see construction begin."

Durant snatched the box from the mayor and began stowing it in his carpet bag.

"I leave for Washington today to talk with the president," he said in half-truth. "The investors and I are impatient to begin. Once Lincoln confirms Omaha as the starting point, activity will pick up. Rusk will keep you abreast of our progress."

"That's good to hear," said Kennedy. "The city leaders and citizens look forward to your success."

When the meeting concluded, Durant and Colton left the general store and conferred outside. Durant's demanding persona reappeared.

"Walking to the steamboat landing will give us more time to talk. Try to keep up," Durant announced, eyeing Colton's leg.

Colton knew the long walk had little to do with time. It was a simple test to measure Colton's fortitude and willingness to endure pain. Colton tightened his grip on Durant's bag and resolved to handle anything Durant could throw his way.

"I am confident," said Durant with an increasingly familiar arrogance, "that we can secure more incentive money and property from Omaha. The conversation you just witnessed is the one you will have with the surrounding mayors. Each of them needs to provide tangible incentives or cash if they want me to represent their cause."

"How will you represent different cities pursuing the same goal?" Colton asked, recognizing a clear conflict of interests.

"I will represent them all, some more than others. The city that provides the most incentive is the one I will represent most vigorously. Obviously I am cajoling the cities into a bidding war."

They trudged two blocks with Durant lost in thought and tugging at his scraggly beard. A strange mood came over Durant momentarily. His wrinkled brow relaxed. He spoke in a low tone.

"My boat should be casting off shortly. How I've longed to depart this town. Do you realize there are no laundries west of the Mississippi that can launder a shirt decently? I want to go home. I miss my cook. I miss my valet, my dogs and horses, even my wife. I'm happy to leave this dreadful city."

Colton said nothing, as Durant no doubt wished. They rounded a corner for the final few blocks when Durant stopped again. His tone turned colder.

"I guess you know General Dodge was at home in Council Bluffs until yesterday. Sick, you know. Now he's returned to the war to take a promotion to Major General." Durant observed Colton closely as he finished the announcement.

Colton was genuinely surprised. "I had no idea he was here. I thought he was in Tennessee with the army. You say he was sick?"

Durant ignored the question and focused on the surprise in Colton's eyes. He recognized an honest reaction.

"Had you known Dodge was in town, I would have assumed you were a spy for him. I would have fired you on this very corner. As I told you, I will test you in ways no one could anticipate. I demand total loyalty."

"And so you shall have it," Colton assured him.

Durant resumed walking. Colton limped along beside him.

"I saw Dodge twice while he was here. I tried to get him to quit the army. Damned fool wants to finish the war no matter what I offer."

Colton was not surprised at Dodge's dedication to the Union's cause.

"I will need your help to hire Dodge. He's difficult to understand at times. I need him, for his engineering and leadership skills, but more importantly for his relationships with Lincoln, Grant, and Sherman. He owes you his life. You owe me Dodge."

Colton thought it would be good to see Dodge working on the biggest project in the nation's history. Two blocks later, a steamboat's whistle pierced the air signaling departure in half an hour.

Durant spoke. "You may charge your expenses to my accounts. You are free to entertain local leaders. These bumpkins generally soften nicely with food and wine. I will send you a pass for transportation on all railroads and reimburse you for cash expenditures."

At the foot of Jones Street they found three steamboats preparing for departure. Doc's boat was the second in line. Without prompting,

Colton carried the carpetbag up the gangplank and stowed it in Durant's stateroom.

"Read my messages closely. A mistake can cost me thousands. Be prepared to travel to Chicago or New York, or even Washington on command. Keep a travel bag packed. Learn the steamboat schedules. Learn the train connections from St. Joseph, Kansas City and St. Louis. Try to avoid getting fired for missing a train in Des Moines."

And so it went until time came to raise the gangplank. Colton disembarked and stood on the landing where Durant could see him.

The frosty doctor shouted parting instructions from the boat deck. "Exercise that leg! When I need it to work, it needs to be ready."

The doctor noted with satisfaction that Rusk remained alert and at the landing until the boat departed and steamed out of sight.

Colton found it unsurprising that Durant left with no handshake or farewell.

* * * *

AS COLTON MADE HIS way from the landing, a young boy approached with labored steps. He looked younger than William by maybe a year and was dirty, thin, and barefoot with holes in his shirt and pants. He appeared impoverished and ready to give up hope.

"Sir, can you help me?"

Colton looked down at the boy. "What do you need, son?"

"Can you spare a few cents for me? I'm an orphan."

"I probably can. What's your name? Where do you live?"

"Name's Sean Cook, sir. Indians killed my parents. I live in a shack with several men here at the landing. I work when I can. I could use some change for food, mister."

Colton took pity and handed the youth a silver dollar. In the boy's eyes he saw the injustice and randomness of life and how his own son could have so easily been the one asking a stranger for help.

"Take this, Sean. Use it wisely."

It was a minor encounter that neither recognized as significant. Neither knew their lives would intersect many times at the boat dock, where Colton would always have a dollar and a smile for the unfortunate youth.

Nor did either realize that destiny held a far darker encounter for them.

Chapter 9

SEPTEMBER 2, 1863 – THE NEW HOME IN OMAHA

George Train and Colton Rusk sat eating breakfast in the Herndon House restaurant. Train was the most noticeable man in town. In fact, he was a shocking sight.

His attire would have been extravagant at a formal dinner in Prague or Paris. In the wild Nebraska Territory, his outfit was beyond comprehension, a fashion statement lost on frontiersmen.

The focus of the ensemble was a brilliant red puff tie. The elegant tie and neckband contrasted with a garish yellow shirt, brilliant blue vest, and dress gloves with dainty pearl buttons. A black frock coat with tails extending half way down the thigh completed the outfit.

Colton was fully engaged in devouring his meal when he noticed George had stopped eating and looked ill.

"You all right?" Colton asked between bites. "You're pale as a dead man."

George leaned back and stared at the ceiling trying to control an involuntary gagging reflex. "In the history of humankind there have never been any worse eggs than these. A museum of horrors would refuse them as too disgusting. I must speak to the manager."

Train turned to the nearby waiter and commanded, "Summon the manager immediately. I need to talk to him."

A stout Italian manager appeared. When he saw it was George Train who sought him, he braced himself. Over the months, Train had proven to be a consistent complainer.

"How may I help you, sir?" he asked in his most pleasing manner.

Train backed his chair away from the table and pointed a finger at his plate. "Just look at this!"

"Do we have a problem, sir?"

"No. I wouldn't call it a problem. I call it a disaster. Remove this hog slop from my presence! How dare you prepare Pommes d'Amour in such a manner. You invariably fail to get it right. Wrong spices. Wrong consistency. Wrong sauces. Take my plate."

"Can I get you anything else?"

"Gad no! I am concerned you'll eventually poison me. Just answer a simple question. Are you intentionally trying to infuriate customers with such horrible cooking?"

"Of course not."

"Then you are guilty of false advertising and blatant lies, sir. This yellow pile may be some savage version of baked eggs, but it's nothing close to Pommes d'Amour. I am beginning to believe I have no recourse than to open my own restaurant. Be gone."

The insult struck home. The manager snatched up the plate, wheeled around, and departed. Meanwhile Colton calmly finished his breakfast and enjoyed the show.

George gagged and fumed several more minutes before recovering. As Colton finished his last bite of toast, he saw color returning to George's cheeks. George took a deep breath and addressed Colton.

"This place has almost cured me from eating breakfast. I want to depart this dungeon the minute your bride and son come down. Shall we?"

Libby and William appeared in the lobby a short time later. George greeted Libby in a manner befitting European royalty, bowing very low. He then donned a sporty hat, like something an English gentleman wears on a fox hunt, and led them from the hotel.

Outside all activity ceased as George Train strutted by in his strange hat and flashy clothes. The hat in particular was a style never seen in the Nebraska Territory.

George Train directed the carriage driver to an address on Capitol Street. The ride took no more than five minutes. When the carriage stopped, Libby and Colton realized they knew the area.

"Ladies and gentlemen," Train announced. "On behalf of Doctor Thomas Durant, I am pleased to present your new Omaha residence."

Libby knew of plans for a carriage ride, but was unprepared for Train's announcement. She was speechless as Train helped her down.

The white, two story house was a typical middle class residence of the day. It was solidly constructed of cedar, meaning the materials came to Omaha by boat. A covered porch adorned with ornate lattice stretched across the entire front. Victorian bay windows gave the house an eye-pleasing appeal.

Train escorted Libby to the door and disappeared inside with her. She was trembling with excitement. Colton and William followed nearly as excited.

Colton stepped through the front door into a twelve foot wide hallway that ran the entire depth of the house. He heard George and Libby discussing decorating options in the sitting room. Colton and William began their own exploration.

"Do you think I'll have a room of my own?" William asked.

After months on the trail, the home tour was intoxicating. Libby memorized every detail of every room from the dining room's decorative crown molding to the fancy indoor water pump in the kitchen. Train was a nonstop fountain of decorating ideas. Long before the visit ended, Colton and William were anxious to move in immediately.

Near noon, Libby and George signaled readiness to return to the Herndon House. They were still in animated chat as George assisted her into the waiting carriage. It was several minutes before Colton could get a word into the conversation.

"George, do we have papers to sign?" he finally interjected.

"It's too early for that, old boy. Doc will have the documents later. For now, move in, get settled, and have a good time." His attention returned to Libby for a discussion about rugs for the office area.

When the carriage arrived at Herndon House, Train made another grand show of helping Libby out.

"I regret I must skedaddle," Train told the family. "Within days I will be leaving for Salt Lake City on business."

"That's a long trip through savage country," Colton commented. "Why are you going?"

"Doc says the Mormon boys will be essential to building the railroad. I'm going to see Brigham Young about contracting his men. I'll handle the preliminaries. Doc will close the deal."

"I wish I could go with you." Colton lamented.

"Ah, dear Colton, you have your own important mission. And so I must say goodbye to you and Lady Libby for now. It is time for you to move into your Omaha mansion."

Libby rushed forward and hugged Train. "Thank you for all your help. This has been wonderful for us."

Train accepted Libby's hug with a mild smile. He faced Colton and shook his own hands as he had done when they had met.

"Will I see you before you leave for Utah?" Colton asked.

"Most assuredly," said Train. "Perhaps we shall compare notes on our unique employer."

And with a sharp whirl that flung his coattails to their full horizontal extent, Train left for his carriage and new adventures.

* * * *

THEY TOOK LUNCH three blocks from the Herndon House at Zack Parker's Café. Libby remained euphoric. Even before ordering, she was almost begging. "I'm hoping we can move into our new house today. Can it be done?"

Colton smiled at the unrestrained excitement. "After lunch we'll check our options. The day is still young."

"Oh, Colton. I am thrilled. It's been years since I felt this way."

William shared the excitement. "I think my room is the best of all. I can almost see the river from my window," he chattered.

When they finished lunch, Colton announced a plan. "I propose that we walk to the livery stable and see what the possibilities are. Perhaps we can turn a good day into a great one."

* * * *

MARCUS HUNT, the boarding stable owner, saw the Rusk family coming and walked into the street to greet them.

"Mr. and Mrs. Rusk. How are you? It's mighty good to see you. And look at this fine young 'un. I bet he'll grow tall as a tree."

The ingratiating manner surprised Colton who remembered the stiff treatment he received in their first meeting. The demeaning tone and high prices had come dangerously close to losing Colton's business. Colton ignored the change and met Hunt in his typical open manner.

"We're fine," Colton said. "We came to ask about retrieving our wagon. We have a new home and want to move as soon as possible."

"Oh? Where are you folks moving to?"

"We have a house on Capital Street."

"I'll bet its one of the railroad's houses near 13th Street."

"Right you are, Mr. Hunt."

"When do you plan to move in?"

"Today, if we can hire men. What little we own is on the wagon."

"Bosh! You don't need to hire anyone, Mr. Rusk. I have two good men here who will be happy to help free of charge. This afternoon will be fine for them. Give them an hour to finish chores, and then we'll hitch up a team. You can make your move today."

"Very good," Colton said. "Meanwhile we need a buckboard."

"That's no problem. You'll be on your way in five minutes. We're glad to have you folks in Omaha, you being a railroad man and all."

Colton responded humbly. "Thank you. We're glad to be here."

Alone, Libby commented. "He seems awfully eager to please. Was he trying to curry your favor?"

"Somehow he's learned about my job with Durant, probably from the mayor. I guess he doesn't want to offend a Durant representative."

Marcus Hunt soon led a horse and buckboard from the barn. They boarded, and at Colton's command, the horse trotted off with its three riders in soaring spirits.

When the shopping was done, they drove the buckboard to their new home and met Hunt's men and their wagon. The move began. Libby watched as each piece came off the wagon and moved inside.

Within two hours the house became a home. Colton released the men and wagon and made a quiet walk-through with Libby.

"This place is as bare as the mud flats. Three rooms are completely empty," Colton said as they surveyed the house.

"Nonsense," she shot back. "The house is perfect. It's our home." She took his hand. "I don't see empty rooms. I see a world of happiness ahead of us." Colton smiled at her conviction.

That night, Colton reflected on the strings attached to the home. He knew why they were in a home. It was because Durant wanted him on a short tether of dependency and obligation. Durant needed control, absolute control, as part of the relationship. The lack of a deed, or sales contract for the home bothered Colton. He resolved to address it with Durant at his first opportunity.

For now, however, Libby was happy. That was more important.

Chapter 10

SEPTEMBER 28, 1863 – ADJUSTING TO LIFE IN OMAHA

Four weeks passed. Libby blossomed in Omaha, taking to city life like she was born to it. She had never seen a community as large as Omaha. For her, the town's eight thousand souls provided a variety and depth that opened a new world to her.

Soon after moving into the home, the Congregational Church came calling. It was Omaha's oldest church. The church ladies pulled her in immediately. Too quickly, Colton thought. Beyond Bible study and regular church services, they invited Libby to social get-togethers, recitals, and poetry readings. They visited her at home and included her in planning future events.

"I wonder whether this church attention stems from genuine Christian affection or our railroad affiliation," Colton casually commented one evening while unloading a box of new dishes. Libby's face fell. He immediately regretted saying it.

"Actually, as long as you're happy I guess I can share you with the ladies," he said jokingly. Inside he anguished over the gaffe and was thankful she was recovering so well from the past.

William, too, adjusted to city life and the Congregational Church School. As a farm boy, William had never attended a real school. His education had come from Libby, who herself was home taught. William thrived attending classes in the church's basement.

William found friends in the neighborhood and was soon a popular ringleader. He surprised his parents by taking a job as a clean up boy at a nearby hardware store.

Colton was happiest of all. He was on the ground floor of a great enterprise, a project rivaling the greatest construction in history.

"I get along well with Mayor Kennedy," he told Libby. "And with the Bellevue men too. It's almost like I was made for this job."

It was true. People found it easy to like Colton's warm manner even if they distrusted the railroad.

Colton had an undeniable gift for coaxing sensitive information from leaders. Something about him made men want to talk. Perhaps it was his cadence, or his soothing voice. Perhaps it was dealing with men who needed to boast, gossip, or share a burning secret.

Each day, Colton sent his coded reports describing the political winds in Nebraska and Iowa. They went to New York, Baltimore, Washington, or wherever Durant happened to be at the time.

Colton could tell by Durant's return telegrams that the information was helpful. Durant kept Colton at a hectic pace, traveling to nearby towns and learning the inner workings of the territory.

In Omaha, Colton spent as much time as possible with George Train. If Colton felt enthused about the Pacific Railroad, Train was obsessed. Colton became almost as knowledgeable and energetic as Train himself, lacking only the brassy showmanship and oratorical skills.

September passed quickly with Colton spending most nights at home. His only time away was a week-long trip to Kansas City to gauge the political situation and check a competitor railroad's construction progress.

Colton used his Omaha time helping Libby turn the house into a home.

"If I didn't know better, I'd say you actually enjoy helping me make curtains and planting shrubs. As much as you work, I'm surprised you have the energy." Libby said one night.

"Actually, I *am* enjoying myself. Fact is, I'd like to take you with me on my next trip to Kansas City. We can have a grand shopping expedition to fill the empty rooms."

Libby appreciated the thought but had a different idea.

"I prefer to furnish the house slowly, one perfect piece at a time. Mail orders at Mayor Kennedy's store are fine with me," she said.

* * * *

IN NEW YORK, Dr. Durant was even busier than Colton lobbying congressmen, raising funds, and planting rumors instead of shrubs.

Chapter 11

OCTOBER, 1863, NEW YORK - DOC'S STOCK SCAM

Two well-dressed gentlemen sat in overstuffed leather chairs in the African trophy room of the New York Yacht Club.

"Forgive me if I'm skeptical, Doctor, but your reputation is terrible, even with me. You're a known scoundrel who will squeeze money from friend, foe, or family. Not that I believe all of it, but that's the word."

Dr. Durant brushed off the comment with a smile that failed to reach his eyes. "You have to remember, Robert, the buyer must always beware. I see you are properly cautious."

"I'm wary of everything about you, Doc. Why have you come to see me?" Multi-millionaire Robert Masterson emptied his cognac glass, set it aside, and waited.

"I'll cut to the chase, Robert. I need your confidential support in connection with my Mississippi and Missouri Railroad. I can offer you an opportunity to make unheard of profits if we play our cards right."

"Tell me about your little scheme," Masterson said leaning forward and grinning at the notorious doctor.

Durant took a serious tone. "When we finish organizing the Union Pacific Railroad next week, I am going to be in charge. For a short time we can make breathtaking amounts of money by manipulating stocks."

"What do you have in mind?"

"The Union Pacific will run from the Missouri River westward. It will need to connect with another railroad running to the East."

"Yes, of course."

"I've been building the Mississippi and Missouri Railroad for ten years. Investors believe my M&M Railroad will be U.P.'s connection. Right now M&M stock prices are sky high. It's time to sell."

Masterson unconsciously licked his lips. Durant continued.

"At the same time I want to buy Cedar Rapids Railroad stock while it's dirt cheap. I need your help keeping my name removed. I simply need you to make my investments for me. You can mirror my investment, if you please, and come along for the profits."

Durant paused to let the message sink in. "When I announce the Cedar Rapids road, not M&M, will be the connection, Cedar Rapids stock, which we will own, will soar. The announcement will wreck M&M prices."

"But you will already have sold out M&M at high prices," Masterson noted.

"Exactly. We can make a killing on these stocks," Durant said.

"And what of the Cedar Rapids stock?" Masterson asked.

"We can make even more profits. As soon as we think the Cedar Rapids Railroad stocks have peaked, we'll quickly sell all we have and invest it back in the depressed M&M Stocks. Then I'll announce that the M&M will connect with U.P. after all, and M&M prices will soar again. We will reap unbelievable fortunes."

"Brilliant. I have to say, Doc, I like your scheme, but it sounds illegal. You're manipulating stocks solely to make a profit."

Durant shook his head and pursed his lips. "I don't agree with your legal interpretation, Robert. Buying and selling stocks is legal. Anyone can do it. So long as we can keep our arrangement confidential, we will make staggering profits."

"Hmmm," said Masterson. His eye slid over Durant's feral face like a poker player reading facial expressions. His heart pumped rapidly thinking of the profit potential in Doc's seductive proposal.

The doctor continued. "Federal regulators are tied up with the war. Stock transactions have almost no oversight. What's more, the regulators who *are* still around are my friends."

"Ah! So you have bribed the stock regulators! They are in your pocket, so to say. How interesting. So tell me, after all your stock manipulation, which road will actually connect to Union Pacific?"

"My ultimate goal is to see the U.P. begin in Omaha and connect with the M&M Railroad. That is where I'm placing all my money. That is where I am going to become richer than anyone in New York, except maybe you. Will you join with me?"

"I will back your plan on two conditions," Masterson said.

"Name them," Durant said. Then he listened closely.

"My requirements are simple. First, you must actually gain control of the Union Pacific. And second, for my protection, we will prepare a written contract for my involvement that I will keep in a safe place."

"Agreed!" said Durant managing a humorless laugh. "I can meet your conditions easily. You won't be disappointed, Robert."

"Then come back to see me when you are ready to move ahead." And with that, Masterson lifted a glass to toast the felonious plan.

* * * *

A WEEK LATER in the ballroom of New York's luxurious Royal Hotel, Dr. Thomas Durant stood like a wolf eyeing a flock of sheep. When he had the room's attention, he addressed the new railroad's twenty-five principal investors.

"Gentlemen, now that the government commissioners are away for the day, we can deal in private. We already know U.P. stock sales are woefully inadequate. I doubt if we can build the first ten miles of railroad with the money we have."

The men around the room grumbled agreement.

"I believe, however, we can follow a solid path to success. I am already the leading stockholder, but I am willing to invest every penny I own. I am already paying private surveyors to plan the line."

The room was silent.

"It is unfortunate that Congress restricted ownership so that no individual can own more than ten percent of the U.P.'s stock. What I propose, then, is a way for me to pump money into the road. First if you will double your investments in U.P. stock, I will personally guarantee you will profit. What's more, if, at anytime you become dissatisfied, I will repurchase your shares with no questions asked. You can find no better investment guarantee in the world. All I ask is to control your voting rights, and therefore the Union Pacific."

The investors buzzed considering Durant's astounding offer. Durant silenced the din with a loud voice.

"Second, if it appears my ownership stake will exceed the ten percent limit, which I hope it does, I will put my stocks in the names of others, keeping only the voting rights and a share of the dividends."

The leading financial wizards of the time looked at each other in eager curiosity and whispered among themselves. They had never imagined such a scheme. The room fell quiet for Durant to continue.

"This stock arrangement will do two things: most importantly, it will get the railroad started immediately. Second, it will allow me, the most experienced railroad builder among us, to retain control. I can assure success and guarantee against failure."

At that, the investors again talked among themselves. One asked, "Are you willing to sign a contract stating your guarantees?"

"Of course I am willing," Durant responded, his lies flowing easily. "My guarantees are rock solid. Write your contracts. I will gladly sign them. My confidence in the railroad and America's future is unshakable. Join with me and prosper."

A round of applause spread across the room as the leading money men of the day lined up to hand their funds to the persuasive and entirely unethical doctor.

Durant leaned back in his chair smiling and momentarily satisfied.

* * * *

DURANT SHOOK Robert Masterson's hand as he entered the elegant library at the Masterson mansion.

Even before they sat, Durant was unable to restrain his excitement. "I've done it, Robert! I have control of Union Pacific."

Robert Masterson acknowledged the news. "The newspapers are talking of nothing else this morning but you and the transcontinental railroad. You have accomplished a feat few men could match."

Robert Masterson poured a drink for his guest. "Naming John Dix as president while you took a vice-president position was a stroke of genius. Well done!"

"I can be president any time," Durant gloated, "but for now I need lower visibility and flexibility. Being vice-president gives me everything I want. John Dix is an old friend. He even looks the part. Better still, he can follow orders."

"Do you realize what a huge task you have undertaken?"

Durant nodded. "I have a plan. Next week I begin a marathon of meetings starting with President Lincoln. I have much to do."

They talked an hour before Masterson turned to other business. "What is the timing for the stock transactions we discussed?"

"I intend to pump up the M&M stock prices for another week by rumor and press releases, and then dump my holdings. Meanwhile I can deliver $3 million to you Monday to buy Cedar Rapids stock while it's still dirt cheap."

"I'll match your money and buy everything I can."

Durant smiled slyly. "The poor greedy bastards won't know what hit them. Prepare to harvest their life savings, Robert."

Chapter 12

OCTOBER 28, 1863 – COLTON TRAVELS

The loud banging didn't register at first. Colton lay exhausted in a deep sleep. The party with territorial representatives had lasted until after midnight. When he became aware of the noise, he roused enough to realize someone was pounding on his front door.

Colton struggled to gain his senses. His first thought was of Libby. He felt her shoulder next to him and knew she was in bed. She slept on undisturbed.

He rose, quickly threw on a pair of pants, and fumbled his way out of the dark bedroom. The banging continued, sounding more insistent with each step. He descended the stairs as quickly as he could, and at the first floor landing, he called out, "I'm coming." The banging ceased.

When he opened the door, Colton saw the night telegrapher on the porch with his hands in his pockets and an apologetic expression.

"I hate to wake you, Mr. Rusk. I have an urgent telegram."

"What time is it?" Colton asked rubbing his eyes.

"Almost four."

Colton took the telegram. "You don't need to wait," he said. "If I need to respond, I'll come down to the office." He reached in his pockets, found two nickels, and handed them to the telegrapher.

"Thank you, sir," and the man left.

Colton retreated down the central hallway to the kitchen and sat at the small table where he opened the envelope by candlelight.

As he suspected, it was from Durant. Colton carefully translated each coded word and read the message three times.

Go now to Bellevue. Get sealed box from Buck Clayton. Provide full security. Sail steamboat to St. Joseph. Ride train to New York and my office. Update me at train changes. Expect you in four days. Contents and transaction are confidential. Repeat: depart immediately.   *T. C. Durant*

Colton knew Buck Clayton and liked him. He was a major landowner in Bellevue who represented Bellevue interests at area meetings. Buck handled himself with an even temper and straightforward manner.

Shortly after the telegrapher's visit, Libby stood at the front door and watched Colton limp toward the street with his carpet bag. She knew he was exhausted after only two hours sleep and worried about his long journey.

As he disappeared in the darkness, she called one more time, "I love you. Please be careful."

"I'll be back as soon as I can," came Colton's voice from the darkness. "I'll be in touch by telegram."

Colton used a night key to enter Hunt's Livery Stable. He lit an oil lamp and penned a simple note:

Per understandings, I have rented saddle and usual horse. Will return before noon today. Please charge to account.
C. Rusk.

* * * *

THE SUN SHOWED promise in the eastern sky as Colton rode from the livery stable onto Farnam Street. He wore plain clothes and a coat. Never a flashy dresser, Colton would be inconspicuous.

The horse, Hero, was a magnificent stallion. During the week, Hunt reserved Hero for special customers like Colton. On Sunday afternoons, Hero filled a different role. After church, when the men and boys gathered west out of town for horse races, Hero proved to be among the fastest horses in Omaha.

Colton had ridden Hero often over the past two months. Man and horse were comfortable with each other.

Colton and Hero passed the Herndon House and turned onto the dirt road to Bellevue. He reached into the carpet bag tied behind the saddle and removed two biscuits and a sausage wrapped in paper. Breakfast on horseback was nothing new to Colton. He ate and thought of Libby and William and the trip ahead.

Hero covered the twelve miles to Bellevue effortlessly in less than an hour. Buck Clayton's homestead was one of the largest in town and stood on a hill overlooking the river. Colton had visited the home twice before to meet with city leaders.

Three dogs rushed from the home to meet Colton while he was still a block away. They provided a noisy escort to the Clayton's front yard.

Colton was ready to dismount when the front door opened and Buck Clayton stepped outside. He walked toward Colton in the dawn light.

Buck's face was familiar, but uncharacteristically haggard and etched with concern. He had the look of one who had made a deal with the devil. He held a brass box like the one Durant had given Colton.

"Morning, Buck," Colton announced from atop Hero.

Buck answered. "I have deeds and incentive payments for Doctor Durant. He wired and said you were coming for them."

"The contents are secret," Colton said. "Doc has forbidden discussion about it."

"How about coffee then? Will he let you come in and relax for a few minutes?"

"Not today. I'd best be going," Colton said. "I've got to hurry back for the morning boat to St. Joseph.

"I understand," Buck said. "This box from the people of Bellevue will satisfy Doc's requirements." Buck handed the box up.

"I'll take you up on that coffee next visit, Buck."

Colton loosened the leather straps that secured the carpet bag and stowed the brass box under the false bottom. Then he wheeled Hero, saluted Buck, and rode off. The noisy dogs stayed with Colton for a quarter mile before returning home.

Colton released Hero to a gallop on the road to Omaha. He would have to push to make the eight o'clock steamboat. He was still two miles south of town when he heard a long, low whistle signaling that a boat would be leaving shortly. He had no spare time to see William or Libby before departure.

On the riverfront, Colton found a carriage driver he knew and paid him to return Hero to Hunt's Livery, then he boarded the steamboat. He traveled light, with only the carpet bag. His wore a travel coat to conceal his easily accessible pistol. The carpet bag never left his sight.

* * * *

IN NEW YORK, Doc Durant sat at his desk consumed in thought over his next moves. He was oblivious to the city activity below his window.

Rumors about his recent stock sales amused him. He was almost impossible to rattle unless summoned before a judge, or unless his own fortune seemed at risk. Who cared if the press asked unanswerable questions about M&M stocks?

It had been a banner month. $6 million in clear profit for him, plus Robert Masterson's take.

"Now to the Union Pacific," he mused. "What is the best way to make millions more?"

A knock at the door broke his concentration.

"Enter!" Durant shouted, his blank eyes now focused on the door.

"Citizen Train here, sir," called a cheery voice through the door.

"George, get in here! You're late. I expected you yesterday."

He watched with narrowed eyes as George Train breezed through the door.

"Washington is a mess, Doc. It was a cat fight getting my business, or should I say *our* business, finished, but now I'm here."

"I reviewed your report on Brigham Young," Durant said in an irritated tone.

"Interesting wasn't it?"

"You wrote it at a 45 degree angle across the paper, George! Your idea of a joke?"

"I wanted to make sure you read it." Train smiled broadly at Durant.

"I did read it. Every slanted word. It was like something from grammar school."

"Fantastic! Then my approach worked, didn't it?"

Durant said nothing.

"Doc, we need to talk about a U.P. stock promotion. We haven't sold many shares. I have some ideas."

Durant still said nothing, but raised an eyebrow for Train to continue.

"The best thing we can do is get the nation talking about the railroad. People are tired of war. They need to embrace a positive cause. Union Pacific Railroad fits that need perfectly. You know what we need, Doc? We need a lavish, fully publicized groundbreaking ceremony in Omaha. The nation will love it."

"Have you lost all sense of reality?" Durant scoffed. "We can't afford an outhouse for such an event much less a spending spree. Besides, President Lincoln is running scared to name Omaha."

"You take care of Lincoln, and I'll get the fine people of Omaha to fund a festival. We'll have a celebration with parades, bands, and the works. Newspapermen will be clamoring to get to Omaha."

"I want nothing to do with it! Even if you have a ceremony, against my will mind you, I won't come. I'll have no part of such a fiasco." Durant's voice was starting to rise.

"Good! Stay away. You're a Scrooge anyway. I'll write an appropriate note for you to send. Your job is to get Lincoln on board."

Durant growled an indistinguishable response and flipped a telegram across the desk to Train.

"My. Oh my. What's this?" Train gushed picking up the message. "Ah! A message from President Lincoln."

Train straightened to a dignified pose and read theatrically.

From the Office of the President
White House, Washington, D. C.

To Doctor T. C. Durant – New York
As I do with others, so I will try to see you when you come.
Abe Lincoln

Durant spoke dryly. "As you can see, I'm working on Lincoln."

"Well, Doc, aren't you the big shot? Very impressive. What else are you going to discuss with Lincoln?"

"You should mind your own business," Durant said leaning back in his chair and examining his nails. "The president and I go way back."

"How so? Schoolmates?"

"No. Abe Lincoln was a two-bit lawyer that I hired to represent me in a lawsuit over a railroad bridge. He stretched the case all the way to the Supreme Court - at my expense, of course. We worked together so long I grew sick of the man. He still thinks we're friends."

"I'm more impressed all the time," said Train. "You get your friend, *Abe*, to designate Omaha as the railroad's starting point, and I'll make you rich beyond your dreams. And at no extra costs, old boy, I'll teach you how to influence people and charm the socks right off them."

"Enough! How could *you* possibly make *me* rich?" Durant snapped, thinking of the $6 million his stock scam had just netted.

"The big money in railroads comes from construction profits, not trains. We need to form a construction company," Train said cocking a finger at Durant. "Lucky for you, I've had my eye on a defunct financial company. We can buy it for almost nothing and use it to build the railroad. It has an absolutely fascinating name. Ready?"

"Yes, George!" Doc's response was unvarnished exasperation.

Train paused for effect. "It is called *Crédit Mobilier*." Train used his best Parisian accent.

"French?"

"Yes. The sound of its name is intoxicating. Just listen: Crédit Mobilier. It has all the charters, stocks, certifications, and endorsements we will ever need. So with your permission I will close the deal for a song. Crédit Mobilier and the companies it hires will perform all the railroad's construction work."

"You're right, we need a construction company, but don't gloat, George, it's an old concept. If we can acquire Crédit Mobilier cheaply, go ahead. Get the details and I'll provide the funds. Give me an initial report on the company in two weeks."

"Oui, Monsieur. So it shall be. We, the railroad, shall hire our Crédit Mobilier to do our work at top rates. With such a cash machine, it won't matter if the railroad ever makes a dime. We'll have our profits anyway." A giggle escaped Train.

"Enough small talk," Durant said. His tone had the same effect as throwing ice water on Train's giddiness. "You seem unconcerned about the gravity of our financial situation."

Train focused.

Durant rubbed his forehead before speaking.

"As competent as I am, this project has the potential to intimidate me. Building a railroad to California is a massive undertaking, bigger than anything ever attempted in America. We may not secure enough money to build this monster. Many people predict total failure."

"It couldn't be that bad, could it?" Train asked.

"I'm telling you, the war is killing finances. Supplies are nonexistent. Sufficient labor is nonexistent this side of Ireland. Congress is allowing the Central Pacific to build east from California. And I'm still unsure about Rusk."

Train spoke reassuringly. "We'll just take the project one step at a time. We can do this. All the issues you mention are known and will seek their own solutions."

Changing the subject, Train continued. "Why do you mention uncertainty about Rusk? Have you seen a problem?"

"The man is unbelievable," Durant exclaimed.

"You can't believe what he says? Dishonesty?" Train asked.

"No, it's nothing like that. The reports he sends about cities and businessmen are extremely detailed and personal. Rusk must have stolen a great deal of the information. No one could legally acquire the information he furnishes me. I've got everything but account numbers. Rusk will likely get us in trouble."

Train laughed. "Only you would complain about a man who is doing exactly what you've asked. Rusk is just what we need in Omaha—someone to counterbalance your ... charm. He's a hero, a confidante, a man with connections. When the Territorial leadership needs a shoulder to cry on, Colton Rusk takes their confessions. He's quite good you know. I call him Father Rusk."

"Well, maybe he's too good. He's probably telling *my* secrets."

George chuckled. "Not Rusk. His heart is good. He believes your railroad is vital to the country. That's why he supports you. He's quite loyal, you know. Ha! He even denies you're a cad. He defends you! Train crossed his arms emphatically.

"I still don't understand how he's doing it. I don't see a single meal or entertainment expense charged at the Herndon House."

Train shuddered at the mention of the Herndon House.

Durant underscored his argument. "No expenses charged for meals or entertainment? Think, Train. Something is wrong."

"Nothing is wrong, Doc. He and his wife entertain almost exclusively at their home, your home, that is. People love to spend time with them. The woman can cook. And when the meal is over, the men retire to the study to talk. That's where the great information harvest occurs with port wine and cigars. And if not in his study, the harvest takes place in *their* homes, or on the streets. He has a homespun, charismatic approach that even I can't match."

Durant scowled and grunted.

"He's very idealistic, yet devoted to you. I think you should keep him clear of your schemes. The man has a conscience."

Temporarily satisfied, Durant moved on. "Maybe you're right. At least I own his house in a city where houses are impossible to acquire."

He tired of Train and moved to conclude the meeting. "I have engagements this evening. Go sell stocks, George. Buy that construction company. Cultivate the newspaper men. I think my work for the foreseeable future will be in Washington."

"And President Lincoln?"

"Don't push me, George. I will take care of Lincoln soon enough."

Chapter 13

OCTOBER 28, 1863 – COLTON GOES EAST

Colton's steamboat trip to St. Joseph was a day-long affair made longer because the river was low and treacherous. Toward evening, the boat maneuvered to shore, sang its arrival with whistles and calliope, and lowered the gangplank.

Colton disembarked and walked to the St. Joseph railroad depot where he confirmed the next train would depart in three hours for a night run to Hannibal, Missouri. He took the short layover as a sign of good fortune.

With ticket in hand, Colton sent a coded message to update Durant on his location. He ate at a local café, then returned to the depot to await the departure.

He felt apprehensive about making such an important delivery to New York City. He knew the city as a huge, crime-ridden place fraught with danger. Gangs had carved the city into fiefdoms, each sector ruled by a ruthless leader.

And then he had to consider the city's Confederate sympathizers: mostly disgruntled businessmen who, until the war, prospered from trade with the south. Now without products, many business owners openly supported the South. Violent outbreaks with Lincoln supporters were common. Some malcontents had talked of declaring New York City an independent country. Colton knew he must guard his support of President Lincoln lest he fan the flames burning in radicals. Any mistakes could risk the mission.

Colton spent a restless night on the train planning and re-planning trip details. In the hours before sunrise he finally drifted to sleep. The train stop at Hannibal jolted him awake.

His goal in Hannibal was to tread lightly around the tension. With many of the town's men serving in the Confederate army, the citizens were rebel supporters. The city itself was in the hands of Union troops.

Colton checked the pistol in his coat pocket and stepped off the train with his carpet bag. Perhaps it was an overly active imagination, but he felt the local citizens were watching him closely. Colton lost no time securing a ticket for the next train. He waited quietly behind a newspaper on the station platform. Soon enough he was rolling eastward again.

The trip required four days with three train changes. Though his seat was comfortable and the meals bearable, Colton was glad when the conductor announced New York City was the next stop.

New York's intensity hit him the second he stepped off the train. Sounds and smells of every description and from every direction attacked his senses. It was worse than he remembered. Everyone seemed to be rushing a different direction. He gained his bearings and moved away from the train, tightening his grip on the carpet bag.

Colton pushed his way out of the depot and hired a carriage. He gave the driver the address: 20 Nassau Street. They left the depot and inched along the crowded streets.

Durant's office and Union Pacific headquarters were in an imposing five story building in the financial district. Colton paid the driver.

"Best step lively, sir," the driver said pointing to a commotion ahead. "Looks like a gang fight. It could come this way. I'm turning around here."

Colton limped inside the building.

The lobby was luxurious and quiet. Colton took a minute to examine his surroundings. The brilliant marble floor extended four feet up the walls. Huge golden chandeliers dominated the room.

"It's magnificent," he told the uninterested lobby guard who directed him to the second floor.

As he limped up the expensive marble staircases, he braced for another challenging meeting with Dr. Durant.

On the second floor Colton instinctively turned toward the front corner offices. He knew power gravitated there and reckoned Durant would have the biggest corner office in the building.

At the end of the hall, he noticed a neatly painted sign on the door that confirmed he was at the right place. Colton stepped inside.

The only person in the room was a small man in a starched white shirt at a desk who looked up from his work at the intrusion.

"You are Colton Rusk?" the man asked.

"I am."

The man seemed unsurprised.

"Do you have the box?"

"Yes."

"Stay here." The man rose and exited through a rear door.

Colton waited. He expected the man to return and escort him to the Doctor. Or, Dr. Durant might emerge from his lair in person. Neither possibility occurred.

The serious looking man returned alone.

"Dr. Durant left for Washington two days ago." He handed Colton a handwritten note. "These are Doctor Durant's instructions to leave the box here and meet him at the Washington Grand Hotel as soon as you can. I am Howard Crane, Dr. Durant's secretary."

Colton recognized the name and warmed instantly. By telegram Crane had helped Colton establish U.P. bank accounts in Omaha and Bellevue. He was also the man who sent Colton's salary.

"By golly! It's good to finally meet you, Crane. You've been a big help for me." Colton grabbed Crane's hand and shook it vigorously.

"Right. Good to meet you too," Crane said mildly, unaccustomed to encountering cheery, outgoing people.

Colton read Durant's note and felt a huge burden lifted from his shoulders. He removed the box from his bag and handed it to Crane.

Crane produced a small brass key.

"Mr. Rusk, I suggest you stay tonight at the Republic Hotel across the street. I have already reserved a room for you. You can leave for Washington in the morning on the eight o'clock train."

As he spoke, Crane opened the box and shook the contents onto the desk.

Colton saw bundled stacks of hundred dollar bills and a folder thick with deeds. His eyes widened, betraying surprise.

"Better get used to it, Mr. Rusk. Doc gets shipments like this frequently. Now that you've completed delivery, I can tell you about the contents. This is a $100,000 gift from the Bellevue businessmen. Take the empty box and key with you. You'll likely need them soon enough."

* * * *

AT NEW YORK'S REPUBLIC HOTEL, Colton found himself energized by the unexpected diversion to Washington. It seemed like years since he'd served in the city as a military liaison. He looked forward to leaving uncouth New York and seeing old friends.

The next morning, Colton rose early, hired a carriage, and went directly to the train station. He arrived two hours before departure to allow for the unexpected.

In the depot, he sent two telegrams. The first was a message to Libby letting her know he was safe. The second was a coded message to Dr. Durant with an estimated arrival time that afternoon.

The trip from New York to Washington was roughly 240 miles and should have required only six hours. It took closer to nine.

Security stops every fourth station and a train change in Baltimore ate deep into the day. At half past four, the train arrived in Washington. Colton knew the area intimately and stepped confidently off the train. The Capitol and the Grand Hotel were less than a mile away.

Colton emerged from the station as a platoon of soldiers marched past. They were young, probably newly drafted. Colton fell in behind the slow formation and followed.

The familiar, bright streets had changed and looked foreboding. Changes were more apparent with each city block. A candy store sat empty and boarded up. A bank now served as a hospital. Grass grew uncut in the medians. Gutters overflowed with uncollected garbage.

Buildings a block away appeared as gloomy apparitions through the army's campfire smoke. Washington was an armed fortress crowded with troops on high alert.

When the soldiers passed the Grand Hotel, Colton stopped and watched until the column turned a corner and disappeared. He missed military life even now as pain shot through his leg.

Colton entered the hotel prepared to register before looking for Durant. Instead, he spotted Durant in the lobby in animated conversation with a well-dressed gentleman. Doc was smiling broadly, his hands waving in exaggerated gestures. Colton had never seen Durant so congenial, so charming.

Durant saw Colton ease into his vision. Doc made eye contact, and then turned away to continue the conversation. Several minutes later he finished with a hearty laugh and warmly shook the man's hand. When the gentleman left, a different Durant addressed his employee.

"Any trouble?" Durant asked bluntly.

"No. I had a pleasant trip," Colton answered.

"I don't care how pleasant your trip was. I couldn't care less about your creature comforts. I want to know if you had a safe trip. Was the box in jeopardy at any time?"

"It was safe. The brass box made it to your office unmolested."

Civil War Construction - The Capitol Dome
Courtesy of United States Archives

"I already know the box made it. You sent me a telegram. Can you remember that? You are telling me things I already know."

When the moment passed, Durant continued. "I have an envelope for you to deliver to Senator Turner. Do you know him?"

"The senator from Connecticut?"

Durant scowled. His voice began to rise in pitch and volume. In his efforts to keep quiet he hissed. "The Senate has only one Senator Turner. You failed to answer my question. Answer it for sanity's sake, Rusk. Stop wasting my time. Do you know him?"

"Yes, sir."

"Good! Thank you for answering me! Think about this: If you need retraining every time we meet, I don't really need you, do I?"

"No, sir." Colton kept his face neutral.

Durant, now vented of his immediate anger, spoke more calmly.

"Get registered for a room first, and then limp along over to the Capitol and deliver my envelope. It goes to Turner, no one else." Durant produced a thick envelope and waved Colton away. "Turner remains in his office until almost dark. You have plenty of time. Meet me here in the lobby after breakfast. We have much to discuss."

"Yes, sir." Colton took the envelope and departed.

This was the first time Colton felt irritated with Durant. Halfway to the Capitol, he concluded he must tolerate the occasional abuse in order to participate in something bigger. He knew his unique role gave him a front row seat to history.

At the Capitol steps, military guards blocked Colton's way. They questioned him thoroughly and, when satisfied, let him pass up the steps and into the building.

Colton knew Randal Turner as a friend and trusted confidante. They had met on several occasions for army business and at Washington social gatherings.

Colton found Turner at his desk working through a pile of papers. The Senator greeted Colton warmly and accepted the envelope without comment. They talked for thirty minutes, filling in the gaps with news about themselves and people they knew. They shared a drink behind closed doors. Colton appreciated the camaraderie.

By the time full darkness covered the city, Colton's exhaustion won over adrenaline. He slept soundly until the early sounds of city life coaxed him awake. It was five o'clock. Colton took an early breakfast at a café he knew. When he entered he saw familiar faces, including a congressman from Ohio. Colton found the food and talk therapeutic.

He returned to the hotel recharged and ready for whatever Durant and the day brought.

When Durant entered the lobby, Colton was waiting for him.

"I am to see the president this morning," Durant announced. "You will accompany me to the White House and wait for me. Afterwards, we will finish our business. You leave Washington in the morning."

"Yes, sir."

"Hail a carriage for us while I speak with the hotel manager."

Colton considered reminding Durant the White House was only a short walk away, then thought better and hired the finest coach he could find.

As they pulled away from the hotel entrance, Durant wasted no time with another surprise.

"In the morning, proceed directly to St. Louis. Make a survey of steamboats for sale or lease. We will need seven or eight big boats to handle the materials we purchase. I need all the particulars about the boats and their costs. It will be two years before the Eastern railroads reach Council Bluffs, so until then most construction materials will move to Omaha by steamboat. The boating operation alone will stretch the limits of our energy."

Durant suddenly became quiet in deep thought; his head drooped forward as he stared blankly at his shoes. The silence became dead air. The carriage moved ahead another city block before Colton gathered courage to speak, "May I ask a clarifying question?"

"Ummm?" Durant responded, roused to consciousness,

"When will we need the boats?"

"Obviously sometime after spring. The rivers will be frozen until then." Durant's sarcasm was bitter and overdone. He looked at Colton as if the question amazed him.

Colton looked Durant in the eye forming an unspoken communication.

"I didn't answer your question, did I? I suppose you want to reprimand me for wasting your time? Is that it?" Durant asked.

Colton allowed a brief smile and nodded once.

"Actually, I'm unsure when we'll need the boats. Just check out general availability, capacities and price ranges. Frankly, Rusk, I have no idea when we'll have enough money to buy anything."

The carriage rolled onto the White House grounds watched by a dozen armed soldiers. They stopped at the guardhouse as Durant finished instructions for Colton's St. Louis trip.

"In St. Louis, be careful about letting anyone know you represent me. Deal with as many steamboat companies as you can find. Tell them you'll need the boats for heavy mining equipment, which is somewhat true. We will need steam excavators, at least. I'll expect a written report in New York in no more than ten days. You can—"

Durant never finished the sentence. A burly guard interrupted, "Gentlemen, please state your names and your business."

Thus began a thorough check for identification, credentials, and purpose of the visit. They checked and rechecked the president's daily agenda. Durant found the process irritating and was tugging at his beard before guards escorted the two into the White House.

They sat silently in a reception room, Durant brooding and Colton wanting to avoid inciting wrath. After fifteen minutes of peace, Durant broke the stillness.

"Lincoln must have a light schedule today. This room is usually full of people, mostly crony Republican friends begging for jobs or army commissions."

Durant's statement called for no response. Colton remained still. Durant was overdue to voice a salty comment on the president's rudeness when the inner door opened and an aide escorted him away.

Now alone, Colton reflected on his upcoming mission to St. Louis and speculated what other surprises Durant had in store. He wondered what the president and Durant would discuss.

Chapter 14

NOVEMBER 2, 1863 – DOC DURANT VISITS LINCOLN

Doctor Thomas Durant sauntered into the president's second floor office as if he owned it. Few visitors had such relaxed straightforwardness, especially New York Democrats like Durant.

President Lincoln stood. He watched Durant remove his coat, fling it on an office sofa, and drop into a chair grinning with arrogant satisfaction.

The act irritated the president who accurately read it as an indication that Durant still did not respect him after all their years of acquaintance. Always the politician, Lincoln said, "Welcome, Doc. Take your coat off. Make yourself at home."

Durant ignored Lincoln's tinge of sarcasm, if he noticed it at all.

"How have you been, Abe?"

The president flashed a knowing half-smile at Durant and sat. They shook hands across the desk.

"I am, as always, exhausted. The nation is run by exhausted people. And you?"

"I'm exhausted too. Building a railroad is hard work," Durant said.

"Tell me about your progress. I lost contact when you dismissed the government directors."

"The investors insisted on more control over their investment," Durant answered, feigning innocence.

"Understandable. What do you see for the future?" This was Lincoln's civilized manner of asking, "What do you want from me?"

Durant was prepared. His requests came neatly packaged and expertly delivered to the president. Lincoln saw his guest still possessed debater's skills almost as good as his own.

"I suppose you realize considerable intrigue exists about where the eastern end of railroad will begin," Durant began. "In fact, the entire project is on hold waiting for you to name the starting point. You've been sitting on this for over a year now. We have things to do. When can we expect a decision?"

"I have spoken with many on this issue. Even Grenville Dodge paid me a visit. He says the Omaha-Council Bluffs option is the most logical one."

"I agree with Dodge. Why don't you name Omaha today?"

"I struggle with the political questions. It's no secret I own land in Council Bluffs. If I name Omaha as the starting point, the Democrats will say I did it solely to increase my land values."

Durant detected weakness in the president's case and latched on.

"Please tell me, Mr. President. Please tell me you are not delaying a question of national importance for fear of offending a Democrat. Is that what you're doing? Shame on you. You need to name the starting location now, and I want it to be Omaha. I see no conflict of interest in naming Omaha. It's merely coincidence that you own property nearby."

The president deflected the attack with a gesture indicating Durant should move on with his requests.

"Council Bluffs and Omaha have more advantages than any other city. I don't see how you can seriously consider any other place. Omaha is safe from the war and the shortest route to the mountains. You owe this to your supporters in Omaha and Iowa."

"Are your strong feelings about Omaha related to the property *you* own?" the president asked.

"Me? Why, no. My property ownership is a fortunate business decision. I own land in other places too." Durant tried to appear slightly offended, but knew he was unconvincing and settled for a devilish grin.

"Move on, Doc. I can dedicate no more time to the starting point."

Durant shifted to his second discussion topic.

"We should talk about the poor incentives in the 1862 railroad act. The financial people are reluctant to invest in a railroad that goes to a desert inhabited by savages."

"So I've heard, and I agree," Lincoln acknowledged. "I have directed Congress to explore enhancing the government incentives."

"Very good, Abe," Durant approved. "I'll work with the Congressional leaders to help things along."

"Did you have anything else to discuss?" Lincoln asked.

"As a matter of fact, I do. I was wondering if you received my telegram asking for military escorts for our survey crews. It's dangerous working with so many Indians out west."

"I received your telegram, but the war is commanding full use of our army. I'm unclear when we'll be able to send men west," Lincoln said.

"It seems," Durant countered with a pull of his beard, "that if the government calls for a railroad to be built, those of us who do our civic duty and place ourselves at risk should be afforded protection from scalping and murder. Am I wrong?"

"Knowing you as I do, I doubt you will ever place yourself at risk of scalping. Nonetheless, you have raised a good point. I can see that deploying soldiers to protect railroad surveyors is appropriate. I'll see what I can do."

The president stood, signaling the conclusion of the meeting.

"Come, Doc. I'll walk you out. I have committed the rest of the day. I'm already late for my next meeting."

They walked from the office and down the stairs. Durant expected small talk, but the president was somber as he spoke.

"As you know, this nation will need an unthinkable amount of healing after the war. A railroad to the West Coat is essential to the country's development. It is also important to the nation's healing—a symbolic joining together, as it were." He interlocked his fingers in an emphatic gesture. "Union Pacific is something we need for many reasons."

* * * *

COLTON SNAPPED TO ATTENTION when the interior door opened and President Lincoln entered the room with Durant. The president took Durant's hand and said, "Keep me informed about your progress, Doc. I'll announce my decision on the terminus soon and send military escorts for you as soon as I can."

Then looking beyond Durant, Lincoln spotted Colton standing star stuck. Durant promptly stepped in. "Mr. President, this is my assistant, Colton Rusk."

The president extended his hand. "I believe we've met, Mr. Rusk, but I admit recalling your name required prompting." Colton saw the astonishment on Durant's face.

"I was a military liaison in Washington for two years, sir. We met shortly after your inauguration," Colton answered.

The president gazed at Colton. "I remember. You made several presentations on enemy troop deployments in Virginia. Am I correct?"

"Yes, sir. That was I." Colton admitted proudly.

"Your name also came before me a year ago. General Sherman recommended you for promotion to colonel. I had already signed the papers when we learned of your wounds and sent a replacement name."

Lincoln's comment stunned Colton. "Was I to be a Colonel?"

"I signed the recommendation, so you actually were a colonel for a time, although you may not have known it. How are your injuries?" the president asked.

"I am still healing, sir, and will never be suitable for active military service, so I've found a new way to serve my country."

"The transcontinental railroad is a great cause. I hope you do well."

President Lincoln turned and walked slowly away. An aide appeared from a doorway to pester him with papers and questions.

* * * *

OUTSIDE THE White House, Durant dropped the friendly facade.

"You never told me you knew the president."

"You asked at my interview if I had met him. I answered truthfully that I had."

Durant, who could not recall the interview details, changed the subject. It was almost as if a visit with the president, an impossibility for most people, had no impact on Durant.

"Do you understand your St. Louis mission?"

"I do," Colton answered.

"When you finish in St. Louis, go immediately to Omaha. You should be home in ten days. Meanwhile, I expect to hear from you daily."

As the carriage meandered along, Durant caught Colton off guard. "How do you like your new home?" he asked.

Colton classified the artificial tone between forced politeness and outright insincerity. He answered hoping Durant was making an effort to be pleasant for a change.

"It's wonderful. Libby and I love it. We are very happy in Omaha." He couldn't be sure, but he thought Durant rolled his eyes.

"I have the papers for your home at the hotel. You can sign them when we get back."

"With all you're facing, I hesitated to ask you about the home."

"We both need a signed agreement. Admittedly, it's overdue."

"I appreciate your concern," Colton said.

* * * *

AT THE GRAND HOTEL, Colton watched Durant charm two senators at the bar. Before they left, the Senators believed they were the two most powerful men in the city. They also were new converts to the need for improved railroad incentives.

As they walked through the lobby, Colton encountered an old friend and made the introduction to Durant.

"Doctor Durant, this is Richard Sybesma, Governor of Vermont."

And to the Governor he said, "Rich, this is Doctor Thomas Durant of the Union Pacific Railroad, my employer."

Formalities finished, Durant suffered impatiently as the two friends spoke briefly about family, friends and the events of their lives.

Durant found it almost impossible to extend five minutes' courtesy to Colton. He shifted his weight from one leg to the other and stared about the lobby with a pained expression.

When the Governor left, Colton saw a disbelieving look on Durant's face. The expression clearly asked, "How could you, a crippled soldier from Maryland, possibly know the Governor of Vermont?"

Colton understood the unspoken question and answered. "Sybesma was in Congress for two years. We played poker every Thursday night while we were in Washington. Now he's Governor."

In Durant's suite, talk returned to business.

"The house is worth $3,000. I am granting a mortgage loan in that amount. No payments will be due to me. The agreement says I will forgive the mortgage, or show it paid, at the rate of one sixth of the balance each year. In other words, the house becomes yours, free and clear, after you complete six years of employment. If you leave my employment, the mortgage is cancelled and the house returns to me. If you agree, sign the contract."

Colton checked the documents and confirmed the terms were the same as Durant had offered in Omaha. Durant had backdated the contract to his first day of employment in August. In six years they would own the house. Colton was happy to sign the papers.

Both men seemed satisfied to have signed copies of the contract. They celebrated a quick toast with Scotch whiskey.

"I have other information for you," Durant said setting his glass down. "For the foreseeable future, I will spend nearly all my time in

Washington. We need to stir this big pot. It is essential that Congress improve the financial incentives. Until I get the legislation updated, I'll be here. Send your daily reports to Washington until I advise otherwise."

"Yes, sir," Colton answered in the short style Durant preferred.

"Do you know an engineer named Peter A. Dey?"

"No I don't know him, but I have heard his name."

"Dey worked for me on the M&M Railroad. He is making surveys for me as far west as Salt Lake City. Get to know him when you return to Omaha."

Colton nodded understanding and waited for more.

"I may replace Dey as the Chief Engineer when construction begins. He is a competent engineer, but I simply don't trust the man. The primary reason I hired you is your relationship with General Dodge."

Colton wondered where Durant was taking the conversation.

Durant continued. "I think Dodge is probably the best person to get this railroad built. He will be our long-term Chief Engineer. I need you to help recruit him to this railroad. Don't do anything yet. I will let you know when to contact Dodge."

Colton was delighted at Durant's comment. He responded without thinking. "Dodge will make an excellent Chief Engineer."

The agreeable conversation turned instantly ugly.

"That's your opinion is it?" His voice took a challenging tone.

"Yes, sir."

Durant's face flushed red with anger. "Stop! If I want someone's opinion about Dodge and his abilities, I will hire an expert. You're a shot-up, low-ranking soldier. You are not here for diversity of opinion. No one really cares what you think. Give me facts only unless I ask for an interpretation. Never burden me with unsolicited opinions again. Am I clear?"

A meeting that started so pleasantly with a home contract and a toast now ended like so many others, with Colton nursing slight wounds and trying to understand Durant. Colton left in silence.

He spent the remainder of the day making travel arrangements and visiting an old contact in the War Department.

Alone that evening, Colton reviewed the home papers by oil light. He visualized the time when, in six years, they would celebrate the mortgage's total cancellation.

"The house will become ours in August 1869," Colton said, announcing his calculations to the hotel room. "William will be over seventeen years old, almost a man."

He locked the mortgage in the brass box and went to bed feeling warm satisfaction about the day. Any day the president can remember you, is a good day, he concluded.

The train trip to St. Louis required more time than Colton expected. First, an early snow storm slowed trains to a crawl, and then rumors of an imminent rebel invasion further clogged rail lines.

Once in St. Louis, Colton struggled to gather the information he needed. Several steamboat owners were away on their boats transporting troops. Other absentee owners, some owning five or more boats, lived on the east coast. Their St. Louis agents took several days to answer Colton's inquiries.

By the time Colton returned to Omaha, almost a month had passed. His family celebrated his return. Libby prepared a wonderful meal. Colton had gifts from Washington and New York and made a merry time of presenting them during dinner.

For Libby he brought a necklace of finely sculpted blue stones held together with a gold chain. He gave William a folding pocket knife.

Colton was able to spend only one uninterrupted day at home, then it was back to work for a hectic finish to 1863.

Chapter 15

NOVEMBER 17, 1863 - THE GROUNDBREAKING

Across America, a war-weary people plodded day to day, hour to hour, struggling to survive until the great insurrection passed. The euphoric patriotism of three years earlier was gone, violently supplanted now by ghastly reality. Hopelessness lay across the nation like a smothering, poisonous cloud. Exhausted and grieving people felt drained of all energy and optimism.

Bad news came daily from every direction: riots in New York, Indian massacres in the west, conflict in Congress.

Thousands upon thousands of boys marched to their deaths at the hands of other boys. Everyone knew someone lost in battle; too often it was a family member.

The people, the government, and even the newsmen longed for good news to balance the losses at Shiloh, Gettysburg and a hundred other battles. They needed positive diversion of massive proportions to offset the coming destruction of the South that would be immense in scale. The downtrodden, the inconsolable, and those who saw no future turned to Omaha for their hope as the war dragged on in its third, bloody year.

* * * *

ON THE SECOND FLOOR of Herndon House Hotel, the bedroom and office formerly registered to Thomas Durant now showed in the name of Union Pacific Railroad. The unassuming rooms were an uninspiring manifestation of America's best hope for healing.

George Train pranced into the office wearing a full length fur coat. It fit tightly against the body and had a bushy collar. "I'm here," he chirped with a broad smile. "And I've got big news."

Colton Rusk looked up from a map of The Nebraska Territory. "Nice coat. Beaver?"

"Canadian Beaver. Mink collar. Custom made, of course." He stroked the fur with long fingers.

"Here it is, old boy: I heard from Doc this morning. Long telegram. He said President Lincoln finally declared Omaha the railroad's starting point."

"That *is* good news," Colton answered, still taking in George's attire. "Doc worked hard for this. He must be pleased."

"I don't think so. Doc said Lincoln scribbled a note as he was leaving for a speech at Gettysburg. He wants us to begin plans for a groundbreaking ceremony."

"Will Doc come for the ceremony?"

"No. He plans to stay east to work on finances," George said.

For the next hour, they pounded out the framework for a rousing ceremony that would include bands, cannons, speeches, and a parade. George correctly assumed he would be the keynote speaker.

"Maybe we should have a city-wide picnic or ball after the ceremony," Colton said. "People love a good get-together."

"Right-O. It would be a perfect setting to mix with the newspaper people. Let's do it," Train agreed.

They divided the work. George recruited newspaper reporters from across the country and invited dignitaries. He obtained congratulatory letters from those unable to attend. Colton's role was to pick the spot, get Durant's approval, and work out details with the mayor.

Colton spent the next two weeks nailing down fine points. He easily convinced the city fathers to host a lavish ball at the Herndon House. Then he arranged for a St. Louis band to march in the parade, and play for the ceremony and dance.

Selecting the actual groundbreaking site proved challenging. Durant suggested a spot two miles north of town to maximize government mileage payments. In a rare moment of uncertainty, he asked Colton's opinion. Colton suggested a location downtown near the river explaining the closer location would bring more participation and national attention. Several days later, Durant demanded the downtown site as if it were his own idea. He set the ceremony for December 2, 1863. He also bombarded Colton and George with unneeded guidance:

Your preparations are behind schedule for this grand event. Pick up your pace immediately.

T. C. Durant.

The mayor was elated about a high-profile ceremony and campaigned vigorously to raise funds for the festival.

"The news coverage alone will bring Omaha new business and families," he told the citizens. Mayor Kennedy mobilized the town and supervised efforts to construct a stage. Excitement grew.

The day before the ceremony every passing steamboat deposited newspapermen, musicians, and dignitaries wanting their name associated with the railroad's start. Hotels filled to capacity. There seemed to be no concern that freezing weather might soon ice-over the river.

George Train arrived for the ceremony the next day leading the marching band. He waved at the crowd to the sounds of drums and trumpets. He wore a brilliant white suit, complete with a white vest, white shoes, and white gloves. Several thousand watched as Train strutted onto the stage. Most were unaware such an outfit existed.

While the band entertained, Train checked the harvest of newspaper men. It was a bumper crop. "We've got reporters from every major newspaper in the country," he boasted to the territorial governor. "Wait until they hear my speech."

The ceremony began. Dignitaries took turns reading laudatory messages including ones from President Lincoln and Dr. Durant. They turned dirt with ceremonial shovels, and gave grandiose speeches. By the time Train began his speech, the crowd was eager to hear him.

As the world expected, Train's speech was a masterpiece. His delivery made it a spellbinder; showmanship at its best. He worked the crowd into a frenzied state about Omaha's rich future. He cited the pyramids, the Suez Canal and the Great Wall of China as lesser projects than the nation's transcontinental railroad.

At the height of Train's speech, and at Colton's signal, two companies of artillery, on opposite sides of the river, fired a thunderous volley. Several women screamed, but most of the crowd exploded into an incredible roar. The businessmen cheered loudest of all.

"The great Pacific Railroad has hereby commenced!" Train shouted in triumph. At that point, every man, woman, and child would have been willing to build the railroad themselves, had U.P. owned any construction materials. Instead they settled for dancing and a banquet.

At the ball that night, the revelers gravitated toward George Train. Train was in his element and soaked up the attention. He entertained with stories of London and Paris, but assured them, "Omaha is my favorite city of all."

Colton and Libby drew their share of attention too. Despite trying to stay in the background, they met and talked with well-wishers much of the night. Long before the party ended, they were exhausted. About midnight they escaped the ball to take a carriage home.

* * * *

"OH NO," LIBBY WHISPERED as the carriage brought them within sight of their home. "That's Mr. Butler on our porch."

Libby looked to Colton. His crestfallen face gave away his disappointment for the inevitable.

"You have a telegram from New York, Mr. Rusk," Butler announced. "I'm glad I found you. The city is having quite a party."

"Do you *have* to go?" Libby asked when Butler had gone. She felt tears coming and fought them off even as Colton opened the envelope.

Eight hours later Colton was headed for St. Joseph.

* * * *

NEWSPAPERS IN EVERY STATE - including several Confederate states - carried glowing accounts of the ceremony and celebrations. Several called George Train's oratory "the most notable speech of the century."

* * * *

TWO DAYS later Omaha still had a splitting headache and a hoarse throat from the wild festivities. Most people were barely sober and wholly unprepared when rumors began circulating.

"Did you hear?" they asked. "Omaha is no longer the starting point for U.P. The railroad is moving to Bellevue. We're destined to be at the end of a minor branch line, if on the railroad at all."

The listeners scoffed. "This can't be true. We just broke ground,"

The rumors continued. People listened and gave them consideration. They could barely bring themselves to accept them as possible, much less factual. How could they be true? Weren't Peter Dey and his grading crews already preparing a road bed?

They became nervous, like sheep sensing the presence of a predator. They fretted. *Was* something waiting for the right moment to bring disaster upon them and their financial future?

The person they sought to confront was Colton Rusk. It was essential that a railroad spokesman immediately address these rumors.

Libby was at home when the mayor and two councilmen knocked at the door. They asked for Colton only to learn he was in Chicago. They left bewildered, trying to control their frustration. The mayor was the first to bluster, "I will telegram Durant today and demand an explanation. We can't wait for Colton to return. This is too important."

"Why give Durant any ideas? Colton will be back soon. Don't let Durant know we're worried," a councilman said.

So they waited. But the rumors persisted as snows blanketed Omaha. Day by day the businessmen became increasingly nervous. In the second week new rumors spread saying that Desoto, barely twenty miles to the north, would be the railroad's starting point.

After two weeks, Colton returned from Chicago on the last steamboat of the season. From the moment he arrived, he perceived the tension. The glares, frowns and a hundred other indicators told him something was wrong.

Libby and William spotted him walking up the street and were waiting for him when he reached the front porch. He hugged them, grateful to be home. They settled in the kitchen.

"Sit down! I have stories to tell and presents to share," Colton said. The family enjoyed a rare quiet evening together.

Before bedtime, Libby told Colton about the rumors and the mayor's visit a week ago. Colton suspected the source of the rumors and felt comfortable he could track the source, probably to Bellevue.

The following morning the mayor and two businessmen knocked on Colton's door. Colton had anticipated the visit and was ready. The three men settled in the study. They bluntly refused coffee and instead poured servings of their own hot anger and demands.

Colton listened to panicked men lashing out at the only reliable railroad contact they had.

"We've given so much! These changes are unacceptable."

Colton tried to calm them. "Doc will be here when the first steamboats are running again. He'll have the answers you need."

It was too little for town fathers who had reputations and dollars on the line. They stormed from the house still unsure how to attack their problem.

Colton would have been surprised had he known the rumors came not from landowners in Bellevue or Desoto, but a landowner in New York, one with a calculating mind and a scraggly beard. Durant.

Chapter 16

FIRST QUARTER 1864 – DURANT RETURNS TO OMAHA

For three months, bitter winter winds battered Omaha, changing life's focus to survival and temporarily freezing the town's distrust for the railroad. Despite their panic, the city fathers realized they could do nothing about Durant until spring and so postponed action. They told themselves the right moment would come soon.

Winter also restricted Colton's travel, holding him in Omaha until the end of February. Daily communications with Durant continued, but with transportation frozen, Colton could do little other than try to pacify the Omaha leadership.

The bitter weather drove Chief Engineer Peter Dey from the frozen prairies to Omaha. He stayed in town most of December where Colton got to know him. The three, Colton Rusk, George Train and Peter Dey shared the Union Pacific office in the Herndon House.

George Train focused on real estate and made a personal purchase of five thousand Omaha lots south of Pacific Street.

"We'll call it Traintown," he bragged to Colton and Dey.

Peter Dey, who worked at a small table in the office, spent his time endlessly reviewing track diagrams and survey reports.

"We'll start grading the roadbed in March," he told his officemates.

Colton spent his time corresponding with the territorial legislators and city leaders from St. Louis to Sioux City.

During this time Colton learned to appreciate Peter Dey as an honest man. Dey was one of the most religious men Colton had ever met, praying before meals and reading his Bible in the afternoons. He had a sense of humor and an honorable way about him that impressed Colton.

Colton recalled Durant's comments in Washington about Dey. He knew Durant intended to fire this fine man. As required, Colton kept the information to himself. For now, Peter Dey was the Chief Engineer and a pleasure to work with.

In mid-February Colton notified Durant the waterways should be open in a week. Durant responded, "I will depart for Omaha within three days. Have Train and Dey available for meetings when I arrive."

Colton spent the next week preparing for Durant's arrival. The three cleared the office and adjoining bedroom of Dey's surveys, Train's real estate documents, and a winter's accumulation of papers.

Preparations finished, they waited. Each morning Colton walked to the Herndon House to check the hotel register and office. He saw no sign of Durant.

On the tenth day, Colton walked before daylight through a spring snow flurry to the Herndon House. Reaching the office, he found Durant with a stranger.

The stranger had a penetrating stare in a face set with a permanent frown. He was a chubby middle-aged man with silver-streaked hair and a matching mustache. His low brow and deep inset eyes gave him a simian look.

Durant looked up at the interruption, saw it was Colton and announced, "Ah, Rusk. I'm glad at least one of you decided to come to work today. Shake hands with Colonel Silas Seymour. Silas, this is Colton Rusk, one of my well-rested assistants."

The two men shook hands.

To Colton, Durant said, "Silas is an experienced engineer. Like you, he is a special assistant. He reports only to me."

To Seymour, Durant said, "Silas, you should know that Rusk has similar status. He answers only to me."

Silas Seymour nodded with a grunt.

Durant turned back to Colton. "Silas' role is to identify construction savings missed in the initial planning. Every penny we save during construction is a penny to profits. His title is Consulting Engineer. I am traveling to Desoto today. Give Silas a tour of Omaha. Show him the planned railroad route out of town. Introduce him to Peter Dey."

While Durant and Seymour finished their conversation, Colton went downstairs to hire an enclosed carriage and driver for Durant's day trip. He also rented a small buggy for Silas Seymour and himself.

Durant gave final instructions. "We'll meet here at daylight tomorrow. Get Train and Dey here too. We have business to discuss."

Seymour suffered through the Omaha tour. He looked bored and preoccupied. Without Durant's orders, Seymour would have cancelled the excursion.

After driving through the town and along the riverfront, Colton drove to the railroad route where one day trains would run. Now the roadbed was an uneven dirt pathway cleared for survey crews. A mile beyond town, they found Peter Dey and a work gang cutting trees.

Peter Dey saw the buggy approaching and greeted the visitors warmly.

Seymour's demeanor changed the moment Dey approached. After riding in a sullen funk all day, Seymour was suddenly overbearing. He unleashed a nonstop stream of criticism toward Dey.

"Why do you have these men so bunched up, Mr. Dey? They seem to be stumbling all over each other. I could get the same work done with half the men. Why so many?" Seymour challenged.

"Why do you have men using shovels when you could fabricate a mule-pulled excavator so cheaply," Seymour berated.

"Why do you plan to dig such a deep cut at this point?"

"I looked at your survey. It seems your current route will require digging up half of Nebraska. Why did you choose this route?"

The harassment was unrelenting. Peter Dey kept his cool, courteously answering all of Seymour's questions. When he tired of the exercise, Dey excused himself and returned to his men.

"I'll see you at the meeting in the morning," Dey called to Colton.

Colton had been was taken aback by the interaction between Dey and Seymour.

* * * *

THAT EVENING, Seymour joined the Rusk family for a fried chicken dinner. After days of travel, Silas enjoyed a homemade meal washed down with three glasses of wine.

After dinner, Colton coaxed Seymour into his study where cognac and a cigar loosened Silas' tongue. Seymour took a hearty tone with Colton. "Exactly what do you do for Durant?" he asked. The condescending tone was unmistakable.

"I give new assistants an orientation and entertain them." The answer was in a friendly tone, but conveyed no useful information.

Seymour knew that Colton had avoided the question and tried different bait. "Durant told me you are a war hero and will be bringing Dodge to Union Pacific."

Colton remained aloof though cordial while pouring Seymour a second glass of cognac. "If you say Doc said such a thing, he must certainly have."

Colton, a masterful conversationalist, toyed with Seymour. After several attempts to pry secrets from Colton, Seymour dropped his own guard with his third glass of cognac. Colton lit a cigar and let Seymour talk. With cognac now in control of Seymour's mouth, the information Colton wanted spilled out.

"I think we'll probably get rid of Peter Dey within a few months," Seymour announced smugly. "I just need to get the cost estimates raised to the proper level before General Dodge gets here. I'll be reducing standards and raising expected expenses like there's no tomorrow."

Colton showed no reaction to Seymour's confessions. Inside, he pondered the statements and the meanings behind them. Colton worried about the need to fire Peter Dey. At the same time, he longed to see General Dodge achieve his life-long dream.

* * * *

OMAHA WAS ABUZZ about Doc Durant's arrival. The appearance of such a powerful industrialist so early in the year was big news for a frontier town. This was the man who would bring the railroad and its promise of wealth to Omaha. Word of his coming spread like wildfire almost from the moment he strode arrogantly down the gang plank with a man described as "a big grumpy ape." Within two hours, Mayor Kennedy's passions about the rumors had reignited.

* * * *

JUST AFTER DAYLIGHT, Durant convened a meeting at the Herndon House office with Peter Dey, George Train, Silas Seymour, and Colton Rusk. Clerk Johnson sat outside awaiting orders.

Durant removed a brass box from his carpet bag and was spreading documents when a knock at the door broke the calm. He railed against the interruption.

"What! This had better be important," he bellowed to Johnson.

The door opened, but it was not Johnson who stepped inside. Instead, Mayor Benjamin Kennedy eased in with his hat off and clutched to his chest. He was a man who looked short of confidence.

"What do you want, mayor? I'm in a meeting here!"

Durant's abrupt tone was the polar opposite of the conciliatory manner Colton had observed in the last meeting.

The mayor spoke hesitantly.

"We're hearing non-stop rumors that you're moving the shops and starting the railroad at Bellevue," Mayor Kennedy stated.

"That rubbish! I don't understand why you people react to every rumor as if it's truth. The railroad will begin at Omaha."

"But we heard—"

Durant cut off the mayor in mid-sentence. "I don't care what you heard!" Durant extended a finger and leveled it at the mayor like a pistol. "The railroad starts in Omaha, or at least it will if you allow me to get my work done. Really, Kennedy, you can do better than this whimpering in front of grown men."

"I'm sorry, Doctor, we just wanted to clear up these rumors."

"Go, Kennedy. I don't have time for this. Reassure your citizens they will get the railroad. I foresee nothing that will change Omaha's situation. Just go. And close the door behind you."

"Thank you, sir." They mayor eased backward out the door and quietly closed it.

Alone again with his staff, Durant continued ranting. "I travel all the way from New York in winter and all I've done so far is get interrupted by a mayor who wants to moan about rumors. Of course he's hearing rumors! I planted them. I planted more yesterday at Florence and Desoto."

Durant paused and fumed a moment, then continued. "Rusk, look at me. When the next round of rumors hit, keep the Omaha mayor out of New York. I don't need him hounding me. You either learn to manage your mayors or I'll get someone who can. Keep the mayor here in the sticks and away from me. Understand?"

"Yes, sir."

Durant laid his head on one shoulder and then the other, each motion resulting in clearly audible popping. The four men watched, hoping Doc's relaxation technique would work. Sitting up again, Durant straightened his collar, popped his knuckles with a loud crack, and began stroking his scraggly beard. "Now let's get down to business."

The four resumed breathing.

"Lincoln's war is going badly. We have little investor money coming in. Our candy-hearted lobbyists are unreliable, so I am temporarily moving to Washington to personally push Congress for more incentives. It will take six months to buy the legislation I want."

Durant turned to Peter Dey. "How many men do you have?"

"The contractor has about fifty men now and will have a hundred more with warmer weather next month. The numbers are inadequate."

"That's still more men than we can afford. Let them get started on the grading with 150 men, mainly to pacify the Omaha people. We'll cut back half of them after a month."

Dey started to protest, but was immediately drowned out.

"You have a better plan?" Durant chided. "Let's hear what you can do with no money, Mr. Chief Engineer. I'd love to hear it. Otherwise, sit quietly and listen. Start your earth work in June and get as much done as you can until I get more financing. Working with half your men is better than working with no men. Get tougher, Dey."

George Train sat with them looking as if he just stepped from the pages of a Paris fashion magazine. He leaned back in his chair and rested his thin soled shoes on the desk. He knew he looked good.

"At the risk of appearing impatient," Train offered, "delays will hurt us and hurt my personal investments here. Maybe I should join you in Washington for the lobbying. You will need help."

Of the four men, Train was the only one permitted to offer strategy suggestions or challenges. He alone could rest his shoes on Durant's desk. He alone could tell the emperor he was naked.

"Perhaps you're right," Durant answered. "Make your plans to join me in Washington as soon as you can."

Train popped a cashew nut into his mouth, celebrating the small victory.

Durant turned back to Peter Dey. "I understand you met Silas Seymour yesterday."

"I did," Dey acknowledged, casting a wary eye at Seymour.

"Seymour's title is Consulting Engineer. He will review our plans to ensure construction is done as economically as possible."

"My plans already take cost into consideration. No one envisions a gold-plated railroad, Doc."

"We'll see. I want your full cooperation with Seymour. I am the final authority if questions arise. Is that understood?"

"Yes," said Dey.

"Good. Let's talk about the four survey teams I'm paying for. I want two teams dedicated to surveying river crossings. Send one team to Bellevue, the other north to Desoto. I doubt if we abandon Omaha, but I need to know my options for other bridge locations."

The instructions staggered Colton and Peter Dey. Everyone recognized the implications. Only minutes earlier Durant had assured Mayor Kennedy that Omaha was the starting point. Now it seemed Durant was actively looking at alternate routes.

Train again spoke up. "How can we justify looking at Bellevue considering the president's orders to begin at Omaha?"

"I'm making these surveys with my own money, George. Union Pacific has no official involvement at all. Can't you see the beauty of it? My personal surveys are in conflict with nothing."

Train whistled. "That's an interesting move, Doc. It will have the Omaha businessmen beating war drums and pounding spears on the ground. I think I'll leave for Washington sooner than I planned."

Train winked at Colton. "May the Lord grant you strength to endure the great wailing and gnashing of teeth about to begin in Omaha." Train made the sign of the cross toward Colton.

"Stop the jokes, Train! This is serious business," Durant scolded.

"Doc, I am serious," Train replied. "When the city fathers see survey crews in Bellevue, they'll want to lynch you."

"Let's move on," Durant remarked dismissing all concern.

He scanned the small audience then continued. "Next month we will complete the purchase of a company called Crédit Mobilier. George gets the credit for the idea. It will be a completely separate company from Union Pacific. Here's the critical part: All construction work will be awarded to Crédit Mobilier."

Peter Dey dared to ask a question. "So Crédit Mobilier will be a general contractor, correct?"

"Yes. Crédit Mobilier will select and pay all sub-contractors."

Dey pressed. "That's why you want higher estimates. The government will pay Crédit Mobilier, and you, top prices based on high estimates, while you pay sub-contractors as little as possible based on my lower estimates."

"It's called making a profit. Is that is a new concept for you, Dey?

The room was silent. Durant continued.

"Know this: every project, every job, every purchase goes through Crédit Mobilier every time. Remember the name well. This is a must."

Durant's visit to Omaha was short—three days in all—but he left behind the same fear and uncertainty a wolf leaves after sniffing around a calf pen. Colton was the one left to deal with the aftermath.

Chapter 17

The orphan boy Sean Cook left the boat landing in the late afternoon and slipped through the river trees to the abandoned shack below the levee. He threw open the door excitedly. "Guess who gave me a dollar again today," he crowed.

Darcy Lonigan, bone tired from unloading cargo off three consecutive steamboats boats, lay on a blanket next to a stolen bag of flour.

"Why would I care who gave you anything?" he sneered.

"Cause it was that crippled guy you hate," Sean said almost taunting.

"The same man I showed?" Lonigan sat up on the edge of the cot.

"Yeah, that's him. Alone this time."

"Coming or going?"

"Just got in from the south. He was really nice to me too."

Lonigan backhanded the child across the mouth, sending him to the floor.

"That's how nice he is. Hand over the money. It's time you paid rent."

"I was here before you. You don't own this place," the boy argued.

"Well it's time you learned about life. No rent means no bed. So, do you want a beating, or will you just hand it over? Either way I'm taking the money."

Sean Cook ducked his head, handed over the dollar, and stepped back out of arm reach, tears in his eyes.

"I still think he's nice," the boy said defiantly and ran out.

Lonigan called out, "He ain't like us. He's a rich man." Then he muttered to himself, "His type will keep us in this shack the rest of our lives."

* * * *

COLTON MADE HIS WAY from the river on Jones Street. He planned to arrive home before dusk after a quick stop for messages.

Rounding the corner onto Farnam Street, Colton spotted Peter Dey in front of the Herndon House preparing to mount his horse. As he approached, Dey spoke.

"How was your trip?"

"Successful enough, I guess," Colton answered. "We've got steamboats available when they're needed. How are things with you?"

"This was a rough week. Seymour has been in my way every time I turn around. Doc is pressing again for inflated cost estimates. He wants the employee count cut in half. And he hasn't paid salaries in two months."

Dey gave the saddle cinch a tug to check its tightness. He waited for the horse to exhale, then gave it a final tug.

"All things considered, it was a miserable week", said Dey.

"Sorry to hear Seymour is so disruptive," Colton said shaking his head.

"You know why Seymour is really here, don't you?" Dey asked.

"I guess not. Tell me," Colton said.

"Seymour is a mediocre engineer. Truth is, his brother is the governor of New York and may run for president. Durant is hedging his bets in case he needs new inroads to the White House."

"I had no idea," Colton answered. "What was that you said about the salaries?"

"It's true. Doc is holding all salaries. Better check your own accounts. You may go hungry this month like the rest of us. He says the company is temporarily short of funds."

"That's strange," Colton said trying to grasp the situation.

"This was predictable. There is nothing strange about it," Dey retorted. "My contacts tell me Durant is having the time of his life in Washington. He's throwing lavish parties and bribing lawmakers. Durant is buying Congressional votes with our payroll money. I hear he's spent over $400,000. That's almost everything Union Pacific owns."

Colton was unsure what to say. He didn't need to say anything. The concern on his face showed in deep lines and furrows.

Dey continued, "I can almost guarantee part of U.P.'s money is in Durant's personal bank account. For the ten years I've worked for him on the M&M he has consistently skimmed company funds for himself. The man has icy greed coursing through his veins."

Colton found it upsetting to listen to Dey's harsh allegations.

"You look shocked, Colton. For your own protection, you'd better wise up. Durant is an expert liar, skillful in telling people exactly what they want to hear. You don't have to believe me, just be alert."

Dey threw out another shocker. "And as for me, I hear my days with Union Pacific are numbered."

Dey mounted his horse looking disgusted. Colton offered encouragement.

"Peter, no one knows what the future holds, but I do know you're a fine man. Things will work out."

"We'll see." Dey pulled the horse around to leave and added, "One more thing, Colton. I have survey crews going to Bellevue and Desoto on Monday. The mayor will probably drop by to see you when he hears about it."

Colton stopped at the Herndon's front desk to pick up messages. He felt relief when he found a paycheck waiting for him.

* * * *

IN WASHINGTON, Durant's creativity worked overtime. Every day brought freshly hatched projects for Colton. In private Libby was grateful for the "schemes," as she called them, for they kept Colton close to Omaha in March and April of 1864.

Colton worked at a feverish pace. One day he would rush to Bellevue to talk with Buck Clayton about land for a depot. The next, it was an emergency run to Desoto to discuss land for a locomotive shop. Two days later he was off to Florence about additional cash incentives. He had no idea what might come next.

Colton saw that Durant had four cities competing with real money and land for a spot on the railroad. Bellevue, Florence, and the Desoto landowners were mounting strong challenges against Omaha.

Durant was impossible to read. Even as an insider, Colton had no clue which cities would win or lose.

Peter Dey's survey crews were on the job a week before Mayor Kennedy, looking very nervous, appeared on Colton's front porch.

"We need to talk," the mayor said.

The mayor was a welcome guest who normally needed no appointment. Colton greeted him warmly and invited him in for coffee.

The mayor was much more confident than during Durant's visit and walked with determined steps to the study where he turned on Colton.

"I'll skip the formalities. We know about Union Pacific survey crews working in Bellevue and Desoto. One of the councilmen rode out and confirmed it."

"I can confirm it also, mayor. Those towns will need railroad service too, even if on branch lines," Colton answered.

"At this point, we don't give a fig about those other towns. They're obviously trying to undermine us. We want to know if Doc is keeping his promises to Omaha.

"Everything I see still shows Omaha as the headquarters," Colton said.

"I want to believe you, but we won't relax until Dey actually starts grading from Omaha to the west. You can understand it, Colton. Omaha has so much money and land invested in Durant that anything short of getting the terminal and shops will be disastrous."

"Peter should start earth work in July, Mayor. The contractors are almost ready to go. You've seen the equipment yourself."

"I've seen it. Let me know if anything changes," he begged.

"I will, as I always have," Colton said.

Mayor Kennedy stayed long enough for coffee and pie, and then left, satisfied for the moment.

Colton was less confident than his voice. He wondered what Durant was really up to.

* * * *

TWO DAYS LATER, George Train surprised Omaha when he arrived by steamboat. Colton cancelled a noon luncheon with a territorial legislator to have lunch with Train hoping to learn the latest Washington news.

They agreed on a restaurant a short walk from the office. Within minutes Train and Colton sat talking at a private table.

"I'm only here for two days. Real estate deed work, old boy. I need to get back to Washington as quickly as possible. Doc was most unpleasant about this trip for personal business."

"From what I hear, Washington is busy as a beehive," Colton probed.

"I'd say it's more like being in a whirlwind. Doc is tireless. Nonstop motion! We're making great progress on getting our legislation."

"I'm glad you're here," Colton said. "Tell me about the legislation. Does it look like we'll have better incentives with the new law?"

"We think land grants will double and other restrictions will loosen. I think we will finally be able to attract investors."

"How about President Lincoln? Is he on board?" Colton's eyes sparkled.

"You put it too mildly. Lincoln and most congressmen are clamoring to get this business finished. We have a couple of senators to coax, but we're getting close. Final wording for the bill is just around the bend. We will finish the whole thing by July."

"What about Crédit Mobilier? Is the construction company in place?"

"We completed the purchase in March. It's ready to go. Doc will charge all expenses to Crédit Mobilier within a few weeks."

"Peter Dey tells me the company is out of cash. What do you know about it, George?"

"He's right. Lobbying expenses are hitting hard. You and I are lucky that Doc pays us directly."

Colton gathered information from George until he felt fully briefed on the Washington scene. George's comments suggested that Dey's story about Durant's carefree spending, bribery, and gift giving were true.

They had breakfast together the next morning, but too soon, George finished his business and was gone again.

* * * *

COLTON CRISSCROSSED Mid-America during the first half of the summer of 1864 promoting the railroad, locating suppliers, and making contacts for Durant. The hidden brass box was always with him. His pistol was always ready under his coat if needed.

In July, a coded message came instructing Colton to pick up a package from Desoto "and deliver immediately to Washington."

Seven grueling days later Colton arrived exhausted at the Grand Hotel in Washington. Doc Durant took the brass box and excused Colton for the evening with no comment.

The next morning Colton was in the hotel dining room when Durant walked in and sat with him. The fact that Durant was smiling gave Colton an eerie feeling. Colton fought the urge to say, "Good morning."

"This will be a day to remember," Durant gushed. "Lincoln signs the new law this morning."

"That's good news, sir."

"You and George shall go with me to the signing ceremony to witness my triumph."

"I will be happy to attend, sir."

"Yes, I know." Durant smirked at Colton

The short ceremony occurred on a White House porch. Seven senators, ten congressmen, and a host of bureaucrats crowded around to hear the president speak and watch him sign the revised Pacific Rail Act.

Following a short reception, Colton and Durant returned to the hotel. The carriage ride proved every bit as interesting as the ceremony.

"Rusk, even you should realize we are in a great position to get the railroad moving along," Durant started.

"Yes, sir."

"Private investors will flock to us soon. The incentives are too high now for them to stay away. Land grants have doubled to 12,800 acres for every mile we build. We get the mineral rights for coal and gold. And for construction we get government payments earlier than with the old law. We can now issue U.P. bonds. Things are definitely looking up."

It was impressive, Colton thought, that Durant had succeeded in getting a generous law from Congress even as war raged around them.

"When you return to Omaha, your focus will be supporting construction. It is essential that we complete twenty track miles to collect the first government payments. Do you recall Collis Huntington at the reception?"

"I recall," Colton answered.

"He is our enemy and in charge of the Central Pacific Railroad. CP is already laying track from California to meet Union Pacific. Every mile they build is money from our pockets. We will be in a frantic race with CP to lay track. The more miles we build the less they will. Peter Dey needs to understand that delays will ruin us."

Several moments passed. Colton cleared his throat to speak.

"We'll need more men," Colton said, breaking Durant's thoughts.

"What's that? More men?" Durant said refocusing on Colton.

Colton explained. "Dey tells me it's impossible to make much progress without manpower. He has no labor sources to draw from, and what he had is now reduced by half. Grading is going very slowly."

"I'm on top of the manpower needs, Rusk. For your information, I've contacted the army. We may be able to use Indian labor. Lincoln is considering railroad jobs for thousands of former slaves. When the war is over, maybe next year, soldiers will be looking for work. Meanwhile Dey needs to get going."

"And my mission will be what, sir?"

"You will keep a close eye on Peter Dey. I distrust him. He's stalling on revising cost estimates. I need to know what Dey is doing at all times."

Colton stared across the carriage at Durant. Spying on a fellow worker was distasteful duty.

"Yes, sir," Colton said, wishing there was another option.

"You will also deal with suppliers and contactors on behalf of Crédit Mobilier. Meanwhile, get back to Omaha without delay. Dey needs to send me his final cost estimates within a month. Push him."

* * * *

COLTON LEFT WASHINGTON within hours on a westbound train knowing he faced an overwhelming workload. During one period that summer he was gone from Omaha six weeks. He missed his family, but tried to work as tirelessly as Durant.

It seemed everyone Colton talked with disliked Durant. Colton still wanted to view Durant as a hero, a man doing a great service for America, yet he understood why people had difficulty seeing past the brash behavior and cold decisions. Colton remained loyal, but no longer blindly loyal. The summer months passed swiftly with Colton defending his boss, soothing hurt feelings, and supplying the charisma Durant lacked.

Chapter 18

A voice pierced the silence. "Sir? Sir, it's almost daylight."

Summer nights in Georgia are always sweltering, and this one was no different. In his command tent, Major General Grenville Dodge awoke to find he was sweating. He remained motionless on the cot gathering his thoughts.

"Sir, I have your breakfast."

Dodge rose grudgingly and forced himself to dress. Still groggy, he moved to a small table and sat facing a tasteless breakfast. An Atlanta newspaper sat next to the plate, freshly smuggled from behind enemy lines. He eyed the bold headline.

YANKEES APPROACHING—CITY PREPARES FOR SIEGE

The General shoved aside the paper and dug into the food. It was a plain breakfast, a soldier's breakfast of biscuits, a strip of bacon, grease, and strong coffee. The coffee was steaming hot on a morning when iced water might have been a better choice.

Nearby, ten thousand soldiers under Dodge's command ate the same breakfast. Like his men, Dodge ate ravenously for it might be the only chance to eat until nightfall. After he sopped up the last of the grease, he used a cloth napkin first to wipe the crumbs from his beard and then to dab the sweat beading on his forehead.

Dodge's command tent was on the outskirts of Atlanta a mile from the front lines. Soldiers had foraged food for the breakfast from local farms and plantations before burning them to the ground. It was a good meal considering the battle conditions.

Dodge thought about the campaign, this long bloody march to Atlanta. He saw his political star rising in the army.

For months, the Union Army, with greater manpower and resources, had relentlessly pushed the rebels deeper into their heartland. Each time the Confederate Army established a defensive position, the Union Army overran it. Each time the rebels mounted a desperate, hopeless attack, the Yankees beat it back. Steadily, the Union Army advanced, burning plantations and towns as they went. Now Atlanta, the crown jewel of the Confederacy, was in sight of conquering army.

Dodge felt good about his troops' victories. He was proud of his own performance, predicting accurately where and when the rebels intended to attack Sherman's flanks. Only two months ago Grant had promoted him from Brigadier General to Major General in charge of Sixteen Corps. His men and his instincts were serving him well.

Now fully awake, Dodge called to the officer waiting outside, "Major, bring my mail."

The tall major came in with a bundle and laid it on the table. General Dodge sorted through the envelopes, quickly arranging each document in priority order. He began reading. Most were routine reports. Two documents, however, drew a second reading. Dodge tucked these two in his uniform coat pocket.

This first document contained written orders from General William Tecumseh Sherman, the commanding officer for all Union forces in the Western Theater. He was the strategist who ordered the scorched earth policy that was demoralizing the enemy. The orders contained nothing unexpected. Dodge was to hold his position and continue fortifying for a long siege against Atlanta.

The second document was a letter from Dr. Thomas Durant thanking him for "wise counsel" in "certain business matters." It also contained an appeal for Dodge to quit the army and lead the construction of the transcontinental railroad.

"Yes," Dodge mumbled as he forced down the last swig of coffee and stood up. "I will see Dr. Durant *after* the war is over."

Dodge exited his tent to face a stressful day. He was anxious to hear from twenty former slaves serving as spies. He was proud of his spies. Their information had proven very reliable over the months. He looked forward to hearing about rebel defenses in Atlanta.

Before meeting his spies, however, General Dodge needed to inspect siege preparations along the front lines.

"Have the horses saddled," he ordered the major. "I want the staff to leave in fifteen minutes to see the rampart work."

Within half an hour, the group was nearing the first stop when they encountered a sentry a quarter mile from the front.

Major General Grenville Dodge
Courtesy of United States Archives

"Sir, you'd best dismount and walk from here behind the tree line. We have rebel snipers in the area. We lost two men yesterday."

"Thank you, son. We'll do that." Dodge said. The General and his staff dismounted and crept forward to the reinforced trench and rampart.

Now in the trench, a young lieutenant gave a progress report. Satisfied, Dodge stepped to a small peephole in the rampart to view enemy positions.

Dodge bent over to look into the opening. He never saw the sniper's muzzle flash or the bullet that flew through the peephole and struck him in the head. Dodge fell back unconscious in a spray of blood. His staff rushed forward. The sad word spread across the army and the nation that Dodge was shot dead at Atlanta.

When Atlanta fell to the Union Army on September 2, 1864, Grenville Dodge was not at hand to experience the historic moment. He was not present to see the population evacuated and the entire city burned to the ground. But neither was he dead. Grenville Dodge survived the sniper attack and, after being unconscious for days, revived and began recovery. When Atlanta fell, Dodge was home nursing serious wounds and dreaming of returning to battle.

* * * *

IN KNOXVILLE, TENNESSEE, General Sherman talked with the top commander of the Northern Armies, General Ulysses S. Grant. They were in a commandeered hotel trying to relax between battles.

"I miss Dodge," Sherman groused. "We need him. His absence exposes our flanks. It will be months before he's ready to return."

Grant took a long draw on his cigar. "We're lucky he's alive. Let him stay home and recuperate, Billy. Fact is, after his recovery I may send him out west. We need someone strong to push the Indians around. He knows the prairies and how to deal with savages."

Sherman protested. "Dodge is one of our best. With all respect, we need him back East. The rebels aren't entirely licked yet."

Grant considered Sherman's appeal for a moment. "No, Billy, I think we need him in the West. We'll win the war without him. Our next war will be with the Indians. Dodge and his family lived in Indian country west of Omaha for years. He understands Indians as few do."

"Is this about the railroad?" Sherman asked.

"Not entirely. It's more about protecting the nation's westward expansion. The railroad will be important, of course, but we need Dodge on the frontier for many reasons. Besides, Dodge told me several times there won't be a railroad until we solve the Indian problems. So, let's assign him to work on the solution."

* * * *

THE SAME DAY, halfway across the continent, Chief Engineer Peter Dey was increasingly agitated with Silas Seymour. The two were near open feuding. At the Herndon House office they squared off in another confrontation.

"Silas, I am fighting non-Christian impulses over your persistent hindrance. Most of your suggestions violate sound engineering principles."

Durant's consulting engineer—frequently referred to as the "Interfering Engineer"—mocked hurt feelings. "Now Peter, I'm just following instructions, please don't get angry with me."

"I'm just annoyed. You are the most irritating person I have ever known. I furnished the construction estimates to you and Doc exactly as instructed. The cost will be about $30,000 per mile. Why can't you leave me alone to do my job?"

"I am afraid, Peter, that we are going to need easier grades and more curves in the track. We'll need new cost estimates for the upgrades." He gave a nervous laugh worried that he was close to breaking the last straws of Dey's self-control.

"That will run the cost sky high," Dey said. "We don't need smoother grades. I've designed the road with the exact standards Congress specified. We don't need more curves. The estimates I submitted are entirely in line with every other railroad in the nation."

"Ah but Doc says we need *higher* standards for the national road. So I suggest you have your team get busy and refigure the costs. We understand the costs will be higher."

"You want a gold-plated road, eh Silas? Off the top of my head I'd say that will increase the cost to $50,000 per mile or more. That's a huge increase over my $30,000 estimate."

"Those aren't my instructions, Peter, they come straight from Doc. Please get going on this right away. Doc wants every man on it."

"What about the grading? We'll need surveyors on site to work with the graders."

Silas replied with a bombshell. "Grading on the current route is no longer important. We'll probably be going to a new route soon. You've already wasted $300,000 with the work you've done."

Dey was livid. "What do you mean we'll probably use a different route? Our route goes due west from Omaha."

"We'll probably change the route to go via Bellevue."

"That's crazy. On one hand you want gold plated estimates for smoother grades, and now you tell me we may send the road by a poor route to Bellevue. Do you know how far out of the way that is?"

"Thirteen extra miles?" Seymour answered with a shrug.

"I think you have gone mad. I'm doing nothing on your authority. I need to hear from Durant before I make another move."

"Very well. Have it your way, Peter." Silas stalked away from Dey toward the telegraph office.

Within twelve hours Telegrapher Butler awakened Dey for an urgent telegram that laid all doubts to rest. Durant demanded new cost estimates immediately. In predictable fashion, Durant's message sounded as if the end of the world was near.

* * * *

WITHIN TWO WEEKS, Dey's team had new drawings and cost estimates. Silas Seymour beat a fast path to New York to make personal delivery to Doctor Durant.

"Here they are, Doc," the exhausted Seymour proudly announced, presenting a rolled set of plans. "I've got the new cost estimates. I did a major part of the work myself, of course," he lied.

Durant seemed unimpressed. "What is the cost per mile on the new estimate," he asked without emotion.

"$50,000 per mile. I've got it in writing."

Now the plans drew Durant's full attention. After a half hour review, during which Seymour remained silent, Durant was ecstatic.

"Good job, Silas. We now have two estimates, one for $30,000, and the other for $50,000."

"Thanks, boss, I really tried hard on this," Seymour lied again.

"Here is how our business will work: We, the railroad, will make a contract with Crédit Mobilier to construct track for $50,000 per mile. The government will approve funds to pay Crédit Mobilier at the $50,000 rate."

"It will be a top-notch railroad," Seymour interjected missing Durant's direction.

"The beauty is we will actually build the railroad using the cheaper $30,000 specifications. We will achieve a clear profit of $20,000 per mile even before we add in a reasonable profit and other incentives."

"I've got thousands of cost saving ideas," Seymour added still clueless about Durant's point.

"Can't you see the brilliance, Silas? We can make a contract with ourselves at any price per mile we choose. Crédit Mobilier will be the only bidder allowed. The government will pay the going rate we charge. The profits will be astounding."

Seymour was beginning to see the reason for two estimates.

"I plan to hedge a bit and award the first contract for $60,000 per mile. The government inspectors will accept it without question." Durant smiled thinking of the profits and how clever he was to harvest money from an entire nation.

"That's $60,000 revenue against expenses of $30,000 per mile. I like the sound of it myself," Seymour added.

* * * *

NOVEMBER, 1864

WITH HIS FINANCIAL structure in place, Durant hatched an overwhelming number of schemes and plans. From day to day, no one, absolutely no one, knew where the railroad would begin or go.

As the city entered winter, Colton received instructions from New York that left him in disbelief. He read the message three times.

Immediately notify Buck Clayton of Bellevue the Union Pacific will abandon the route running due west route and will instead build track from Omaha to Bellevue before turning west.
T. C. Durant

In Bellevue, the news thrilled Buck Clayton. "The railroad will make Bellevue the city of the future. All we need is a bridge over the Missouri River and Omaha will be on the dead end of a branch line."

Returning to Omaha, Colton suffered dismay knowing Durant's announcement would devastate his friend Peter Dey. As it turned out,

Colton never saw Dey again. He simply never returned from an urgent trip to New York.

Two weeks passed before word about Dey arrived from New York in the form of a suddenly jovial Silas Seymour.

"Did you hear?" Seymour bubbled to Colton. "Peter Dey resigned after his meeting with Doc. I am the new acting Chief Engineer. I will finally show the world how to get this project going."

Colton was saddened yet unsurprised by the announcement. He would miss Dey.

"I suppose I should congratulate you, Silas," Colton replied.

"Oh, I don't deserve congratulations yet, Colton. My real success will come in the revolutionary ideas I introduce. Experience tells me it is cheaper to support rails with timber that runs long way rather than cross ties, so I am going to try a section of track with no cross ties. We're going to give it a try, and with available wood."

"What's available?" Colton asked, looking out a window, "Cottonwood?"

"That's right. Cottonwood trees are abundant in Nebraska."

"Cottonwoods seem like a soft material for a railroad," said Colton not bothering to mask his skepticism.

"You will see," said Silas opening Dey's map case. "I've got a lot to do before spring."

* * * *

1864 GROUND TO A gloomy end in a ten inch snow. Colton fought despair from every direction. All the cities he dealt with were unhappy. Investors still avoided Union Pacific's stock, thinking it was a reckless gamble. Worse yet, U.P. had no tracks and only twenty miles graded. More discouraging, Durant stopped all work indefinitely for lack of cash.

It seemed Omaha had only three happy people. The first two were Libby and William. They were content to be snowbound in their comfortable home with Colton. The third was Silas Seymour who spent his winter altering maps intended for the government.

For Colton, memories of the huge groundbreaking celebration were growing fainter. For a man who sold optimism for a living, it was hard to see the possibilities of better days ahead.

Hope would come with the end of the Civil war. Action would come even sooner with President Lincoln interceding to help.

Chapter 19

I guess you're wondering why I summoned you to Washington."

Oakes Ames, the United States Senator from Massachusetts, looked across the table at the very unhappy Doctor Thomas Durant.

"The question did cross my mind while I was sloshing through snow in two cities. I am normally afforded an agenda for meetings, sir. Obviously, I have no idea why I'm here." Durant's tone approached disrespect.

The Senator looked squarely at Durant. "I met with the president last month. He is a strong advocate for the Union Pacific. He asked me to invest heavily in the road from my personal funds."

Durant straightened in his chair, losing his defensive attitude. He knew the senator was rich, disgustingly rich, from family-owned manufacturing businesses.

"Tell me more, Senator."

"President Lincoln believes that if I attach my name and money to the railroad, more people will invest in the stock. You are here, Doctor, to convince me your railroad is a worthwhile investment. I am hoping you can impress me."

"How much money are you talking about?"

"I am considering numbers that will fund construction to the last spike, an investment that will enable you to build this road from start to finish," Ames responded. "My investment will also ensure my full influence in congressional matters."

Durant, now smiling, assumed his charming salesman persona. "Before we talk about railroad stock, Senator, let me tell you about a great company called Crédit Mobilier."

Durant performed well, and within a month money began to rain heavily into the nearly dry Union Pacific accounts.

By April 1865, while the nation mourned the death of Abraham Lincoln, Durant was busy siphoning money from Senator Ames and his brother.

$$* \quad * \quad * \quad *$$

Bellevue, Nebraska – The Oxbow Incident

BUCK CLAYTON'S DOGS sounded alarm and charged into the street all teeth and threats to intercept the approaching stranger.

Inside, Buck heard the commotion and tore his eyes from his newspaper's horrific headline. He glanced at it a final time in disbelief:

PRESIDENT LINCOLN ASSASSINATED

He pushed the curtain aside and saw at once why the dogs were barking. It was Colton Rusk riding in on Hero.

As Colton reined Hero to a stop, Buck opened the door and called out, "Come in, Colton. I had a feeling you'd show up sooner or later."

They sat in the living room and spoke of Lincoln's death in somber terms.

"I thought we were going to have a good April considering the war ended. And now this. Who would have believed this could happen? I hope you have something good to tell me. I could sure use a lift."

"Doc announced today that the railroad will build south from Omaha to Bellevue before turning west. It's official. Government approval is pretty much pro forma. You can count on it, Buck. Bellevue will be on the main line."

"That's news that could cheer anyone from Bellevue." Buck broke into a smile.

"Doc said grading expenses are too high for a route due west from Omaha. The grades are easier via Bellevue. He's calling it the Oxbow route for the big U-shape the road will follow."

"Did he send word about the shops and headquarters?"

"No," said Colton

"What about the bridge?" Clayton asked. "The bridge is a critical factor."

"His message said nothing about the river crossing," Colton answered.

"I'll bet the Omaha people are in shock. They never thought Bellevue might be in competition for the bridge and yards."

"They are quite concerned," Colton acknowledged, minimizing the heart-stopping panic ten miles away.

Buck expressed his first doubts. "I'll admit I have my own concerns about this announcement. Durant could be playing another game to squeeze money from all of us: Omaha, Desoto, *and* Bellevue. He'd just as soon have all the cash in Nebraska and give nothing in return."

Buck Clayton read the consternation in Colton's expression.

"What? You doubt me?" Buck asked. "I've heard about the fortune Durant is spending in New York. The newspaper says his special bred horses and luxurious carriage are the envy of high society. His new yacht is in the news too. He needs money. Union Pacific has no tracks or trains. How do you suppose he generates his money?"

Colton had seen the articles and actually ridden in Durant's magnificent carriage with its thoroughbred horses.

"Until today Omaha has been arrogant. Now they see they could lose everything," said Buck.

"That thought has crossed minds in Omaha," Colton admitted.

"You can bet Bellevue will be pushing hard to get the shops built here. This will be a real battle."

* * * *

THE MOOD IN Omaha grew darker and more desperate every day. It was obvious Durant ignored all telegrams from the Omaha mayor and businessmen. Mayor Kennedy, with no other choice, called for an emergency trip to New York to confront Durant.

The very day the mayor and ten prominent citizens prepared to depart, Durant arrived unexpectedly in Omaha on a steamboat. He walked arrogantly down the gangplank into town.

A showdown was imminent. It occurred the following morning in the Herndon House dining room. Mayor Kennedy and three citizens, bolstered with courage, confronted the financial giant as he calmly ate breakfast with Colton.

The mayor began the verbal assault as Durant munched French toast.

"Durant, it's time we talked about your shenanigans! This is the third time I've talked with you or your people about the Bellevue rumors. What do you have to say?"

Activity in the room halted. All eyes turned to Durant's table.

"Sorry, mayor, I don't recall having an appointment with you this morning. Maybe we can talk tomorrow. Shall I check my calendar?"

"There is no tomorrow! We talk now! We want to know why you abandoned the direct route to the west and diverted to Bellevue. You must have wasted a hundred thousand dollars on the grading. Now we hear you have surveyors looking at bridge sites in Bellevue."

"OK. We're old friends. I'll entertain you for a minute," said Durant. "Fact is, mayor, the change is more than just a simple route adjustment. We intend to move the entire operation to Bellevue or Desoto. Sioux City is also in the running. They've all given us a better deal. I suggest you get used to the idea that Omaha may be on the end of a branch line. Sorry to break the news to you this way, old friend."

Colton and the Mayor were dumbfounded. It was the mayor who spoke first.

"You can't do that!" Kennedy screamed. "We gave you money, property and commitments. We understood the railroad was to begin in Omaha. We have signed contracts with you."

Durant smacked his lips enjoying a bite of toast most unconcerned. "I admit that was my intention at the time."

The doctor casually picked a piece of French toast from between his teeth and examined it. "Things changed."

"We have contracts for every dollar and acre we gave you. Besides, the president directed the railroad to start in Omaha."

"Poor President Lincoln, God rest his soul, did not require that the railroad *remain* in Omaha. He merely stipulated the railroad was to *start* here. We met our obligation with the groundbreaking ceremony that started the road. Now we're moving elsewhere."

"We still have the contracts."

Durant shook his head with mock pity. "You made those contracts with me personally. They contain no mention of Union Pacific. The railroad company was nonexistent at the time. Unfortunately for you, the terms guaranteed I would make every effort to get the railroad to Omaha. I've done my part. If the railroad chooses to do something else, that's the railroad's decision. Those contracts do not guarantee actual results. Check them yourselves. Nonetheless, I am very grateful for your generous payments and the land transfers."

"But you *are* the railroad! You're the top man."

"You're wrong," Durant lied. "I am merely a humble vice-president, who reports to a president, and he reports to the Board of Directors, and they report to the stockholders. I fulfilled the contracts you had with me. My new obligation is to the stockholders. I must act in their interests. Good business requires me to rethink staying in Omaha."

"Why are you doing this to us?" The mayor felt dread return.

Durant rolled his eyes as if dealing with a balking mule. He exhaled with an exasperated snort. "Come now. You're being ridiculous. This is business."

The mayor and his delegation stared in disbelief at the New York financier. Durant's confidence was unnerving. The realization hit them that Durant had legally fleeced them. They had been picked clean by a professional.

The mayor now resorted to empty threats. "Now listen, Durant," he shouted. "You can't come here and kick us around like this!"

"Oh can't I? You think I don't understand your plight? I understand your situation completely. The main line will *not* come through Omaha. You need to accept this new reality. Do we have anything else to talk about?"

"But, -"

"Ah. See? The more you argue, the more I can see your little town was never worthy of my investment. I am increasingly confident abandoning Omaha is the right business decision. I will feel no guilt whatsoever seeing your muddy streets revert to pasture land."

From this point the encounter deteriorated into a screaming match. Threats and counter threats continued for fifteen minutes. When voices were at their angriest, the Omaha delegation stormed from the Herndon House still shouting.

With the mayor and his party gone, the dining room was deadly calm. The onlookers, enthralled with the thunderous drama, returned to their meals. Durant's demeanor changed instantly. He wasn't entirely pleasant, but was unquestionably calmer. Colton wasn't sure what to make of Durant's performance.

"I think that went pretty well," Durant commented with a slight grin.

"If you think that went well, I'd hate to see a bad meeting," Colton replied. For Colton, the screaming match was unforgettable.

Durant's expression was deferential, a mood Colton took as an invitation to comment further. Seizing the opportunity, Colton asked, "How do you want me to handle the cities? I have no idea which way you will end up going."

Durant answered smugly. "I can tell you exactly what will happen. First the Omaha men will fully realize they are still in the running for the railroad. Don't contact them. In about a week they will approach you. They will choose you instead of me because they think you are a nice man. At any rate they will ask you how much incentive it will take to keep the railroad in Omaha."

Colton listened and understood that Durant was probably right.

"You will tell them my further influence will require a $10,000 cash payment. That amount will guarantee a favorable decision and start construction of the permanent shops. I refuse to negotiate, haggle, or sign a contract. Tell that hick mayor if Omaha doesn't pay in hard cash, the city is doomed. Before I'm through, cattle will be eating grass in deserted streets."

"Do you think they will believe me?"

"They have no choice. Tell them I prefer to keep the railroad here, if they are accommodating. Show them the plans for the engine house, machine shop, sawmill, and tie treatment plant. They'll dig deep when they see we're ready to build."

"And if they don't dig deep?" Colton asked.

"I will assume Omaha has decided to forego a railroad. We'll move to another town. It's just that simple. Be prepared to deliver a brass box to New York about ten days from now. If Omaha calls my bluff, be prepared to spend more time in Bellevue, Desoto and Sioux City. Either way, I have the surveys to immediately start construction anywhere I want."

Colton knew he was at the spear point of an intense battle. He would be the first to know where the railroad would begin.

Durant broke Colton's thoughts. "Hire a carriage for us. I want to see the grading work."

They inspected the railroad work and Durant's properties the remainder of the day. In late evening, Durant mentioned Seymour.

"I will meet with Seymour tomorrow morning. I am displeased with the work I saw today. We will eventually need Dodge as our Chief Engineer. Seymour is having trouble leading fifty men. He certainly can't handle the largest American project in history."

Colton was careful to voice no opinions.

Durant continued. "Here's the situation, Rusk. Union Pacific now has money to begin construction. Before the assassination, Lincoln gave us a magnificent investor. The problem is labor. The government denied my request to hire freed slaves for the job. They denied Dodge permission to provide low cost Indian labor. That means we will wait for soldiers to be discharged. We'll hire as many as can make their way here. We'll advertise for them soon."

"That could take months," Colton acknowledged.

"Until men arrive, we need to prepare. You will continue to work with the city governments for another month. After that, you will work almost full time with suppliers and contractors as I direct."

Durant departed the following morning. He left Colton a long list of projects needing immediate attention. It was enough work to keep an entire department busy for months.

Durant was wrong on one thing. It took less than a week for the mayor to come calling. Four days after the confrontation at the Herndon House, Mayor Kennedy came to the Rusk home. Colton delivered Durant's demand adding his own hope that the railroad would stay in Omaha. On the sixth day the mayor delivered a thick envelope which Colton locked in his brass box. The following morning, Colton quietly left for New York.

Six days later, a flurry of telegrams arrived in Omaha triggering the beginning of construction.

> *Work will begin immediately on tracks and shops. The oxbow route via Bellevue remains because of severe grades west of Omaha. Railroad operations headquarters will be in Omaha.*
> *T. C. Durant.*

With money in the coffers and work underway, the days and weeks passed swiftly. Silas Seymour for all his bluster and giant ego was caught flat-footed and unable to get things moving. By anyone's measure, his start was inauspicious taking two months to gather enough untrained Irishmen to begin any work.

For his slow start, Seymour drew ridicule from Eastern newspaper reporters watching the ballyhooed road. Seymour endured scrutiny from every direction. Newsmen saw the weaknesses and told the world about his failure to get things going. Seymour's antics provided some of the best news stories since war's end

* * * *

IN NEW YORK, Durant fumed too. He threw a newspaper at the wall and shouted, "Will he *ever* lay the first rail?"

Chapter 20

MAY 1865 – THE HUMAN RIVER

With the end of the war, changes came that fed Durant's urgent need for labor.

From New Jersey, Massachusetts, and New York, a trickle of men who read the Union Pacific brochures began moving west. Yankee soldiers from Ohio and Pennsylvania joined the flow making it a stream. They were no longer fierce, but ready for work— any work— with or without a rifle.

And from Tennessee and Arkansas defeated rebels, thin, resentful, and despairing, traveled west in tattered gray uniforms.

As the human stream moved through Indiana, it added men, starving but hopeful. Illinois provided hundreds more, swelling the human stream into a small river. Rumors of railroad jobs guided the flow inescapably to Omaha.

Thousands of hungry, jobless soldiers descended on Omaha seeking to enlist in Durant's army of railroad builders.

"I seen a flyer in Toledo that you need men."

"No. I got no back problems or ailments."

"Pa learned me to shave boards from a tree when I was fourteen."

"Indians don't scare me as near bad as starving in Ohio."

"I'm a hard worker, mister."

Durant's construction bosses accepted them, fed them, and sent them to battle deserts, mountains, and Indians. Their new leader was a doctor in New York they seldom saw, if ever. He was a different kind of hero than Grant or Sherman, but in their desperate minds, Doc Durant was the all-powerful man responsible for feeding and employing them.

Omaha grew. New businesses followed the workers. Union Pacific's steamboats worked non-stop bringing men, materials and the nations' future to the frontier.

* * * *

IN JUNE 1865, while Colton was away, the Postmaster delivered an unusual letter.

Libby noticed the bright yellow envelope right away and pulled it from the bundle. It was the first colorful envelope Libby had ever seen, and was made of thin delicate paper. The handwriting was unusual too, cheery and feminine. The address read simply:

Libby Rusk
Omaha, Nebraska

It surprised Libby to see a letter addressed to her. The markings and return address showed this letter came from Council Bluffs.

She fought the temptation to tear open the envelope in the post office and instead took it home. For an hour she did chores. Then, when she could stand the excitement no longer, she carefully opened the envelope and read the note.

Dear Libby,
I trust this letter finds you in good health. I have heard so many nice things about you and your husband that I would love to know you. Please join me for lunch at my home next Friday at eleven o'clock. Our husbands served together in the army.
Yours truly, Annie Dodge

Annie Dodge. Libby knew the name. She was General Dodge's wife. The next day Libby mailed an acceptance note and made arrangements for William to stay with a church lady. She looked forward to the opportunity to meet Mrs. Dodge.

Libby knew the Dodge family by reputation. She was aware the Dodge family owned banks and businesses in the area, and she hoped Annie would not be a pretentious person. Libby would soon experience was how delightful Annie Dodge was.

When the day arrived, Libby hired a carriage and traveled to Council Bluffs by ferry.

They dined alone in Annie's parlor on a meal prepared by household staff. Libby learned Annie was a strong person who had faced challenges similar to her own. Annie, for example, came to Nebraska by covered wagon. She struggled with the Pawnee Indians and suffered early business failures. Now, despite her wealth, Annie retained a simple, unassuming approach to life.

"Libby," she said toward the end of the visit, "I host a card game here once a month. I would be delighted if you will join me and several Council Bluffs ladies. You will have a very pleasant time with us. Please say you'll come."

Libby found a special friend in Annie: someone to admire, someone whose husband, like hers, was away for long periods. Every good weather month, Libby left William with friends and traveled to Council Bluffs for a day of playing cards and enjoying in new friends.

She looked forward to the monthly gathering. Perhaps, in time, she thought, she would even host the get-together in Omaha.

* * * *

JULY 2, 1865 - OMAHA

GEORGE TRAIN RAISED his arm, pointed downriver, and broke into a wide smile.

"Here she comes, boys, just rounding the bend. I proudly give you the first locomotive to arrive in the Nebraska Territory. What an historic day for Omaha!"

The dignitaries at the foot of Chicago Street strained to look at the barely visible shape coming into view. The steamboat 'Colorado' was emitting huge plumes of black smoke as it struggled against the swift Missouri River currents.

George Train turned to Silas Seymour on his right. Silas managed a half-hearted smile. Train goaded Seymour for everyone to hear.

"Just think, Silas, if we had any track, we could take our distinguished guests on the first train trip in Omaha."

Seymour's smile disappeared into a frowning crimson face. He held his tongue, knowing better than to match wits with Train.

Three newspaper reporters exchanged grins and winks knowing Train's jab stemmed from their scalding reports about Seymour's poor progress with Union Pacific construction.

As the boat pulled to within a half mile of the landing, its steam calliope filled the air with lively music. The new locomotive was still a barely distinguishable black spot on the boat's white deck.

At a quarter mile out, the locomotive was clearly visible lashed to the boat deck. The waiting guests soaked in each detail as it approached. After waiting so long, they were at last seeing a major step toward making the railroad a reality.

George Train shouted, "Look! That's Colton Rusk standing on top. Now that's a sight for sore eyes, if I've ever seen one."

From atop of the locomotive, Colton saw the group and began waving, his arm high above his head. On shore, they recognized their friend and returned the greeting.

"It's good to have him back," the mayor told the Congregational Church minister.

* * * *

A WEEK LATER, on July 10, 1865, Silas Seymour and his men began laying the first rails westward from Omaha.

For a month Durant threatened to name the first side track "Thank God" in honor of Seymour's producing a miracle by laying rail.

Bare Hands And Muscle On U.P.
The Andrew J. Russell Collection,
The Oakland Museum of California,

Chapter 21

SEPTEMBER 1865 – COLTON FINDS GENERAL DODGE

I don't mean to cry," Libby said, wiping her eyes with a handkerchief. "It's just that I couldn't bear to lose you."

"I'll be fine. The prairie is so vast I doubt I will see any Indians at all. George Train made the trip two years ago without any problems."

"That was before the Indian War. It's unfair, him sending you into rough country alone. How could you ever hope to find General Dodge?"

"He shouldn't be hard to locate. I'll follow the railroad maps to the outposts. Soldiers or wagon trains, or even hunters will be able to help. I won't be alone all the time."

"Read it to me again," she pleaded. "Maybe you misunderstood."

Colton patiently unfolded the coded telegram and read it aloud.

Depart west at once to find General Dodge. Inform him it is urgent that I see him as soon as possible. I want him to meet me at St. Joseph in four weeks concerning employment with Union Pacific. Find Dodge immediately. My entire investment is at stake. You must succeed in this mission. All depends on you.

T. C. Durant

He refolded the paper and returned it to his shirt pocket.

"One man traveling alone can move very efficiently, maybe a hundred miles per day on flat ground. I'll be on Hero, the strongest, fastest horse in the territory. I'll exercise caution, and when I find the General, I'll have a whole army to protect me. Things will be fine."

She allowed him to persuade her that all would be well. When he rode out the following morning, Libby shared his confidence and longed for the day he would return to her.

* * * *

EVERYTHING WEST of Omaha was Indian country. Colton knew it, and knew he must keep a sharp eye for his safety no matter what he'd said to Libby. The friendly Pawnee held the lands for a hundred miles west of Omaha. Here travelers passed in relative safety.

Beyond the Pawnee mud lodges, Indians were hostile. The Cheyenne and Sioux hated the white invaders.

If Colton had learned one critical thing from Dodge, it was the importance of planning every mission. He studied the maps and notes left by Dey and concluded there was but one option. He would follow the wagon ruts and telegraph lines along the Platte River. That was how George Train and a scout had done it, and it was how he would find Dodge.

The bluffs above the Platte were not beckoning lands, far from it. From his own experiences, he knew that any high ground would be threatening and ominous with Indians, wild animals and treacherous ground. He would avoid the bluffs if he could.

He moved steadily west, riding Hero and leading a pack horse. The first day he covered eighty miles without difficulty. He saw no one.

Colton loved the smell of the prairie flowers, sage, and fresh air. He loved seeing the huge eagles and other birds of prey in their long slow circles overhead. And he loved the first coolness of fall.

During the war, Colton developed a sharp eye for trouble. It was still with him. Passing into Cheyenne country on the second day, Colton saw the first signs of Indians in the form of two sets of fresh tracks left by shoeless horses. The first set indicated eight riders, the second set fifty or more.

Late on the third day, Colton met two white hunters moving east with several horses loaded with buffalo hides. They warned him of trouble ahead.

"The Cheyenne have war parties looking for wagon trains and soldiers. You'll see five burned wagons and nine graves 'bout ten miles ahead. The rest of the wagons left after the battle. We're going east until Dodge restores peace."

Moving on, Colton found the burned wagons and graves the hunters had described. The scene told a brutal and tragic story that reminded him of the ghastly images on his own farm in Maryland.

He rode five more miles before making a hidden camp for the third night. The horses were in good health and feasted on the rich grasses along the riverbank. Colton knew a campfire was unsafe. He would endure the night chill and a cold meal.

Colton was tired after three days' hard riding. He figured he had traveled close to two hundred fifty miles from Omaha. In the gray light between dusk and night, he thought of the fresh graves at the massacre site and longed for Libby and William. He finished a cold biscuit, wrapped in his blanket, and slept on the hard ground.

Daylight came with a brilliant cloudless sky. The sun shone on the grass sea bringing out all its vivid green hues. Colton pushed on in a pure, unadorned world of blue and green. He took nothing for granted and frequently turned to check behind him. An hour after leaving camp, Colton turned in his saddle and squinted into the morning sun. He was surprised to see two silhouetted riders on the horizon. His gut told him they were Indians.

As a precaution, Colton hid the horses in the river bottom trees. He removed his rifle from the saddle holster and made sure it was fully loaded. It was. He already knew it was, but it was better to check it again than find otherwise at a bad time. He concealed himself to watch and tensed as the two figures drew nearer.

The two Indians rode by, distracted in conversation. They were strong-looking warriors, the larger one with a single red feather tied in his hair. The buckskin clothing identified them as Cheyenne.

Colton could have shot them on the spot and considered it, but for many reasons he remained silent and allowed them to pass. Neither Indian ever sensed his presence.

He never suspected they were father and son or that the two, White Eagle and Running Elk, were discussing the chief's plans to move the tribe to winter camp.

After fifteen minutes Colton remounted and followed their tracks until they left the river and disappeared into the bluffs. Colton wondered if the two were part of the band that attacked the wagon train.

He reached the spot where the North and South Platte Rivers joined. It was a wide, shallow place where wagons crossed the river. Colton crossed too, pausing only to check his map and bearings. He was two hundred eighty miles from Omaha. He reckoned he would reach Lodgepole and the army outpost the following day.

At noon on the fifth day, Colton rode into the dusty army post at Lodgepole. He was let down to learn the General was further west. The base captain, a tall red-faced man from Pennsylvania, welcomed Colton and spoke freely with him.

"General Dodge left a week ago with two hundred men. He is on an expedition to the Black Hills to learn more about the Indian situation. I doubt that he'll return for a month, sir. I advise against following him. Hostilities are increasing."

Colton smiled remembering how Dodge had told him a major problem for the transcontinental railroad was finding a route through the daunting Black Hills. Colton wondered if Dodge was pursuing two goals with his expedition.

He happily discovered the telegraph lines did more than pass through Lodgepole. The military post was a wayside relay station complete with a qualified telegrapher. He used the opportunity to send an update to Durant and a message of assurance to Libby.

By the time the horses were fully rested two days later, Colton had received two coded telegrams from New York. Durant was adamant.

Continue your mission the instant you are able. All depends on your success. Seymour's construction performance is a national disgrace. T. C. Durant

Against the base captain's advice, Colton departed deeper into hostile territory. He was well-stocked and confident, but cautious.

Colton rode west in awe of the enormity of the prairie. It was perfect, pristine land offering enormous promise for the nation. Its sheer size made encounters with others rare. The prairies had thousands of people, but spread across millions of acres so that the country seemed empty. All day he saw no one. Telegraph poles and wagon ruts were the only evidence humans had been present at all.

About noon, Colton encountered a herd of buffalo. To get around them, he climbed a bluff where he saw the herd was even larger than he had thought, extending almost to the horizon. He knew Indians would likely be near such an important food source and felt vulnerable on the exposed bluffs. He remained fully alert even after returning to the pole line two hours later.

Toward the middle of the afternoon, Colton came across one of Durant's survey crews. Nearby, twenty soldiers guarded against Indian attack.

Colton approached the men and introduced himself. The surveyors were immediately friendly. The lieutenant in charge of the soldiers was leery at first. He warmed up only after he realized the newcomer was a former officer and friend of General Dodge.

"I'm searching for General Dodge. The captain at Lodgepole said his expedition was going toward the Black Hills. Have you seen him?"

"Yes, sir, he passed by here three days ago," the lieutenant answered. "He said he was working his way west to the hills."

"I'll be moving on while it's still daylight, but if you have any coffee in that pot, I could sure use a cup," said Colton.

The surveyors took a break to talk with Colton, eager to hear news from civilization.

Colton remained with them an hour, sharing what he knew of national events.

Before Colton mounted up, the lead surveyor gave a final caution. "You'd better be careful. We've seen a lot of Sioux in the area and they're on the warpath. I'd be scared myself if it weren't for our army escort. The Indians don't want to tangle with them. If you insist on chasing Dodge, I suggest you travel only after dark and find a place to hole up during daylight."

On the trail again, Colton decided the advice to travel at night was sound. He slowed his pace the rest of the afternoon stopping only once for water. Eventually, the sun sank behind the western horizon. Colton rode on in the darkness.

The mild weather that night was perfect for travel. Overhead a bright, full moon lighted the night beneath a clear sky. Colton rode beside the Platte River silent as a shadow, keeping a steady pace and remaining alert for hazards. So dazzling was the moonlight on the prairie that even pebbles were clearly visible from atop Hero. The small furry night creatures and their night predators were there too, more obscure, but still observable. He watched them all.

About midnight he saw campfires burning ahead and stopped to gaze at them. He was unable to tell if they were from a wagon train or a Sioux war party. For safety, he rode well clear of the location and kept going. In total he covered over sixty miles without difficulty.

Dawn was still two hours away when Colton came to a running creek in a broad, deep ravine. It was a perfect refuge out of sight from the surrounding plains. He tied Hero and the pack horse in the lush river grass and ate dried beef and bread from his saddle bag

As the sun rose, Colton lay on his blanket and thought of Libby. Within minutes he drifted to sleep to the peaceful music of the stream and summer crickets. He slept with his pistol in his hand.

Four hours later he was jolted awake. Sounds came to his awareness, neither crickets nor stream, but something else, something familiar. He listened and looked but saw nothing. The sounds grew louder now, clearly coming from the ledge above. Horses approaching!

He tightened his grip on the pistol and crawled slowly up the embankment. The hooves were now thundering. In the bright sun he saw them between the bushes. It was a war party, thirty or more Indians, riding hard east. They were close, barely thirty feet away. Colton could see human scalps, still red with fresh blood, tied to their horses.

He lay motionless knowing that if discovered he would have no chance of survival.

Are the horses out of sight?

He couldn't be entirely sure because he had tied them in darkness. If they spotted them, he would be good as dead. He held his breath as the war party rode past. Colton remained motionless until the sounds faded to silence.

Sleep was impossible. Colton checked the horses and found them sufficiently rested to continue. Despite the bright daylight, he departed westward immediately, in the opposite direction from the war party.

Time and twenty miles passed with no sign of Indians. Ahead, Colton spotted a herd of antelope. They were beautiful animals, lean and graceful in movement. They remained unconcerned even as Colton approached within a hundred yards.

He stopped and dismounted to stretch his sore leg and let the horses rest. He watched as the antelope grazed in the foot tall grass.

Suddenly, in unison, the entire herd raised their heads and stiffened in full alert. Something Colton could not see was alarming them. What was it? In one move the antelope fled at full speed. Colton scanned the horizons.

"Indians!" Colton gasped. He mounted Hero in a flash.

They appeared from nowhere, swooping down on horses from a bluff where they had a commanding view. He saw at least fifty, a combined war party of Cheyenne and Sioux. Perhaps the group he'd seen earlier had doubled back.

Colton had no time to plan or assess the situation. Instinct took control. He loosened the reigns and urged Hero into a full run. Hero responded immediately.

The Indians surged down the bluff at full speed trying to cut Colton off and force him off the wagon trail. Hero and the lightly loaded pack horse ran their hearts out. When the Indians reached the road, they were fifty yards behind and closing. He cut loose the slower pack horse and urged Hero on. For several minutes neither Colton nor the Indians knew how the chase would end. Then, Colton began to see that the Indians were steadily losing ground. Matched against Hero running alone, it was a race the Indian ponies never had a chance to win. Colton looked back and saw them capture the pack horse.

The pursuit continued. Bullets kicked up dust around Colton, near enough to be a concern. Hero steadily widened the gap, until several miles later the Indians recognized the futility and gave up the chase.

Colton continued the all-out pace a mile further before slowing his horse, safe at last. He owed his life to Hero's speed and surefootedness. Hero was magnificent, never wavering once when everything was on the line.

The rest of the afternoon Colton held Hero to a walk and kept a wary eye in all directions. With the packhorse gone, he had no food, extra ammunition, or blanket. Lesser men might have felt panic. Colton pushed on.

About four o'clock Colton found fresh horse tracks crossing the wagon trail leaving a path of trampled grass It was impossible to estimate how many because they had crossed the wagon road in two straight columns. "Come on, boy, let's go," he told Hero excitedly "These horses have shoes. Government horse shoes! It's Dodge!"

Colton left the wagon trail and telegraph poles and boldly struck out toward the dangerous bluffs. Within an hour he found sentries. Not long after, Colton was in camp receiving bear hugs from an elated and genuinely surprised General Grenville Dodge.

* * * *

COLTON AND DODGE spent the evening in a long overdue reunion. Dodge produced a bottle of brandy from one of the supply wagons.

"This will help wash down your buffalo steak," he said.

They sat by the campfire outside Dodge's command tent and talked for hours under a star-filled sky. Both appreciated the protection of 200 veteran soldiers equipped with the new Henry repeating rifles. Colton relaxed for the first time in a week.

Their comradeship went beyond shared army experiences, even beyond Dodge's debt to Colton for saving his life in battle. They genuinely enjoyed each other's company.

Late in the evening with brandy low in the bottle, Dodge turned to business.

"You said you have a message from Doc Durant?"

"You haven't shown much interest in Doc. Aren't you curious what he wants?"

"No," the General responded. "I already know what he wants."

"You do?" asked Colton, not hiding his surprise.

Dodge grinned. "Sure I know what he wants. Doc is predictable as cold weather in January. He probably has an emergency and needs to talk to me immediately. I just don't know the details."

"You're right about what Doc wants. Construction on Union Pacific is moving at a snail's pace. Silas Seymour has become the joke of every Eastern newspaper. Doc wants you as Chief Engineer."

General Dodge hesitated. "I suspected as much. I will think about it for a day. Meanwhile I am touring the Black Hills in the morning with my engineers. Come with us. We'll talk further in the field."

The following morning Colton mounted Hero and met the engineers as General Dodge gave final orders to one of the colonels.

"After you break camp, ride west along the base of the bluffs. We'll be above you on the ridges. If we get in trouble we'll fire signal shots or light a fire. We should be all right. Most of the war parties are east of us."

The scouting party set out with ten persons. In addition to General Dodge and Colton, the group had two surveyors and the company clerk. Five sharpshooters rode as escorts.

All morning they explored the crest lines and valleys. Occasionally they saw the main company below, but were mostly out of sight.

The general confided the true purpose of the excursion. "Colton, it's no secret the railroad has yet to find a route over the Black Hills. With all the deep ravines and steep grades, no one knows whether we can afford the tunnels, high trestles, and grading that we'll need."

Colton had heard this before. "Peter Dey and Silas Seymour have lost sleep worrying about these hills," Colton said.

"I'm worried also," Dodge confessed. "The more I see of the Black Hills, the more I realize we may never find a good route over them."

They came to a deep gorge and worked their way carefully to the bottom. As they started up the opposite side, Colton heard the echoes of rifle shots bouncing off the rock walls.

"Indians!" cried Dodge, quickly sizing up the situation. "They're too far to get a good shot at us. Their bullets are falling short. Let's make a run for the top."

Halfway to the ridge, they saw the Indians, still out of rifle range.

"They're following us up the ravine. Looks like two hundred or more," a scout shouted from the rear.

Dodge considered their options. They were hopelessly outnumbered. The main body of soldiers was far away and out of sight.

"We can make it to the top of the ridge and hold the high ground against them. They'll find ten men with repeater rifles have the firepower of a hundred. To the crest, boys!" Dodge shouted.

At the top of the ravine they watched and waited behind rock outcroppings. Soldiers lit a large signal fire that sent smoke billowing. Two hours passed with neither army reinforcements arriving nor Indians attacking.

Reality dawned on Dodge. "They've come up another path. They should have arrived here long ago. They'll probably attack after dark." His gut told him to stay and fight. His men were capable fighters, as good or better than any soldiers he'd ever seen. His training, however, told him not to fight. They were badly outnumbered. The best option was to make a run for it.

They built the fire higher both as a signal and a diversion for the Indians, then mounted up to escape down the ridge line. After a mile's hard riding, Dodge shouted at Colton. "Look! We can see all the way to the plains. This is it, Colton! This is the pass we've been searching for. It's an uninterrupted gentle grade all the way down to the Laramie flats. Perfect for the railroad!"

"Perfect, but only if we save our scalps." Colton shouted pointing back to the war party chasing them.

Fifteen minutes later and three-fourths down the slope, the excursion party met a hundred mounted soldiers charging at full speed up the slope. When the Indians saw blue-coated reinforcements, the chase ended. The war party faded away into the hills.

"I was hoping to engage them." General Dodge's disappointment was obvious. "The Sioux have no idea what they'll get facing a hundred repeater rifles. We have yet to fire a shot. They attack wagon trains and lonely farms, but run from us."

General Dodge Discovers Sherman Pass

Mosaic by Stephen McDowell in cooperation with 1st Cavalry Regiment, Volunteer Brigade

In camp that night, Dodge and his men spoke of the narrow escape and missed battle. Dodge was euphoric about finding the long-sought route through the Black Hills. "We have it at last. From this day on we shall call it Sherman Pass in honor of General William Sherman's bravery. The route we discovered today solved the biggest physical problem facing Union Pacific."

Before retiring, Dodge spoke privately with Colton. "Tomorrow I am sending a twenty-five man detachment east. You will ride with them. Tell Doc I will meet him in St. Joseph in three weeks."

"He'll be glad to hear it," Colton replied.

"I wonder if Doc wants me badly enough to give me complete control in the field. I know he's a sharp businessman. Now I'll see how well he negotiates. Fact is, I have better cards than Doc for this poker game."

Chapter 22

NOVEMBER 1, 1865 – THE FIRST EXCURSION TRAIN

From July to November, 1865, Seymour laid only fifteen miles of railroad. Telegrams from New York poured into Colton's mailbox.

What is Seymour doing out there? Why is construction moving so slowly?

T. C. Durant

And, the next day:

What can Seymour do to speed production? It is critical. Respond immediately.

T. C. Durant

In a world dominated by huge egos, Colton knew to avoid getting between Durant and Seymour. Durant, it seemed, begged Colton for his opinion, at least on production matters. It was one of the few times. Colton sidetracked direct involvement by wiring,

Seymour needs your personal attention and motivation. Per your earlier instructions, Seymour refuses to respond to me.

Colton Rusk

Durant wired back.

Like you, Seymour has stopped answering my questions. I will arrive at Omaha within two weeks. I will bring General William Sherman and others with me. Get with George Train and arrange for an excursion train to the end of track. I'll need a dozen rooms at the Herndon House. Rename locomotive No. 1 as the William T. Sherman in honor of our guest.

T. C. Durant

Colton was energized by the news that Sherman was coming to Omaha. Sherman was the most famous General in the nation, after Grant. Colton, with George Train's help, set to work organizing a banquet followed by the train excursion.

The railroad owned but one locomotive and a mere handful of construction cars. With options limited, they decided to build wooden benches on two flat cars, and have a grand picnic at the end of the line fifteen miles away.

Colton's telegram to Durant describing the plans caused disappointment in New York, but no better ideas came back.

A picnic? That's about what I expected from you. If that is the upper limit of your creativity, proceed with your plan. I can't do everything myself.

T. C. Durant

* * * *

DURANT ARRIVED in Omaha two weeks later with General William Sherman, two senators, and an English Duke. He also had his own press corps from the major Eastern newspapers.

Durant disembarked the Union Pacific steamboat surrounded by reporters. He was smiling and pointing out Omaha's sights.

"Look at those reporters," Train whispered to Colton. "I'm going to have a field day. By the time I'm through with them, everyone in America will want to buy U.P. stock."

General Sherman knew Colton from his War Department days and went to him to escape the crowd. While Durant and Train charmed their guests and directed them to carriages, General Sherman and Colton chatted during the short ride to the Herndon House.

With the travelers in their rooms preparing for the night's banquet, Durant cornered Colton.

"I've decided to keep you off the train tomorrow. Get four carriages and shadow the train all the way to the picnic area. I'm worried we'll derail on Seymour's track. Stay out of sight unless you see the train is in trouble."

"Yes, sir," said Colton, wondering how only four carriages would be of much use to thirty guests.

The next morning Doc Durant beamed as the train prepared to leave. Durant and General Sherman sat on special bench seats built higher than the others.

Just before boarding, guests admired the freshly cleaned locomotive now sporting the name "William T. Sherman" in tall, gold letters. They found gift bags next to their seats with liquor, snacks, cigars, and printed descriptions of the work they would see. Most of the Easterners were excited to see that their bags included real Indian arrowheads and necklaces as souvenirs.

T. C. Durant, (standing on far right) and UPRR department heads
Public Domain Photo by John Carbutt
Courtesy of New York Public Library

At precisely ten o'clock, the General Sherman blew a long whistle blast and started down Seymour's rickety track. It was as interesting a party as Omaha had ever seen with people sitting and standing on two flat cars drinking, talking, and laughing as they journeyed toward a picnic at the end of track.

* * * *

A MILE DOWN THE TRACK, Darcy Lonigan heard the locomotive's whistle blow and stepped clear of the rails. Lonigan disliked his new job building railroad bridges, but the work was easier than unloading cargo from steamboats. This job would do until a big score presented itself.

Lonigan and his fellow bridge workers waited on both sides of the track for the train to come. Their work securing additional bracing to the new bridge could wait until the special train passed.

In the distance the locomotive whistle blew again, this time closer. The worker next to Lonigan gently elbowed him in the ribs saying, "Tis a beautiful sound, eh Lonigan? Finally we hear the trains in Omaha."

Lonigan said nothing. He was neither a team player nor impressed with the appearance of Omaha's first train. He had seen trains before, in his childhood. He still remembered how his friend lost a leg to a train in New York. No, he felt no excitement for the approaching train.

The excursion train rolled past with alcohol and good cheer flowing. Darcy looked for the railroad man he detested, the one who had humiliated him, the cripple. If the cripple was on the train, he was hidden among the passengers.

The train gone, the foreman called for the men to return to work. It was then that several wagons and carriages approached on the rough construction road beside the track. Lonigan spotted Rusk instantly and looked long enough to examine his nicely dressed enemy. How high and mighty he looked above them, following the others with food and drink.

Lonigan turned away before Colton could look down on him. He spoke to the co-worker who had nudged him in the rib. "Did you see the food stacked high in that wagon?"

"Aye. It's for Doctor Durant's honored guests."

"Keep this in mind, O'Toole," Lonigan said sourly. "They would see us starve to death before sharing a single bite of that bounty."

O'Toole stared at Lonigan wondering at the bitterness. Then he returned to work.

* * * *

AT THE END OF TRACK, Colton caught the train and helped serve food. He found the group vibrant, with spirits soaring, appetites healthy, and conversation energetic.

At the picnic, George Train, Durant, and Territorial Governor Saunders gave rousing speeches about the future of America. An hour later when the train left to return to Omaha, Colton found only enough scraps to make three sandwiches. Colton skipped lunch that day to make sure the other drivers ate.

The trip to Omaha was a reverse move of the outbound trip with the engine simply pushing the cars ahead rather than pulling them. The guests remained lively and were even better-oiled. They punctuated the mood with champagne-enhanced yelps and boisterous laughter. The excursion was a great success that left the participants encouraged about the railroad's future.

When the party was over and the grandiose statements completed for reporters, General Sherman pulled Durant aside for a strong dose of reality before boarding a steamboat to St. Louis.

"Durant, at the rate you're going you'll never get a railroad built to the Pacific in my lifetime. My grandchildren will be lucky to ride on your railroad. The worst thing for you personally is that if you don't reach the Hundredth Meridian before the Kansas railroad, you'll lose it all. I suggest you get serious about building this railroad. There lies your challenge, *Doctor*," he said emphatically.

Sherman's caustic comments shot through Durant like a bullet. For three days, the wounded doctor raged about the Herndon House lashing out at anyone unfortunate enough to encounter him. The hotel staff cowered in fear of yet another thrown ashtray. On the fourth day, Durant summoned Colton for a private announcement.

"If Silas Seymour doesn't lead us to our doom first, Dodge will be Union Pacific's Chief Engineer next year. We've made a tentative deal, but it is secret until he actually resigns from the army. I have a brass box for Dodge. He is in St. Louis. We leave in the morning to deliver it to him. Hang onto your hat, Rusk, your life is about to get very busy."

Chapter 23

By the time General Dodge and his entourage rode horseback from the Jefferson Barracks military base to downtown St. Louis, Dodge was twenty minutes late.

He found Durant and Colton waiting in the dining room of the Jacobson Hotel. The General excused his staff and sat with the two railroad men.

Durant blurted without greetings the instant he saw Dodge. "Have we reached an agreement on the terms of your employment?"

Dodge ignored Durant for the moment and turned to Colton. "How is Libby? I heard from Annie she has been sick."

Colton knew Dodge's snub would begin a slow boil in Durant. "She is much better now, General. It was the flu. Thank you for asking."

Dodge, having taken control of the meeting, turned to Durant.

"The salary and duties are agreeable. They are, in fact, quite generous. Only one question remains. Your expertise is finance, Doc. We must avoid wasting time bumping heads with each other or with Seymour on specifications or routes. I must have absolute and final authority on all construction decisions. Is that agreeable?"

"It is," Durant lied, avoiding eye contact. "You shall have unlimited authority in construction matters."

"Very well, Doc. I'll be on the job as soon as I can put the army's affairs in order and resign."

Durant smiled broadly. It was the end of a three-year campaign to hire the best-qualified man in America.

Dodge turned to business. "In our last meeting I urged you to hire the Casement Brothers. General Jack Casement is an expert track man who can meet any challenge. We're going to need him."

Durant agreed at once. "By all means have General Casement establish a construction company and we'll get him started laying track. You can make him our lead sub-contractor for track construction, working through Crédit Mobilier."

ON FEBRUARY 18, 1866, Omaha lay frozen and still. At sunset, the temperature, pushed by a strong wind, plunged well below zero making the post-holiday gloom even bleaker. Omaha resembled an abandoned city. Few dared to venture from their homes.

In stark contrast, the atmosphere in the Rusk residence was warm and friendly. Two fireplaces roared keeping home and guests comfortable. Three couples sat eating in the dining room.

Before dessert, Territorial Governor Alvin Saunders guided the dinner conversation away from weather and food.

"Doc Durant announced in January that Dodge is the new Chief Engineer, but that was a month ago. No one has seen him yet. Why?"

"General Dodge is finishing military duties. He'll be here soon," said Colton.

The governor was skeptical. "I helped break ground over two years ago. Since then, U.P. has built only forty miles of track. That's a miserable performance in anyone's book. Omaha's population doubled last year because of the railroad. Problem is, we don't have a railroad that goes anywhere."

George Train spoke up. "That's only partly true, Governor. We have workers arriving every day. We have completed the engine house, sawmill, machine shop and a cross tie treatment plant. 1866 will be a banner year for the Union Pacific, our first full year of construction."

The governor pushed. "It had better be a good year. The Kansas Pacific Railroad is making good progress toward the Hundredth Meridian. If you don't beat them, Congress will remove your funding. We're applying for statehood this year. Nebraska needs this railroad."

"With Grenville Dodge as Chief Engineer and Jack Casement building, we have every intention of succeeding," George boasted.

"Waiting for U.P. is like watching crops grow. It's infuriating," the Governor groused. He turned to fresh apple pie for relief.

* * * *

TWO WEEKS LATER, as winter considered melting away, Colton traveled to Des Moines. The closest rail head, it was still over a year away from reaching Council Bluffs. Colton organized suppliers and freight haulers from seven states to ensure a steady flow of materials for Jack Casement's construction crews.

Track supplies arriving by railroad at Des Moines soon stretched across Iowa to Omaha in hundreds of wagons loaded by U.P freight haulers. In Des Moines, Colton coordinated shipping schedules and procedures.

Colton returned to Omaha after six weeks to coordinate steamship and U.P. train schedules. He established a practice of sending wagons directly to bridge builders and graders as far away as Utah.

Rails, cross ties, food and countless other essentials rushed west to the end of track where Jack Casement was now in charge and already starting to make a difference.

The people of Omaha grew used to the loud train whistles at all hours, and welcomed them as sounds of progress.

* * * *

WARMER SPRING WEATHER finally arrived in late March, 1866 with dazzling lightning displays and soaking rains. The brown prairie turned green with new spring grasses that shot skyward, transforming the bland plains into a beautiful sea whose waves ebbed and flowed with the spring winds. A thousand varieties of colorful wild flowers accented the countryside giving it a splendor that impressed even the calloused railroad workers.

Animal life became part of the transforming landscape. Half a million sand cranes danced and made music with millions of snow geese and ducks as they rested in Nebraska on their long migrations. The season's fledglings dotted the sky, perfecting flying skills, and darting here and there with abundant springtime energy.

General Jack Casement's men brought their own spring transformation to Nebraska. Production tripled as new track advanced west. Workers spread across a thousand miles to grade earth and build bridges in advance of the track layers. Thousands more manned the material yards, steamboats, and supply wagons that now stretched from Iowa to the Black Hills. The new shops in Omaha worked around the clock treating cross ties, building railroad cars, and assembling locomotives.

* * * *

IN NEW YORK, Durant found the Ames brothers, Oakes and Oliver, were not the pushovers he'd expected. Along with their money came rigid scrutiny. The big money men showed a particular interest in Crédit Mobilier, recognizing it as a profit generator. They also showed distrust in Durant and relentlessly pushed to keep him in line.

"Actually, Doc, we think you should leave your new yacht and fine horses to go west. You need to ensure Union Pacific is the first to reach the Hundredth Meridian. We'll watch the finances and Congress. Go run the railroad."

By July, Doc Durant bent under the pressure and headed sourly west.

"I, not the Ames brothers, am the financier. I am the proper one to buy influence. I am the one who should hand out Crédit Mobilier stock to congressmen."

Durant arrived in Omaha like a wolf hell-bent on protecting its kill. By telegram he ordered his three assistants to assemble at the Herndon House for a Tuesday morning meeting.

On the scheduled day, Colton Rusk, George Train and Silas Seymour assembled before dawn and waited nervously for Durant's arrival. An hour passed in edgy silence before George Train spoke up.

"I hope he remembered to get off the boat last ni-," George began.

Before he finished, Durant threw open the door and emerged from his burrow. He moved, scowling, with a slow, deliberate tenseness, inspecting them with darting eyes.

Recognizing danger, no one moved or spoke. At the desk, Durant stood looking down on them before exploding into a screaming, wild-eyed fit. He pounded the desk with his fist.

"We're in a life and death race to the Hundredth Meridian, and you three don't seem to be helping! It's pathetic that I have to leave important work in New York to check on you. By the time I leave Omaha, I should fire the whole sorry lot of you!"

Silas Seymour was by far the most anxious of the three. He avoided Durant's eyes, but Durant detected the fear and focused on him, the weakest and most vulnerable prey in the group.

"Silas," Durant began, "I'm surprised you bothered to come today. I figured you would stay in bed. Admit it. You thought about skipping my meeting. Am I right?"

"No, sir, I've been very b-," Seymour started to say.

"Silence! I can't bear your whining. I am forced to endure it in your sniveling telegrams. I have no intention of listening to it in person."

From two seats away Colton saw Seymour hang his head. It was strange to see such an overbearing, obnoxious bully humbled so quickly. Durant added his finishing touches.

"I demoted you for good reason, Silas, and you're lucky I don't fire you right now. Don't think I haven't thought about it. You haven't come up with a realistic money-saving idea since Casement arrived. Your idea to reduce cross tie thickness by fifty percent is still drawing hilarious laughter at dinner parties."

Silas kept quiet and accepted the browbeating. He filled with self-doubt, something rare for him, and was thankful for his brother's political influence, the principal reason he would keep his job.

Durant's face had the look of a wild animal who had just subdued prey. When he saw Seymour was properly shamed, Durant turned to Colton who met him eye to eye. Unable to think of any deficiencies in Colton's work, Durant threatened, "Don't think you're clear of the trouble, Rusk. If I decide to clean house, you go too."

He turned to George Train and lowered his voice.

"George. George. George. It is true that I am dissatisfied with Seymour's results, but you? I expected so much from you. You're the biggest disappointment of all. If I had it to do over again, I doubt I would even hire you. I'd fire you now except you're a loose cannon. You'd do more damage outside the railroad than in it."

Train was unfazed by the rebuke. "Be careful, Doc. I'll bet this is how you felt before you fired Lincoln as your attorney. That didn't turn out so well, did it? You seem to be feeling a bit testy today."

"Testy! Yes, I'm testy. You're spending too much time on personal business. You're supposed to be selling stocks. Instead you're stepping over cow patties and selling your private lots to people who live in wagons."

"What about the positive publicity I've generated, Doc? You can't pick up a paper anywhere without reading about you and the railroad. You're the emperor of railroading, remember?"

"Your publicity was supposed to sell stock, George. I don't see anyone investing. If the stock prices don't go up, we have nothing."

"Stock prices will go up, Doc," Train retorted.

"The fat dividend checks from Crédit Mobilier are making you lazy. I'm unimpressed with your results."

"OK, Doc. You're right. What should I do differently?" George asked in a mock conciliatory tone.

"What should you do differently? Are you insane?" Doc raised his voice, infuriated by George. His face turned red as he flung a stack of maps across the room.

"You want suggestions for doing things differently? How about this: Sell stocks! How about making *my* stock prices go up? How about impressing *me* for a change! That really would be different!"

Doc trembled momentarily, like a volcano about to erupt, and then lost all control. He ripped off his coat and hurled it against the wall, his feet stomping. "What can you do differently? I want you to *earn* your extravagant salary. I want you in New York. I want to feel good about keeping you on the payroll. That would be different."

Train, still unruffled, remained calm as the mighty industrialist stood over him panting, disheveled, eyes and veins bulging.

"I will immediately go to New York ... after my vacation, that is. Don't let the pressure get to you, Doc. We're still on course to meet our goals. It would be very helpful if you ran real freight trains instead of non-revenue construction trains. I don't have anything tangible to sell yet."

Durant sank into a chair, exhausted from his performance. He turned to Rusk, "As for you, Mr. War Hero, I've changed my mind. You're fired! Limp out of my life forever. Go. I can't afford you anymore. Get out!"

Colton stood in shock. Fired! He was stunned. Perhaps he would protest later, with no audience. He turned toward the door.

Durant turned his frustration on George Train and addressed him with fiery eyes. "I'll deal with you later, George."

Chapter 24

Colton reached the door and pulled it open. He was heartbroken. *Fired! For no real reason. What will we do? My poor family.*

Durant's voice shrieked as Colton stepped into the hall. "Stop, Rusk. Go get us four horses and arrange to take them with us on a special train. We'll travel to the end of track by train. From there, we'll go by horseback to see bridges and grading work."

"But you just fired me," Colton answered in confusion.

"Well, you're hired again, but don't push your luck. Get my train ready. I want to leave Omaha in two hours."

Was it Durant's gallows sense of humor, or did the incident convey a deeper message? Either way, Colton found it desperately humorless.

Three hours after his brutal dismissal and immediate reinstatement, Colton Rusk and Omaha railroad workers had Durant's two-car train almost ready. Colton's arrival at the U.P. yard had triggered the mobilization of fifty men to assemble equipment, gather provisions, and check a thousand details for the special train.

The locomotive was new and ready for its first road trip. Behind it the crews attached a box car furnished with hastily built wooden stalls where four horses stood on straw-covered floor. They were the best horses from Hunt's Livery Stable, including Colton's favorite, Hero.

The last car was a second-hand office car Durant had purchased in Ohio and shipped west. To railroad men who slept in tents and on the ground, the second-hand rail car was luxurious. It had three private bedrooms, a dining room, and a kitchen. An observation room at the rear gave a full view of the track behind the train. Two efficient attendants met every need from cleaning to cooking.

Once fully ready, the train sat in the huge U.P. complex, waiting for Durant's arrival. All around it, the new shops and yards bustled with activity. Hundreds of men labored to build railroad cars, assemble locomotives and sort the flow of material arriving by boat and wagon.

* * * *

DARCY LONIGAN stopped working and stared across an open storage area watching the crippled man limp beside the train. He watched him talking with the conductor and supervisors. Lonigan's hand closed around the knife strapped to his leg in a daydream of sorts.

Lonigan often had secret fantasies about dealing with people he hated. Twice he had actually settled scores with enemies, serving his revenge like a cold sweet dessert. He felt the same hatred toward the limping man who had humiliated him in Council Bluffs.

Lonigan watched the men share a laugh. Whatever their joke, Lonigan felt only resentment. He wiped sweat from his forehead with a dirty rag and kept watching. He detested working as a bridge man while lesser men, like Rusk, sat in the lap of luxury and did almost no work at all.

Lonigan was dog-tired from loading bridge timbers onto railroad cars. He twisted from side to side trying to ease muscle cramps and fatigue. He rested, watching as the men greeted a carriage. A finely dressed, slump-shouldered man climbed out and boarded the train.

A second man emerged from the carriage and carried luggage. Lonigan recognized him. It was Seymour, the reviled manager who had twice visited bridge sites and criticized the work. The bridge gangs had nearly revolted over his demands to extend their twelve-hour work day beyond dark.

Around noon, after the special train departed, Lonigan's foreman called lunch break. Instead of eating, Lonigan walked to the far end of the storage yard looking for the Bridge Superintendent. He found Mr. Lutrel measuring huge wooden beams. Lonigan removed his hat and played the subservient employee. He used his thickest Irish brogue for a fellow-Irishman.

"Beg ye pardon, sir. I noticed a limping man boarding the special train a wee bit ago. I've seen him before, maybe thrice. Would you be knowing his name? He looks very important indeed."

"Aye. You are speaking of Mr. Colton Rusk. Fine man he is. Special Assistant to Doctor Durant," Lutrel answered in the same Irish accent. "Quiet man, but very tough, they say. Mr. Rusk knows all the top people, even the mayor and governor."

Lonigan nodded his understanding. In his mind he repeated Colton Rusk's name until he had etched it permanently into his memory.

"Don't just stand there with that blank look, Lonigan. Go rest, man. Eat your lunch. Your crew has much to do this afternoon."

* * * *

ON HIS PRIVATE CAR twenty miles out of Omaha, Durant raved about every issue troubling him. With no reporters, investors, or congressmen present, his behavior was out of control.

He ranted about slow payments from the government, cursed the iron suppliers, and swore vengeance on a steam excavator company slow to deliver earth-moving equipment. He threatened Seymour with ejection from the train on the hostile prairie.

Twice, the train stopped to take on water and firewood. Twice, Durant stayed on the car refusing to meet the station agents and maintenance foremen who came to greet him.

Durant ordered the train stopped for the night at Columbus, Nebraska. The only track available was next to the main line and less than fifty feet from tents used by local track workers. Five minutes after stopping, Durant instructed the attendant to close the window shades to block the views.

Seymour stayed busy scurrying to and from the local telegraph office with urgent messages. Colton met the station agent and confirmed arrangements for the train and horses. He also spent an hour talking to workers at their campsite by the train.

Durant remained secluded on the car for the evening, venturing out neither for fresh air nor human interaction. After retiring, he spent a troubled night shaken awake repeatedly by trains roaring past.

Next morning, despite the beautiful day, Durant showed up in the dining room tired and ill-tempered. He ate in silence across from Seymour and Colton until the strong coffee freed his tongue.

"Rusk, did you know that Indians attacked one of our trains?"

"Yes, sir. It occurred two days ago, twenty miles west of here."

"And our losses?" Durant asked.

"The Indians killed the six man crew and mutilated the bodies."

Durant glared at Colton, stern impatience in his eyes. "I was asking about monetary losses. How much did it *cost* us?" he asked icily.

"We incurred no equipment damage, sir. Train traffic stopped for seven hours. Total cash cost was about three hundred dollars."

Indian Attack

*From the Bostwick –Frohrdt Collection, Owned by KM3TV and on permanent
loan to The Durham Museum, Omaha, Nebraska*

"What about today? What is your plan for my safety?"

Colton felt vindication. He saw that Durant, too, felt the terror the Indians cast on the land. Durant listened as Colton laid out his plan.

"Twelve sharpshooters will board the train at departure. Three will ride on top of the cars. The rest will be with the horses or on the locomotive. They can easily fight off sixty Indians if needed. They'll be with us to Lone Tree. We'll ride by horseback from Lone Tree to the end of rail. You'll have an army escort. You should be all right."

Durant grunted a noise that Colton interpreted as approval.

* * * *

THE RUN TO Lone Tree siding was uneventful. By eleven o'clock, they had the horses unloaded and saddled. The cavalry escort arrived just as Durant mounted his horse.

Durant and the army Captain rode at the head of the column. Durant forced a fast pace. To Colton's surprise, Durant was an excellent horseman who showed no fatigue during the long ride.

They weaved around two hundred supply wagons. Soldiers and wagon drivers waved as they passed. The sight exhilarated Colton. Durant viewed the railroad activity without emotion.

By evening, they arrived at General Casement's camp. Casement was prepared to host Durant and the escorts for the night.

At dinner, Casement was informative and proud of his men's progress. "These Irish trackmen are the most efficient railroaders I've ever seen. They will impress you when you see them. We'll reach the Hundredth Meridian before Kansas Pacific. Count on it."

"Talk is cheap," Durant replied curtly. "I'll know more about how good you are after tomorrow. Lord knows you're spending a lot of money. I hope you're worth it. "

At daybreak, they gathered to continue inspecting the new railroad. Rumors of Durant's presence had spread miles west. Every work gang and train crew knew the big boss was near.

With the warm morning sun to this back, Durant led the procession at the leisurely pace of the supply wagons. He was quietly scrutinizing every detail and listening to Jack Casement's explanations.

As they rode past, construction activity paused long enough for the men to remove their hats respectfully and get a look at the man spearheading the transcontinental railroad. They wanted to see him, talk to him, and admire their leader. To them he was a hero, a great benefactor who had saved them with food and jobs.

Colton knew Durant had no interest in the workmen despite needing them as tools to build his wealth. Durant stared ahead ignoring them.

"How do, Mr. Durant," they called in Irish accented voices.

"'Tis good to see you, sir. Good morning."

"May St. Patrick guard you, sir."

"Top o' the morning to you, Doctor."

At first Colton chuckled at the irony of men admiring someone who detested them, someone who hated being told 'good morning.'

As the hours passed, Colton recognized parallels in his own relationship with Durant. Like the workers, Colton admired Durant, but rarely saw any acknowledgement of his efforts. Too often his rewards came in the form of additional work that seemed more like punishment. For now though, it didn't matter. He was enjoying his part in the magnificent quest.

They came to a stream where a bridge towered over a ravine. The riders watched as a supply train rushed westbound across it. Scaffolding and supplies suggested a crew had recently been working. Silas Seymour cleared the trail dust from his lungs with a loud cough and spoke.

"Doc, see the stone work on that bridge? It's more extensive than we need. We can adjust our standards and realize huge savings."

"Let's take a closer look," said Durant, suddenly perking up. He dismounted, giving Casement his reins. Seymour handed his reins to Colton then walked under the bridge with Durant.

As Durant and Seymour poked around the stone abutments, a dozen workers rose from eating lunch nearby and approached. They knew the visitor could be no other than Doctor Durant. Innocently, they encircled him desiring to talk.

Durant feared being in the midst of these… mere workers. It wasn't in his thinking that these thin and calloused, hard-working men made it possible for him to be wealthy. He saw them as dirty, dangerous beings smelling of sweat. Mixing with them was a risky waste of time that could be spent on more profitable tasks.

The alarmed doctor forced a smile and attempted small talk. Even as he did, his words had a hard, insincere edge. "Good morning. Glad to be out here with you men. Hope everything is going all right for you."

Supply Train and Wagons Near The End of Rail
From the Bostwick –Frohrdt Collection, Owned by KM3TV and on permanent loan to The Durham Museum, Omaha, Nebraska

Durant quickly slipped away to more predictable company. He longed for the security of his private railroad car.

On the move again, they rode past a stopped construction train that included a complete blacksmith shop capable of mending wagon axles and tending the thousands of shod horses. There was a kitchen car, two dining cars with long tables, and a combined physician and payroll car.

"From here, the railroad makes a sweeping curve around a bluff," Casement announced. "We will ride a mile cross country to get to the other end of the curve and ahead of the work. I have a viewing tent waiting for us with food and drink."

They rode on to the tent and found themselves at a place with no railroad at all. The only evidence of track was a graded roadbed stretching to the horizon, materials staged along each side. Casement spoke again.

"West of here, thousands of men are grading, blasting tunnels, and building bridges, depots, and water towers. They're stretched nearly all the way to Ogden. They'll be ready when our rails reach them."

The party dismounted at the tent and drank sun-heated water from shared tin cups. They had rested only a few minutes when a mass of men and wagons approached.

The scene grew hectic and noisy. Amid shouted communications, several hundred strapping men rushed to unload cross ties from dozens of wagons and place them on the bare roadbed. The men almost ran to the roadbed with their ties. The end result was a corridor of equally spaced wooden cross ties advancing at a walking pace past the viewing tent. Durant watched without speaking as the tie gang passed.

Shortly behind the cross ties came more wagons and hundreds more men who lifted rails and positioned them with experienced hands onto the cross ties that had been laid only minutes earlier. These iron men, equally powerful as the cross tie installers, moved the work westward at a steady gait.

A constant flow of iron rails arrived from the rear. Within the huge gang, men moved precisely, each with his role in advancing the end of rail. As soon as a rail was placed, the men hurried to bring another.

Colton found the coordination and teamwork inspiring. The influence of military organization and discipline was obvious.

Next a throng of several hundred, half-naked men, with sledge hammers appeared around the curve securing the rails to cross ties. They had tough, calloused hands from work. None wore gloves.

Their activity was as intense as that seen with the cross tie crews and rail gangs. The spikers quickly secured the rails, ten spikes to the rail, three powerful blows to the spike, the blows sounding like clanging music.

They attached the rails just enough to allow construction trains to move forward, pushing rather than pulling, a long string of cars within a few feet of the advancing work.

Durant was rarely given to express appreciative feelings, but General Casement expected at least acknowledgement of his men's efficiency. What he got was a coldly asked question.

"How can you go faster? It is urgent, critical even, that we build tracks faster than this."

Casement hid his disappointment.

"These are the fastest track layers in the world. When they broke records last month, the newspapers called you the Napoleon of railroads."

"It's not fast enough," Durant said flatly. "The world record pace doesn't impress me. You need to work faster, even it if kills you. And if you don't get faster, that's actually not a bad idea."

Casement deflected the offensive comment.

"Next year we will be faster with better supply lines and dormitory cars to reduce camping time. World records will fall again."

"Humph!" Durant exclaimed. "You just don't get it, do you?"

* * * *

TWO DAYS LATER in the private car parked on the siding at Columbus, Nebraska, Colton still felt exhilarated from the immense scale of work he had seen. The operation had impressed him more than he had ever imagined.

Dodge and Casement could overcome *any* difficulty they faced. Nothing, it seemed, could stop the momentum of this gigantic construction operation.

It was unthinkable at the time that the well-organized construction organization would soon grind to a dead stop.

Chapter 25

AUGUST 1866 – THE NEW RAILROAD CARS

Colton awoke in dim morning light to the sound of a man shrieking. Apprehension rocked him. Unsure of the situation, he lay motionless gaining his bearings.

He focused on mahogany walls fitted with fine brass lamps and knew he was in a bedroom of Durant's private car. He heard nothing for a moment. Colton reached for his pistol.

It was Colton's eighth morning on the siding in Columbus, Nebraska. Like a king in exile, Durant was tending business from his temporary headquarters on the plains.

The shrill, panicked voice began again. "I want …. in fact, I demand you stop all construction immediately."

That's Durant's voice.

Colton heard a reply. "I will comply, but this is no way to run a railroad. Your conflict with the front office will lose the race to the Hundredth Meridian."

It's Dodge. He must have just arrived.

"Right now I don't care about the race. Senator Ames needs to learn the difference between investment ownership and professional management. I review my own contracts! I grant my own permissions. I *am* Union Pacific. Order must be restored. Stop all work!"

Dodge argued. "Stopping the work of thousands of men across eight states will create chaos. You'll create the opposite of what you hope to achieve," he said.

It was as if Doc had lost all memory of his edicts for faster production. "This is about control. The Senator needs to know who is in charge. I don't need his approval for decisions. Stop laying track!"

Colton returned the pistol to its holster as a door slammed at the back of the car. He pulled on his pants and eased down the hallway to the observation room. Durant was at his desk writing furiously.

Hearing Colton's approach, Durant called out. "Rusk, take this message to the telegraph office immediately. Stay until it is transmitted. Alert the train crew and dispatcher I want to leave here for Omaha as soon as possible. Go!"

Colton reached the telegraph office in time to find General Dodge sending instructions to stop operations. Dodge looked at Colton, smiled, and shook his head. "Doc is in rare form today. I probably should have warned you about his quirks a long time ago."

"It's part of his charm, I suppose," said Colton returning the smile.

"No doubt you're here with a message for Senator Ames."

"Exactly. Doc is notifying the Senator about the work halt."

"Mark my words, Colton. The senator will surrender soon. He has too much to lose. We'll be back to work in two days."

* * * *

ON A MAGNIFICENT Omaha morning when the sun peeked over the Iowa bluffs in a brilliant sunburst, when the air, sweet and clean from the night's thunderstorms, gave energy to all living things, Colton stepped from the business car with his carpet bag.

Love pointed his footsteps homeward as briskly as his legs allowed. He hoped to arrive early enough to gently kiss Libby awake.

She awoke overjoyed to see him. They went downstairs in the quiet morning while William slept. They drank coffee and talked with the tender words of lovers. They discussed church activities, Will's progress in school, and local news. In time Colton's excitement about the railroad bubbled over.

"Libby, the progress occurring on the prairies is amazing. New towns pop up overnight. Where the land is desert one day, the next you find stores and homes and people. Union Pacific is building hotels, eating houses, and water towers all along the line."

She listened, eager to hear his stories.

"General Dodge has an entire department of surveyors laying out towns. They're planning repair shops and locomotive roundhouses. I've seen hotel dining rooms that can hold an entire trainload of passengers. We're building depots at regular intervals. People are buying property and building businesses. We're civilizing the West!"

Libby knew all this was true. She and William had witnessed Omaha's transformation from a small town into a roaring base camp. They watched the gigantic railroad shops rise above the levees then expand again to meet every railroad need. They saw the towering stacks of rails and cross ties waiting for shipment.

She knew about the thousands of men who came to Omaha hoping to continue west with the cross ties, rail, and supplies, a sort of commodity that arrived with the railroad's other freight. She knew that until they secured jobs, they were homeless and hungry men who longed for the better life the railroad promised.

Libby was vaguely aware of the filth and poverty along the river, but never witnessed it. She never saw the gamblers, thieves or prostitutes who arrived in a steady flow. She heard from friends about the drinking binges and occasional murders.

"Doc was impressed with the inspection trip," Colton continued. "He wants trips arranged for investors and legislators to see Casement's operation. I'm sure to make more excursions."

"Is your job changing?"

Colton laughed. "My job changes minute to minute. I'm going east in two days to bring back Doc's new private car. It'll be a beauty. No expense spared. Doc also purchased President Lincoln's private car. It's almost new. I'll be escorting both cars and attendants to Omaha."

Libby sat spellbound. "I can hardly wait to see them."

"Senator Ames may have banned him from Washington and New York, but Doc still knows how to entertain and influence. He's planning a major excursion if we beat the Kansas Pacific to the Hundredth Meridian. General Dodge thinks we'll win the race easily."

"That reminds me," said Libby. "Annie Dodge told me her husband is running for Congress."

"Doc put him up to it. Frankly, General Dodge seemed unconcerned. He doesn't even plan to campaign."

They spent a pleasurable afternoon attending a play at William's school. Colton proudly noted that William, now fourteen, was growing into a fine young man. Colton pictured William attending college in the East or perhaps helping establish a family business after the railroad was completed. After the play, father and son made plans to go fishing the next morning near the ferry landing, their favorite place.

All day long, Libby tiptoed around an unpleasant subject she wanted to discuss. It was late before she eased the conversation into sensitive territory. "I guess you realize Doctor Durant is distrusted all over Omaha. You're one of the few people who defend him."

Colton's response was predictably loyal. "People criticize Durant for personality quirks, and his exceptional business sense. His friends are men like Lincoln, Grant, Sherman and senators who do only good for America. I think it is an error to judge Doc too harshly."

Libby's face grew serious. "Many people think Doctor Durant has a much different agenda than doing good things. Have you read what the newspapers are saying?" she asked.

"No, but I talk to reporters almost every day," Colton answered.

"Some newspapers have concerns about Crédit Mobilier and Doc's ethics. They say the nation may be paying double what it should."

"I doubt it," said Colton. "I've negotiated competitive pricing in the contracts I've worked on. Most contracts have rock bottom prices."

"But could Durant be doubling his prices to the government?"

Colton's mind tumbled back to Peter Dey and his concerns about Durant inflating estimates. In the end Colton shrugged his shoulders and admitted, "I don't know how much he charges."

"I worry you're doing the devil's work without knowing it. Just from your stories and the things I read, I believe the man is greed with skin and bones. I sense something in him that represents the darkest wickedness of the human mind. I can feel it."

"Now really, Libby," he tenderly chided. "That's a little strong. You make Doc sound like a representative of Satan himself. I have seen no evidence of it in him."

She saw his innocence and incurable optimism.

"All I ask is that you recognize evil may be around you. Look for it. Lessen it where you can, but above all remain the same man I love."

In the forty-eight hours Colton stayed in Omaha, he came to two conclusions. First, he concluded Libby was almost fully recovered from the ordeal in Maryland. She was strong and well-adjusted.

Second, he affirmed he loved his role in building the railroad. He vowed to ignore Durant's abuse. He had no choice, really. Where else could a crippled veteran find work that included a home? And besides, he didn't see Durant all that often. Maybe Doc was crooked. Colton wasn't sure, but he knew his own conscience was clear.

* * * *

COLTON SPENT A WEEK in Chicago at the Pullman Sleeping Car Company where Durant's car was receiving final touches. Colton had never seen anything so sumptuous and extravagant. The luxury stopped just short of being gold plated. Stepping onto Doc's car was like entering the finest hotel suite in New York or Paris.

Working with George Pullman, Colton updated final orders to purchase everything from sheets and china to enough custom repeater rifles to arm a platoon. He interviewed twenty trained attendants and hired four, two each for Durant's car and the Lincoln car.

His second day in Chicago, Abraham Lincoln's railroad car arrived, now property of Union Pacific. Pullman's crews worked the car from top to bottom making it ready for assignment on the plains. It was heavy, built with bullet proof iron, and in perfect shape with original tapestries and furniture.

George Pullman showed Colton six additional coaches and sleeper cars, built to Durant's expensive taste. Colton found them almost as dazzling as Durant's private car. The only change Colton recommended was adding rifle lockers. Durant gave quick approval by telegram.

When Colton left Chicago with the cars, he rode to St. Louis in the lap of luxury. The attendants showered Colton with fine foods and service. It was a rare and enjoyable work assignment.

In St. Louis, Colton waited two days for workers to load the cars onto U.P. steamboats for the journey to Omaha.

As in Chicago, Colton kept abreast of construction progress by reading the local newspapers. America clamored for updates on Union Pacific's progress. Daily telegraph dispatches reached every major newspaper east of Omaha. With such notoriety, it was easy to keep track from afar.

Relaxing on Durant's car in a St. Louis railroad yard, Colton read two exciting news articles in the St. Louis Dispatch. The news caused him to lift a wine glass and toast his comrades.

The first article noted that Union Pacific laid one and three-quarter miles of track the previous day breaking the world record. Colton knew that with tracks extending entirely across Nebraska, new freight and passenger trains would join the flow of construction trains.

The second article reported that George Train had just broken the record for the fastest trip on record from Omaha to New York, making the trip in eighty-nine hours. Colton laughed aloud knowing with almost certainty that Durant was behind George Train's frenzied effort. Colton winced picturing Durant screaming at Train.

* * * *

DURANT WAS FUMING on the Omaha waterfront when the steamboat arrived with Colton and the railroad cars.

Skipping all fanfare, Durant greeted Colton with the warmth of a broken bottle. "Where the hell have you been? What took you so long? If you really cared about your job you would have arrived long ago."

Colton smiled, slightly defiant, and replied matter-of-factly, "No one but you could have done it faster, Doc. Come see your cars. Beauties they are, sir, perfect in every way."

"They had better be. We have a trip next week with the governor and the territorial legislature. Move out of my way. I'm going aboard."

* * * *

THE GOVERNOR'S EXCURSION trip was elegant and carried off with precision. Four chefs prepared continental cuisine that even George Train enjoyed. Durant, under Train's tutelage, was becoming an increasingly skilled host. Colton watched Durant's performance and listened to the grand talk. He also saw a forced politeness in Grenville Dodge who, Colton knew, preferred work over entertainment.

During the buffalo hunt near Columbus, Durant cornered Colton. "Make sure any buffalo they shoot get processed and packaged to return home with them. Have the hides made into long coats or rugs, their choice. Stay with the Governor. Make sure he bags a buffalo."

When the trip ended, Durant was already thinking ahead. He gathered Dodge, Colton, and Train. "This trip was a success, but could have been better. Next trip we shall improve the shops tour. We need more entertainment. The next trip will be one for the history books."

"What do you have in mind?" George Train asked.

"When we reach the Hundredth Meridian and lock up the government contracts, we'll have the grandest excursion anyone has ever seen. Dodge, you need to figure out special entertainment for the prairie. George, start planning a guest list that will give us maximum exposure. Colton you need to get back to Chicago to make sure George Pullman delivers the executive coaches and sleeping cars on schedule."

An hour later, while Durant created havoc at the cross tie plant, Colton escaped to the Herndon House where he found General Dodge.

"I should be planning tunnels in Utah," Dodge said. "Do you know what I'm doing instead? You'd never guess. It's ridiculous. Doc has me planning a fake Indian raid for his next excursion!"

Colton shook his head sympathetically. "You're right, General, someone else should plan the entertainment."

"It's not fake Indian raids I'm worried about. It's the real ones. I'm waiting for a message now from General Sherman about sending more soldiers to protect us. Trouble is increasing with each mile we build."

"Everyone agrees Indian hostilities are worsening," Colton said.

"We won't finish the road until the Indian problem is solved."

* * * *

FOR COLTON, THE REMAINDER of summer passed in a blur. He made trips to Chicago, New York and Washington carrying brass boxes heavy with clandestine cargo.

By late September, construction was going well, pushed along by Durant's *encouragement*. Doc still ranted about slow production.

On October 6, 1866, Colton was in Omaha when Casement passed the Hundredth Meridian. Durant personally announced it to Colton.

"Rusk, we have finally guaranteed our irrevocable right to continue building west. The race with Kansas Pacific is over. Now we celebrate with the grandest excursion ever seen! Everyone is going; even your wife is to come, if you're still married."

To the Herndon House management's delight, Colton leased the entire hotel for the railroad party. To General Casement's delight, Doc Durant worried about party plans instead of track construction. To Colton's delight, Durant left for New York two days later. The only person with anxiety was General Dodge who chafed in Omaha and longed to be west.

"The Cheyenne and Sioux are in their winter camps. They will be quiet for the trip," Colton assured Durant. Nonetheless, Colton arranged for military patrols to sweep the countryside of Indians.

* * * *

COLTON SHARED THE trip plans with Libby as they developed. Her anticipation increased daily. She arranged for William to stay with church ladies the week of the trip.

Libby surprised Colton one afternoon when she stepped into the study wearing a new outfit and looking more beautiful than ever.

"Will this do for Mr. Durant's train ride?" she asked twirling.

Colton grabbed Libby around the waist and planted a kiss on her lips.

"Does that answer your question?" he smiled.

The Lincoln Car
From the personal papers of Dr. Thomas C. Durant
maintained in the Levi O. Leonard Collection, University of Iowa

June 6, 1866, Dodge wires headquarters "100 miles of road built."
From the personal papers of Dr. Thomas C. Durant
maintained in the Levi O. Leonard Collection, University of Iowa

Chapter 26

OCTOBER 1866 - THE GRANDEST EXCURSION EVER

The October sun slipped over the Omaha horizon, its dimming glow bathing the town in a beautiful golden hue. Trees rained leaves onto the streets and yards and rooftops.

Colton and Libby stood on the riverfront in the cool fall air, hands locked in each others. They watched two steamboats turning slowly toward the landing. Grenville and Annie Dodge stood with them, along with the mayor, territorial governor, and a dozen railroad officials. Behind them, fifty carriages waited—probably every available one in Omaha and Council Bluffs.

The Union Pacific boats carried Doctor Durant and 250 dignitaries. The lead boat sounded a long blast of the steam whistle and eased to the landing, its calliope playing rousing music. Elegantly dressed people crowded the deck. The second boat pulled in beside the first.

Annie Dodge leaned close to Libby.

"That's Durant standing next to George Train," she whispered too loudly. "Look at the smug face on that slump-shouldered rat. He's *such* a pompous ass. He just named himself president of Union Pacific."

Grenville gave her a stern look which she completely ignored.

Libby shuddered involuntarily at the sight of Durant and then carefully examined the man she had heard so much about. Something about him, some indescribable quality, frightened her. She felt guilty knowing this was the man who gave her husband the job he so loved.

"I couldn't have picked him from the crowd," Libby answered.

George Train was the first person off the steamboat.

"We'll form a receiving line here," George chirped to the reception committee. He took the head position to begin introducing guests and hosts. He directed the new arrivals to the carriages for the ride to the Herndon House and the waiting banquet.

Libby was awed meeting such famous businessmen, politicians, financiers, and journalists. Many brought their wives. Libby found them charming. She met senators, representatives, European earls and even a marquis. She knew the names Robert Todd Lincoln and George

Pullman. Pullman greeted Colton with a bear hug. She was surprised that such a feared employer should seem so friendly. Pullman's reputation as a brutal taskmaster was legendary.

Intentional or not, Durant walked past Libby without speaking.

The U.P. Steamers *Colorado* And *Denver* Arriving Omaha With Durant's Guests For The Grand Excursion to the Hundredth Meridian
Courtesy of the Douglas County Historical Society

The banquet that night was regal, made more impressive by anticipation of the upcoming trip to Indian country. Many guests were disappointed when Durant ended the event after the governor's speech.

"I know many of us want to dance to our band's fine music," he said. "But tomorrow will be most demanding. I encourage everyone to rest tonight, that is, if you want to fully enjoy the Wild West."

The next morning, guests toured the new railroad shops and massive locomotive house. Then, with the railroad cleared, a special train departed Omaha at mid-morning. Doc Durant passed from car to car chatting with his notable guests.

"Tonight we camp on the plains at Columbus, Nebraska," he announced. "This will be a camping experience like no other," he promised. "For anyone interested we will have a buffalo and antelope hunt tomorrow. For the rest, we offer a French cuisine picnic with a string quartet for entertainment."

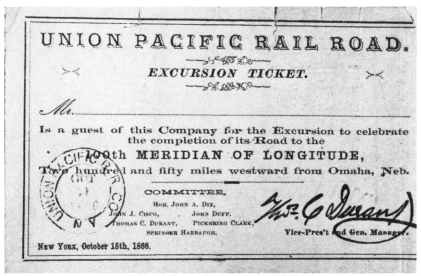

An Unissued Excursion Ticket
From the personal papers of Dr. Thomas C. Durant
maintained in the Levi O. Leonard Collection,
University of Iowa

The train started after a water stop at Fremont. Colton and Libby sat with a senator and his wife. Colton was taking his first sip of coffee when something caught his eye out the window. He glanced in time to see a familiar face passing slowly by.

He was repulsive all right. It took only a moment for Colton to recognize the man. It was Darcy Lonigan, the troublemaker who had accosted Libby three years ago. Lonigan, looking evil and frightening, stood on a pile of bridge timbers watching the excursion train pull out. Colton made unflinching eye contact. Both showed recognition of the other. It was over in an instant, but the sight of Lonigan stayed with Colton for days.

True to his word, Durant's campsite near Columbus was unprecedented; nothing like it had ever been seen on the prairie. Arriving guests found a city of gleaming white tents erected around a huge fire pit. Libby and Colton used an engraved map to find their tent.

"Oh my," Libby said as she entered the tent. "This is nicer than a hotel room." On their comfortable cots, they found canvas bags packed with commemorative items, snacks, and essentials.

General Dodge explored his tent and grumbled to Annie over the extravagance.

"In the army even General Grant never had a command tent this large." Then, spotting the feather pillows and down quilts, added, "or as comfortable."

For an October night the air was warm enough to enjoy Durant's excellent entertainment. Large campfires lighted a banquet of expertly prepared prairie game. After dinner, the mock Indian raid shocked the refined guests. More than a few felt raw terror when Indians with war paint ran into the gathering screaming and waiving war axes. Later, with order restored, the Pawnee demonstrated native dances for entertainment.

The following morning, the excursion train ran to the railhead to witness General Casement's inspiring progress. "Each mile of track requires forty railroad cars of material," Durant bragged. "We're at least a year ahead of schedule."

Guests posed for pictures with trackmen and Pawnee Indians. They ate more fine meals and enjoyed the sights. Shortly after lunch, word spread that Grenville Dodge had just won the election to the U. S. House of Representatives.

After dinner the second night, a vaudeville show, direct from New York, kept guests laughing for hours. The grand finale on the last night was terrifying and beautiful. Durant ordered a twenty mile stretch of prairie set on fire. Even from a safe distance it was a remarkable spectacle. Flames from the dry grass reached unbelievable heights creating their own fire tornadoes. To some, Colton in particular, it was a careless waste.

It was a three day party that no one would ever forget, a well-orchestrated trip of a lifetime.

As a result of George Train's mentoring, Durant had developed his self-promotion skills to an unprecedented level. The stocks and bonds sold on the trip and afterward easily justified the trip's heavy expenses.

U.P. Directors Pose At The Hundredth Meridian
247 Miles From Omaha
Courtesy of United States Archives

Back in Omaha, Doc and his privileged guests hurried to homes in London, Paris and twenty cities across America. Dodge left for his new congressional position in Washington. As Durant boarded a steamboat, he grabbed Colton's coat sleeve and pulled him roughly aside.

"I'll winter in New York, but I'll be keeping an eye on you. Your work on the excursion was barely passable. I'll expect better performance from you in the future. Go to Bellevue. Let Buck Clayton know I still plan to build my bridge in his city. Tell him Omaha just raised the stakes by increasing their incentives."

"Yes, sir."

For all Colton's work on the excursion and for all the praise from others, Doc had offered no hint of recognition or appreciation. It was always this way with Durant. Deep down it hurt. Each day was like starting from scratch.

* * * *

THE BONDS THAT connect men are among the strongest forces of humanity. Allegiance drives men to endure intolerable hardships, persevere against unbearable pain, and march willingly to certain death in battle. Loyalty and faith, it is said, can move mountains or, as Colton was witnessing, build railroads.

When men begin to doubt their beliefs, when faith is chipped or cracked, there may be a time of uncertainty before shattering and complete loss. It is a lonely feeling when a man confronts his suspicions. In the final days of 1866, Colton felt such loneliness.

Doubts crept into Colton's mind like a poison ivy, inching slowly, unalterably up a tree. The gnawing feeling in his gut wouldn't leave. He wanted to know the truth about Durant, but at the same time he was afraid of it. Even if he discovered the worst, he had no choice but to continue. His leg would never permit physical labor again. He saw no option to leave, so he stayed as the railroad marched ever westward.

* * * *

COLTON'S MISGIVINGS WERE in the back of his mind as he dismounted at Buck Clayton's home and accepted Buck's invitation to come inside. It was easy to put off thinking about Durant.

Buck tossed an extra log in the fireplace and handed Colton a full brandy snifter. Buck was glad to see his old friend and joked with him.

"Your visits normally cost me a lot of money," he said. "I'm afraid I don't have a brass box for you this time."

"I'm not here to pick up anything," Colton said, returning Buck's smile. "I'm here with a message."

"From the Doctor, no doubt. One of my favorite people." Buck's tone was facetious. "What urgent information does Doc have for me?"

"He asked me to tell you he still plans to build the bridge at Bellevue."

"Please tell me more. Surely he sent some other tidbit, some nugget of wisdom. What could it be?" Buck said, adding a pinch of cynicism.

"You're right. I have more," Colton said. "Doc wanted you to know a delegation from Omaha is going to New York to increase their bid for the Missouri River Bridge."

Buck dropped the theatrics. "You understand, of course, this was a predictable move. Durant completely drained cash from Omaha and Bellevue three years ago. Now he intends to renew the bidding war."

Colton's heart sank with the realization his suspicions may have merit. He couched his next question more as a challenge than the inquiry it was. "Come now, Buck. Are you saying Doc is doing something illegal?"

Buck took a long draw on his pipe and contemplated.

"No. Doc is simply a tough, selfish businessman who knows how to wield power. If I saw anything illegal, I'd be the first to sound alarms."

Clayton's comments, thin as they were, strengthened Colton.

* * * *

WITH THE FIRST severe blizzard, Jack Casement stopped most construction and retreated to Omaha. He was proud. The end of track was at North Platte, Nebraska, 260 miles from Omaha.

"General Jack" planned to spend the winter months in the U.P. shops preparing a dormitory train, a city on wheels. He had simple goals: bunks would replace tents; kitchen cars would replace chuck wagons. Dining cars with long benches and tables would give the men a place to eat prepared meals. A clerk's car crammed with desks, a payroll safe, and telegraph keys would fine tune the administration.

In late December, 1866, a coded message came for Colton.

Go see what Casement is doing. I'm seeing heavy expenses for unnecessary comforts. He ordered hundreds of rifles at my expense. Report immediately with full details. My suspicions are growing.

T.C. Durant.

Colton arrived at the Omaha shops so casually that General Casement never suspected he was on a mission from Durant. The general proudly escorted Colton through the shops, showing the work on his dormitory cars.

"We'll be able to build several miles per day. 1866 was good, but 1867 will be even better. I plan to build all the way from the Platte River to the Black Hills before the end of the year."

Casement opened a bunker in one of the cars revealing fifty rifles.

"That's a lot of firepower," Colton said, examining a carbine.

"We face two major problems," Casement answered. "The Indians will be the worst. We'll need these weapons next year. The army doesn't have enough men to protect everyone, so we must protect ourselves."

"Doc and Dodge regularly request troops in their weekly communication with the president and General Sherman," Colton offered.

"One thing seems certain, Colton. Without thousands of troops, the Indians will never allow settlers on the plains. Even with our new rifles and more soldiers, I worry if we can keep the railroad together. Our Pawnee scouts say the Cheyenne and Sioux are planning bigger raids after winter. Fact is, the country will have to eliminate the Indians if we intend to use the plains."

"Most Americans agree with you," Colton said. "You mentioned two big problems. What is the second one?"

"Hell on Wheels."

Colton grimaced involuntarily.

"Is that wretched outfit still around?"

"Ever since we've built west from Omaha, Hell on Wheels has followed us like a shadow. It's nothing but gamblers, outlaws and prostitutes who prey on our workers. They've got dance halls and saloons that move from camp to camp as fast as we do. The territorial government has almost no law enforcement west of Omaha. When we stopped for the winter, we were losing two men per week to murder or disappearance. Just as bad, drunken workers can't build track."

"Maybe a strong winter will drive out the bad elements."

"Hell on Wheels is at North Platte dug in like a badger den. Our men are flocking there by the hundreds for entertainment. The gold they worked so hard for is professionally stripped from them."

"What's the answer?" Colton asked.

"Maybe I'll have to appoint myself sheriff, judge, and jury," Casement said.

"And executioner?" Colton added, raising an eyebrow.

General Jack Casement smiled. "We'll see, Colton. For sure, we'll see interesting days ahead. Come. Let's see the other dormitory cars."

As Casement turned leading the way to the next shop, Colton was formulating his report. Durant would be pleased. All was well with Casement.

Chapter 27

FEBRUARY 1867 – AN ACTIVE SPRINGTIME

Union Pacific's workers returned to work in mid-February. Many arrived from Eastern homes via the new Cedar Rapids & Missouri River Railroad, the first railroad to reach Council Bluffs. Others, the survivors of Hell on Wheels, crawled dead broke from the appalling dark dens and squinted in the freezing sunlight.

By the time the ice pack broke on the Missouri, the railroad had dug itself out of the snow and laid twenty miles of new track with pre-positioned rail and cross ties. Material flowed west again, now faster with many shipments arriving Council Bluffs by rail instead of wagon.

On the plains, General Jack Casement's new dormitory train was successful in supporting every aspect of construction. In New York, management was pleased with progress. Across the nation the newspapers praised Durant, Dodge, and the railroad's march westward.

* * * *

NOT EVERYONE was happy with the railroad's advance. Hidden among the vivid colored wild flowers, a Cheyenne war party crouched low watching the railroad. Among them, a warrior with a single red feather in his hair studied three steam locomotives pushing the huge dormitory train along the track.

White Eagle listened to the great devil horses scream at the evil white men. The horrifying shrieks he heard were actually whistle signals. He watched the great iron horses breathe smoke and fire into the sky. He watched the white men serve.

"Devil horses," he said with fear and hatred in his voice. He remembered Running Elk's vision from four years earlier of the Great Wolf whom the Devil Horses obeyed. He searched the scene for the great wolf, but did not see him.

General Jack Casement Walks Alongside A Dormitory Train
(Note: Workers pitched tents on the tops of the cars for extra space and fresh air.)
The Andrew J. Russell Collection, the Oakland Museum of California

* * * *

AT THAT MOMENT, three hundred miles east, the Great Wolf was at the Herndon House Hotel tearing through croissants and gulping tea. The three men with him were his closest assistants, though none felt any closeness. Durant scowled listening to George Train's worn-out complaints about the food.

"I've never had a croissant made with bacon grease and prairie flour. It's quite ghastly." Train wrinkled his nose and returned the pastry to his plate. Within a minute Silas Seymour slipped a fork into it and claimed it for himself.

Durant, ignoring Train, turned to Rusk. "I'll leave Omaha in three days. Arrange to ferry my private cars across the river to Council Bluffs. Get with the CR&M about operating a special train to New York. I'll need security, so arrange it. I'll have several brass boxes. You follow my meaning?"

"Yes, sir," Colton answered. "Shall I accompany you east?"

"No. I have other plans for you."

Durant now addressed the entire group. "I've been considering our options. It looks almost certain that Nebraska will become a state this year. Congress votes on the application this week. We need to play every political card to our benefit."

He checked to ensure he had their attention and then continued. "Omaha people believe they deserve the state capitol. One of the biggest shocks these hicks could receive is if the state legislature established the Nebraska capitol somewhere other than Omaha."

"Why should we care about the capitol's location?" Train asked.

"Think about it, George. If we can pull the right strings, the Omaha people, insecure as they are, will have another identity crisis. That means they'll pay a lot more to guarantee they get the railroad bridge."

"So you intend to put Omaha in another high stakes bidding war?" Train asked.

"Certainly. It's only when they're scared that they open their bank accounts." Durant smiled.

Everyone at the table knew Durant's assessment was accurate.

"Next week, George, I want you to contact the legislators. Make sure the capitol ends up in another town. If we invest ten thousand dollars to secure their votes, I'll bet we can reap a twenty-fold return in bridge incentives. Omaha will dig deep to get the bridge."

178

"I'll see what I can do," Train answered. "David Butler will be the first state governor. I know him well. He'll work with us."

The breakfast meeting broke up. George Train and Silas Seymour scurried away on urgent missions. Colton hired a buckboard and waited to escort Doc for the day.

"Are you armed?" Durant asked as he climbed onboard.

"Pistol," Colton answered.

"I have three appointments. You will remain with the carriage while I conduct business. First stop is the ferry landing. Go!"

Colton's doubts mounted each time Doc returned from an appointment with a brass document case. He noticed their heaviness and strong padlocks as he stowed them away. The box from the ferry owner was particularly heavy.

Yes, it's suspicious, but there is no proof of wrongdoing.

That night, Colton told Libby about the day. "Those boxes contained gold. I'm sure of it. I don't know what he's up to."

Libby took a cautious approach. "It may seem suspicious, but keep in mind Mr. Durant owns property in Omaha. Perhaps he was delivering deeds or picking up rents. I know you suspect illegal kickbacks, but you need more than suspicion."

"Maybe I'm too paranoid. I'm starting to feel disloyal for doubting my boss," he confessed.

* * * *

AS PLANNED, COLTON drove Doc to Council Bluffs where the special train waited to transport the boss comfortably across the nation.

Five nervous railroad officers also met them and boarded the train with maps, plans, and drawings. They greeted Doc like an honored benefactor. Durant greeted his managers with cold sneers.

On board, Durant was ready to analyze details of Union Pacific's progress. He wanted not an overview, but a penetrating reexamination of every decision. Seymour was present too, armed with his own documents to supply Doc with doubts, criticisms and cost saving alternatives whether sound or not.

Colton left the train glad to remain in Omaha and relieved to miss the inquisition on the train. Yes, it was good to skip this trip. He had his own mountain of work to conquer, everything from auditing expenses and verifying supply inventories to dealing with new suppliers across several states.

Durant In His Private Railroad Car

Dr. Thomas Durant (seated second from right) gazes toward
Consulting Engineer Silas Seymour (seated at left) as U.P. officers look on.
The Andrew J. Russell Collection, the Oakland Museum of California

* * * *

SIX WEEKS PASSED before Colton saw George Train again. They met at the Herndon House the morning after Colton returned from a three week trip to Chicago, Cincinnati and Pittsburg.

Train greeted Colton with genuine enthusiasm. "Well if it isn't Father Rusk! You're back, old boy! How was your journey? Better than mine, I hope."

"It was an exhausting trip," Colton said. "Doc had me hopping like a frog in a skillet. What about your New York trip?"

"Sit down, Colton my friend. I have plenty of news."

Colton pulled up a chair. "Let me brace myself."

"You already know about the trouble at the top. Things are getting worse all the time. Doc almost came to blows with Senator Ames last week. Ames is trying to boot Doc out of the company. They've demoted him to vice-president, and they're trying to take over Crédit Mobilier. The new president is Oliver Ames, Senator Ames' brother."

"Sounds like Doc has a heckuva fight on his hands," Colton said.

"Doc can handle it. Last week, he filed a lawsuit against Ames and his group, and he's threatening to stop all construction work again. He may also report Senator Ames for improper activities."

"What kind of activities?" Colton asked.

"Can't tell you details, Colton. I'm sworn to secrecy, you know. Let me simply assure you Doc knows how to take care of himself. I think he'll reach an agreement with the Ames Brothers soon. At least I hope so."

"Has the new Nebraska legislature selected a location for the state capitol yet?" Colton asked.

"Governor Butler selected a spot south of the Platte close to his ranch. It will probably be our new capital city. They will name it Lincoln."

"Lincoln, Nebraska," Colton said aloud. "It's a solid, patriotic name. Just what the state needs."

"It's just as Doc wanted," Train said. "The people I dealt with sold out cheap! I actually returned some of Doc's cash."

Colton wondered how much cash Train had "invested" in the Nebraska legislators. Instead of asking, he chose to change the subject. "Can you believe the progress Casement is making? All America is watching. It's incredible."

"Even the Indians are cooperating," Train answered haughtily.

Colton raised his eyebrows. He had his doubts about the Indians.

"I spoke with a construction boss last night at the boat landing," Colton said. "Every day our men see warriors on the horizon or in the bluffs. Sometimes they see a hundred or more. So far, they are staying out of rifle range and watching. They haven't attacked the large work crews, but when a war party finds a smaller group, they slaughter every man."

George shook his head. "Those random tactics won't slow down the railroad. Soon enough the savages will move somewhere else."

"You're underestimating the Indians, George. The Cheyenne and Sioux are going to fight. We're ripping apart their way of life. They're warriors who have everything at stake. We're in for tough times with the Indians."

* * * *

Early Scene - Union Pacific Shops, Omaha, Nebraska
The Andrew J. Russell Collection, the Oakland Museum of California

Chapter 28

AUGUST 1867 – THE PLUM CREEK DISASTER

By the time Colton awoke, Libby was already up and dressed. He lay in bed and realized it was the smell of cooking bacon that had awakened him. He stayed in bed for a few relaxing moments enjoying the soft morning breeze and the birds singing somewhere nearby.

He pulled on a robe and went downstairs to find Libby in the kitchen. He gave her a long hug and was leaning in for a morning kiss when she asked, "Do you know what today is?"

"Sure. It's a rare day when I get to relax at home."

"No. I mean what is the significance of today?"

"I don't know. Don't tell me you are filling the house with church ladies again," Colton joked.

"It was four years ago today that we reached the top of the high bluff and looked down on Council Bluff. We were so excited."

"How do you remember these things?" Colton asked.

They reflected on how life had changed and held hands over breakfast. Colton was on the verge of concluding life couldn't get any better when Telegrapher Anthony Butler knocked on the door and broke the spell.

"Urgent telegram, Mr. Rusk. I brought it up right away."

Butler presented the envelope and smiled sheepishly. They both knew whom it was from.

Colton returned to the kitchen and read aloud for Libby.

Dodge unable to leave Washington for railroad duties. In his place, travel west immediately by train and update profiles for each town along line. Report political situation, contacts, business overview, and population. Need is critical to ensure best political positioning. Leave tomorrow. Also pick up locked box from Grand Island Mayor. Advise daily activity by telegram. Further instructions to follow.

T C. Durant

The demands for instant action were exasperating. Colton sent a dozen telegrams canceling meetings for the rest of the month. He left the telegraph office with his neck and shoulder muscles tight from stress. His mind raced, hoping he had remembered everything important.

By daylight the next morning, Colton was at the riverfront railroad yard boarding a train. There was nothing luxurious about the twenty-car freight train. Most of the cars carried rails, cross ties, and spikes. Three loaded box cars carried merchandise for Kearney, Nebraska.

Toward the middle of the train, two flat cars carried a steam excavator, and behind it, a high-sided gondola car with fifteen workmen to operate it. They were tough, new arrivals, with a look that spoke of energy and longing for adventure. Most wore blue or gray uniform pants. Their destination was the dangerous Black Hills where grading was behind schedule. All had rifles.

The last car was an ancient wooden passenger coach car now converted into a bunk car. Crude wooden beds lined the walls. The only rooms were a tiny kitchen in the center of the car and a small observation room at the rear. It was in this last car that Colton rode, along with seven surveyors making their way to Utah.

Colton planned to ride to the end of rail, making notes on each settlement. With any luck he would visit General Casement and give him the latest newspapers. The return trip would be slower, stopping at each settlement to gather detailed information. It should be an easy, though time-consuming, assignment.

As the train rolled west, Colton sat at a table, notebook in front of him, and watched the sights unfold. He noticed the track gave a smooth ride. Most of the rocking and swaying of previous trips was gone. Since construction, General Casement's gangs had worked and reworked the tracks until now trains could speed along smoothly at thirty miles per hour.

Hours and miles passed. At the water stop in Grand Island, the conductor came into the observation room and stopped to talk with Colton.

"I thought you would like to see one of the train orders we just received. It sounds like the Indians are becoming more active."

Colton read the train order to the surveyors. The two men sharing his table laid down their playing cards and listened closely.

Cheyenne war parties reported west of Kearney. Exercise caution. Avoid unnecessary train stops. Report any Indian sightings at first open telegraph office.

Chief Dispatcher.

Colton arched his eyebrows at the conductor as if asking a question. The conductor saw the alarm in the car and offered encouragement.

"Don't worry, boys. We get these messages all the time. Sometimes we see Indians in the distance. but that's the most of it. They keep their distance."

Despite the calming words, Colton checked his pistol before going back to work. The surveyors put away their cards to watch for trouble.

Miles passed with no sign of Indians. Calm returned to the car. By the time they passed Kearney, the surveyors returned to their card game. Men talked or slept and enjoyed the peaceful clickity-clack rhythm of the rails passing under the car. No one expected what happened next.

Without warning, Indians attacked both sides of the train. They appeared from nowhere riding skillfully on fast, barebacked horses. Many fired rifles. Others had bows and arrows.

In the rear car, a bullet slammed through a window and into the face of a surveyor sitting two seats from Colton. The man fell instantly dead.

Colton instinctively dropped to the floor and yelled, "Everyone get down!"

At first the other men failed to comprehend what was happening. Then, as reality set in, they panicked. Several rushed terror-stricken through the car. Colton rose and led two men to a rifle locker. Soon they were returning fire.

Several cars ahead, the Indians faced a tough bunch. When the attack came, the men in the high-sided gondola had been caught off guard. Within seconds they grabbed their rifles, stood behind the car's protective sides, and responded with a fierce volley of return fire.

The Indians had picked the wrong opponent in former soldiers who loved a good fight and knew how to shoot. Their fire was accurate, and they delivered a devastating hail of bullets. The Indian horde wilted under the workers' defense. Colton saw the Indians take heavy casualties, as the experienced marksmen shot them off their horses.

AT THE HEIGHT OF the battle, a Cheyenne warrior reined his horse and dropped from the horde. He turned and galloped back to the spot where a comrade lay wounded and gasping the last breaths of life.

The warrior pulled his horse to a stop and dropped to the ground by the wounded man's side. Blood poured from the dying Indian's chest, its red color matching the deep red of the single feather still tied in his hair.

"My father, what can I do for you?" Running Elk cried.

The dying warrior struggled to speak. "It is too late, my son. The devil horse of your dreams has taken me. Go. Be with our brothers. Soon you will celebrate victory when the devil horse is defeated."

"No, Father. I will not leave you. You cannot die."

The response was soft and difficult. "Do not worry for me, Running Elk. I go to join our ancestors. They rejoice in my arrival."

They looked in each others eyes for half a minute longer, the younger Cheyenne warrior grief-stricken, the older man accepting his fate. Then it was over. White Eagle's body relaxed into the prairie grass.

ON THE SPEEDING TRAIN, the situation eased as more Indians died. At last the horde melted away. The workers had started congratulating themselves when the locomotive whistle began shrieking. All eyes strained looking toward the locomotive.

They watched horrorstruck as the engine derailed, turned over, and disappeared into a ravine. They heard its whistle scream over the deafening crash. Behind the locomotive, moving cars overturned one by one. Equipment, lading, and men flew in all directions, a dozen killed instantly as railroad cars rolled over and crushed them. Colton had little time to assess the situation.

Seconds before the last car overturned, a brakeman cried out, "We've derailed on a barricade, boys! Every man for himself!"

Men, footlockers, bunks and everything inside the car went airborne. Most of the surveyors landed against the car's wall with bone-crushing force and suffered injuries. Two men crashed through windows and went to their deaths under the tumbling car. It was a horrible, chaotic scene. A fire started in the kitchen and spread rapidly in both directions, accelerated by spilled fuel oil.

Colton was one of the fortunate who avoided instant death in the wreck. He was momentarily dazed from tossing about in the car but quickly regained his bearings.

Even in the smoke-filled car, panic failed to overcome Colton. He calmly checked for his pistol and then looked for a way out. He fumbled along in the overturned car until he saw a broken window above him. With all his strength he climbed up and onto the side of the car. He looked in disbelief at the devastation and carnage around him then dropped to the ground.

Near him, another man struggled clambered out of the car and was shot down before he could join Colton. The fire was growing. Heavy smoke floated toward the engine covering the area. Only the smoke cloud allowed Colton to make his way unseen toward the head end of the train.

Though he could not see Indians, he heard them talking excitedly on the opposite side of the train.

God willing, they'll stay there. Otherwise, any step might be my last. I've got to find a safe hiding place.

As he inched forward he came across the bodies of three U.P. workmen. One lay under a twisted piece of the crumpled excavator. Two others lay among uprooted ties, rails, and railroad car wheels.

The Indians suddenly grew louder. Colton heard war cries, and for a moment he thought they had spotted him. When no one attacked, he paused to steal a look around the end of a car. Through smoke, he saw the Indians had captured four workers and were torturing them. Colton raised his pistol to fire, and then realized the futility of fighting forty or more Indians alone.

With no option, he moved on, no place to hide, no horse to steal, no one to join. He heard screams behind him. Perhaps the Indians had scalped their captives or thrown them into the raging fire. Colton shuddered.

Reaching the box cars, Colton heard Indians nearby, yipping with delight. Again he peered around a railroad car. This time he saw Indians fully engaged in plundering cargo. A Cheyenne pony and its rider raced around the wreckage with an unrolled bolt of calico streaming behind.

The wrecked cars surrendered whiskey and household goods. The Indians celebrated their treasures and drank while plundering cargo with excitement.

Thirty yards later, Colton reached the edge of the ravine. Below, the locomotive lay on its side barely visible through the rising steam and smoke. The derailed tender was upside down. Two cars lay nearby.

Colton was about to descend into the ravine when he saw a shadow slinking around the end of a derailed car next to him. Alarm pulsed through him like electricity. Without wavering he aimed his pistol at the spot the Indian would appear.

Tense, breathless moments passed before a human figure emerged. To his relief, it was the train's conductor instead of a Cheyenne warrior. The man was injured. Colton lowered his pistol and rushed to help.

"Have you seen anyone else?" Colton asked.

"Dead. They're all dead," the conductor mumbled. "You're the only living person I've seen."

"We need to find cover. The Indians will be here soon."

The dazed conductor stared blankly. He grabbed his side as pain shot through him.

From the opposite side of the train Colton heard the thunder of hooves and the yips of newly arriving Indians.

"Let's move," Colton whispered. We'll be dead in minutes if we stay here."

Colton took the conductor's arm and pulled him along into the ravine.

Ahead, the overturned tender was half buried in the wreckage, its firewood scattered across the ravine. It would make a perfect, armored hiding place, if he could find a way inside.

They crept along as quickly as they could, the conductor's face contorting with pain.

Reaching the tender, they found a small opening where iron seams had wrenched open in the crash. Colton helped the conductor crawl through the gash and into the darkness. Inside, Colton closed the opening with uprooted cross ties.

Small holes in the tender's metal sides allowed a dim light inside. The largest hole was a split seam no more than a foot long and two inches wide. The other three holes were round, perhaps an inch in diameter left when rivets popped out. More important than light, the holes gave Colton a safe view of the world outside. He could see smoke drifting past, but no Indians.

They waited, silent in the grayness, straining to hear any sounds. The only sound was the pounding of their fearful hearts.

"Do you have a weapon?" Colton asked.

"Pistol and cartridge belt," the Conductor managed to say.

"We're going to need it. I have a pistol too."

Three long hours passed in the dimness. They heard nothing nearby. Colton thought of Libby. He pictured her beautiful face, her smile, her voice. Just thinking of her gave him strength and affirmed his need to stay alive. William needed him too. There was still much to teach a son who just celebrated his fifteenth birthday.

Eventually the silence broke with the sound of Indians laughing, closer now, rummaging through unexplored wreckage in the ravine.

Colton whispered to the injured conductor. "Be very quiet. We may be able to live through this. They won't expect people in the tender."

War cries penetrated their iron shelter. "Maybe a rescue party has arrived. I'll look," said Colton.

He carefully approached a rivet hole and peered out. No more than fifty feet away, twenty Indians surrounded a captured man. Colton recognized him as one of the surveyors who had been playing cards. He had somehow made it into the ravine. Warriors had probably discovered him hiding in the wreckage. He looked no more than eighteen years old.

In Colton's clear view, the Indians pummeled the young surveyor to the dust and brutally cut a wide swatch of scalp from his head. His screams echoed through the tender. As the Indians danced, wildly waving the bloody scalp, the surveyor stood and ran. The Indians let him run fifty bloody steps before shooting him down and returning to plunder and savage celebration.

Colton collapsed in a corner from the horrible sight. The Indians' loud, liquor-fired party dragged on for an hour.

"Maybe they'll leave soon," Colton whispered. "They must know soldiers are stationed at the next town. Our train is badly overdue. A platoon will be out to check on it."

An hour later, it was clear the conductor's condition was deteriorating. He became delirious, talking of senseless things. His moaning grew louder until Colton grew concerned someone would hear.

Outside, a warrior walked past the tender and heard something. He stopped and listened. He heard moaning in the overturned tender. He walked completely around the tender eventually finding the one inch split in the iron side. He listened and again heard the white devil inside. The Indian gripped his war club and called threateningly.

A shot rang out. A thick fountain of blood exploded from the Indian's skull. He fell dead. Indians ducked and scattered in thirty directions unsure where the shot originated. Within twenty minutes, however, when they found no one, the warriors returned to the tender. They swarmed and attacked.

Shots exploded through the rivet holes into the tender, but no one was hit. Bullets flattened on the iron sides and dropped harmlessly to the dirt. Colton knew the darkness made him invisible to the Indians. He found he could time his shots perfectly. When an Indian withdrew his gun from an opening, Colton instantly positioned himself to fire. In this manner he felled six warriors before they retreated.

Colton knew they would return. He knew what they would try next.

"They'll be back to burn us out," he told the conductor.

He was right. The Indians approached from Colton's blind side with dry brush and splintered boards. Colton heard them, but could see no one. He moved between the slits and rivet holes trying to see what was happening.

First he saw the smoke, not a lot, just a few wisps floating past the viewing ports. Nonetheless, it was fresh smoke, clearly distinguishable from the train wreck smoke that hung over the area. Then he noticed the heat. He felt it first in his face and in his lungs, then over his upper body and arms as the temperatures rose steadily.

He laid the conductor flat, below the most intense heat, and returned to the slit. Something was happening. Indians running! He heard shots. On the top of the ravine he saw three soldiers, then twenty.

Instantly, Colton rushed to the cross tie barricade at the entrance. The heat was unbearable. With all his strength he moved the cross ties and pulled the conductor to the opening and out to safety.

* * * *

THE NEXT MORNING, as daylight broke in Omaha, news of the train wreck reached the telegraph office and filtered into the city. The massacre was the talk of the town. About noon, rumors began spreading that a mass of Indians was approaching Omaha to destroy it.

As Colton helped with the burial duty, panic gripped Omaha. Men desperately prepared for a battle that never came.

Libby and William suffered two days of uncertainly about Colton, and the fear of an imminent attack in Omaha. When Colton's telegram came two days later, his family rejoiced. Its simple reassuring words meant the world to them.

Resting at Julesburg today. Moving west in morning. I am in good health. Will arrive in Omaha in ten days.

Colton.

Chapter 29

Colton faced Durant in Union Pacific Railroad's handsomely appointed New York headquarters. He opened his carpet bag, carefully removed two locked boxes, and placed them into the doctor's outstretched hands.

"I am dissatisfied with the town profiles you provided. Even worse, your report was late. Senator Ames belittled me for not knowing the details of our situation. You failed miserably."

If Colton had been new to these situations, Durant's coldness might have surprised him, but it didn't. He expected derisive comment.

"The train wreck delayed me, sir." Colton spoke respectfully, without defensiveness.

How long can Doc nurse a grudge? This matter is already over a month old.

Durant's eyes burned with fury. "Ah. The train wreck delayed you. Did it now?"

Durant's tone mocked Colton.

"You waltzed away footloose from that derailment without a scratch. Don't try to cover your incompetence with Indians and train wrecks. A devoted man would have immediately continued west on his mission. You failed me."

"I lost time helping to recover and bury our men. I had an obligation to the men who died at my side. Only two of us lived through the ordeal."

Durant stared blankly at his desk shaking his head in incomprehension. When he looked up his wild eyes bulged. He began with a forced calmness, a controlled, shaking rage.

"During the war, was it your practice to bury your dead during battle? For example, did you ever bury casualties while surrounded and taking enemy fire?"

"No, sir. We waited until after the battle."

Durant sprang to his feet screaming. "So, why did you stop fighting *my* battles to take care of the dead? Are *my* battles not important enough for you? We have people to take care of cleanup. Burial duty is not your job. Do you not understand your role? Your position exists to take care of *me*. Taking care of me *is* your job, your *only* job. You could cost us victory with your soft attitude."

Colton's face flushed as his temper rose. Durant's battle analogy was a poor one. It was an insult. Building U.P. was commerce, not war. Colton refused to disrespect the men who died beside him. He trembled, choking back hot words with doubled fists.

Neither man spoke for a moment, both reining in raw emotions.

When the passions faded, Durant jerked his ruffled coat lapels straight and sat hard in his chair. He ran a finger inside his shirt collar and turned his head side to side to ease neck tension. He unlocked one of the brass boxes and dumped the contents onto the desk. It was cash, hundreds of bills bundled into neat stacks and secured with paper wrappers.

Colton watched as Durant skillfully counted a small fortune. Wasn't this evidence of dishonesty? Was any further proof needed?

In mid-count Durant awakened to Colton's staring. "Refund of overcharges," Durant stated flatly. He continued counting.

It wasn't anything Colton said, for he said nothing, but when Durant looked up he instantly recognized revulsion painted on Colton's face.

"What is that look on your face?" Durant snapped.

Colton ignored the certain consequences of speaking honestly. "Sir, there are newspaper reports that question your integrity. I thought you should know."

Durant erupted in a new tirade. "Of course I know. Do you think I don't read the newspapers? Fact is, Rusk, you're not asking about newspaper reports, are you? You're asking for yourself. You're downright nosy. Even worse, I think you're accusing me of something. I see it in your eyes."

Colton stood silent and unflinching, stoking Durant's tantrum.

"What smugness from a crippled man! You look upon me with disgust. You can't understand how a man like me operates. Fact is, Rusk, I'll accomplish more in my life than you could accomplish in six lifetimes."

"You look at me like I'm the problem here, but you're the one who has a narrow view of the world. If I weren't building this road, someone else would be. I am in a unique position at this time in history to profit from events that will occur with or without me. The forces at play are bigger than any of us. The economic tides driving us are more powerful than Congress or the president or any individual.

"You despise me for making profits? Without the profit motive, the nation would not have its railroad in a hundred years. Lincoln knew it. That's why he set the incentives as high as he did.

"I disgust you? It's mutual, Rusk. You disgust me with your innocence, your weeping for the workers. They begged me for jobs. I gave work to those men who died. They accepted the risks without a second thought. They gambled on an unforgiving job and lost.

"You don't understand how business works. Forget the rumors. Keep your faith in my ability to complete this project. It is my tenacity that will make America great. Just remember, Rusk, people who are universally loved have no character.

"Now get out! Get out before I fire you. Go back to Omaha. Let me know in a week if you intend to meet the requirements of your job. I insist on total loyalty as I have from your first day." Durant paused momentarily to point a threatening finger. "You *cannot* abandon me to bury the dead in the midst of the battle."

* * * *

FOR THE FIRST TIME in his years with Durant, Colton was full of doubt. He abhorred Durant's manner, but at the same time recognized Durant was right about some things. The need for the railroad *was* bigger than any individual. Durant was as much a tool of the nation as the nation was a tool for him.

Colton returned to Omaha under a dark cloud of uncertainty. The money he had seen proved nothing. Gut feelings and intuition were not proof. He had to accept Durant's actions at face value for now.

If Durant was a crook, he was not just an ordinary one, but a brilliant villain, smart as Satan. Colton was glad to be away from him for a while.

In the following months, Colton kept these thoughts to himself.

* * * *

Omaha, Nebraska, December 31, 1867
IN THE BALLROOM OF George Train's hilltop mansion overlooking the Missouri River, twenty finely dressed men and women

sat at a long dining table. A dozen servants scurried serving drinks and taking dinner orders from a special menu printed for the evening.

The guests included mayors, the governor, and a federal commissioner. Grenville and Annie Dodge, freshly arrived from Washington, sat across from Libby and Colton. Annie and Libby chatted as close friends.

Their host was dressed in a lavender tuxedo with white gloves and matching shoes. The other men wore tuxedos and sat with ladies wearing long, formal gowns.

Colton looked handsome in a new tuxedo and new dress boots. Libby was the only person who knew how uncomfortable he felt. She was as stunningly beautiful as he had ever seen her in a long blue gown with her hair up.

After drinks and appetizers, Train stood at the head of the table and tapped his wine glass for attention.

"My dear friends, thank you for coming tonight. I appreciate your braving the bitter cold weather to celebrate New Year's Eve with me. As we say goodbye to 1867 and welcome 1868, I propose a toast to a man who is unable to be with us tonight, one who continues his work tirelessly in New York. Please raise your glasses with me.

"I offer this toast to Doctor Thomas Durant, the heart and soul of the Union Pacific Railroad, the man who has led construction of over 500 miles of track to the new city of Cheyenne in the Wyoming Territory, to the man who has inspired our workmen to continue laying track in the dead of winter. I toast the man who very soon will build track through Sherman Pass with its elevation over 8200 feet above sea level, the highest railroad on earth, the man who will see us to victory in the all-out race with Central Pacific Railroad. We toast you, Doctor, as you toil at this historic hour for the betterment of America and mankind. May the world praise your successes forever."

Glasses clinked, and wine flowed. Libby and Colton toasted Durant with the others. Their eyes met sharing their mixed thoughts of the benefactor tyrant.

"Before we enjoy a fine dinner, I have a few words, and an important announcement," Train said.

A loud groan came from the far end of the table.

"I heard that. I will try to be brief, Governor Butler." Train smiled.

Laughter rose and fell as the Nebraska Governor's face reddened.

Train continued. "Omaha and God have been good to me. This home stands as testament of my faith in the future of America. Long after we are gone, long after people forget George Train and those of us in this room, this house will stand as a monument to what happened in Omaha and the events that opened the American prairies to civilization.

"I chose this site for my home for two reasons. First, from this high point, I can see the five hundred structures currently under construction. These will provide homes for thousands of new residents. Train Town has made me proud to be a part of Omaha."

"Train Town has also made you rich," said a voice that sounded suspiciously like Governor Butler's.

Laughter filled the room. Even Train smiled, and then continued.

"The second reason I chose this hilltop location is its view of the railroad and all it brings to the city and the lands beyond. Even today, I looked from library window onto the railroad's newest engineering marvel. I speak of Union Pacific's ice bridge. Imagine it. A railroad laid on the ice of the frozen Missouri River. It is a tribute to you, General Dodge. It excites all who see it."

A round of applause filled the room as all eyes turned to General Dodge.

"And now, ladies and gentlemen, it is time for a personal announcement. I know it will come as a surprise for I made my decision only today."

He paused.

"At the direction of my heart and morals, I will soon leave the railroad."

Gasps and murmuring spread around the table.

"Why you leavin', George?" a man's voice asked.

"Last September I joined a cause even more important than the transcontinental railroad, a cause greater than any effort I have ever committed to. My friend, Susan B. Anthony, has shown me the need for women to have the right to vote. If women can successfully rule countries as queens, they can also vote competently in republics."

The ladies in the room clapped. The men exchanged curious expressions, as if Train was speaking a strange language.

"I am considering many other things. Irish independence appeals to me. The Australians are asking me to run for their presidency. After the transcontinental railroad is complete, I may try to break the speed record for going around the world. I believe a person can probably travel around the world in less than eighty days."

Several at the table chuckled at the absurdity of what they considered dinner humor. Those who knew Train better listened carefully to his unusual wisdom in foretelling future developments.

"I may run for president of the United States. Again! I know not where I will end up but within a week I leave for Europe. Meanwhile, my friends, let the New Year's Eve feast begin."

Train clapped his hands twice as a signal. Servers entered through two doors with trays loaded with fine foods. A small band played party music. The guests chattered excitedly about George Train's announcement.

1867 ended grandly for Colton and Libby with bright lights, friends, and happiness. Their hearts brimmed with love and optimism.

Leaving the party in the first hours of 1868, Colton saw her as he often did—beautiful and the love of his life. In the carriage her face was radiant in the light cast from Train's windows. She smiled tenderly, and he knew she wanted him to kiss her. She wrapped her arms around him and held him tightly as the carriage descended the icy hill toward their home on Capitol Street.

Years later, when she grew to be an old woman, Libby thought of George Train's elegant party and remembered it as one of the best evenings of her life.

Chapter 30

FIRST QUARTER 1868 – THE RAILROAD ADVANCES

The first months of 1868 were harsh, even in a land known for blizzards and snowfall. The river remained ice-bound twelve weeks longer than usual. Ferry boats sat idle, tied frozen to moorings while U.P. trains delivered materials over Dodge's ice bridge.

By the time people ventured from their homes to check for signs of spring, General Casement's army was already at full strength and laying track west of Cheyenne. Behind the railhead, crews rebuilt and shored up track laid on snow. Ahead, thousands toiled preparing roadbed for General Casement's advance.

Casement's construction train was now at eighty cars with a new bakery, saddle car, and additional bunk cars. There was even a bath car to encourage employee hygiene.

Since passing the 100th Meridian, bond sales had boomed. People now considered U.P. bonds among the safest and best investments in America. Money poured into the U.P. coffers only to pass soon enough to Durant and his cronies at Credit Mobilier.

Durant's obsessions grew more intense. The best way to make money was laying as much track as possible. The construction effort he controlled was without parallel. He looked greedily ahead to the mountains and increased government incentives.

Rail after rail was laid in perfect alignment relentlessly moving the Union Pacific west. Mile after mile the road advanced, pushed along by Durant's telegrams from New York demanding faster production.

Faster! You must go faster! What do you need? We must beat Central Pacific to Ogden. Immediately increase working hours. Double the wages.

T. C. Durant

As the leader of one of the nation's two largest companies, Durant's influence extended from coast to coast. To those closest, it seemed Durant's greed was driving the entire country.

A Paystub For Work On Union Pacific Railroad
From the personal papers of Dr. Thomas C. Durant
maintained in the Levi O. Leonard Collection,
University of Iowa

* * * *

ON A CRISP MARCH morning, a train from Omaha stopped in the hectic Chicago depot and released a steam cloud that covered the first three cars. Veiled by the steam, the baggage car door slid open and a man climbed to the ground with a carpet bag. He walked with a pronounced limp through the steam toward the depot building.

In his pocket, he carried an unused pass that would have permitted him to ride the first class coaches. Instead, Colton Rusk preferred riding with employees in the baggage cars and cabooses. He felt camaraderie with the men. He loved their shop talk, stories and coffee. More importantly, he felt more secure with his brass boxes when slightly removed from throngs of strangers.

Emerging from the steam cloud, he heard someone call his name.

"Colton? Colton Rusk!"

He turned to see Buck Clayton, his old friend from Bellevue.

"Buck! What a nice surprise to see you here. You're sure a long way from Bellevue." They exchanged smiles and a hearty handshake.

"I'm headed back home," said Buck. "Been in New York. I guess you heard what happened with the plans for the high bridge?"

"Actually I haven't," Colton answered. "I've been helping organize towns, and now I'm on my way to Milwaukee. Tell me about it."

Buck seemed exasperated. "Doc called in the contenders for the Missouri River bridge. He required all the cities to come to his office for negotiations. I should have suspected what he was up to. It turned out to be another session to wring cash out of us."

"Tell me who went to New York?" Colton asked.

"I represented Bellevue. Omaha sent a delegation, and several landowners came from Desoto. Three groups in all. Doc stalled two days before he talked to anyone. He kept us isolated in hot offices and eventually met with us individually. He drove up the incentives with every conversation."

"So, does Bellevue get the high bridge?" Colton asked.

"No. We couldn't meet Doc's demands or match Omaha's money. Omaha won, but believe me they will pay dearly for it. They're donating hundreds more acres and guaranteeing huge bonds. Durant took ruthless greed and manipulation to a whole new level."

Colton was stunned by the story but kept a poker face. It seemed almost unthinkable that Durant, a mere man, had the power and cleverness to pit entire cities against each other for his own gain.

"I guess my grandchildren will still be paying for the bridge," Colton offered.

"Probably your great-grandchildren too," Buck added. "Other railroads are coming. Some day we'll get a railroad bridge at Bellevue. Desoto will probably get one too, but it will take ten more years. Omaha will grow into a huge city while Bellevue waits as a small town. It's disappointing."

"I suppose the Omaha delegation was happy," Colton said.

"The Omaha men left with mixed emotions after long, ugly negotiations. Durant threatened to pull out all the shops and depot if they didn't pay up. Omaha threatened to sue. In the end, Omaha paid for an iron-clad agreement. When it was over, Durant laughed at them and called them hicks. I tell you Colton, no one wants anything in the world as badly as Durant wants money. He will stop at nothing to get it. He will crush anyone who stands in his way."

They entered the depot building still wanting to talk, but neither had time to spare. Within minutes they parted, with Buck boarding a Council Bluffs-bound train. Colton departed an hour later for his meetings with timber suppliers in Milwaukee.

* * * *

DURANT RETURNED to Omaha while the vast grass ocean was still green from late rains, before the summer heat that would paint the plains brown.

On June 15, 1868, Colton kissed Libby and left for the railroad yard under a sky full of stars. Railroad workmen had labored through the night to spit-shine and load provisions in five of U.P.'s newest cars. Colton arrived and found preparations still underway for Durant's special train.

By the time Colton checked the train and confirmed arrangements along the line, the sun had almost shown itself. Colton saw Doc's carriage arrive and hurried to finish his duties with the train dispatcher and yardmaster.

Ten minutes later, when he boarded Durant's car, Colton found Doc alone with the conductor. He was already caustic and sarcastic.

"Ah. Mr. Rusk has finally struggled out of his bed to join us. May we depart now? How are your bed sores? Should we send someone for ointment? I wanted to leave at daylight, but because of you, we'll have people down the line standing and waiting for us."

Durant expected no response and received none. He turned to follow the conductor onto the car's back platform.

"Let's go. Get this train moving!" Durant's voice was turning shrill even before breakfast.

"Sir, I'm waiting to hear from the mechanical inspectors. They'll let me know when work on the train is finished. I can't move the train until then," the conductor answered.

"Do you think I'm stupid? These cars are new. There are no mechanical problems with them. Look up the train! Use your eyes, man! You can see all the way to the engine on both sides. Can you see any workers?"

"No, sir. I can't."

"Of course you don't see anyone. They're all standing at the shanty getting paid for doing nothing. Look for yourself. They're drinking coffee. They've had all night to get this train ready. Let's go."

The Conductor looked toward a small shack and saw five men loitering well clear of the train.

Durant persisted. "Obviously they've finished. Who said they're still working?"

"No one, sir. It's our procedure to— " the conductor did not finish.

"I dictate the procedures here. I control this railroad. I tell you we're ready to go. Get this train moving! We have a long way to go today. People higher paid than you are waiting for our arrival."

The conductor leaned out and looked again at the train, first up the up the right side, then the left. He saw nothing. Still he felt reluctant to do anything.

Durant was screaming. "Do you have a family, Conductor?"

"Yes, sir."

"Then if you want to continue feeding them, I suggest you get this train underway. Otherwise I'll fire you on the spot and get someone who can properly perform the job. Do you understand?"

The conductor strained and squinted in the dawning sun to check the train a final time. He saw no one on either side. At the shanty, three mechanical department employees sat on a wooden bench outside the door. Two others stood talking nearby.

The conductor's resolve collapsed under Durant's threats. He leaned out and raised and lowered his lantern giving the signal to proceed.

Five cars away the locomotive engineer saw the signal he was waiting for. He released the engine brake, blew the whistle, and pulled the throttle lever. The train lurched forward.

They moved no more than a few feet when the workmen at the shanty came alive. They rushed toward the train frantically waving their arms in panic.

"Something's wrong!" cried the conductor. He swung his lantern wildly, giving emergency stop signals to the engineer.

But the engineer, who had acted on the signal to proceed, was watching the tracks ahead as the train gained momentum to climb out of the river bottom.

Durant looked curiously at the frenzied conductor. He saw the panicked men outside, one wringing his hands in despair. Now calm, Doc waited for his slow-moving train to build speed.

They had moved no more than three car-lengths when Durant's palace passed over and revealed a man's twisted body lying between the rails. His legs lay severed at the knees in a pool of dark blood. Colton, Doc and the conductor stood on the back platform and realized the contorted mass was a worker. The man's head lay twisted and watched them with blank, lifeless eyes.

The conductor continued swinging his lantern with emergency stop signals. At last the locomotive fireman saw the conductor's lantern light. The train made an easy stop with the dead man still in clear sight of Durant's car.

Durant's anger reignited. "What the hell is going on? Why are we stopped?" he screamed, wild eyes darting about.

The conductor doubled his fists but controlled himself. "We departed too early. One of the mechanical department men was still working under the train. We've killed him."

"Oh," said Durant. The compassionless, single word was the closest Durant ever came to acknowledging regret. Recovering quickly he demanded, "How long will this take?"

The conductor ignored Durant, stepped off the train, and ran back to his fallen comrade where the mechanical employees now hovered in shock over the gruesome sight.

With the conductor gone, Dr. Durant turned his wrath on Colton. "Don't just stand there. Do something. Get us moving again!"

"Doctor, we've just killed a man, one of our own. It's going to take a while to clear up this tragedy."

Durant was out of control. "Get him off my tracks. Not only has he delayed my train, he's going to delay every other essential activity around here."

Colton felt his own ire rising from the total disrespect for a fallen employee. "I'll see what I can do," he said curtly.

It was two hours before the train was underway again. In the interim Durant sat on the car alone, except for the valet and chef who managed to stay at the opposite end of the car. Durant sulked.

"Did you wire ahead to Seymour and the others about our delay?"

"Yes, sir. They are waiting for us at Fremont," Colton answered. He was appalled that Durant was devoid of sympathy. There was no interest in the dead man whatsoever, other than the train delay.

Colton brooded silently on the run to Fremont with a new understanding of a man without empathy.

Durant stayed busy reviewing charts and documents. He never mentioned the incident again.

At Fremont, Silas Seymour climbed on the train with a host of railroad officials. Only Seymour and Colton rode with Durant. The rest waited in other cars dreading an inevitable summons before the great wolf.

Durant was quite talkative with Seymour for it had been several months since their last face-to-face discussion.

"The newspapers say the bridge agreement is done," Seymour probed.

"I had the Omaha men outgunned from the start," Durant said with a wicked smile. "They never realized there is no real option but to build at Omaha. They failed to read my bluff, and it cost them dearly."

"I figured as much," Seymour laughed knowing the proper way to respond to Durant's levity.

"How is Dodge doing handling two jobs at once?" Seymour asked in a slightly snide tone.

"Dodge is spending too much time in Washington and too little time pushing Casement. I overestimated the man thinking he could handle both jobs."

"I've developed several route changes that Dodge should consider," Seymour offered. "My proposals call for more track miles and fewer bridges, as you like. The improvements I propose will have no impact on the railroad's completion date."

Durant's face lit up. "Finally something positive from you! More miles and government incentives. Fewer bridges. Same construction timetable. I like your plan already. Show me the details," Durant said.

Seymour had a map at hand and unrolled it on the table.

"Dodge will veto the extra miles and curves, of course. He is a straight-line engineer," Seymour worried.

"But Dodge isn't here, is he?" Durant shot back. "Dodge can't properly make these decisions while serving as a Congressman."

"I'm worried Dodge will go berserk if you change his plans without talking to him. You gave him full control over engineering and route matters," Seymour warned.

"I don't care, Silas," Durant said firmly. "Dodge is out of the picture. I'll change any plans I want. Fact is, I've been thinking about firing Dodge for a while now. I don't need him any longer."

Colton cringed at the mention of firing Dodge.

"And as long as we're changing Dodge's plans," Durant continued, "you might as well know I've decided to move the Cheyenne shops to Laramie. I've sold all my Cheyenne property, but lots in Laramie are selling too slowly. Moving the shops should pick up sales."

Colton, still distressed over the employee death in Omaha, now had the shock of hearing Durant might fire Dodge out of greed and selfishness. And what about the people of Cheyenne? Hadn't they purchased property and staked their futures on the promise the city was planned as a major point for Union Pacific?

As the train rolled on, Colton felt a change sweep over him as profound as any man can feel when the limits of tolerance and self-appeasement are exceeded. He knew in that moment he must oppose Durant, if not for Dodge and the country, then for his own conscience.

The remainder of the trip galvanized Colton's resolve.

* * * *

DURANT SUMMONED the materials superintendent to his car as the train rolled through Grand Island. He arrived with a satchel of documents and reports, but he never got the chance to unlatch the hasp.

Durant began with blunt facts. "You're buying cross ties from an unauthorized company instead of Chicago Timber Company. Why?"

It was an easy question for Union Pacific's top purchaser. He answered confidently. "Premier Woods produces better materials at a third less price. They deliver anywhere along the line while Chicago Timber delivers only to Omaha. Also, Chicago has furnished too many cross ties that fail to meet our minimum size standards."

"Do I need to remind you that policy, my policy, is to use favored vendors only? You are buying from a non-favored company. If you want to continue working here, you will use only the vendors that management specifies."

"But, sir—"

"Stop!" Durant roared, holding up his hand and slicing through the air like a knife. "One more insubordinate word from you and I'll fire you and have you thrown off the train right here. Now, will you follow my instructions, or will I have to hire someone who will?"

He answered submissively avoiding eye contact. "I will follow your policy, sir."

"You don't deserve to be in my presence. You're lucky I'm feeling benevolent. I'll wait until the next stop to eject you. Get out of here. Gather your things. You have materials orders to cancel."

"Yes, sir," came the dejected, humiliated reply.

Silas pounced when the materials superintendent left. "I tried to tell him the same thing, boss. Told him again and again. Use Chicago Timber, I said. He refused to listen. He thinks we're silent partners with Chicago Timber."

"He can prove nothing," Durant said. "I wouldn't care if he could."

A memory flashed in Colton's mind. Silent partners? Chicago Timber, the preferred vendor, regularly delivered locked brass boxes to Durant. In theory Durant could be buying timber at inflated prices, and taking a discount in gold. Colton worried he was an unwitting participant. His gut told him something was crooked.

"Rusk! Wake up! Go get the general agent," Durant barked. "Silas, while we're waiting, show me the tunnel proposal for Weber Canyon."

Colton jumped to his feet and made his way through the train. The general agent, a man named Lawrence Phipps, was two cars ahead with his staff.

He was a tall, silver-haired man dressed immaculately in a business suit. Durant had personally hired him for his salesmanship skills and a long track record for cultivating railroad traffic.

The general agent strode into the observation room, handed Durant a twelve page report, and confidently sat down. Despite his composure and professional appearance, the agent's time with Durant went badly.

Nothing ignited Durant as quickly as low revenues and a poor plan. It took Doc less than five minutes to reduce the general agent to confused blabbering. Reaching the end of his tolerance, Durant lashed out.

"It's as obvious as rain that you don't have the first clue about what business we enjoy or how to increase it. There is nothing of substance in your report. Exactly how incompetent are you?"

Phipps mounted his defense. "We don't have much of a working railroad yet. Populations are still too small to support industry, especially in hostile Indian Territory. And I do have a plan. It's right there in my report, on page nine."

"You call this a plan? You dedicated two paragraphs to Salt Lake City? There's nothing in here detailing industrial potential. There's nothing about agricultural products or markets. This is the worst report I've ever read. Here's what I think of your plan," Durant shouted.

Red-faced and pulsing with anger, Durant threw the reports at the general agent, hitting him squarely in the face.

"Get off my train! Get out of my sight." Durant screamed. "If you don't generate more revenue, we'll be out of business in a year. I'd better see improved numbers in a month or you're done here!"

In a final flash of rage, Durant threw a candy dish as the general agent scurried to leave. From a bad aim, the dish hit the overhead doorframe showering the agent and room with candy mints.

It was a long, bruising afternoon. Colton and Seymour watched as Durant chewed up and spit out railroad officers, one after the other. By the time the train stopped for the night at Lexington, Doc had ejected all but a handful from the train.

He turned out the division's top track manager for a track section with a rough ride. He threw off the top mechanical man for having too many expensive repair parts at his shops. The land agent from Laramie won his ejection at a wayside station for setting real estate prices too low. Durant was like a rampaging wolf in a sheep herd.

In the siding at Lexington, Durant grew moody and sat staring blank-eyed at the wall. An hour passed before Colton found the courage to break Durant's trance.

"Excuse me, Doc. Shall I invite the managers still on the train for dinner?"

"No. Lord, no. I have to work tonight. You and Seymour will dine with me. Just the three of us," Durant answered.

Now focused on Colton, Durant's voice turned forceful. "What are our security arrangements for tomorrow?"

"The army has extra patrols out, and our train will have twenty-five sharpshooters. The Indians are quiet, just breaking winter camps."

"After the derailment last fall, General Sherman promised to send more troops. Did I get anything more than lip service?" Durant asked.

"New troops are arriving every day, sir," Colton answered. "Colonel Newman expects another five hundred soldiers before the end of the month."

"I guess it's better than nothing," Durant said, unsure if he was satisfied with the answer or with Sherman.

In a private car dining room that would easily accommodate sixteen people, the three men ate French cuisine in silence. Not even the table's flower centerpiece brought the slightest comment. Durant had no small talk for his assistants. They knew to keep quiet.

After dinner, Durant kept Colton and Seymour on standby while he wrote a dozen telegrams. When he finished, he thrust the messages at Colton.

"Have these sent right away, and then make sure the arrangements for my end of rail news conference are finalized."

Colton was glad to break away from the business car. As he walked onto the back platform, Durant was already raising his voice at Seymour over a depot blueprint that seemed too extravagant.

Colton watched the local agent transmit Doc's telegrams and then sent two of his own. His first telegram was to Libby. The second message, coded, went to Washington with no regret, no second thought and no disloyal emotions. He knew the second telegram would incite swift action.

* * * *

THE FOLLOWING MORNING, Durant's special train left Lexington, Nebraska, loaded with sharpshooters and a fresh crop of grim-faced railroad officers.

Before they traveled a hundred miles, Durant fired two officers and ejected three others in a hail of threats. So it went over the next two days as the train passed North Platte, Julesburg, and Cheyenne. On the fourth day, they approached the railhead and the news conference.

The newspaper reporters who followed the railroad's progress were starving for new information. Excitement built from the moment they learned of the upcoming press conference. Durant's train pulled into the railroad's newest siding near the end of track and found thirty reporters eager to hear fresh news.

For Colton, it was no surprise when Dr. Durant emerged on the back platform smiling brightly. He was a different man than the tyrant of the last four days. Durant greeted the media with handshakes, pats on the back, and knowing winks to the ones he knew.

"Gentlemen of the press," he began with a sugar-coated tone. "Thank you so much for coming today. I will begin by reading a prepared statement. Afterwards, I will take any questions you have. Your readers have a right to know about the historic work underway."

He said all the right words in the right tenor and with a faultless delivery that made an insignificant announcement about new train services sound sensational. The reporters melted like butter in his hands. He extolled General Casement's miraculous progress, championed the American dream, and promised to give the nation the finest railroad in the world.

He opened the train's dining rooms to the group and fed them a delicious lunch on fine china. By mid-afternoon, the happy reporters departed, eager to expand the Durant myth.

News dispatches telegraphed from the frontier that night carried high praise for Durant. Morning newspapers across America and Europe portrayed Doc Durant as an energetic leader, a hero accomplishing the impossible. One newspaper proclaimed, "Thomas Durant is the foremost transportation expert in the history of the world. Because of him, men are accomplishing feats heretofore unseen by mankind."

* * * *

WHILE THE WORLD read of Durant's achievements, Jack Casement scraped the mud off his boots and entered Doc's car.

Durant approached the breakfast meeting knowing he must be careful to avoid angering General Casement. The little man had a big reputation for toughness and a hot temper.

"I was hoping to see your construction further along," Doc said between bites of Quiche Cher.

"We continue to work at world record pace," Casement replied. "I calculate we'll have the road completed seven years ahead of plan."

"Seven years early. Yes. That is good, of course," replied Durant. "Yet I wonder how we can do better. There is danger that Central Pacific will reach Ogden before you. In my estimation, you should be thirty miles further west than you are. Have I not given you everything you've asked for? Have I not paid you well?"

"You have provided everything I've asked for, Doctor."

"Then why can't you go faster? And what is this manpower problem you seem to be having? The morning reports show that your man counts vary from day to day as much as a hundred men."

"Hell On Wheels takes a huge toll on us," General Casement answered.

"I've heard of it. So what?"

"We're losing up to five men per week to murder and gamblers. Hundreds more can't report because they're drunk in the mornings. I'd fire them, but we have no replacements."

"Are we paying them too much? If so, I can solve that problem."

"No, Doc. If you disrupt their pay, you won't have any men at all."

"What about the law? Are they helping?" Durant asked.

"No. The Territorial Marshall is more concerned with wagon trains than our workers. He doesn't have the men to take on Hell on Wheels."

Durant was losing control. He struggled to keep his voice at a normal volume, but his fierce eyes were those of a wild man.

"Are you so weak you can't run off a few prostitutes and gamblers? Do I need to send in a stronger man, like Rusk here, to clean up Hell on Wheels? You're not getting the job done, Casement. You either figure this out or we'll renegotiate your contract."

"I plan to take care of Hell on Wheels. Rusk has other important duties to take care of," General Casement replied.

"You should have already solved this problem long ago," said Durant, barely controlling his annoyance.

Durant calmed himself.

Casement felt embarrassment at Durant's slap on the wrist. Such a dressing down was unusual for a general.

Colton felt relief that dismantling Hell on Wheels would fall to someone else.

Dr. Durant Plots His Next Move At The End Of Track
Original Photograph by Andrew J. Russell
Public Domain Image Courtesy of New York Public Library

Chapter 31

Congressman Grenville Dodge was about to vent his frustration on an aide. "I came to Washington to make laws," he said. "Why must I spend so much time listening to citizen grievances and bureaucrats?"

"That's the way Washington works, sir," the aide responded, laying a stack of letters and telegrams on the desk.

"I detest paperwork! I can hardly wait for my next trip west. I need to be on the railroad with my construction crews and surveyors. Here I am, stuck in an office."

The aide was uninterested in Dodge's complaints and turned to leave. "Let me know if you need anything," he said blandly as he closed the door.

Dodge grudgingly began opening mail and making notes about how he wanted each item handled. The ninth envelope was a telegram. He saw at first glance the message was in code. A bolt of recognition ran through him causing him to sit upright.

He transcribed the message easily. It was the code he had created for his staff in the Iowa Fourth Infantry. Clearly, the unsigned message was from someone he had served with in the war. It read:

> *Durant has taken personal control of railroad construction and is making major changes per Seymour's recommendations. Your instructions are countermanded. Railroad shops are to be moved from Cheyenne to Laramie. Route, bridge and tunnel changes are planned to maximize government payments.*

Dodge's eyes lit up. "This is from Colton Rusk," he exclaimed. Within an hour, Dodge was packed and had his private car hooked to a locomotive in Washington station. He sped west to Council Bluffs, arriving on the third day in time to spend the night at home while crews ferried his car across the river. The next morning he raced westward from Omaha.

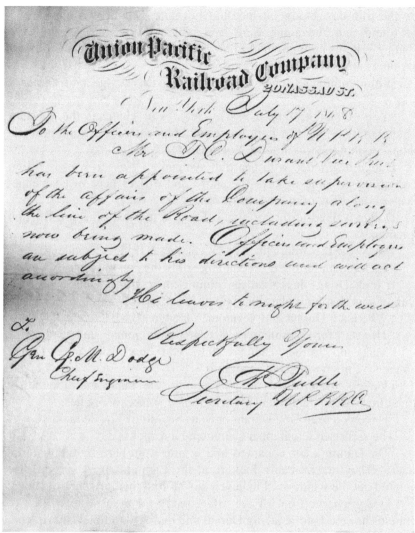

July 17, 1868, notice issued at New York on Durant's instruction:

"To the Officer and Employees of UPRR.   Mr. T. C. Durant Vice Pres't has been appointed to take supervision of the affairs of the Company along the line of road including surveys now being made. Officers and employees are subject to his directions and will act accordingly. He leaves tonight for the west."

From the personal papers of Dr. Thomas C. Durant
maintained in the Levi O. Leonard Collection,
University of Iowa

By the fifth day, Dodge arrived in Cheyenne. Durant was nowhere to be found, but the signs were everywhere. Scores of people were loading wagons and moving to Laramie. Men labored to dismantle new buildings and ready them for transport.

Within minutes, angry citizens recognized Dodge and cornered him.

"You're bankrupting us! Why have you changed the division headquarters point? We built homes and businesses here, and now the shops are moving to Laramie. You misled us."

Dodge responded with heartfelt sympathy. "I assure you I will do everything possible to keep the shops and offices here in Cheyenne. Please hold off your move a while longer."

Dodge walked to the railroad office and met with the construction foreman.

"Show me the orders for all plan changes," Dodge demanded.

The foreman unrolled several large drawings on the table.

It took Dodge less than ten minutes to confirm what he feared. Durant was changing plans in mid-construction.

"Where are Durant and Seymour?" Dodge asked.

"They left for Laramie two days ago," the foreman said.

"Make no further changes until you hear from me," Dodge ordered. "I'm on my way to Laramie."

Dodge's train rolled on to Laramie. He burst into the newly constructed depot and found the telegrapher sorting messages.

"Have you seen Doc Durant or Silas Seymour?" he demanded.

The surprised telegrapher stammered a response.

"Dr. Durant's car is parked half a mile from here by the material stacks. They are probably looking at the Laramie street survey." He pointed out the window. "I believe you can find them in that direction."

Dodge charged out of the office ready for a showdown. In five minutes he stood alone facing Durant and his staff on the dusty streets.

Durant saw Dodge was red-faced and spitting mad. "What are you doing here, Congressman?" Durant's face showed surprise and alarm.

Dodge lashed out. "You are guilty of changing my plans without talking to me. You violated our clear eye to eye agreement about my authority. I will *not* allow you to change my plans."

"Oh, that. Well, the directors have given me broad authority to make any changes I see fit," Durant retorted with an ugly smile.

Windmill and new shops at Laramie, Wyoming
Original Photograph by Andrew J. Russell
Public Domain Photograph courtesy of New York Public Library

"No. I'm holding you to the agreement we made when I resigned from the army. I make the decisions about routes, and town locations. I set the specification for bridges and tunnels, not you. You are to stay out of it. That was our agreement." They now stood toe to toe.

No one watching dared say anything as all semblances of good terms evaporated.

"Unfortunately for you, our agreement has changed," Durant said. "I am taking more control here for the good of the stockholders."

"One more word from you, Durant, and I'll take control of your scrawny throat. You've made your last change reducing standards on this nation's railroad."

Dodge was ready to fight, but no one moved to counter him. Dodge was shorter but fully trained for physical action if needed. Durant, taller, puffed up and looked down menacingly on Dodge.

They stood staring at each other for a full thirty seconds, Durant bluffing, and Dodge ready for combat on Laramie's newly staked streets. Durant was the first to blink. He merely turned and walked away.

Dodge shouted at Durant's retreating back. "You are going to learn that the men of Union Pacific take orders from me, not you! If you try to interfere with me you will have serious trouble from the government, the army, and the men themselves. This road is going to be built properly for the nation, not shoddily for your profits. You are the New York finance man, nothing more!"

* * * *

DURANT AND HIS assistants, including Colton Rusk, walked quickly to their private car. Durant locked the doors, visibly shaken from the encounter.

"Rusk! Get this train rolling. We're going to Omaha. Silas, you will get off at Cheyenne to keep an eye on Dodge. Firing Dodge may be harder than I thought, but I am already working on the plan."

Twenty minutes later Durant's train moved the half mile to the Laramie telegraph office and stopped. Colton dropped off the car to send telegrams and update the train dispatcher. From the door Colton saw Dodge writing his own telegrams. Dodge looked up at Colton and smiled.

"Thank you," Dodge said privately. "Your telegram will save an entire town. I came as quickly as I could. A lot of people and the railroad would have suffered without your intervention. It was the right thing to do."

"Be cautious, General," Colton said. "You won this battle, but your war with Durant isn't over. He's already plotting the next attack. Fact is, Durant is out to fire you."

"I wish I had time to worry about Doc, but between Congress and railroad duties I'll have a hard time keeping an eye on him."

Ten minutes later, Colton was steaming toward Omaha and home.

* * * *

DARCY LONIGAN SAT alone at a table in a scalding tent saloon in Wyoming. It was a miserable place to drink rot gut whiskey and spend a half-day off, but it was all he had. He welcomed any rest for his aching muscles. Working with bridge timbers was backbreaking work.

Outside, the tent bore a weathered plank sign reading "Rails End Saloon." The tent had been at this location for thirty-six hours. A week earlier it had housed a thriving business on the outskirts of Laramie. Three weeks before that it had been a popular saloon in Cheyenne.

The Rails End Saloon was an anchor establishment in Hell On Wheels. Like the other gambling houses and saloons, it existed for the sole purpose of separating railroad men from their wages through any means necessary, legal or not.

Lonigan drank and watched a woman dancing on a makeshift stage made from two tables shoved together. She was nineteen years old at most, yet bore the unmistakable weathered look of a hard life.

Dance music clinked from an ancient piano that had seen its best days long ago, even before moving countless miles in the back of a wagon. No one seemed to mind the tinny sound or out-of-tune notes.

The patrons, including Darcy Lonigan, were filthy, shaggy men with heavy beards. They thirsted for whiskey and reveled in escape from the harsh rigors of railroad construction. Nearly all, when sufficiently intoxicated, would be lured into gambling against experts who kept the odds heavily in their favor.

Lonigan brooded over his pathetic condition. "'Tis unfair," he lamented. "I'm as fine a man as the next, certainly better than me railroad bosses." A deep-seated hatred surfaced. He whispered to his whiskey glass. "People like that cripple Rusk are lower than the dirt under me finger nail. He's a waste of a man - and a fine woman as well."

The bartender came from behind the bar and approached the familiar customer.

"Ready for another hit?" the bartender asked. "An Irishman is never drunk as long as he can hold onto one blade of grass to keep from falling off the earth, eh, Lonigan?"

"I'm a wee bit low on cash. I'll pay on credit this time until payday in two days. I've been a regular here for the last 600 miles."

The bartender's chummy attitude turned sour. "I don't take anything except gold," said the bartender. "No gold. No whiskey. You know the rules."

"Not even one drink on credit, after all the gold I've given you?"

"Ah. See? You Irishmen can understand the rules. No drinks on credit. Not ever. I have a cash business, and it will remain so. Either lay down gold, or get out. This table is for paying customers."

Lonigan felt the fury rising in him. When pushed, something in his elemental nature required him to push back. He had no more control of his instincts than a wounded animal that bites its keeper. This headstrong bartender had gouged him regularly. Lonigan wondered how much gold he had given this money-grubbing bartender for watered-down whiskey. He felt his face redden in anger.

The two stared at each other, tensions intensifying. Both knew Lonigan was debating action.

As Lonigan reached for his knife, a gunshot shattered the moment. Lonigan and the bartender shifted their focus to a gambler standing nearby over the lifeless body of a railroad worker. The gambler holstered his pistol. Lonigan could see the dead man was a workman from his gang.

The piano music and the dancing girl stopped and stared. The red-faced bartender threw his towel next to the whiskey bottle on Lonigan's table. He rushed toward the dead man and the card shark.

"Calm down, Marsh," the gambler called to the bartender. "He accused me of cheating. Called me a bald-faced cheater. I had to protect my honor."

Lonigan ignored their confrontation and poured a free drink from the unattended bottle. He watched the familiar scene, one he had witnessed three times before.

The saloon keeper closed in on the gambler screaming wildly. "That's the fourth man you've shot in my saloon. And it's the last one. Get out! You'll not set foot in my place again."

Before the gambler could argue, a dozen armed men stormed in the front of the tent. The saloon remained silent. All eyes now turned to the intruders.

The leader turned to his men, "Get this poor, dead soul out of here. See if you can identify him. He looks like one of ours." Then to the crowded saloon he shouted, "You railroad men, teamsters, and mule whackers have five minutes to get out. This slime pit is out of business. The tent and all contents will be burned. Get moving. All Union Pacific men will assemble outside."

To the saloon owner, the leader said, "General Casement wants you to know you've killed your last railroad man. You're on railroad property. Clear out of the territory or you'll hang tomorrow."

The saloon owner rushed behind the long bar and retrieved a pistol. Three gamblers pulled pistols to defend their lifestyle. It was over in seconds. The hail of fire took down the saloon owner, the three gamblers, and two Union Pacific workers who were unable to get out of the way.

In the confusion, Lonigan managed to commandeer the unattended whisky bottle and take the cash box from behind the counter. He escaped out a tent flap as the remaining U.P. workers assembled for a sobering lecture.

Lonigan was more than half way to the railroad camp before he slowed. He heard distant gunfire and looked back at Hell on Wheels. At least four tents and temporary buildings were on fire with flames blazing high and lighting the night sky.

He checked to ensure he was alone and then stepped out of sight behind a rock outcropping. Five minutes later, he had the cash box and whiskey safely buried. Lonigan continued to the railroad camp.

After midnight, when he retrieved the cash box, Lonigan found disappointment inside. It contained two hundred dollars, not nearly enough to leave the railroad. Bitterness flared inside him. He was stuck in the desert with no saloon. Lonigan transferred the stolen money into a small canvas bag and hid it among his belongings. Tomorrow he would return to his job cutting, shaping and moving bridge timbers

"What kind of railroad would shoot its own employees?" Lonigan mused, staring at an empty bunk.

Chapter 32

JULY 7, 1868 – ULYSSES GRANT INTERCEDES

In the early days, Omaha had a small freshwater lake near downtown. It is still there. Then, as now, the lake blocked Howard and Harney Streets from reaching the Missouri River. Farnam Street, however, was different in that it ran past the north lakeshore and continued to the riverboat landings.

Nature formed Heartland Lake, as it is now called, long before the white man came. It was created when the river, in one of its moody phases, suddenly grew tired of its course and moved east. The lake it left became one of nature's better gifts to Omaha.

The Indians considered the lake a holy place set aside from the muddy river to quench the Great Spirit's thirst. The Omaha Indians buried their dead overlooking the lake to bring them closer to their gods. The burial mounds still dotted the banks when Lewis and Clark visited the site and wrote about them in 1804.

After the white man came, the lake met different needs. As far back as anyone could remember, it had served as an ice skating area in the winter and a swimming hole in the summer. The little strip of land between Farnam Street and the lake became Omaha's beach resort.

July 1869 was hotter than normal causing the grasses to turn tan and Omaha's dirt streets to fracture into fine powder. Early summer rains had filled the lake to capacity, so that when July was at its hottest, the lake still had a good swimming depth.

William Rusk had no thoughts of the Great Spirit or Indian graveyards as he hurried down Farnam Street toward the lake. Now seventeen years old, his thoughts were of meeting friends and cooling off after a hard day's work at the hardware store.

At work, he had impressed his boss, Mr. Witliff, long ago, earning him responsibilities beyond stocking the shelves and stacking boxes. Now in his fifth year, William had authority to verify and sign for shipments, order merchandise, and keep accounts. Customers praised Mr. Witliff for having such a fine assistant.

"How many part-time employees can recommend the perfect valve for a two inch water line?" Mr. Witliff once bragged to Colton.

From a window of the Union Pacific offices in the Herndon House, Doctor Durant looked across the street and onto the lake.

"Frivolous teenagers," he scoffed. "Wasting their lives. Their time would be better spent working or studying."

Durant watched a handsome teenage boy walk onto the dirt strand never realizing it was William Rusk. How could Doc know the boy? He had never taken any interest in meeting Colton's family. It was a social slight Colton and Libby made excuses for but never forgot.

Across the room, Colton continued working without responding to Durant's remark. Neither did he see his son enjoying the afternoon.

"General Grant is coming west, you know," Durant said turning away from the window.

"I had no idea. What is he coming for?" Colton stopped working.

"It's part of his presidential campaign. He wants to show America he's knowledgeable about the plains and the Indians. He'll get headlines for coming to check on Union Pacific. He wants his name in the paper, and we're big news. Visiting U.P. is very presidential."

"Will you meet with him?" Colton asked.

"I plan to. After all, Grant will probably be our next president." Durant suddenly changed the subject. "By the way, where is Dodge?"

Colton knew it was more than a random question. Doc never used a phrase like "by the way" unless he was plotting.

"The morning report shows Dodge is in Utah reviewing Seymour's recommendation to build around a mountain rather than bore a tunnel. He plans to work his way to Green River and Cheyenne," Colton answered.

"Good. Get my train ready. We're going west to wait for Grant."

* * * *

TWO WEEKS later Dodge stood with a construction superintendent and two surveyors on the rocky banks of the Green River in the Wyoming Territory. Above him Citadel Rock stood bare and foreboding. Behind him a water tower neared completion for the railroad and the new town of Green River.

"By the time Brigham Young gets his eight thousand Mormon boys to Echo and Weber Canyons," Dodge told his companions, "Union Pacific will have almost thirty thousand men working in one way or another. It's more men than I ever commanded in the war. I'm a bit awed by the size of our operation."

He examined the line of wooden stakes marching down to the riverbank and up the far bank marking the planned bridge location.

"We can't wait for the permanent bridge," Dodge suddenly exclaimed. "Casement is pushing west so hard we won't have enough time to build it before the track layers arrive. We need a temporary bridge downstream," he said, pointing.

He turned to the construction superintendent. "Assign your bridge makers to build it. Get it done, and then move them on west. Leave a fifth of the masons here to work on the permanent abutments. They can take their time and build a first-class crossing."

Green River Wyoming
Original Photograph by Andrew J. Russell
The temporary bridge and abutments for the permanent bridge.
Public domain photograph courtesy of New York Public Library

Dodge was still pondering the best spot for the temporary bridge when a rider caught his attention. He was coming in hard from the direction of the new telegraph office at Green River.

"Urgent message for you, General Dodge. It just came," the rider announced.

Dodge opened the envelope expecting a new life-death crisis from Durant. It was a coded message, as expected, but the code! This was another message from Colton Rusk using Dodge's own code.

Before the sun disappeared behind the Wyoming mountains, Dodge was on a stagecoach headed east at full speed to Laramie.

* * * *

July 26, 1868 - Fort Sanders, Laramie Wyoming
AT LARAMIE SIDING, four men stepped off the business car and mounted horses for the three mile ride to Fort Sanders. They rode southeast following the railroad tracks, departing in ample time for Dr. Durant's nine o'clock meeting with Ulysses S. Grant.

Durant took the lead position, as he always did when there were no recent reports of Indian sightings.

Colton and Silas Seymour followed in their assigned spots. The fourth rider was Sidney Dillon, a U.P. Director and Durant's crony.

"My top goal today," Durant had bragged to Dillon at breakfast, "is to cultivate the right environment to fire Dodge. Everything I say to Grant will cast Dodge in bad light. I intend to announce Dodge's firing at the meeting. Don't let your jaw drop in surprise."

* * * *

AT FORT SANDERS, General Grant waited for Dr. Durant in the base commander's office. He was in good company. General Sherman, General Harney, and General Sheridan stood at his side giving counsel. Before the meeting, they briefed the future president on the tricky financier. Grant had heard such warnings about Durant before.

The four riders soon saw Fort Sanders looming. Colton's first thoughts on seeing the fort was how flimsy it looked. The wooden walls would easily fall to any foe with cannons. It was fortunate, he thought, that the Indians lacked heavy artillery.

Durant led the way through the fort's gates and onto the parade grounds. Colton gave the barracks and officer quarters a passing grade. He knew the fort was only two years old, built to protect settlers and wagon trains moving along the Overland Trail. Now, with the railroad, the fort was helping to protect thousands of U.P. workers.

The meeting began on time at nine around a conference table.

General Grant wore a dark business suit. It was a different look from the military uniforms Colton was accustomed to, and it took a minute to adjust to it.

Durant too noticed the suit. To him, it looked like a cheap garment purchased off the rack at the Laramie general store.

"Probably bought it yesterday," Durant whispered to Dillon. Both wore perfectly fitting custom-made suits that would have cost an average man a year's earnings.

Colton watched Doc as he sized up the most famous military general since George Washington. Durant considered Grant in the same category as Lincoln. They were both public servants, fed by the people, and performing the intellectual equivalent of charity jobs.

Colton recalled hearing Durant rave about Grant's failure as a businessman. "He would have been nothing without the war. Killing people doesn't take a lot of skill," Durant had chuckled with mean-hearted satisfaction and the full support of expensive cognac.

Colton remembered Durant's comments about public servants. "Who do you think controls this country, Rusk?" he had asked at the time.

"You probably think that government officials and military leaders guide our country. That's what you think, isn't it?"

"Truth is, Rusk, even the president answers to money and the captains of finance. Popular vote may elect presidents, but it's money and people like me they answer to. You ask about congressmen? I can't name one I wouldn't kick in the shins. I've done it many times."

Durant raged on. "Lincoln? Even he was a hired hand, just like you. Believe me, Lincoln answered to money too, just like all the rest."

Remembering that distasteful episode, Colton was uncertain what to expect from Durant. He was surprised when Doc spoke respectfully.

"Thank you for meeting with me, General Grant," Durant began.

Grant was equally civil. "I saw your construction teams from a bluff yesterday. Thousands of men. All very engaged. I had a chance to talk with General Casement. He seems to be doing to superb job."

Durant responded, "Counting the iron plants, timber and other suppliers, plus the freight haulers and steamboats, we have close to thirty thousand men employed for the project. We expect to reach Ogden in January ahead of Central Pacific. We should finish the entire railroad before June next year."

Grant smiled broadly. "An 1869 completion? That *is* good news. People have criticized me for supporting the railroad with so many troops. The quicker you get this railroad completed, the sooner we can close redundant forts in the west. A mobile army will be less expensive."

Durant detected opportunity and seized it.

"Frankly, General Grant, I need to share my concern over a serious threat to completing the railroad."

Grant gestured for Durant to continue.

"We are desperately tight on finances, and the responsibility fall to one man," Durant said. "It saddens me to tell you that Chief Engineer Dodge's work is unsatisfactory. He's saddled us with bad routes, expensive tunnels, and unneeded bridges. I'm disappointed he's not up to the job. To our credit, we've made progress despite Dodge, not because of him."

General Grant's brow furrowed.

"I'm going to have to replace him," Durant added. "I thought it was important for you to hear it directly from me."

Before Grant could answer, a commotion outside disrupted the meeting. General Sherman rushed to the window to see what the uproar was.

"It appears a stagecoach has arrived at full speed," Sherman announced. "It stopped just outside. I have no idea what—. Wait. Well, you won't believe who is coming in," Sherman said grinning.

Grenville Dodge threw the door open and stepped in. The surprise was so complete, so unexpected, that Durant was left sitting with his mouth wide open. The last thing Durant expected was a showdown with Dodge in the presence of the future president.

Ulysses Grant was the first to grasp the moment and speak.

"Ah! General Dodge. You have blessed us with a very timely appearance. Doctor Durant was just telling me how he is going to fire you. Please continue with what you were saying, Doctor."

Grant looked at Durant with a half-smirk.

Durant tried to rally his presentation to save face.

"Well, as I was saying, General Dodge has become incompetent. His routes are impossible. His standards are gold plated. The railroad, indeed the nation, cannot afford such luxuries. His ineptness has reached such extremes that I have had to step in to personally countermand many of his decisions."

Silas Seymour nodded his approval of Durant's statements. Durant concluded his case.

"I have the revised drawings if you care to see them. Dodge's poor work speaks for itself," Durant said with conviction.

Ulysses Grant nodded, and then turned to Dodge. "What about it Dodge? What say you?"

Dodge appeared relaxed, his fury suppressed.

"Even a broken clock shows the right time twice a day, but in Mr. Seymour's plans, I haven't seen anything right yet."

Grant chuckled. General Sherman shot a menacing look at Seymour as Dodge continued confidently.

"Indeed, I encourage you to examine Mr. Seymour's plans. You will quickly conclude they call for needless construction miles. For that, we will build a less direct railroad with little available water. The only thing we will get more of is sand, something we don't need. Mr. Seymour's plans give more immediate profits to Doctor Durant while strapping the railroad with terrible long-term operating expense."

Dodge paused a moment and unrolled one of Seymour's plans. "Unlike these plans," he continued, "my plans meet strict engineering standards. The government's own inspectors have approved my plans."

Grant gave a slight nod of understanding.

"Let me conclude by saying this: If anyone changes any more of my plans without my authority, I will resign and go to another railroad. I will take with me my loyal surveyors, construction chiefs, and any working man willing to join me."

The room was silent. Everyone waited for Ulysses Grant to speak. Colton was breathless. He knew he was witnessing a remarkable moment in history.

When Grant spoke his tone was sharp, honed as fine as a skinner's knife. He directed his sternness at the entire group.

"The government expects this railroad to be finished. The government expects the railroad company to meet is obligations to the people. And the government expects General Dodge to remain with the road as its Chief Engineer, fully in control of the routes and construction."

Grant then spoke directly to Durant with narrowed eyes.

"If you want to take me on by firing Dodge, then roll the dice, Doctor. See how smoothly your government funding and land grants go. See how effortlessly your road passes government inspections. Maybe we need to examine how many government inspectors own Crédit Mobilier stock."

Grant's strength was surprising, and for a moment Durant remained in stunned silence. Feuding with the man who was sure to be the next president was a course Durant could not take. He recognized defeat.

"I withdraw all my objections," Durant said without emotion. "We want Dodge to stay with Union Pacific."

The meeting broke up with a photographer posing the group to make a record of the occasion. Then all scattered to their separate worlds. Grenville Dodge gave Colton a secret pat on the back as the groups filed out the front door.

Durant returned to New York to fight with Senator Ames. He gave Colton a contemptuous glare as he mounted his horse. He had no reason for such hostility except it made him feel better. Durant never suspected it was Colton who had informed Dodge of the meeting.

That day, newspapers across the country reported that General Casement advanced the railhead west two miles.

Chapter 33

Colton holed up in the frozen confines of Omaha from the end of 1868 until late February, conducting business by mail and telegram. Colton slept at home every night while the snows swirled and built tall drifts against the homes and buildings.

Twelve hundred miles to the east, Durant wintered in New York, presumably with his family. Colton suspected Doc was actually renewing his feud with Senator Ames and the Union Pacific directors. Whatever Doc's real reasons, Colton enjoyed the time away from him.

Colton knew Durant would return soon and spend increasingly more time on the railroad as completion neared. Just last year, Colton had spent months with Doc watching him pester construction bosses and "tweak" Dodge's plans.

By March 1869, Union Pacific was laying track faster than ever. The race with Central Pacific brought daily headlines in newspapers around the world. Durant, Dodge, and Casement became household words. In Europe, the major newspapers followed the frantic construction race almost as closely as in America.

In one phenomenal day, Union Pacific workers built over seven miles of track. From New York, Durant bet $10,000 that his railroad's record would never fall, yet only a few days later he lost the bet when Central Pacific's Chinese workers laid over ten miles in one day.

* * * *

AGAINST THIS BACKGROUND, Colton lay awake in the predawn hours on a Sunday morning. His mind raced about the work he faced. Libby stirred next to him, awakened by the change in his breathing.

"You're awake," she whispered.

"Just thinking," he said softly.

She leaned into him and kissed his shoulder. "I can tell you're worried. Is everything all right?"

"Doc departs New York in two days for Omaha," Colton said. "I'm leasing a home for him today, probably the vacant Lutheran parsonage. Will you go with me to look at it?"

"You certainly know how to show a girl a good time," she joked. "Of course I'll go. Is Doc tired of the Herndon House?"

"It seems so, but I don't know for sure," Colton said.

They lay contentedly enjoying the silence for a moment before he spoke again.

"Dodge says we will complete the railroad in about six weeks. It's hard to believe. The nation will celebrate, politicians will give speeches, and then thousands of men will move on."

Libby asked the question he knew was coming. "What will become of us when the railroad is finished?"

"I don't know yet," Colton confessed. "I just don't know."

* * * *

DURANT'S TRAIN rolled into Council Bluffs at night under a black, violent thunderstorm, the worst the area had seen in years. In Omaha trees toppled and several roofs blew away.

Colton waited for the train in a punishing downpour punctuated by wind, hail and lightening. As the train pulled in, preparing to stop, six luxury cars passed in the dark. In a brightly lighted dining car, he saw a loud party: men drinking, laughing, and playing cards. Then, the party faded as Durant's private car reached him and the train stopped.

Colton was soaked to the bone when he climbed aboard the car. He found Durant sitting comfortably in the observation room with a tall, beautiful woman. Durant made no introduction. He seemed to be stone sober and impatient. If he had attended the party in the dining car, he had avoided drinking to excess.

"Do you have a covered carriage for me?" Durant greeted Colton.

"Yes, sir. It's waiting at the depot."

The rain was slowing.

Durant said, "Show me and my"—he paused—"my nurse to the new accommodations."

"You will be at the Lutheran parsonage, sir. We have a four month lease while they find a new preacher. What about the passengers, sir?"

"They're newspaper reporters. Go tell them I'm sick. Tell the station master they can stay on the train for the night."

Durant sprang to his feet and grabbed his bag as well as those of the elegantly dressed "nurse." He escorted her attentively to the carriage. The spring in his step and glint in his eye belied illness.

* * * *

IT IS IMPOSSIBLE to know if Durant's arrival and the thunderstorm were connected or mere coincidence. The horrible storm drew the attention of Libby's Bible study group the next day. Several ladies said the severity was a bad omen. Libby kept quiet.

Years later, she wondered if the storm had, in fact, been a sign of things that were about to happen.

* * * *

DURANT DISAPPEARED into the parsonage for a week. Colton visited twice daily to deliver telegrams and newspapers, and to check on his ailing boss. He always found outgoing messages on the front porch with orders for food and medicinal Scotch whiskey. He never saw Durant or the woman. No other signs of life came from the church's residence other than smoke from the chimney.

Colton concluded from the blunt outgoing messages that Durant was feeling well enough to remain in complete control. He gave crystal-clear instructions to the New York accountants.

We're out of money. Let the bills pile up while we finish the railroad. We'll sort out the finances after government funding. The important thing is to finish the road. Keep ordering what the railroad needs, but hold the bills. Stop all payments. T.C. Durant

To Casement and Dodge he wrote:

The question is no longer whether we can beat Central Pacific to Ogden. The question is how far we can get, how much land we can win before we meet CP. The new goal is winning land grants. Go all out for the finish. Spare no expense. Double the work hours if necessary. T. C. Durant

The Omaha Reporter noted Durant's arrival from New York and his lengthy illness. According to the article, Durant suffered a week before emerging. The article made no mention of the beautiful nurse who quietly slipped onto an eastbound train and returned to New York.

When he gained sufficient strength to walk about, Durant appeared, seeming fully recovered. He burst into the Herndon House office booming orders. By evening Colton was on Durant's private train traveling west.

Doc was in rare form lecturing managers at each station like a fire and brimstone preacher. Clearly he felt energized and ready to take dictatorial control of everything. True to his style, he shouted or threatened the strong managers into submission. Those already submissive, he trampled.

The only two escaping Durant's wrath were General Casement who ignored him, and Grenville Dodge who was in Washington negotiating the final meeting point for the two advancing roads.

After three grueling weeks on the railroad, Durant returned to Omaha, his voice reduced to a hoarse whisper from screaming. A messenger waited for the train and offered Durant an envelope. Durant hissed an inaudible response and grabbed the envelope. He read its contents, smiled and thrust the telegram at Colton.

Washington, D. C., April 8, 1869

Dr. T. C. Durant – Omaha

Central Pacific has agreed to meet our rails at Promontory, Utah. President Grant threatened to decide the point if no agreement was reached. C. P. agrees Promontory is best. I am coming west for the completion and ceremony.

G. M. Dodge

Durant gloated with satisfaction. He had beaten Central Pacific to Ogden and cornered them at a God-forsaken point in the Utah desert.

"If Central Pacific wants to buy our line into Ogden, I will sell it to them," he boasted to Colton. "But it will cost them dearly."

* * * *

Original Photograph by Andrew J. Russell
The approach trestle to Promontory, Utah.
Public domain phototraph courtesy of New York Public Lbirary

DURANT CANCELLED Colton's normal duties for the remainder of April and assigned him full time to preparing for the completion ceremony at Promontory. Durant knew his time to bask in glory was at hand. He craved having the world witness his crowning achievement.

"It is appropriate," he said with sparkling eyes and a healed voice, "that the last spike will be solid gold. I have long pictured myself striking the final blows."

Colton worked marathon hours coordinating travel plans for dignitaries and newsmen. He planned with the Western Union Telegraph Company so the actual sledgehammer strokes to the last spike would be transmitted to the world with a specially wired spike and hammer. He watched as workers stuffed every square inch of Durant's train with the best foods, delicacies and whisky available.

Perhaps someone should have told Doc, but no one dared. Someone should have said, "Doc, it's not all about you. It's about the railroad and the nation." No one said it. His huge ego could never have accepted it. Union Pacific was *his* railroad. This was *his* victory, *his* accomplishment. He was the great builder of the age.

New York, Washington, Philadelphia, San Francisco and hundreds of towns planned celebrations for the railroad's completion. It was a grand, national event that generated collective excitement never before felt in America.

On May 4, 1869, Durant's train left Omaha loaded with railroad executives, reporters, and dignitaries. The world's newspapers reported it in flowery praises that made Durant seem almost god-like in his power and achievements.

On the train, a non-stop celebration was underway. The party train rolled west through Fremont, Kearney and North Platte headed for history. At Cheyenne, Colton picked up telegraph reports that rains were causing problems in Western Wyoming. They charged on.

* * * *

THE PROMONTORY TRAIN left the main track at Buford, Wyoming to take on water and firewood. Dr. Durant stepped from the boisterous revelry onto his car's peaceful rear platform. His throat was beginning to hurt from thick clouds of cigar smoke and boisterous talk. He relaxed alone, looking up at the bluff next to the track.

The land here was rocky and almost barren. Here the prairie grasses grew thinner and the wild flowers fewer. It was the kind of harsh land Eastern journalists referred to as the uninhabitable American West.

But desert life thrived in the bluff above the train as it did throughout the West. Dozens of insect species inhabited the area feeding on scrawny semi-arid plants that also fed ground squirrels and birds. Higher up the food chain the predators, owls, snakes and an occasional coyote made their homes on the land.

Durant climbed off the car and without a word began climbing the bluff. Colton watched Durant nearly fall as his thin-soled French shoes slipped on the loose shale. The prairie grasses on the slope brushed against his dress pants depositing grass seeds and dust.

Colton watched from a window and wondered what Durant was doing. His instincts for trouble kicked in. It was a bad move for a tenderfoot to charge alone into this unforgiving environment. Colton pushed through the noisy party to the back platform and followed.

Stepping from the train, Colton saw Durant was well above him, silhouetted against the sun. He looked like a great man surveying his empire, a man who could conquer anything. Colton ignored the pain in his leg and climbed.

Durant reached the top of the bluff and was turning to enjoy the view when movement at his feet drew his attention He looked down on a coiled rattlesnake ready to strike.

The deadly reptile's threatening rattle froze Durant in terror. He gasped for breath and was unable to make a sound or stop the tears welling in his eyes. He was scared motionless, except for uncontrolled trembling.

Colton reached the top of the bluff and quickly assessed the perilous situation. He looked at the paralyzed man in front of him and said, "Stay very still, Doc."

With placid face and cool emotions, Colton eased out his pistol, pulled back the hammer, and shot the snake in the head. The loud report jolted Durant into a pell-mell run down the bluff to safety.

Colton holstered his pistol and watched Durant's almost comic flight. He saw irony in Durant's panic.

"So," he thought with satisfaction, "the scourge of working men and businesses, the dread of employees can himself feel terror."

Colton worked his way down the hill and entered the private car. Durant was shaking as he attempted to pour a glass of scotch whiskey. He related his version of the story in a clipped, excited voice.

"Damned thing struck at my leg. If I hadn't been so quick, it would have bitten me. It was huge. Calling it a snake is an understatement, like calling the Mississippi River a stream. Lucky I am so fast." Durant awed the audience with his bravery.

Bolstered by whiskey, Durant joked. "For a minute, Jake Rattlesnake had me convinced that I was wearing my burial clothes."

His admirers laughed. From a corner of the observation room, Colton waited and listened. His disgust with Durant's lie was total.

* * * *

DEPARTING LARAMIE that evening, Colton stood on the rear platform watching as they passed the depot. The agent suddenly burst from the door and ran toward the train waving a piece of paper. Colton leaned out barely in time to take the telegram. It was bad news from the Superintendent in Utah.

Colton made his way through the crowded car to Durant. "I have a telegram here, Dr. Durant. We have reports of heavy rains and flooding ahead in Utah. We may incur delays until the water goes down."

"We will not be delayed. I won't tolerate it," Durant sneered. "We have an appointment with history. Arrange to get us through the area."

"I'll do what I can, sir, but the flooding is beyond our control."

"Go! Solve this little problem." Durant returned to his guests.

At the next crew change point, Colton checked the latest weather information. Reports of heavy rains pointed to delays ahead.

They stopped for the night in Rawlins. Colton stayed up late communicating with managers in the flooded areas. The reports looked bad. The Devil's Gate Bridge was at risk of washing out. Dodge was on the scene directing repairs.

* * * *

THE NEXT MORNING, the train resumed its trip in light rain. Destiny had determined it was to be a bad day, one with a horrible alignment of bad weather, hot emotions and life-threatening revolt.

Approaching Piedmont, Wyoming, the passengers noticed the train bumping to a hard stop. They looked at one another curiously. Less than a minute later the train moved slowly ahead again. Everyone clearly saw the train was entering a side track.

The further the train moved, the more apparent it became that something was awry. Colton saw workers, tie cutters by the look of them, throwing down their tools and walking toward the train. Something was wrong, dangerously wrong.

Colton entered Durant's private car and made his way to the observation room.

"What the hell is going on?" Durant barked at Colton. "We're running late. I want to know who is delaying me."

"I'm unsure what's happening. We're leaving the main line and entering a side track. When we stop, I'll step down and find out."

As the train came to a final stop, they watched twenty men rush forward with heavy chains and secure Durant's car to the rail. The same was happening up and down the train, rendering it immovable.

Durant and his guests stared through the windows at the wild-looking workmen outside. Several had rifles. None looked happy. Two spokesmen stepped forward from the crowd. Colton recognized the first man immediately. It was Darcy Lonigan, looking tawny and mean.

The man with Lonigan could only be described as a brute. He was tall, at least six feet four inches and heavy, probably weighing close to three hundred pounds. He held an ax in his hand. His full, dirty beard, long hair and several broken, jagged teeth did nothing to sway Colton from his realization that the man was probably fearless.

Lonigan stepped to the car's rear platform and hollered up, "Durant, come out here! Now!"

Colton looked to Durant for instructions. The sullen-faced man said nothing. Colton reacted. For a lesser man, facing the angry workman would have been an act of madness, but not for Colton. With his coat on and his pistol hidden from sight, he stepped onto the car's back platform to face axes and rifles. He stood alone against a mob that looked ready to attack. He looked squarely at the two men facing him.

"What do you want, Lonigan?" Colton asked.

"Well. Well. 'Tis Mr. Rusk, his very self." Lonigan looked surprised at Colton's appearance. "Here's the deal, crippled man. I have about four hundred men here who haven't been paid in six months. Durant owes us over $250,000. We're not letting the train go until we get our wages. Either that or the train burns. It's just that simple."

Colton said nothing.

Lonigan took another step forward. "I want Durant out here, so I can tell him myself."

"Keep your distance, Lonigan. One of the trigger-happy, half-drunk politicians on board could start a war. You're the closest target. Actually, I already told them to focus on you if the shooting starts."

Realizing the car was probably heavily armed for Indian attacks, Lonigan was wary. He and the brute with the ax took a step back.

Colton addressed Lonigan. "I can't much argue with your position. I'll go in and tell Mr. Durant what's going on, and we'll try to get you paid as soon as possible. I know these men are ready for their money. Problem is Mr. Durant doesn't carry that kind of money with him."

The brute boomed out rejecting Colton's conciliatory tone. "We want our money, and we want it now, Rusk. Now!" The workers behind him shouted their support, shook fists, and spat on the ground. The entire mob stepped forward at once.

Colton looked beyond Lonigan and appealed directly to the horde.

"You men go back to work. I understand the problem and will take care of it. No one wants to do anything regrettable."

Colton's clear voice resonated with the men. They were former soldiers who recognized leadership. Some turned and trudged back to their tools. Many more stood uncertainly, unsure what to do.

Lonigan seethed, anger churning.

Colton reentered the car to find Durant irritated and twitching.

"They want you to come out, but I can't allow that. It's too dangerous for you," Colton explained. "They say you owe them six months wages, over $250,000."

Durant was dubious. He divided looks between Colton and his guests.

"These scoundrels can't hold me for ransom," he blustered. "Are any troops nearby?"

"The closest soldiers are over a hundred miles away," Colton said. "I suggest we get these men paid before they get violent."

"They'll get their pay in due course. They're of no concern to me now. We need to get to Promontory. Go out and tell them to move out of the way. We're leaving."

Colton responded with the grim truth about their circumstances.

"Here's the reality, Doctor. These men are dead serious. If you make the wrong decision now, they will burn this train to the ground. The wrong decision will likely see you dead within the hour. The train is chained to the rail and the locomotive boiler fire is doused. Our lives are in danger, especially yours."

Durant considered what Colton was saying. Slowly, the cold truth gripped him. As the gravity of the situation soaked in, fear squeezed him tighter and tighter until he strained to breathe.

"My God! They've kidnapped me," Durant gasped. "What are we going to do?" There was no thought for the other passengers, men now at risk of blazing death because of his selfish greed.

Colton watched Durant transform from an industry giant into a pathetic coward.

Durant's voice trembled. "Go talk with them. You take care of this. Send a wire to New York authorizing a special train to come with money. Wire Dodge in Echo Canyon. Have him send troops. Don't let those people near our car. I don't want trouble, Colton."

It was the first time Durant had ever called him "Colton." Colton returned to the back platform. Lonigan was waiting.

"You again?" Lonigan snarled. "Where is Durant?"

Colton ignored Lonigan and spoke directly to the mob.

"Doctor Durant is deeply embarrassed about the accounting issues. He sincerely apologizes and will immediately make things right for you." Colton knew his fabrication would save lives. "Doctor Durant was totally unaware of this situation. I am on my way to have your pay sent without further delay."

Lonigan resented Colton ignoring him as spokesman. "If I don't see a copy of the telegram within an hour, one car will burn. Get my drift?"

"Sure, Lonigan. We're getting the payroll. Be patient a bit longer."

"Patient, Hell!" Lonigan shouted. "Give us our money!"

Thirty minutes later Colton returned from the telegraph office and read a copy of the telegram to the crowd. Most seemed satisfied. They were, after all, hardworking men who had accomplished the impossible. Only rabble-rousers like Lonigan remained discontent.

"You may pay these men, but it won't be over between us," Lonigan said.

Colton saw the hatred in Lonigan's eyes. It was the look of a deranged man hell-bent on inflicting pain, death, and destruction.

Colton worked around the clock to counter Lonigan's violent message. He mingled with the tie cutters, apologizing for the payroll shortage, praising their work, and promising quick resolution. Colton's effort was the only force that kept Lonigan in check and Durant alive.

Two days passed before the payroll train arrived with gold and payroll records. Lonigan moped while workers queued up to collect past wages. Now out of the mainstream, it was as if he preferred battle to resolution. Colton encountered Lonigan while returning from the telegraph office. Their eyes met.

Lonigan couldn't let the moment go. "Mark my words, Rusk," he said. "This ain't over."

When they paid the last man, the trip resumed and the tyrant returned.

"Rusk, you've failed me miserably this time, like no other failure. You've publicly humiliated me in front of the entire nation. You should have shot the leader of that gang when he first approached the train. Because of you, we're two days late to a ceremony the entire world is awaiting. You've delayed the entire world."

Colton ignored Durant's offensiveness and presented a telegram.

"We heard from Dodge at Echo Canyon. The rains washed out the bridge at Devil's Gate. We may incur more delay. Dodge is doing his best to open the line."

They stood regarding each other for a moment, each feeling disdain for the other. From the cold look in Durant's eyes, Colton could tell that his time with the railroad would end soon. Durant would fire him, this time for good.

* * * *

THE TRAIN REACHED Devil's Gate Bridge only to find the river still raging. Several timbers had already washed away from the just-completed bridge.

The locomotive engineer pulled nervously at his beard and shook his head. "See those missing supports? This bridge won't hold a locomotive. The best I can do is free-roll passenger cars across. They weigh less. They'll do fine, but you'll have to bring a new locomotive from Ogden to take the train on."

Durant knew it was useless to threaten the engineer, especially on a safety issue. "OK. Roll the passenger cars across," he conceded.

Durant personally supervised the move from a safe distance. Emotions raced as the train crew cut the cars loose to coast across the weakened bridge. The bridge trembled almost as badly as the passengers inside. Colton stayed with the dignitaries calming them as the cars rolled slowly to safety. Durant casually followed on foot.

Engine 119 soon arrived from Ogden, and the train resumed its historic mission to Promontory.

* * * *

DURANT AND HIS GUESTS arrived at Promontory for the Golden Spike Ceremony two days later than scheduled. Durant was sick from celebrating his escape "from kidnappers who threatened my life for ransom money." He barricaded himself in a bedroom until shortly before the ceremony.

From the west, Governor Stanford of California, also president of the Central Pacific arrived to represent the western states. Pulling his train was "Jupiter," a beautiful locomotive with a flared smokestack. With him, Stanford brought California blue skies, bright sunshine, and a solid gold railroad spike for the ceremony.

United States government officials, soldiers, a military band, newsmen, and several hundred workmen assembled at the windswept, desolate spot.

Colton stood away from the crowd and looked at the two locomotives. Union Pacific 119 and Jupiter stood facing each other. Then Colton looked at the workers. United here was a diverse group, the Chinese, Irish, Negro, and Mexican. They were a mixed lot but

239

representative of the thousands who toiled on the road. He saw Durant, walking alone from his car nursing a terrible headache.

He watched as the last rails were laid. First, Union Pacific Irishmen laid the north rail with precise, experienced hands. Then the Central Pacific Chinese expertly laid their rail in place.

Colton's eyes sparkled with pride as the workers spiked down the last rails until finally only one spike remained. This was Colton's dream, the reason he had come to Omaha. He knew he had made a difference and felt pride in his accomplishment.

After speeches, prayers, and music, California Governor Stanford stepped forward with the golden spike, the final piece of the transcontinental railroad. He placed the spike and took up the specially wired sledge.

All over the world telegraphers waited for the clicks that would mark the railroad's completion. Cannons, bands, bells, whistles, parades and fireworks waited for the signal. Governor Stanford swung the big hammer, and missed the spike entirely. The workers, both Chinese and Irish, broke out in laughter.

Then Durant, still in the throes of a hangover took his turn. His mighty swing missed as well and drew even more laughter. Durant dropped the hammer and tried to hold his splitting head together. Finally a burly foreman took the sledge and drove the spike home flashing the signal around the world.

The telegraphers told the listening world. "It is done! 2:47 P.M. Utah time. The nation is spanned. UPRR runs 1,086 miles east from Promontory and CPRR runs 690 miles west. The nation is united!"

So began the largest celebration the nation had ever seen. All thirty-seven states responded simultaneously. A seven mile long parade marched through Chicago with over ten thousand people attending. Bells pealed in New Orleans, New York, Atlanta, and hundreds of cities across the country. In Philadelphia the Liberty Bell rang out. In San Francisco, two hundred cannons roared tribute. In Washington, a hundred cannons saluted. Across America people celebrated with parades, picnics, and dances. In Salt Lake City, seven thousand Mormons crowded into the tabernacle to sing and celebrate.

National pride was restored. The American continent was spanned overcoming Indians, storms, deserts, and the direst predictions of the pessimists. At Promontory, Durant and Governor Stanford provided food and drink for all. The food sat mostly uneaten. The booze flowed freely.

The Golden Spike Ceremony At Promontory, Utah. May 10, 1869

Chief Engineers Grenville Dodge of Union Pacific (right) and Samuel
Montague of Central Pacific shake hands celebrating completion of the
transcontinental railroad.
Courtesy of United States Archives

Omaha, too, participated in the celebration. Libby and the church ladies made fried chicken and picnicked at the town lake listening to band music until late. William and his friends helped with a fireworks display that impressed all.

* * * *

THIRTY-SIX HOURS LATER, Durant stumbled from his bedroom reeking of spent booze. He made his way to the observation room and fell into a cushioned chair. He leaned forward, elbows on his knees, and held his head in his hands. He had no memory of Colton carrying him passed out from Governor Stanford's car back to his own. He had no idea how he made it to his bed.

Durant looked up and noticed Colton sitting across the room. Their eyes met. Colton spoke.

"I kept people away while you slept. Can I get you anything, sir?"

Durant said nothing and resumed holding his head.

It was an hour before Durant spoke. When he did, his voice was soft-spoken, deliberate and icy sober.

"I'm through with you, Rusk. You've been a poor assistant."

Colton sat stunned waiting for more.

"We want different things from life, Rusk, so I am sending you where you will be happy. You're dismissed. Fired. Go home. You aren't very good at this, anyway."

Durant continued. Colton listened, but his mind began to close with rejection. By the time Durant finished, Colton was disconnected to the point it didn't matter what Doc said. Colton knew he was jobless.

"Go on, now. Leave your transportation pass on the table. Get your bag and leave." Durant's command brought Colton to awareness again.

Colton half-smiled at the ridiculousness of the situation. "I knew the job wouldn't last forever, but I'm a little surprised you're firing me in the middle of the Utah desert."

"You're a grown man. You can find your way home. I'm going the opposite direction. We're sort of in the same boat, Rusk. I'll be out of a job in a few days too. I've decided to sell all my stock and leave the railroad."

"Frankly, Doc, I am not disappointed one bit to see you leave Union Pacific. Neither is anyone else who knows you. You can't name a single person, except Seymour, who won't rejoice to see you go.

Omaha and Union Pacific will be far better without you. Even so, I am grateful to you for allowing me to be a part of it all."

Colton rose, packed his bag and within minutes stepped off Durant's car, jobless in the vast Utah desert.

* * * *

IN LESS THAN two hours, Colton had a comfortable seat in a bunk car on a homeward bound train.

Colton reflected during the long trip home. Working on the nation's railroad had been his dream, and now his dream was fulfilled. He saw no cause for self-pity, or resentment toward Durant. It was simply time to start over.

He thought of Durant and admitted he still had a degree of respect for the man, at least for his part finishing the railroad. Mostly he felt sorry for him.

He had seen the rich. They were no different than people struggling for a living. Both the upper and lower classes were insecure; perhaps the rich were more insecure. Both were consumed with meeting immediate needs.

Colton considered his future and dreamed of a life that included more time with Libby and William.

Chapter 34

Omaha basked under a warm, hopeful sun the morning Colton returned. From the train he saw the Union Pacific flag flying tall over the shops as if reminding the world of the achievements celebrated at Promontory.

He worked his troublesome leg into working condition and walked up the hill from the riverside yards toward home. Colton welcomed this beautiful day and was thankful to be home.

His hope and optimism endured even as he adjusted to the reality of being jobless. He cared little about losing his job. He was ready to move on. His sole concern was Libby. When she learned, she would worry needlessly. He decided to postpone telling her until the right time.

Through the morning they talked of the celebrations across the nation and the activities at Promontory. He presented her with a small, perfectly carved wooden spike no more than three inches long.

"Where did you get it?" she asked. There was excitement in her voice.

"The last cross tie was beautiful California laurel wood polished to a brilliant shine. After the ceremony, Governor Stanford saved the golden spike, but the men removed the tie and cut it to bits for souvenirs. A foreman gave me a piece. I carved this miniature spike for you. It's a memento from the great event. See, I've carved the date and your name in tiny letters."

She examined the shiny carving and read the inscription. "To Libby. May 10, 1869."

She clutched the little spike close to her heart and then wrapped it in a lace handkerchief. "Thank you, Colton. I will treasure it forever, my love."

He spoke of the railroad. She listened intently to every word. She cherished the sound of his voice and was happy to have him again.

"They say a person can now travel from Omaha to Sacramento in ten days," he said. "Wagon travel takes ten months. What progress the world has made!"

It was afternoon before Colton decided to break the news. He sank into a chair and said, "Libby, come sit with me. We need to talk."

He spoke straightforwardly. "I am no longer in Mr. Durant's employment. For the time being, I don't have a job."

"Did he fire you?"

"I guess you could call it that. My position is no longer needed. Nothing happened really. It's just that the road is finished, and Doctor Durant is leaving. He released me."

"What do you mean he is leaving?"

"He's spending two weeks with Governor Stanford, and then returning to New York. He told me he is selling his U.P. stock as soon as he gets home."

"Oh, Colton. What are we going to do?" She grabbed his hand.

"We have the house. I'll get a job, perhaps with Dodge. Or, maybe we can open our own business. Omaha has plenty of potential. It's on a growth spurt. Maybe I'll try real estate. Why, George Train himself taught me about the real estate business. Who better than George?"

He saw the concern in her eyes.

"Maybe I'll work for U.P. or one of the other new railroads. With Durant gone, U.P. will be run by railroad men, rather than money men."

They talked through the afternoon, treasuring each other's company.

By six o'clock, William returned from the hardware store and ate dinner with his parents. The talk continued. The more William heard, the higher his spirits climbed.

"Pa, this is wonderful," he exclaimed. "You can stay home every night. We have so many work opportunities. What about building homes? That's it! The need for houses is overwhelming. With your contacts and my hardware knowledge we can take the town by storm."

In the end, William's enthusiasm carried the day, turning Libby's concerns into anticipation. By the time they cleaned the dinner dishes, Libby felt as optimistic as her men.

* * * *

THE END OF THE DAY came and the twilight stars emerged flickering above the town. Two hours after sunset, Omahans began snuffing out their oil lamps preparing to retire for the evening. Only essential businesses remained open. The saloons, telegraph offices and the railroad shops continued their activity oblivious to nightfall.

In those days, when people tended to retire early, the Rusk home was dark by nine o'clock. At half past ten, Colton was still awake and staring at the blackness. He listened to the night sounds and thought about the future. For the moment he was content to be home with his family.

At his side, Libby slept peacefully. He listened to her slow rhythmic breathing and thought of his love for her. In the distance, he heard a train whistle, followed by the barking of several dogs. He said a prayer of thanks, breathed the cool air from the open window, and drifted to sleep.

* * * *

THE TRAIN COLTON HAD HEARD but disregarded, crept around the long curve behind the town lake, its stabbing headlight searching Omaha's shadowy underside. On it rode two hundred men returning from Wyoming.

With the completion of the line, the railroad released thousands of men, up to two-thirds of the construction force. Most headed east to build other railroads. Only a third of Dodge's workers remained to shore up and rebuild the frantically-constructed road.

On the train, one returning worker was different than the others. The unsightly Irishman on the third car, the one with neither home nor family, was also the one with the darkest heart. Lying alone in the midst of other men, he obsessed over sinister plans.

When the train stopped in the dark railroad yard north of downtown, the men gathered their belongings and began scattering. They made their separate ways to company tents rentable for a quarter per night, or to the company canteen to eat, or to the nearby saloons waiting to solve their problems with whiskey.

Darcy Lonigan rose and stretched his lean muscles. He spat. The man in front never noticed the spittle on his bed roll.

He returned to Omaha knowing he had no chance of working for any railroad. Kidnapping Durant's train closed that door forever.

He sulked over General Casement's investigation identifying him as the ringleader. In the heated struggle that broke out with one of Casement's men, Lonigan drew an angry knife and narrowly escaped being shot.

The confrontation marked him as a chronic troublemaker. He was lucky to have slipped away on the eastbound train to escape Casement's punishment.

Those things didn't matter now. Bitterness boiled in him. He had a score to settle with the crippled man who had repeatedly humiliated him, the man he would forever loathe, the person who most likely gave his name to General Casement.

Lonigan knew Omaha well from the early days when he worked on the boat landings. He knew the streets. He knew the businesses and gambling houses. And he knew the home where Colton Rusk lived.

Lonigan walked south from the rail yard, passing between the river and the Herndon House. He continued to the steamboat landings and the shack near the foot of Jones Street.

* * * *

AT ONE O'CLOCK in the morning, fate pounded on Colton's door. He grumbled his way into pants and down the steps. When he opened the front door, he found himself facing a boy no more than fourteen years old.

Recognition came quickly. The boy was older, better nourished and clothed, and had a nice look about him, but clearly the same boy.

"You're the orphan boy Sean…," Colton paused uncomfortably trying to remember a last name.

"Cook. Same old Sean Cook, sir," the boy responded, smiling awkwardly.

"What do you want, son?"

"You're to come to the Missouri and Western Telegraph office, sir. We have an important message coming across that needs an answer."

Colton was confused. It must be a message from Durant, or maybe Dodge. It was probably Durant with a crisis on his hands. He didn't know.

"Tell the telegrapher I'm coming. I need to get on shoes and a shirt. I'll be along shortly." He flipped two bits to the boy and went upstairs to finish dressing. The boy dropped Colton's quarter in his pocket next to the silver dollar he had just earned.

Colton dressed and departed out the door for the telegraph office. He felt pain in his leg and limped more than normal. It was his body's punishment for not stretching before rushing into the cool night.

He cursed himself for responding so energetically to Durant's call. He had no obligation to accept Durant's messages, much less rush out in the middle of the night. What could Durant possibly want? He pictured himself like an old fire horse who, after being put to pasture, still responded to fire alarms the rest of his life. Was this how it was with old soldiers? He walked on.

He was still a block away from the telegraph office when he walked past the Red Dog Saloon. Sounds of piano music and a lively crowd spilled into the street. From the alley at the far end of the saloon a figure suddenly stepped from the shadows, blocking Colton's way. "You're out mighty late, Rusk," said an Irish accented voice.

"Who is it?" Colton said. He stopped abruptly to avoid colliding with the man.

"'Tis your old friend Darcy Lonigan," an ominous voice whispered.

"Darcy Lonigan? What are you doing here?"

"I have unfinished business in Omaha," Lonigan said softly.

Lonigan's eyes were cold and lifeless. In the dimly lit street, Colton recognized the look. It was the same resigned blankness he had seen in the eyes of battle weary soldiers in the minutes before a charge into enemy lines.

"Rusk, you've been a thorn in my side for six years now. You are everything I hate."

"What do you mean, Lonigan? You're a thorn in your own side. Now step aside. I've got business to attend." Colton was more irritated than defensive. He felt no fear of this worthless troublemaker.

Lonigan stayed his position, his blank look turning into a sneer.

"You think you've got it all, don't you? You spit on the little man." Lonigan paused, and then added, "You don't deserve what you have."

"You're wrong about that," Colton laughed. "I'm scraping by just like every man out here. I just lost my job like thousands of others."

Lonigan raised his voice slightly, his anger building. "You're a liar, Rusk. You're a flat-out lying dog. I've seen you on the private cars sipping wine, eating fine foods. You're pompous and rich. You couldn't do a day's work if you had to."

"You've got it all wrong, Lonigan. What do you really want from me?"

"What do I want? I want a tad of respect. I want you to talk with me a few minutes more. I want to put our problems behind us, Rusk."

Colton considered the pathetic dirty creature before him. His hat was filthy. He wore a shabby, long coat in the cool evening. Lonigan stood with shoulders slumped, hands thrust deep in the coat pockets. Rusk's good heart melted with pity.

"I appreciate your need to put the past behind us. People need to resolve disputes before they fester and rot. Let's make a new start. I've found that deep down all men are basically the same. I'll bet you're good at heart."

Colton smiled warmly and extended his hand to Lonigan. "I offer you my friendship. I hope you will take it. Let's start over."

The fugitive track worker looked at the hand offered in friendship. He shuffled a moment as if deciding whether to accept friendship, then looked up at Colton. Lonigan's hardened face slowly turned into a half-grin that gave Colton encouragement.

Then Lonigan's half-grin turned into a chilling, deranged smile. For the first time, Colton felt uneasy and unsure if Lonigan would accept a handshake. He never expected what came next.

Quickly removing a hand from his coat pocket, Lonigan extended his arm full-length toward Colton's face and fired his pistol with cold, precise calculation.

Colton died instantly and collapsed to the dirt street without a sound. Lonigan watched blood rushing from a small hole above the right eyebrow, then fired a second bullet through Colton's already stilled heart.

The loud reports shattered the calm on 11th Street. A woman screamed inside the saloon. Music and voices went silent. Lonigan knew the next sound would be that of boots running to the door.

Lonigan's fiendish eyes glared at Colton's body. He kicked his lifeless ribcage hard. "I'd say our problems are finally resolved, Rusk."

He threw the gun on the closest roof, and after checking to make sure he was unseen, disappeared into the alley.

Men rushed from the saloon and saw the body in front of them. No one noticed the man slipping into the darkness toward the river.

One cried out. "My God. It's Mr. Rusk. How could this happen?" The speaker removed his hat and clutched it to his chest. It was the conductor whom Colton had saved in the train wreck at Plum Creek.

Before they could organize to search for the murderer, Lonigan was in a tent at the edge of the rail yard.

* * * *

IT WAS FOUR O'CLOCK in the morning when City Marshal Hollins knocked on the Rusk front door.

Libby woke in fright the instant she heard the knock. Where was Colton? She knew instinctively that bad news was at hand.

She met William in the upstairs hallway as he came out of his bedroom. They hurried downstairs together to open the front door and let their nightmare begin.

Neither Colton nor Libby had thought about their final arrangements. Libby's burden to make burial plans was so overwhelming that church members had to take over. The outpouring of sympathy for Libby and William was enormous. The entire community was in shock. The Governor attended the funeral. The house was full of people for the three days before the funeral. Libby didn't notice.

In another week they were alone again, feeling the same helplessness they had experienced in the Maryland farmhouse so long ago. This time, Colton would not come to save them.

No clues. No suspect. No motive was ever found. No explanation was ever attempted for why a man of Colton Rusk's reputation was shot dead outside a rough Nebraska watering hole. People wondered and raised eyebrows when the subject came up.

Libby and William mourned, cheated of the man they loved and needed. They had neither recourse nor understanding. Libby's grief turned inward, paralyzing her to the world. William's grief turned to unresolved anger.

* * * *

TWO WEEKS AFTER the funeral, Telegrapher Anthony Butler came to the Rusk house. Libby invited him into the long hallway.

In him, Libby recognized sincere sympathy. "Mrs. Rusk, I am truly sad to deliver this telegram. I knew your husband. He was a fine man and always treated me with respect. From the first day you folks arrived, he was very kind to me."

His comments brought tears to eyes already red and swollen. She wiped them with her apron. "What do you have for me?" she asked.

"It's a message from Dr. Thomas Durant."

"What does it say? Will you read it for me?"

From upstairs, William heard voices and came down just as the telegrapher opened the sealed envelope and began reading in a reluctant voice.

To the heirs of Colton Rusk:

Under the provisions of your mortgage agreement dated August 29, 1863, you stand in default of your obligations for the residence at Capital and 14th Street in Omaha, Nebraska. Under the agreement, all interests in the residence revert to the undersigned effective immediately. Please promptly arrange to vacate the house and surrender the keys to the Union Pacific Agent.

T.C. Durant

Butler folded the telegram, retuned it to the envelope, and placed it in Libby's trembling hand. "I must be going, now," he said. "I can see myself out. I am very sorry for all your troubles."

When he gone, Libby turned to William. "What does it mean?"

William was in disbelief. "Ma, it means Dr. Durant is evicting us."

"How is it possible? Doctor Durant paid for the house as part of your Pa's salary. He reduced the mortgage every year. Our time is completed."

"I don't know, Ma. Is there a contract Pa might have signed?"

They searched Colton's desk, the same desk brought by wagon from Maryland, and soon located the mortgage papers in a box. William examined his father's signature then read the document carefully. Twice more he read it. Libby stood watching for any reaction that might reveal important information.

She recognized bad news was coming by the way William's face tensed and his shoulders slumped as he cast the papers onto the desk. William remained motionless, withdrawn into himself in deep thought. He stared with blank eyes toward the bookcases along the wall.

"What's wrong, honey? What does it say?"

"It says the same thing the telegram says. It requires completion of six full years work to complete the loan forgiveness. Anything less than six years is the same as nothing and the house goes back to Doctor Durant. I just counted the time. Pa was fired about three months short of completing the sixth year."

"And we must leave our home now?"

"Apparently so," William responded. He was trembling with anger, his face reddening. "I need to find Doc Durant and talk to him. I don't believe anyone, even Doctor Durant, could disregard Pa's years of dedication so impersonally. He cannot be that cruel."

"Your Pa would want you to talk to him. He always believed rational men can reach understandings. He believed people are basically good. Maybe you can make a deal with Dr. Durant."

"We already know Durant has a selfish streak, Ma. I'm worried his timing was intentional in firing Pa. He might have planned this surprise six years ago."

William's mind drifted into deep thought. He looked at his mother, but did not see. He heard her voice, but did not listen. Instead he bent over, kissed her on the cheek, and walked out the front door. "I'll be back," he said.

* * * *

WILLIAM WALKED AIMLESSLY for half an hour through the Omaha streets. He had no destination, only fury growing with each step. Three times, as frustration and rage reached a boiling point, William momentarily drew back and tried to hope. He visualized reaching an understanding with Durant.

He walked to the telegraph office and found Anthony Butler at his desk sorting papers.

"I am looking for Doctor Durant. His telegram is dated today from Omaha. Is he in town?"

"He's in town. He plans to leave Omaha soon to return to New York. He's already picked up his messages. He had his private rail car ferried to Council Bluffs this morning. He'll probably depart tonight."

William thanked the telegrapher and crossed the street to the Herndon House. In the lobby he faced memories of happier days when his family stayed there almost six years ago. Now the same lobby where he had felt such joy held nothing for him. He looked at the people and the hotel register, but seeing no evidence of Durant, he left.

William decided to wait at the U.P. ferry landing near the spot he and Colton had fished many times. He topped the levee at Izard Street and looked across the bare mudflats. The ferry was on the Iowa side of the river discharging railroad cars. On the Nebraska side, a steam locomotive sat idle near the ferry landing.

William crossed the mudflats to the one rom shanty next to the landing. He had been to this rickety place once before when his Pa had brought him there to talk to the railroad men.

Inside, William heard the railroad crew fully engaged in a card game. He decided it was best not to disturb them.

A pony switch engine working in the Omaha rail yard, 1869
Original Photograph by Andrew J. Russell
Public domain phototraph courtesy of New York Public Lbirary

He moved past the shanty and sat against one of the landing's hefty pylons. From here William had a good view of the wide mudflats and levee. He decided to wait for Durant, if he came at all.

William waited alone with heavy thoughts. He considered what to say to Durant. Would there be sympathy for his mother's plight? Did Durant even know about what had happened? If his talk with Durant failed, he had no backup plan. He would be left with hatred for the man who would pile poverty onto grief.

At sunset, the silhouette of a man carrying a bag appeared in the sun on top of the levee. He stopped momentarily, perhaps surveying the mudflats or the ferry as William had done an hour earlier. William watched the figure descend and move toward the landing.

Durant walked alone, something not so unusual for him. He felt relief that construction and festivities were over. His fortune was assured. In only a week he would sell his stocks and be done with it all. No more governors, congressmen or senators to pander. He planned to relax in luxury before moving to other projects.

William had seen Doctor Durant only once and worried he might not recognize him. He studied the figure against the blinding sunset looking for something familiar. It was impossible. He waited, maintaining focus on the approaching man.

Without warning the ferry boat arrived and bumped against the solid, wooden pylons jolting William to his feet. As the man came into focus, he saw it was Durant walking at a fast gait. He was sure of it.

As Durant closed in, William spoke. "Excuse me, Dr. Durant. I need a word with you, please."

Durant was anxious to visit the Captain's quarters and the bottle waiting for him on the table. He never broke stride. He brushed past William and stepped onto the boat. Then, the leader of industry, the builder of the transcontinental railroad, the emperor of thirty thousand men wheeled around, still holding his carpet bag and jeered, "What do you want, boy?" He eyed William suspiciously.

"My name is William Rusk. Colton Rusk was my father."

"So?" came the unconcerned answer.

"Maybe you don't know. My father was killed two weeks ago."

"I'm aware of it."

"My mother received a telegram from you this afternoon telling her to vacate the house immediately. Do you know about it?"

"Yes, I sent the telegram. Is there something you people don't understand?" Durant eased toward the wheelhouse and the bottle.

"Ma is still grieving since the funeral. I don't think she can move out right now." William stepped onto the ferry boat.

"Let me make it clear: that house is no longer your home. Your father defaulted on his contract."

"The reason he defaulted, is because you fired him just short of the required time." William felt tears of anger flowing into his eyes.

"Very perceptive, young Rusk. I did do that. Whether your father lived or died, he was going to lose the house. That's the way business works."

"If Pa was alive he would not allow you to easily strip away his home. You have to realize that."

"You're right. His death made it easier. It saved me the cost a sending a telegram from New York to the sheriff. Probably saved me legal costs too. Was he angry when I fired him? Did he even realize he was going to lose his home?"

William stood astonished and speechless.

Durant continued. "No. I can tell from your gap-jaw, country look that he never grasped the implications of the mortgage agreement."

"No. He trusted you as an honorable business man."

"Well ho-hum. As I've always said: Let the buyer beware. Go on boy, I've got things to take care of."

"Are you saying you won't do anything to help my mother keep the house? We're willing to make an arrangement."

Durant began to grow loud. "No. You don't seem to understand. I want you out of the house. I want you out now. You can live anywhere you want, but not in my house. I'm going to sell it to a family with a working father, preferably one with two good legs and a job."

William's fury neared the breaking point. Mighty Durant raged on never sensing the coming eruption.

"I'm going to turn a dandy profit on that house and buy a new barn for my champion horses. The only point that matters is that your mother is in violation of the contract."

Durant showed no kindness, no sympathy, nothing but self-serving greed. William's wrath exploded. He rushed Durant, unstoppable as divine punishment. Durant was able to take one step back before the bodies collided. Both tumbled overboard and into the dark, turbulent river. Both flailed, William trying to strike blows, the other trying to swim to the boat. Durant's carpet bag floated slowly south for a minute then sank below the surface.

Two deck hands pulled Durant from the black waters and onto the boat deck. They pulled William from the river and shoved him face down to the deck planks.

Durant cursed the loss of his bag and its most important lading: a cash box chock-full of deeds and gold, including his poker winnings from Governor Stanford.

"No one can treat me this way! Get the marshal. I want this thug hung before morning!" he screamed at the boat captain.

As William tried to stand, deck hands attacked like wolves swarming prey. Their vicious payback by boot and fist continued until William lay motionless.

Durant, still wet and chilled, watched it all but made no effort to intercede. When it ended, he left for the wheelhouse and liquid consolation.

* * * *

Absolute, total darkness. Pain.

William came to on his back with terrible weight pressing down on him. His first awareness was his own moaning and the unbearable pain required to breathe. He was unable to move. He never felt pain like this before.

He struggled to open one swollen eye, then the other. He felt a thick wetness that blurred his vision. He could make out the indistinct shapes of two men looming above against a black, starless sky. He gasped a shallow, panicked breath and felt stabbing pain shoot through his chest.

He began to comprehend they were standing on his outstretched arms bearing down and pinning him to the boat deck with rough boots. A third man, heavy, foul-smelling, and still panting with exertion sat across his knees dripping water onto him. William could not move, nor did he want to.

He let his head roll slightly to look at the man standing on his right arm.

"Lay still, boy, or you'll feel more broken ribs. Or maybe you'd rather have a boot crush your nose. It's your choice. Lay still!"

William tried to say something with a dry mouth and swollen tongue. The pain rippling through his body was too great. The words he tried to form became an agonized moan.

Another voice, deeper and harsher, spoke. "We don't take kindly to thugs in Omaha. We know how to handle 'em. Likely you'll be hanging from a tree before long. Marshal's coming for you."

William struggled to think, to respond, to breathe. The treacherous, horrible events that had driven him to desperation flashed through his brain. Then all went dark and silent again.

THE HOUSE ON CAPITAL STREET was no longer a home, only a dispirited structure with memories. The shades were drawn tight, darkening rooms and spirits. Despondency hung in the air like an inescapable coldness. Wooden crates and boxes half-full, cluttered the walking areas throughout.

Libby sat in the kitchen crying softly. This had been one of her favorite places to talk with Colton and share life. It seemed impossible that she and William were alone. Poor William. What would become of him? Would they hang him? Libby's soul was nearly dead. She looked as if she had not slept in three days, which was the truth of it.

At first she did not hear the knocking at the front door, and when she finally did, she ignored it and withdrew again into herself.

She heard distorted, unrecognizable voices passing the side window moving toward the back of the house. She ignored them and drifted into her own world.

The tapping started. Someone was tapping at the back window.

"Libby! Libby, honey. Let me in."

"Go away," she muttered never looking away from the cabinets.

"Now you get up right now and open this door. Can you hear me?"

Libby turned and looked toward the window to see Annie Dodge's face, etched with concern. Her husband, Grenville, stood behind.

"Open the door, honey," Annie called.

Libby stood and shuffled to the door dragging her feet the entire distance. She slowly pushed back the latch.

When the door opened Annie rushed to embrace Libby, tears streaming down her face.

Annie regained her voice. "Oh my God, Libby. We're just back from Boston and heard the terrible news. We can't believe it."

Grenville Dodge stepped forward, gave Libby a tender hug, and took her hand in his. It was cold and frail. "We're so sorry," he said.

Annie Dodge took charge. "Grenville, go open those curtains. Let some light in here. Move those boxes. We need a place to sit."

Grenville Dodge moved to follow her orders and waded into the disarray of moving day.

Libby grasped at dignity while drowning in grief. "Please come in, Annie. I'll make tea."

"You'll do nothing of the sort. Grenville will make tea for us."

Over the next hour, they tenderly coaxed the story from Libby. They tried to fit the pieces together from the unknown messenger and Colton's murder to Durant's telegram and William's arrest.

"Durant is evicting us with a trick deed," she said. "He never paid Colton for his last two months work and never will. The Marshall says William will probably go to prison for attempted murder. He said he's under pressure from big people."

Annie and Grenville saw her condition was worse than grief. It was as if Libby had lost all reason for living.

Grenville Dodge choked back tears and fumbled with words.

"Colton saved my life in battle. Without him, I would not be alive today. And during the past six years, he continued to save me. I swear to you Libby, I will not rest until your house is rescued and William is safe at home. I will continue Colton's job of guiding him."

Annie Dodge spoke up. "You will come with us. You will stay with us until you can return."

Libby climbed into the Dodge carriage without protest. She was too numb to know or care what was best for her.

The next morning, Grenville Dodge embarked on a mission he considered one of the most important undertakings of his life, a personal quest more imperative than building the transcontinental railroad and more honorable than serving in Congress.

He owed the gift of life to a loyal friend. He would stop at nothing to repay his debt to Colton.

EPILOGUE

The blazing sun bore down searing the West Texas landscape driving all but the heartiest creatures into the shade or underground.

Grenville Dodge, now president of the Texas and Pacific Railway, sat on his horse above the Pecos River valley scanning the riverbanks with binoculars. Below, the river was a slender, brown ribbon threaded across the parched desert.

Spotting the railroad survey crew, Dodge stowed his binoculars and eased his horse in their direction. He was grateful to locate them so easily.

Soon he identified William Rusk directing the crew as they drove stakes to mark the railroad's approach for the Pecos River Bridge. Dodge hoped to come in quietly and hear their interaction. He should have known he would never hear a word. As he closed in, they recognized him. All work stopped. The men removed their hats in respect for General Dodge.

Dodge tipped his hat in return and addressed William.

"May I have a word with you in private?"

They moved together out of earshot and talked in the shade of a mesquite tree. Dodge's voice had a certain pleading.

"When you finish the Texas and Pacific surveys, I need you to come back to Omaha. I need a good man at one of my banks."

William, now in his late twenties, wiped the sweat from his forehead and subconsciously shook his head.

Dodge continued. "I'll have the best men in the banking business train you until you're ready to take charge. You have every skill needed for the job. I rode out here to personally ask you to do this for me."

"Sir, I went to college to learn this trade. I'm good at it."

"Yes. Yes. The Chief Engineer tells me you're not just good, you excel. I know you have a lot of talent William, but I'm hoping you will accept the offer. It would put you back in Omaha. Your Ma misses you

259

horribly. She's angry with me for taking you so far away. For sure, Annie is upset. I really need you to return when this survey is finished. Your future is in Omaha."

William met the eyes of the man who saved him from hanging, the man who rescued his mother and "persuaded" Doctor Durant to hand over a clear deed for the home on Capital Street.

"I'll return to Omaha. After everything you've done, I can't say no, General."

Dodge visibly relaxed.

As they returned to the surveyors, Dodge tossed in the deal closer.

"My pretty niece from Delaware is in Council Bluffs. She looks forward to meeting you."

The General had lunch with the men and entertained them with stories from the war and the transcontinental railroad. The surveyors wanted to hear about his meeting with President Lincoln in Council Bluffs and the second meeting in Washington during the war.

When work resumed, Dodge watched with a knowing eye. When they offered the transit level, Dodge sighted in several benchmarks for a curve. From his unambiguous hand signals to the distant rod man, the crew saw he still had an expert surveyor's touch.

Toward mid-afternoon, Dodge mounted up for the ride back to the Pecos village. William stepped in close to say goodbye.

"Take care, General. Tell my Ma I love her and I'll be in Omaha by October."

The General held the energetic horse in place. "Anything else?" he asked admiring William almost like one of his own sons.

William smiled up at his benefactor.

"Yes, sir. You can tell that pretty niece of yours that a young man named William will be coming to call."

AUTHOR'S NOTES

This book is a work of fiction. To construe it as an historical treatise or anything else would be an error.

The story is set within a framework of actual past events and figures. Within this context, Colton Rusk, his family, and his activities are a product of the author's imagination.

Dr. Thomas Clark Durant was a real person. While his treatment in the novel may seem unkind, there is ample historical evidence to justify the unflattering portrayal. His depiction as a cold scoundrel and petty tyrant are most likely very close to the truth.

In Omaha, there are no honors for Dr. Durant. No Durant Street. No library. No public building. No park. No historical marker.

Dr. Durant may not have been lovable, but he did achieve greatness in what he did for the nation. The positive effects brought by the railroad far outweigh his character flaws. Historians generally agree the transcontinental railroad was a bargain even with Dr. Durant's inflated expenses, profit skimming, and nonstop shenanigans.

In seeking a degree of fairness, I spoke with Dr. Durant's Great-Great Grandson. He offered insightful wisdom when he said, "Great men often have faults equally as great as their achievements."

He was right. Charisma is not a requirement for greatness.

I encourage readers to draw conclusions about Dr. Thomas Durant from the broader perspective of his accomplishments. Without his efforts, the continent would have opened for settlement much later. America's transformation to an industrial power would have been delayed for years while the nation languished in a wagon-drawn, agrarian economy. America owes Dr. Durant a debt of gratitude.

George Train, too, was a real person, and probably more eccentric than suggested in the novel. He was more than a railroad promoter and Omaha developer. His national prominence led him to run for president in the 1870's. He was a remarkable orator, a noted suffrage advocate, and a friend of Susan B. Anthony. Because of his world travels, Train was said to be the model for Phileas Fogg in Jules Verne's book Around the World in Eighty Days.

Grenville Dodge also was a real person and national figure. He was a noted engineer, military general, and U. S. Congressman. He is still revered as a hero in Iowa and on the Union Pacific Railroad.

Please accept my apology for any factual discrepancies resulting from my efforts to craft an enriching work of fiction. Errors, intentional or otherwise, are my own.

Following is a sampling of documented occurrences interpreted in the novel:

- President Lincoln's support for the Pacific Railroad
- General Dodge's battle wounds at Pea Ridge and Atlanta
- General Dodge's spy network and all black regiments
- Dr. Durant's profits from Civil War cotton smuggling and his early employment of Abraham Lincoln as an attorney
- General Dodge's discovery of the Black Hills route while under Indian attack
- The Battle of Antietam (Sharpsburg, MD, 9/17/1862) - the bloodiest single-day battle in American history
- General William Sherman's stern warnings to Dr. Durant during Nebraska's first train excursion
- U.P.' s acquisition of President Lincoln's private car
- Nebraska's first legal execution in August 1863
- Dr. Durant's grand excursion to the Hundredth Meridian
- Dr. Durant's stock deals, unethical lobbyist activities, and endless negotiations for the railroad terminus and bridge
- The "Oxbow" route change to Bellevue, Nebraska
- Work stoppages stemming from Dr. Durant's conflicts with the Ames brothers and other U.P. stockholders
- George Train's mansion (now Omaha's Dahlman Park)
- The residential development known as "Train Town"
- George Train's unresolved conflicts with the Herndon House that led him to build his own Omaha hotel
- Crédit Mobilier – created by Durant and Train that lead to a major national scandal for conflict of interests
- Senator Oakes Ames and brother Oliver Ames participation as principle investors in Union Pacific
- Nebraska's first locomotive arriving Omaha July 2, 1865
- The 1867 Indian-caused derailment at Plum Creek
- General Dodge's showdown with Dr. Durant at Laramie

- Dr. Durant's lease of the Lutheran parsonage in Omaha
- The existence of "Hell on Wheels" and General Casement's enforcement actions (actual occurrence was at Julesburg, Colorado)
- U. S. Grant's dramatic support for Dodge at Fort Sanders
- Dr. Durant's kidnapping by tie cutters for back wages while traveling to the ceremony at Promontory, Utah
- Coasting occupied passenger cars across the Devil's Gate bridge
- The Golden Spike ceremony on May 10, 1869 and the national celebration that followed
- Dodge's lifelong friendships with Sherman, and Grant
- Dr. Durant's sell-off of UPRR interests after completion

Other factual references relating to the novel:
- Union Pacific purchased The Herndon House Hotel in 1911 for its first headquarters building.
- Other railroads eventually built bridges at Desoto and Bellevue but too late to impede Omaha's development.
- David Butler, first state governor of Nebraska was impeached for ethics violations not related to George Train or Union Pacific Railroad.
- George Pullman, mentioned in the novel, was a noted capitalist so reviled for his cruel treatment of employees that upon his death was buried at night in a lead lined coffin under tons of concrete and steel to prevent employees from desecrating his body.

Union Pacific Railroad construction reached the 100th Meridian on
October 5, 1866. The Cozad, Nebraska Chapter of the D. A. R.
replaced the original sign in 1933. Photo taken in 2013.

The Plum Creek Train Wreck
A trackside monument near Lexington, Nebraska marks the site where Cheyenne Indians attacked, derailed, and burned a Union Pacific train on August 7, 1868. Photo taken in 2013.

The Ames Monument is a 60-foot tall pyramid built to honor the contributions of brothers Oliver and Oakes Ames to the transcontinental railroad. It is located near the ghost town of Sherman, Wyoming. When completed in 1882, it marked the railroad's highest point, 8247 ft.

President Rutherford Hayes attended the dedication ceremony. In 1918, the tracks were shifted three miles south leaving the pyramid alone in the desert. The monument is listed in the National Register of Historic Places

Notes

Author Lawson McDowell is a long-time employee of Union Pacific Railroad and its predecessor lines.

After college, Lawson began his railroad career riding trains as a brakeman in Austin, Texas. Since then he has served in many capacities and locations including superintendent on two divisions and corporate safety director for Southern Pacific Lines and the Cotton Belt Railway.

Lawson and his family live in Omaha, Nebraska, where he is headquartered at Union Pacific's historic Harriman Train Dispatching Center. He serves as Director of Network Operations for intermodal and automotive trains.

In the photo above, Lawson stands in front of an historic photograph showing the unethical Dr. Thomas Durant (seated third from left) in his regal private railroad car. The scene shows expensive gilded mirrors and crossed repeater rifles for fending off Indian attacks. The photograph hangs in the train dispatching center in Omaha.

For more author information, visit: www.lawsonmcdowell.com

Made in the USA
Coppell, TX
08 May 2021